DEVIL'S GARDEN

By Aline Templeton

DI KELSO STRANG SERIES

Human Face

Carrion Comfort

Devil's Garden

DI MARJORY FLEMING SERIES

Evil for Evil

Bad Blood

The Third Sin

DEVIL'S GARDEN

ALINE TEMPLETON

Allison & Busby Limited
11 Wardour Mews
London W1F 8AN
allisonandbusby.com

First published in Great Britain by Allison & Busby in 2020.
This paperback edition published by Allison & Busby in 2020.

Copyright © 2020 by Aline Templeton

The moral right of the author is hereby asserted in accordance with the Copyright, Designs and Patents Act 1988.

All characters and events in this publication, other than those clearly in the public domain, are fictitious and any resemblance to actual persons, living or dead, is purely coincidental.

All rights reserved. No part of this publication may be reproduced, stored in a retrieval system, or transmitted, in any form or by any means without the prior written permission of the publisher, nor be otherwise circulated in any form of binding or cover other than that in which it is published and without a similar condition being imposed on the subsequent buyer.

A CIP catalogue record for this book is available from the British Library.

10 9 8 7 6 5 4 3 2 1

ISBN 978-0-7490-2611-0

Typeset in 11/16 pt Sabon LT Pro by

Th
has bee
fi

LONDON BOROUGH OF
WANDSWORTH

9030 00007 2725 5

Askews & Holts

AF CRI

WW20006757

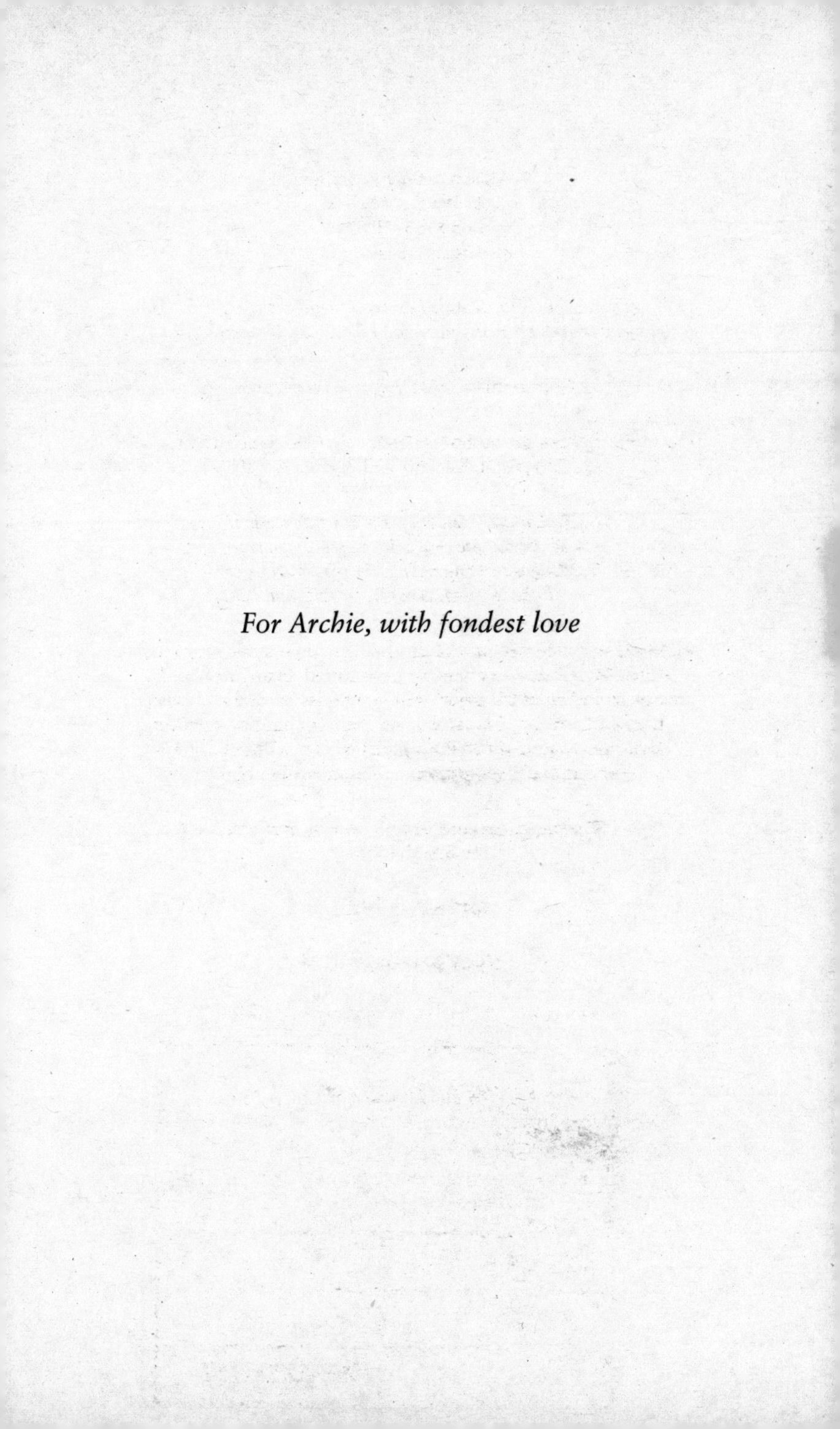

For Archie, with fondest love

PROLOGUE

They left at first light, just as the thin, fiery streaks of dawn edged the great peaks of the Dolomites behind them. It was still too dark to see the terrifying drops on either side as the battered taxi negotiated its way round hairpin bends on the road leading down to the valley floor.

The two women sat in the back in silence. One stared straight ahead; the other, as the road twisted, glanced back each time at the village clinging precariously to the heights, where in the huddled houses lights were starting to appear like stars on the darkness. It dwindled into the distance until at last it disappeared as if it had been a mirage. A place where secrets could be left to disappear in the same way.

Further down the road, another woman stood looking out of the window to watch the new day arrive and saw the taxi pass on its way, though she didn't know what she was seeing, barely registering it with her mind on what lay ahead. From the bed behind her, her husband's voice spoke.

'Excited, love?'

She could tell he was smiling. A little shudder ran through her, but she said, 'Oh yes, excited,' though to her ears the words sounded as hollow as a cracked bell.

CHAPTER ONE

It was a sharp February day with a low sun; on the horizon the Eildon hills looked softly smudged against a bleakly grey sky. There was snow lingering in the ditches and behind drystone walls, a sign of more to come. They were still forecasting hard weather ahead.

Cassie Trentham stared blankly out of the window of the big black car as it swept into the drive of the Borders crematorium at Melrose behind the hearse carrying the mortal remains of her brother Felix.

Felix – an ironic name for a tortured soul. Her own, Cassandra, fitted better. Like the priestess, she had warned him and warned him and had suffered the helpless agony of seeing her warnings ignored. They'd been so close – little more than a year apart – yet there had been nothing she could do.

But then when he was at his lowest ebb she'd managed

to coax him back to live with her here – in safety, as she had thought; she'd actually been sure she had saved him and the dark days were behind them, so the shock of his death had been devastating. She wouldn't have believed it could happen if she hadn't learnt from bitter experience that addiction breeds an uncanny talent for deception. However hard it might be, she had to accept that she'd been wrong.

She turned her head to glance at her mother. Anna, impassive, was coolly elegant as always in a black collarless coat with a grey silk scarf at the neck. Her make-up was flawless and there wasn't a hair out of place in her glossy angled bob. Was she feeling anything at all? Grief? Guilt?

She should be – guilt, anyway. In Cassie's eyes she was to blame for what happened to Felix. It had always been clear that Anna's children bored her. Absorbed in her own literary world she had given them money to make up for lack of love or even interest – money to leave her alone, really. Money that had subsidised Felix's quest for perdition in Edinburgh. And he had found it.

Cassie's throat constricted. She coughed, looked at her watch, changed her position; anything to distract herself and stop the tears coming. It would never do to be photographed sobbing when she emerged from the car. That would be bad for the dignity of The Brand. Because there they all were. 'Private funeral', the notice had said, but even at this early hour they were lying in wait: journalists making notes, cameras poised, someone holding a fuzzy microphone. Not that it would be headline news; just a snippet at the soft end of the national bulletin if it was a slow news day, the local programme if not, and a short paragraph on an inside page of the dailies.

They'd come anyway, along with a contingent of people from the town who would probably claim they had come to 'support' their famous neighbour and 'show respect', but their eyes were gleaming with prurient curiosity.

The cars stopped and the doors were opened for them. Anna got out and walked to the door of the chapel, through the blitz of flashing bulbs and machine-gun rattle of shutters as if she hadn't noticed that they were there. As she went inside, the storm abated and Cassie, walking behind, heard a nearby reporter say into a microphone, her voice dripping with synthetic sympathy, 'And here is Anna Harper arriving along with her daughter to mourn the loss of a son and brother . . .' Cassie turned her head to give the woman a furious glare and had the satisfaction of hearing her stumble over her words.

The media would have been feeling cheated anyway that no famous literary names or actors who had starred in the films had appeared. Anna had seen to that – or rather, Marta had. She'd have done her 'scorched earth' act to protect Anna's privacy, like she always did when that was needed.

Marta Morelli – housekeeper, secretary, close friend and handmaiden to genius – was waiting for them now, square and sturdy, as she stood with the celebrant in the blessed quiet of the chapel vestibule. Despite the expensive tailoring of her black dress and jacket, she still looked like an Italian peasant woman with her greying hair scraped back, though she was younger than Anna. Today her olive skin was grey-looking and she had dark shadows under her brown eyes. Beside her Anna looked ageless, Cassie thought, as they were escorted into the chapel.

There were no more than a couple of dozen people there who had survived her mother's exclusion process: her agent, her publisher, some others Cassie didn't know. None of her own friends had been asked and none of Felix's either, though she didn't mind that considering the company he had kept.

Nor their father. Had Anna even told James Trentham? If she had, would he have come from Los Angeles for the first time in fifteen years, now when it was too late for him to have any relationship with his needy son? No, Cassie didn't mind his absence either.

They took their place in the front row. Anna folded her hands in her lap – elegant hands with slim fingers, the nails painted in a suitably muted pink – then sat entirely still throughout the short service, expressionless.

Impervious, Cassie thought as she struggled with her own composure. She didn't believe Anna was experiencing any deep emotion of any sort.

She was wrong. Inside the carapace of Anna Harper The Brand, Anna Harper the woman was very, very afraid.

Kelso Strang was standing at the farther end of the living room drinking his breakfast coffee, looking out of the window at the view over Newhaven harbour and pretending not to hear his niece.

Betsy was finishing her breakfast. 'Want Unkie to take me to nursery today,' she demanded again.

His sister Finella was having her usual morning panic about assembling packed lunches and collecting up papers she'd been working on to shove in her briefcase. She said wearily, 'No, Betsy. Unkie's too busy.'

'No he isn't,' her daughter pointed out with ruthless four-year-old logic. 'He's just standing there. I want Unkie to take me.'

Kelso sensed his sister's hopeful glance in his direction but ignored it. It wasn't good for Betsy to get away with being a monster because they couldn't face the hassle of taking her head on. He took his mug across to put in the dishwasher, then began to clear the plates from the breakfast table. If he left Fin to stack it there'd be no room for the supper dishes tonight.

He hadn't expected to still have house guests all this time later. When Finella left her partner Mark and she and Betsy had turned up so unexpectedly on his doorstep, he'd thought it would be a week or two, a month at most, before her lawyer could get Betsy's father out of the Morningside flat and them back in.

But that was before Mark was arrested on a charge of embezzlement. Finella had seen it coming; he hadn't been clever enough to cover it up and it had been pitifully obvious what he was doing. Kelso had even gone round to warn him that he wouldn't get away with it but only got sworn at for his pains.

Now, of course, there was no Morningside flat any more. Their parents had rallied round, offering Finella a home with them in Perthshire or help with rent for a flat in Edinburgh so she could go on with her work as a solicitor. But Finella, always so calm, so reliable – stalwart, indeed – had buckled under the strain.

'I couldn't bear to go home to them,' she had said pitifully. 'Mum's all right but Dad blames me for all of this.'

Kelso didn't try to deny it. Major General Sir Roderick Strang had found so much to disapprove of, even before things fell apart – his daughter's choice of Mark in the first place, and then her carelessness in failing to get respectably married before she had a baby – and it was hard to imagine him keeping his opinions to himself as details emerged at the trial.

'Well, he'll be glad now that you weren't married,' was the best he could offer.

'It's very good of them to say they'll help me rent a flat, but – but I just don't think I could cope.' She gave a watery smile. 'Sounds feeble, I know, but Betsy's been so confused and unsettled, I just dread upsetting her all over again. You saw her when Mark said he was coming to take her out and didn't turn up. I didn't know what to do.'

Oh yes, he'd witnessed Betsy's bewildered distress and been seized with a murderous rage; if he could have got his hands on the rotten bastard at that moment he'd have been the one up on a charge. With Finella so upset herself, it had needed Kelso to soothe the poor little thing with cuddles at first and then distraction – or bribery, to call it by its proper name. He could see what was coming.

There were tears in Finella's eyes. 'Oh I know, it's an awful cheek. But you've been wonderful and I just don't know what I'd do without you. Betsy adores you and I know you love her too. You wouldn't mind if we stayed just a bit longer, would you? Just till we find our feet again?'

'No, of course I don't mind.' What else could he say? But it shocked him to realise quite how much he did mind.

He loved kids. He and Alexa had been on their way to having their own, before the accident that had killed them both and left Kelso with a scar down the side of his face as a memento. The emptiness of the house – an old fisherman's cottage on the shore at Newhaven in Edinburgh – had oppressed him at first, but in time he had come to relish it as an oasis in his stressful professional life. Having been an army sniper he had always been comfortable enough with his own company, and being DCI of the Serious Rural Crime Squad was a maverick job that could mean being sent solo anywhere in Scotland to direct operations at the local level where there was only a scaled-down CID.

Your own child is one thing; someone else's child quite another. He'd never felt inclined to create a shrine of any sort, but in the little yellow-painted bedroom, so hopefully prepared as a nursery, there had lingered if not quite a ghost then the gentle spirit of the child who had never been. Now it resounded to Betsy's cheerful chattering and her toys lay so thick on the ground that you could hardly see the carpet.

And when he had come home after being away on a job to find that Finella had emptied out all the kitchen cupboards and reorganised them, he'd had to get out of the room so that he wouldn't explode.

'It's much easier for breakfast now,' she had said happily to his retreating back. 'Much more logical. I can't imagine why you would want to have the coffee in this one, and the cereal right along there at the other end.'

Because that was where my darling Alexa put it, he said silently and savagely to himself in his bedroom. It was ridiculous to find tears in his eyes over something like this. When was the last time he'd actually cried? But he had so little left of Alexa now, and yes, cereal at the far end was illogical. He'd said that himself but she'd ignored him; leaving it where it was had meant that now when he wanted cereal he'd often thought of her with a little smile. Bit by bit, the house was being scourged of the past he and Alexa had shared.

He put the cereal packet back in its sensible place on the shelf below the coffee. Betsy was scowling now, the big blue eyes stormy. 'Mummy, I said I – want – Unkie – to – take – me,' she whined.

It was Finella's turn to become absorbed at the far end of the room. Kelso could perfectly understand why she ducked confrontations. Having got away with far too much recently, Betsy had become adept at escalating a whine into a full-blown tempest of tears, which would leave everyone exhausted apart from her.

With an inward sigh, Kelso said, 'Why don't you ask me, Betsy?'

The storm clouds vanished and she beamed. 'Please, Unkie, will you take me?'

He sat down opposite. 'Well, Betsy, I can take you. But if I do, I will be in a very bad temper because you know you're being naughty. I won't speak to you, I won't put on the radio so you'll just have to sit and think about whether this has been a good idea. Or you can go with Mummy as usual and I'm sure she'll be much nicer.'

Betsy looked comically crestfallen. She shot him a look under her lashes and then got down from her chair and went over to her mother without saying anything, her thumb in her mouth.

It was no fun having to be the bad cop, but it worked. 'That's a good girl,' he said cheerfully. 'And I tell you what – I'll even read you a Peppa Pig story at bedtime tonight.'

Finella gave him a grateful look. 'Now that really is heroic,' she said. 'Thanks, kid. And thanks too for—'

'Aw, shucks,' he said, and smiled at Betsy. 'Am I forgiven?'

Still pouting a little but pragmatic, she came across to kiss him goodbye. '*Two* stories?' she said, with a cajoling smile.

'It'll depend how good you've been,' he warned as she set off with her mother.

Kelso looked at his watch and sighed. Time he was off too. It went without saying that he loved his sister and his wilful little niece had a firm hold on his heart, but he couldn't help hoping that another investigation would come up soon to take him away from Edinburgh. Preferably to the Outer Isles.

As they drove back from the crematorium along the high street in Halliburgh, Cassie Trentham leant forward to the driver. 'Let me off here, please. I'm not going up to the house.'

For the first time since they had left that morning, Anna Harper had a spontaneous reaction. Her head whipped round to look at her daughter. 'We have guests coming back. As Chair of the Foundation, you're a hostess.' The car was slowing down; she raised her voice to say to the driver, 'You have your instructions already. Drive on.'

'Your guests, not mine. I've done enough for The Brand today and that's it.' Cassie turned to the driver. 'I'm getting out here whether you stop or not so I think it would be wiser if you did.'

She could see him stifling a smile. 'Right you are, miss. I'll pull in further along there.'

Anna said coldly, 'I'm not going to have an argument with you—'

'No, you're not,' Cassie said with something of her mother's hauteur. 'Thanks very much,' she added to the driver, reaching for the door handle as the car stopped.

Marta, sitting between them, put a hand on Cassie's arm. 'This is a very difficult day for your mother, Cassie. Don't make it worse.' She still retained an Italian accent but her English was perfectly fluent.

Cassie's dark blue eyes blazed with anger. 'A difficult day for my *mother*? When she's arranged to have a party while my brother is even at this moment being reduced to ashes? Oh puh-lease!'

'You know she has a duty,' Marta said stiffly, but she was speaking to empty air. Cassie had jumped out and was hurrying away. She turned to look anxiously at Anna. 'Are you all right, *cara*?' she said, lowering her voice so that the driver could not hear.

Anna bit her lip. 'It doesn't look good. We should be presenting a united front. You know how the press picks up on these things.'

Trying to reassure her, Marta said, 'It's only your friends coming back to the house, after all.'

Anna gave her a level look. 'Friends? You're the only friend I have. These are potential enemies who must be neutralised before the next gossipy literary party.' She sighed. 'I'll just have to say I could see how distressed Cassie was and I ordered her home to rest. That's the best I can do.'

* * *

Blinded by tears, Cassie stumbled away from the car and heard it move off behind her. How *dare* Marta talk to her about Anna's 'difficult day'? Not that she was surprised. Marta saw everything through the prism of Anna's wishes.

She was warm-hearted enough: in many ways she'd been more of a mother to Cassie and Felix than Anna had ever been, but it was affection at second hand. Children need to be loved for themselves, but Marta only loved them because they were Anna's. In any clash of wills – and there were plenty of those – there was never any doubt whose side Marta was on. She might listen to their complaints, might even sympathise, but her advice would always be the same: do what your mother says. By and large, Cassie had. Felix hadn't.

And look what came of that, she thought.

They'd be arriving back at the house now, ready to greet the 'mourners' – and that was a joke. Cassie doubted if any of them had even met Felix and she knew what their immediate reaction had been to the news of his death: damage limitation. She'd actually overheard a publicist saying, 'Last thing we need just before the launch of *Jacob's Angel*.'

By now they'd be accepting carefully judged canapés along with some suitably unfestive, but of course expensive, choice of wine. Marta would be sure to have found the appropriate ones to accompany the hostess's son's body being burned.

God, she wished she hadn't thought of that. She

couldn't get it out of her mind now – Felix, the flames, the smell . . . She gagged, afraid she would vomit, right there on the street.

She'd turned off the high street into a side street that led uphill and out of the town towards her cottage. A sullen sleety rain had set in now and the rounded hills circling the valley where the little town lay felt oppressive today, as if they were coming in closer, closer.

She was passing the Foundation building on the other side of the road now, closed today of course. It was very stark, very modern compared to its traditional neighbours; there had been a lot of opposition at first but of course Anna had got what she wanted. She always did.

Cassie's hair was soaking but she barely noticed. Walking with her head down she'd been aware of one or two passers-by glancing at her, but only briefly; the ghouls wouldn't have had time to get back from the crematorium and now she'd reached the thirty-mile sign she should be safe enough.

After the turn-off it was another steep and very wet half-mile along a narrower road before she reached her cottage, standing on its own in a little walled garden. Today it looked grim but on a sunny day the position was idyllic, looking out over the valley to the gentle hills on the other side. Cassie had been charmed when first she saw it. It was built of old grey stone with a rustic porch and a slate roof and had arched dormer windows like eyebrows that gave it, she thought, a rather fetching quizzical look.

'Small, but perfectly formed,' she had said to Felix.

'Oh bijou, darling, positively bijou,' he had drawled, and then said, 'Gilded cage?'

She had flushed. She knew exactly what he meant; Anna was luring her back to take charge of running the Foundation and this was the bribe: her very own home, no strings attached. The thing was, it was an alluring job – liaising with publishers and film-makers, answering enquiries, overseeing the charity side – and the alternative was job-hunting on her own merits with an unexciting arts degree.

She'd let herself be bought and she hadn't regretted it. She loved the work and if she was honest it had satisfied, too, the craving for her mother's attention that she still hadn't managed to kick even as an adult. But if she'd turned it down, she thought now as she unlocked the front door – tastefully painted in Farrow and Ball Dix Blue – she'd have been in Edinburgh with Felix, perhaps might have been able to curb his self-destruction.

It was undeniably charming inside too. Marta had found the interior decorator for her with some skill; somehow the woman had known just what Cassie wanted but wouldn't have been able to organise for herself and she'd always felt a little buzz of pleasure as she came into the sitting room that now ran right across the front of the house – a calm, welcoming room with big glass lamps on low tables and a couple of squashy sofas with white loose covers and scatter cushions that provided clever accents of colour.

She didn't feel that now. The whole house was tainted with the memory of Felix's death.

A couple of men had brought him there from the bus shelter in the village where he'd been found collapsed, comatose, drooling, snoring; the ambulance, they said, was on its way but it didn't arrive in the half-hour it took him to die while Cassie screamed at him, weeping, as she tried to get some response. Her screams seemed somehow to have permeated the very fabric of the place, even though Marta had seen to it immediately that all visible signs be removed.

Cassie walked straight through to the kitchen at the back, sleek and modern with its polished granite worktops, and extended into a glass conservatory looking out at the hillside rising just behind. The sleet was heavier now and despite the heating the room felt cold and she shuddered. She didn't know what she wanted – a cup of tea, a glass of wine? Brandy, probably, only she didn't have any. She hardly had the energy to fill the kettle or open the fridge.

She sank down on to a chair beside the dining table. She could just sit here and cry some more, though she felt dry, shrivelled, as if she'd no tears left. Her mobile was lying on the table in front of her and she picked it up listlessly, by way of distraction.

There had been a number of calls and texts from friends, three from Gil Paton, but she swiped through them all. The last one was from Kate Graham. She hesitated, then clicked on the name and read the text message, which was brief. 'Here if you want me. Free until eleven.'

Cassie looked at it for a long moment, then texted, 'Thanks. Yes please.' She sat staring out at the sleet while she waited for Kate to arrive.

The media packed up and departed and the crowd around the crematorium dispersed. A Ford Fiesta was trundling out in the stream of cars leaving the car park.

'Lady Muck didn't seem too upset, did she?' the driver said acidly.

There were two other women in the car. Her front-seat passenger sniffed. 'That's right, Moira. Just looked straight through us when she came out – not even a smile to thank us for bothering to come.'

'Cassie looked really upset, though, Denise,' the woman in the back seat said. 'I thought she was going to burst into tears.'

'I didn't say anything against Cassie, Sally. She's all right – and Felix too, poor laddie. Terrible thing. All that money, and this is where he ends up. Just shows you.'

'You get what's coming to you,' Moira said wisely.

Denise nodded. 'Right enough. It's all about money, with Anna. Shoves it in our faces, to show what she's got compared to us peasants. It sticks in my throat the way we have to grovel just to get a bit of it for the community.'

'Well don't take it, then,' Sally said tartly. 'She's a right to do what she wants with her money – she's earned it.'

A chill descended on the car. After a pointed silence Moira said, 'Well, I suppose, if you call it earning just to sit down and scribble a load of rubbish. Sally, I'll drop you off first.'

'That's great. Thanks, Moira.' It would mean driving past Denise's door but Sally was unsurprised. She'd gone along out of genuine sympathy with the bereaved family and her unhelpful remarks were spoiling their fun. Once they got rid of her they could go back to slagging Anna off as much as they liked.

She was a relative newcomer to the area and had been naively shocked that a nice, friendly wee town like Halliburgh could harbour so much animosity towards someone who was so much their benefactor. The trouble, she supposed, was that Anna gave the impression that she'd bought a fiefdom where she could behave as she chose. Objections had poured in to the plans for her house and the Harper Foundation building which were totally out of keeping with the local architecture but the council seemed to be putty in her hands. There were rumours, too, that a housing development application by a local builder – Moira's husband, in fact – had been turned down because Anna had felt it encroached on her privacy.

No one expected a world-famous author to base her social life here, but if she'd actually turned up to even some of the events that kept the heart of the community beating strongly, instead of sending a cheque or authorising a grant when asked, it might have been different. But she didn't; she wasn't interested in Halliburgh except on her own terms as a country retreat where her money could ensure that her privacy was ruthlessly protected.

Death didn't respect the power of money, though, and now Sally thought about it, too much probably did every bit as much harm as too little – and being rich and famous was no consolation if it led to losing your only son.

For once she didn't sigh over the state of the paintwork and the sagging gutter that dripped water on her head as she let herself into her modest semi.

CHAPTER TWO

The cars following the funeral limousine swept through the town in a decorous procession. The stop, apparently to let Anna's daughter get out, was unexpected. At the wheel of the third car Anna's editor Janine White grimaced sympathetically as she drew up.

'Can't cope with the wake, poor girl? I'm not surprised. She looked as if she was on the verge of breaking down in the chapel.'

As the leading car moved on again her passenger Richard Sansom said, 'Her mother wasn't. Not even a decent quiet tear – looked as if she was carved out of granite. Probably he was a liability, given the drug problem. Hard as nails, our Ms Harper.'

Janine gave him a sharp look. 'Heading up publicity for her you can't even afford to think that thought.

Anna's just a very private person who doesn't wear her heart on her sleeve.'

'Oh sure,' Richard said, but there was a satirical edge to his voice. 'I don't have to believe it to say it.'

Janine frowned as they turned up the hill towards Anna's house a little way out of the town. She wasn't entirely happy about Richard, who had recently joined the PR department in Harrington Publishing. He was a self-confident thirty-something, fair-haired, blue-eyed though not as good-looking as he thought he was and hard as nails himself, in Janine's estimation, but he was extremely efficient and so far Anna had made no complaints – they'd lost two or three people before on that count – and perhaps he'd settle in to it.

'Why does she live out here, anyway?' Richard asked. 'Back of beyond – wouldn't think it would appeal.'

'I think the global success of *Stolen Fire* came as a shock. She actually said in an interview at the time that she was completely thrown by the stress of it all and she'd come here once early on to do an event and just felt that it was somewhere wonderfully peaceful. She's got that nice little pied-à-terre in Holland Park when she wants a bit of civilisation.'

'Odd that she's not launching *Jacob's Angel* from there, then. She's only been to London twice for about ten minutes since I joined the company. The last time it seemed as if she couldn't wait to get away.'

'Yes, she's certainly been more reclusive lately. Working on another book, maybe? We can always hope. You're staying on here, aren't you? With the Foundation Writers Retreat on just now she'll want to be sure you're on hand and I suppose you can do quite a bit in the run-up to the launch too. Where are you staying?'

Richard grimaced. 'There's a pub in the village that isn't too dire, I suppose. I'm braced for fire-fighting in case someone does a snarky, "How come the woman who embodies the dreams of hope for all the world has a dysfunctional family?" piece.'

Janine shuddered. 'Don't even think that.'

Highfield House was just coming into view, its white bulk looming up out of the sleety drizzle. With its sharply art deco lines and expanses of plate glass, it was jarring against the backdrop of a comfortable rural landscape and the soft grey and pink stone of the buildings in the town below. Janine, who had been there before, still found it startling. Richard, who hadn't, whistled.

'Wow, that's giving them the finger isn't it? Malibu Beach comes to Halliburgh!'

Janine said, uncomfortably, 'I think there was a little bit of opposition. Here's the gateway now.'

There had been a police presence at the crematorium and there was a police car parked outside the house, a deterrent to ambitious journalists, but there was no one around as Anna's car came up to the front door. Janine drove on round the side of the house to a tarmac car park area to stop beside a caterer's van and a couple of other cars.

As they drew up, Richard said, 'So – what do we say to her as we go in?'

There was a sort of suppressed excitement about him that Janine found distasteful. 'You don't need to say anything much. "Sorry for your loss," that sort of thing. Just remember you're talking to a bereaved mother.'

'If you say so,' Richard said as he got out.

There were curved steps leading up to the imposing flattened arch of the front entrance. A waiter was acting as doorman, and James Harrington, head of the firm, was already on his way in, followed by the CEO.

There was no sign of Anna or even Marta in the wide hall, minimally furnished with an art deco wooden table in the centre with a Lalique glass sculpture sitting on it and a pair of wooden settles against the end walls. A gallery ran high above along the back, and another waiter came forward to show them up wide, shallow stairs to the sitting room at first-floor level, looking out over the town in the valley below. It was well heated but a fire was blazing in the pale stone fireplace and Anna, a glass already in her hand, was standing beside it as if she welcomed its warmth. Marta was hovering at her side as James went up to greet her.

'James!' Anna said, leaning forward to kiss him on either cheek. 'So good of you to come. Sorry Cassie isn't here to say hello. I know she was looking forward to having a chat, but she was so upset, poor child, I insisted that she just went home. She and Felix were very close. Do forgive her.'

‘Of course, of course,’ James boomed heartily. ‘Entirely understandable. And how are you, my dear?’

‘Oh—’ Her hand waved away a question. ‘Keeping busy. Now, I did just want a quiet word with you . . .’ She linked arms with him and drew him to the far end of the big room.

The other guests appeared, pausing uncertainly on the threshold, then forming an awkward grouping beside the window, lamenting the weather that was spoiling the view across the valley. Marta, who had disappeared, came back escorting two waitresses with trays of tiny sandwiches and croustades and glasses of wine.

It was obvious there would be no question of formal greetings. The conversations, stilted at first, gradually fell into the usual pattern of chat and gossip and the volume level rose. After a little while Janine withdrew herself and went across to where Anna and James were still deep in conversation. She hesitated, wondering if James was in need of rescue, though not wishing to butt in, but as she came up Anna turned to include her.

On the outskirts of the group, Richard looked on, his eyes cold and cynical. He had seen Felix Harper consigned to the flames; now he was watching him, with his inconvenient weakness, being buried.

PC Kate Graham checked her phone once she’d finished hoovering and clicked on Cassie Harper’s text. She’d been planning to go to the crematorium where perhaps she could have caught Cassie’s eye encouragingly as she went in, but someone else had been assigned to do the police presence bit – not that any problem was expected, but given Anna Harper's profile it was always possible.

She hadn't been at all sure what it was likely to say and she was pleased to be wanted, even if it did mean a dash to finish up here before she went on duty.

Kate was worried about Cassie's state of mind. When the 999 call came in she'd arrived at Burnside, Cassie's cottage, before the ambulance did; helplessly watching Felix Trentham die had been one of the most hideous experiences in her professional life. She'd joined in Cassie's frantic efforts to rouse him, knowing they were pointless, and the scream Cassie had given when she realised they had lost him still echoed in her own dreams. She didn't dare to let herself imagine what it had done to Cassie.

She had asked to be assigned as family liaison officer. Her approach to Anna Harper had been met with chilly courtesy and the promise that she would contact DC Graham if she felt it would be useful, her manner suggesting that hell would freeze over first.

It was different with Cassie. By then she was back in Burnside and when she opened the door she collapsed into Kate's arms, sobbing. 'You tried,' she said. 'Thank you. You tried.' Then they had talked for many, many hours as she ranted about her mother and obsessively went over Felix's history.

'I'd almost given up hope. I didn't even know where he was – he hadn't been in touch for months. And then, thank God, he was arrested and he was scared enough to get in touch. He'd been sleeping rough, permanently stoned, and got into some kind of trouble and was picked up. It wasn't anything major – just a fine and a slap on the wrist – but he agreed to come back here. He knew he couldn't go on like that – he didn't want to, I know he didn't. And I thought he would be so safe here. How could there be drugs in a place like this?'

Kate had given a wry smile. 'These days it's everywhere,' she said.

'But I don't believe he'd have gone out looking for it! He'd started to enjoy life again – putting on weight, planning to go back to uni. Someone must have done it deliberately, discovered his problem and offered it to him.'

It wouldn't have been difficult. Everyone in the town knew Felix Trentham was a druggie; there was no such thing as anonymity when you were Anna Harper's son. 'I expect that's right,' Kate said diplomatically.

Cassie leant forward to grasp her hand. 'So will you find out who? It was murder. They killed him.'

Kate had made some anodyne reply about investigations being under way but she knew it would come to nothing. Whatever his sister might like to think, the person who had killed Felix Trentham was Felix Trentham.

Cassie had been in shock at the time. Now, Kate thought, it was more as if she was suffering post-traumatic stress – having flashbacks, not sleeping, not eating. The funeral would have been hard indeed.

She hoped Cassie wasn't going to ask her about progress with the enquiry. The death certificate had been issued, the case had been closed and she couldn't herself see any reason why it shouldn't be. It would be hard for Cassie to accept that someone was just going to, as she saw it, get away with murder.

Kate sighed as she put the hoover away, checked that her father's lunch was laid out ready for the carer and fetched her coat.

'That's me away, Dad,' she called.

'All right, love. You just take good care of yourself, now,' he called back as he always did when she went out to work the mean streets of Halliburgh. Kate was smiling as she drove away. He was very uncomplaining, her dad, however frustrating he found his limitations.

She drove up through sleet that was getting thicker by the minute to Cassie's cottage. It was certainly picturesque, but she wouldn't choose to live out here in winter when the smaller roads were so frequently blocked with snow.

At the cottage, she tapped on the door and walked in calling, 'Hello!' Cassie must be in the kitchen as usual; Kate wondered if she'd ever sat in the front room since that terrible night. She hurried through it herself.

Cassie was sitting slumped in a chair at the table in the conservatory, her face as bleak as the dreary landscape outside. She turned her head and made an attempt at a smile.

'Thanks, Kate. I'm sorry to bother you. I don't even know what there is that you can do.'

'Make a cup of tea for a start,' Kate said briskly, switching on the kettle and picking up a tin. 'And there are some chocolate digestives I brought last time – unless you've eaten them all? No, I didn't think so. Right – now tell me about it.'

Angry colour came into Cassie's face. 'Would you believe my mother said nothing – nothing? Not a word, not a look, until she tried to make me go to this party she arranged.'

'Party?' Kate was startled.

'I suppose she'd call it a wake. But none of them cared about Felix, Kate. Most of them didn't know him at all. It was a public relations exercise to protect The Brand.'

Kate had heard all about The Brand, to which everything else had to be subservient. She brought over the mugs and biscuits and sat down, taking a biscuit herself and putting one in front of Cassie. 'So what are you going to do now?'

Cassie bit into the biscuit, almost absent-mindedly. 'I suppose I'm going to get up tomorrow and just keep buggering on. What's the alternative?'

'Will you be happy to go on working for your mother, after what you've said to me?'

Cassie gave a deep, deep sigh. 'If I resigned the only

person it would hurt would be me. She wouldn't care.'

Anna Harper, as portrayed by her daughter, had no emotions recognisable as human. Kate had felt the icy edge of her personality herself, but Anna had taken some trouble to keep her daughter close. Affection? Expediency? She wouldn't presume to know.

'Are you going in tomorrow?' Kate was concerned. 'You're looking shattered. Should you not take a few days off?'

Cassie gave a short laugh. 'And do what? Sit here staring out at that?'

The sleet was turning to snow, the flakes thicker, dancing a silent ballet against the grey backdrop of hill and sky. She was probably right to keep herself busy, but when Kate left she was still concerned. The problem was she couldn't think what else to suggest. She certainly couldn't see Cassie going to her mother so they could grieve together.

The guests had lingered at Highfield House as if no one quite liked to be the first to go. With the leaden sky the light had been fading even before they left and now it was quite dark. The fire in the stone fireplace was dying, just a few smouldering embers in their pile of ash. A basket heaped with logs stood beside it, but Anna Harper made no move to put them on, and though there were several table lamps casting pools of ambient light she had chosen to sit in a corner where no light fell. The floor-to-ceiling windows that ran right across one end of the room with no curtains to mar their architectural elegance were great squares of blackness.

She didn't turn her head when the door opened. Marta's voice said, 'Anna?' and then, 'Oh, you are there. At first I didn't see you. And the fire – it is going out.' She bustled over to create a base of kindling then logs piled so skilfully that they caught at once. 'That's better. I know the heating's on but you always like to see the flames.' She turned round.

Anna was sitting on a cream leather sofa with a glass in her hand and Marta frowned. 'You are drinking all day, *cara*. How many pills did you take?'

'Not enough.'

Marta sighed then went over to the drinks cupboard, which was standing open, and poured herself a glass before she came back to sit at the other end. 'You managed.'

'I got through it, yes. But Marta,' her voice was thick with tears, 'Cassie thinks I didn't love him. I did, you know I did!'

'Cassie's upset. She doesn't really mean it.'

'Oh yes, she does, and I know why. I've been an odd sort of mother. It's just that when I'm writing, I'm possessed, as if somehow I'm being forced to write, and I get so absorbed that the books are more real than reality. Real people seem sort of – faded, I suppose, compared to the characters. Real people are, well, out there, whereas they're in me, part of me, all the time.'

'I know, I know.' Marta reached across to pat Anna's hand. 'You do what you must do. You were given the gift for a purpose and right from the day when *Stolen Fire* was published, you have been changing people's lives, right across the world. How many of your readers have written to thank you? Hundreds – thousands, even! And your children – they have wanted for nothing.'

Anna looked at her, mouth twisted in a cynical smile.

'Wanted for nothing,' Marta repeated firmly. 'But they could not have *everything*. They wanted all of you – that's what every child wants – and they couldn't have it. What does he say – the writer you like? You march to a different drum?'

'Thoreau,' Anna said. 'Oh yes.' She took another sip of her wine.

'Anyway, it was all right today, do you think?'

Anna sighed. 'I hope so. They seemed to accept Cassie not being there.'

'That was natural – she is a girl who has lost her brother. They were sympathetic.'

'It's just we can't afford scandal, Marta – not right now with so much attention on the book coming out.'

'Not scandal. Just tragedy.'

'Yes.' Anna shifted in her seat. 'It's just . . . well, you know. With this hanging over us . . .'

'It's gone quiet these past two weeks,' Marta said. 'We don't even know what it is all about – we are only guessing. And here we have good security.'

'Yes of course, it could be anything and we're just hypersensitive. But whatever it is, how did he know we were here? How did he even know my personal addresses? The last note came here, right after we left Holland Park. I feel he could be watching us at this moment. I feel trapped – it's like being imprisoned. And how can you go to the police when you're a criminal yourself? Did you look at the crowd at the crematorium this morning?'

'Of course. No one seemed strange, but then I don't know what I look for. Not even if it is him or her.' Marta leant forward to look the other woman in the face. 'Anna, you always said you didn't know. Now, I have to be sure – was that really true?'

'Oh yes,' Anna said heavily. 'You remember – they'd said it would be best, given what I fed them about the father having got custody and taking it away. And I certainly didn't want to know.'

Marta sighed. 'Yes. They were right, I think, but now . . . Could a woman be so cruel, ruthless, like a man would be?'

'Why not? "More deadly than the male," you know. And probably more subtle too.'

'I suppose, maybe. But we must not be frightened into being stupid. It is all about money, I think. Blackmail. You have money. Pay him to go away.'

'But there's no contact! How can I, when all we get is these notes, with no way to get back to him? He doesn't mention money.' She looked up to meet her friend's eyes. '"You know what you have done", and then all the guilt and atonement stuff. Perhaps he is just a random religious nut, but I don't think so and neither do you. He means to frighten us, and he does. I'm afraid, Marta – I'm so afraid!' Anna drained her glass and got up to refill it.

Marta got up, determinedly practical. 'If you drink any more you will not be more brave, you will just be ill. You need to eat. I will make you an omelette, yes?' She didn't wait for an answer before she went downstairs to the kitchen.

Anna took her full glass and went to stand by the window, looking out. All she could see was her own reflection and beyond it the reflection of the lamps in the room, dancing on the darkness. Was he, or she, out there looking in? She shuddered, suddenly feeling vulnerable, a target in this lighted room, and fled back to her shadowy corner.

She heard Marta's footsteps coming back up the stairs, quick footsteps, her shoes clicking on the polished wood floor. Too soon to have made the omelette. With sudden foreboding, Anna swung round.

Marta's face was pale. She was holding out an envelope addressed to Anna Harper, in block capitals and black ink. 'On the hall table,' she said. 'I only noticed it when I switched the lights on just now.'

Anna took it, though her hands were shaking so much she had to take two attempts to slip her thumb under the seal. She drew out the note inside and Marta came to stand beside her so that they could read it together.

It was computer-printed on ordinary paper, as usual, and it was brief, as all the notes had been. Just two words.

'Payback time.'

CHAPTER THREE

Kayleigh Burns took an anxious glance at her watch and gave a final polish to the gleaming black marble surface beside the sink in Anna Harper's kitchen. She undid the strings of the smart black and white-striped linen apron inherited from the previous cleaner, which tied twice round her slim waist, and went to put it away in the cleaning cupboard. It swung open to a fingertip touch and she hung it on the hook below the label marked 'apron' in Marta's firm script.

She gave a final glance round to make sure nothing marred the pristine surfaces: no garish bottle of cleaner, no blue rubber gloves carelessly left out to spoil the chilly purity of the black and white room. It was a kitchen meant for cooking in, not for being the cosy hub of the house, and Marta was apt to behave as if someone had goosed her if she came in and found something out of place – dried up old bat! She wasn't sure how Anna would react; she wasn't entirely sure that Anna had ever been in the kitchen. Not that she was 'Anna' to Kayleigh. Presumably she was Mrs Trentham, though Marta always referred to her as Ms Harper. Kayleigh hadn't as yet really had occasion to call her anything.

In addition to her routine cleaning, the caterers had left her with all the clearing-up to do, though she obviously hadn't been considered worthy of the honour of handing round drinks to the guests. There hadn't been that many of them but from the sound of it they'd enjoyed themselves all right – lots of chat and even laughter, empty bottles and hardly any canapés left over for her to finish off.

Anna hadn't been exactly in pieces, then. That figured; Kayleigh hadn't seen any sign that she'd been devastated when it happened, either. Cold-blooded, she'd been. Showed what sort of mother she was, caring so little about her child.

It made Kayleigh think about her own son. She glanced at her watch again. She'd been hoping to get back to the flat before he got home from school. She was running late; Jason, her partner, was always irritable if Danny interrupted his writing schedule and if Danny found that she wasn't in he was likely to go straight back out again. She was worried about the company he was keeping; he was a big boy for twelve and some of the kids he ran around with were years older. She knew all too well the sort of stuff they were into and the thought of Danny getting drawn in scared her rigid.

With a last glance around the big room that under the LED task lighting looked as sterile as an operating theatre, Kayleigh hurried out. It fell into darkness behind her as she pressed the switch but as soon as she stepped outside the security lights came on.

There was a soughing wind now and the soft, wet snow was falling fast. It wasn't lying, though; the tarmac on the area here at the back where she parked her elderly Fiat was glistening black. She drove down to the electric gate and got out to key in the code. The gate swung open obediently and she drove off down the hill. As she took the turn on to the road the car slid just slightly and her heart missed a beat; the road surface was greasy under the worn tyres she couldn't afford to replace and if she wrote off the car she'd lose her job and that would be a disaster. She got it back without mishap, though, and parked it outside the flat in a side road just off the high street.

'Hello!' she called as she let herself in, brushing a few snowflakes off her hair.

There was no reply and her heart sank. She knew not to expect a response from Jason if the writing was going well but by now Danny should be home. 'Danny?' she called, going along to open the door to his bedroom. It was empty, if you could describe as empty a tiny room so crammed with random objects. She was forbidden to tidy it, but she picked her way across to collect up the dirty glass and plate with toast crumbs from the top of the pile of stuff on the table by his bed.

In the galley kitchen, almost comical in its shoddiness compared to the one she had just left, a jar of Nutella stood on the chipped red Formica surface with a knife still stuck in it alongside a half-empty two-litre bottle of Irn-Bru with the cap left off. She sighed as she screwed it on again and put it back in the fridge. She couldn't see the Nutella lid but she washed the knife and put it back in the drawer, her stomach knotting with tension. She should have left earlier but Marta Morelli would be on her case if there was so much as a mug on the draining board.

Where was Danny? There was often a gang of them that met up round the bus shelter and once or twice she'd actually braved his fury and gone down there to fetch him home, but apart from that Kayleigh wouldn't begin to know where to look for him – and surely they wouldn't be outside on a night like this?

She hesitated. Was there any point in disturbing Jason to ask if Danny had spoken to him? It would certainly put Jason in a bad mood and he was unlikely even to have seen him. Then she heard him opening the door of their bedroom where he had fitted up a corner as a workspace.

'Oh good!' she said. 'Jason, have you seen Danny?'

He looked at her sardonically. 'Not, "Hello, love, have you had a good day?" No, I haven't. I heard him come in and I heard him go out again about ten minutes ago.'

'Oh. Well, I expect he'll be back when he's hungry.' Kayleigh managed a smile. 'So – how was your day, then?'

Jason shrugged. 'Got a bit done. But more to the point, how were things at Anna's palace?'

'Busy. People came back after the funeral and I'd a lot of clearing up to do—'

He made an impatient sound. 'I meant, how's she taking it? Quite a humiliation for the Queen of Perfection to have to admit to a crackhead son OD-ing. What was she wearing?' His tone was unpleasant.

'I didn't see her.'

'Of course, with you working below stairs, you wouldn't. Didn't come and give you a twirl once she was ready to go? I wondered, you see, if she'd go deep black for mourning or a defiant bright red to pretend it was a service of thanksgiving – unlikely that, I suppose, since she must be pissed off as hell that he did it just before the big launch we've been hearing so much about. Do you suppose he did that deliberately, to spoil her fun? She certainly asks for it.'

Kayleigh knew all too well why Jason was bitter. It was a grievance he rehearsed so regularly that she could have recited it in unison with him. The local paper had interviewed him when his debut novel came out and, clearly taken with the notion of two great novelists in one small place, made an unfortunate reference to 'a young Anna Harper in the making'. The review that had appeared in the *Sunday Times* the following week had been pitiless and the fortune the book was going to make him had never materialised. Having read *The Dark Hunger* herself, Kayleigh was fairly certain that it hadn't been going to anyway – there had been no other reviews – but Jason claimed that Anna had the critic in her pocket and that he'd been a victim of the Harper curse. Her reaction to anyone setting even a tentative toe on her territory was reputedly brutal and he had just been unlucky.

It was all the more surprising that he'd applied for a place on one of the Harper Foundation's Writers' Retreat weeks – not only that, but for this particular one, where Anna Harper gave her once-a-year masterclass. It had, of course, been heavily oversubscribed but local applicants usually got preferential treatment. And maybe Anna had felt a bit guilty about that review, but if she thought this would soften him up, she'd another thing coming.

Kayleigh had thought too that he'd object when she announced she'd got the job at Highfield but he'd only said, 'Might as well get something out of the old bitch,' and it certainly paid better than anything else around here. She was permanently skint, though he always seemed to have money for whatever he wanted to do. His only reply to Kayleigh's suggestion that he should get a job was, 'I have one already. I'm an author.'

He liked to indulge himself with constant gibes like, 'Do you have to turn your face to the wall and curtsey if you meet Her Majesty on the stairs?' and there was no doubt he was relishing what had happened.

'I don't suppose so,' she said flatly, then, 'Danny didn't speak to you, then?'

'No.' Jason's voice was equally flat.

'Right. I'll go and start the tea, anyway.'

Kayleigh went through to the kitchen loosening her dark hair from the ponytail she wore to work and running her hands through the curly mass, still damp from the snow. She rubbed her forehead; a muzzy headache had come on. It usually did when she got home, as if her body was reacting to the poison gas of hostility in the air. Next week, with him mostly along at the Foundation, would be a relief.

They'd only met after she'd arrived here a few months ago and it hadn't taken him long to move in with her. She'd hated being a single mother, anyway. She'd been in care as a child with no family for support and it was very lonely, particularly once Danny was past the cute, affectionate stage.

She'd been flattered at first by Jason telling her she could be his muse. He was quite sexy, with a dark, two-day stubble style, and he could be very charming when it suited him. Kayleigh had believed him when he told her he was going to be rich and famous, in that confident, expansive way he had. She didn't believe him now and he'd mostly stopped bothering to be charming unless he wanted something.

It would be good for Danny to have a man around as

he got older, she'd thought, but he and Jason had never clicked. A couple of weeks ago they'd had a screaming row about something – neither of them would tell her what it was – and now the only way she could keep them both in the same room for any length of time was when she put a meal on the table and wouldn't let Danny take his plate to his bedroom. Now, when Kayleigh was so worried about her son's activities, it would have been good to talk it through with Jason; he had good mates in the polis, after all, but when she tried he just shrugged and looked bored. If she was honest with herself, she didn't even like Jason much any more and Danny might have waited for her to get home if Jason hadn't been here, not just gone back out again.

She wasn't sure about that, though. If she did tell Jason to leave and Danny left home the minute he could, she'd be on her own again. And she hadn't liked that either. As she put the burgers in the frying pan she heard the flat door open and shut. 'Danny! In here!' she called and her son slouched in. 'Where have you been?'

He was a nice-looking boy, with reddish-fair hair and blue eyes but his face was set in a sullen expression. 'Just out. You weren't here,' he said in an accusing way.

'Sorry, sorry. It was a busy day at work. You know – I told you it was my boss's son's funeral.'

'Yeah. Whatever.' He went out again and when she called after him, 'It'll only be five minutes till your tea,' he didn't reply.

* * *

It had felt a long, long day after Kate Graham's visit. Cassie Trentham had been afflicted by the terrible inertia of grief; there was nothing she wanted to do, yet if she didn't find occupation all that was left to do was weep. Been there, done that, and now her puffy eyes and smarting cheeks were an active discouragement.

She'd turned on the radio but music too easily set her off again and she couldn't concentrate on discussions. There were the phone messages to reply to, but Cassie didn't trust herself not to break down. Then her eye fell on the pile of personal letters of condolence sent across from the Foundation that she'd left lying on the table in the conservatory after she'd read them, almost all from business contacts she'd had through managing The Brand. None of them were very meaningful – they hadn't known Felix – but they were well intentioned and deserved a response. There was even one from the star who'd got her big break all these years ago in the movie of *Stolen Fire* – very sympathetic, very kind.

That would be something she could do. Once she'd worked out a form of words, copying it as many times as necessary wouldn't be difficult. She fetched notepaper, envelopes, a pen, and sat down again at the table in the conservatory. But darkness had gathered, the wind was moaning and the naked windows made it feel cold and depressing. She hadn't sat in the sitting room since it all happened but now she told herself firmly that unless she was going to spend the rest of her life sitting on a hard chair in the kitchen, this was as good a time as any to confront her demons. She could switch on the lamps, draw the curtains, write her letters on her knee and try to adapt to the new normal.

The room sprang to life as Cassie turned on the lamps. There were flowers she had been sent and barely noticed in vases Marta had placed around the room; the delicious perfume of freesias hung on the air. With the heavy cream linen curtains closed against the night there was at least the illusion of comfort, and as she bent to her task the faint queasiness she had been feeling all day subsided.

A click – the sound of the garden gate being opened – shattered her peace. She jumped in alarm: there was someone there! Who could it be at this time of night? Living out here, she never had unexpected visitors. She stiffened and the sick feeling came back again. It couldn't be Kate who had said she was on a late shift. Surely it couldn't be the press – even they would have the decency to leave the family alone, for today at least? They were hardly known for sensitivity, though, and she hadn't heard a car, either. When the knock came on the door, she glanced through the peephole then frowned before she opened it.

The man standing in the little porch, snow falling behind him, was huddled into a parka, stout walking boots on his feet. He was smiling a little nervously.

'Hello, Cassie,' he said. 'I . . . I hope I'm not intruding. It's just – well, I've been thinking about you all day, hoping you were all right. I did phone, but—'

'Oh – Gil,' Cassie said, her voice flat. 'Goodness, have you walked all the way up in this weather? You'd better come in.'

He looked doubtfully at the pale grey carpet in the sitting room. 'I think I'd better take these off here.' He gestured towards his boots and she didn't stop him, watching as he wrestled with the leather laces and set them neatly on the boot shelf in the porch then stepped inside in his socks. As Cassie shut the door behind him, he took off the wet parka, shaking it and sending a misty spray on to a side table. 'Oops! Sorry!' He pulled down the cuff of his Aran sweater and rubbed at it.

Gil Paton was thickset with a swarthy complexion and dark brown hair already retreating; his round face was fringed with a thin beard that somehow emphasised the hint of a double chin. He was her deputy at the Foundation, a relatively new appointment and good enough at his job, but they were often thrown together as a result. She was afraid that he was starting to blur the edges between a professional and a personal relationship and she certainly wasn't going to encourage that by offering him a drink.

'Do sit down,' she said. 'It's very kind of you to bother.'

He sat down on the sofa opposite. 'Not at all. You know, I'd have come to the service but—'

'Yes, I know. You said. It was just that my mother felt she could only cope with the small number of people who know her best. We didn't want to make a big thing of it.'

'No, of course not. How is she taking it, your mother? Is she all right?'

'Yes, fine. Thanks for asking.'

'Must be terrible for her. Oh, and you, of course. Were she and your brother very close?'

'Yes.' It was the quickest thing to say and now she just had to get him sidetracked. 'You all had the day off, of course. What did you do with it?'

He had no alternative but to answer, though she sensed a reluctance to abandon the subject. 'Wasn't much of a day, really, what with the weather, and a couple of the Retreat writers were arriving in the afternoon so of course I had to be back here to welcome them. So I just did some stuff then got in an Asda shop over in Gala. They've good ready meals. Do you like Chinese?'

'Not really,' Cassie said as repressively as she could, before he could suggest that they sample some together. 'Who's arrived?'

'Two of the ladies – Sascha Silverton and Marion Hutton.' He gave a little snicker. 'Bit of a contrast – can't really see them hanging out together much.'

Cassie remembered them both from their application forms. Sascha, apparently a struggling writer of chick-lit but with literary aspirations and a lifelong desire to meet Anna Harper, 'my idol', had attached a glamour photo exhibiting luxuriant chestnut hair, a peach complexion and light brown eyes. Photoshopped, Cassie had suspected – and her name had more than likely had cosmetic treatment as well. Marion's, on the other hand, was one she'd probably had taken for her passport and showed a lady of a certain age with untidy grey hair and unbecoming spectacles. As a retired primary teacher, she now apparently had time to pursue her dream of 'a late blossoming' like Mary Wesley and Fay Weldon.

Cassie never knew how Anna picked the writers she did; on the whim of the moment, probably, as she read through the applications. 'Is everything ready for them?' she asked.

'Running like clockwork.' He sounded faintly huffy, as if even asking was an insult. 'I've introduced some new procedures, so that should tidy up some of the loose ends that were cluttering up the system.'

She tried not to bridle; she'd organised it until this year and it had always run perfectly smoothly, but he went on, oblivious, 'This is the showcase week so for the sake of our reputation we can't afford any hitches.' He was always very proprietorial about the Foundation.

'Absolutely,' Cassie said. He was right, of course; the Foundation offered half a dozen Writers' Retreat Weeks throughout the year in the Hub at the back of the building, designed with this in mind – free accommodation, food and quiet working space – but this was the only one where Anna got personally involved and given her reclusive nature it always attracted attention. Virtue-signalling on the cheap, she had often thought, cynically, for just the cost of heating and catering in the Hub, which also offered space for conference talks and local events.

'My one anxiety is that Anna won't be able to do the masterclass. You said she was very close to your brother – how is she reacting?'

Again, she sensed an unpleasant voyeurism in his interest and she ignored the question. 'My mother is always extremely professional. I'm sure it will go ahead as arranged. Anyway, I'll be in myself tomorrow and we can check through the arrangements together.'

Gil was taken aback, and quite obviously displeased. 'Oh, there's no need to drive yourself, Cassie, after all you've been through. I can cope. Take a rest – you look shattered.'

She seized her opportunity and stood up. 'I have to admit I am, yes. I'm planning on a very early night, but I want to keep busy. We'll be at full stretch again when *Jacob's Angel* launches.'

It gave Gil no alternative and once he had struggled into his boots Cassie shut the door behind him with considerable relief. She had to work with the man; it really wouldn't do to let him get under her skin, but five more minutes and she'd have come out in hives.

There were three men standing together as PC Kate Graham came into the general office in Halliburgh police station. She had heard a gust of laughter but now there was a sudden silence.

One of the men was PS Colin Johnston. He was holding a formal-looking letter, which he folded up with a sideways look at her as she came in. DS Grant Wilson was still grinning.

'No problem then, pal,' he said. 'Right, boss?'

DI Steve Hammond said, 'Right,' and as Johnston went out saying, 'Thanks, boss,' he turned his dark, narrow-eyed gaze on Graham.

'Well, how did it go?' he said.

They were an unhealthy trio. She could feel herself stiffening, becoming awkward. 'How did what go?'

'The Harper funeral.'

'I wasn't there. Someone else was assigned to it.'

'I know that. Have you checked on the family?'

As so often, she found herself on the defensive. 'As you know, Ms Harper has refused help. I did see Cassie Trentham briefly afterwards, but it was really just a short chat.'

'Have you filed a report?' He raised his eyebrows as she hesitated. 'Better to keep things formal, don't you think? Just do it by the book, Kate. All right?'

'Sir.' She went across to one of the computer stations and began typing. It wouldn't take long. There was no way she was going to put up any of Cassie's confidences for everyone to read.

There had always been an element in the Halliburgh force that she'd been uncomfortable with, grouped around DS Wilson. If you liked red hair and pale skin you might even say he was quite fit and he fancied himself as a bit of a ladies' man; she thought he was creepy and even though he was more careful about sexist remarks now with all the new directives, that only meant he didn't make them to her face. The quiet sniggering with his own little coterie was bad enough, and he homed in on new young officers to groom them too.

It certainly hadn't got any better since Hammond had arrived from Edinburgh, an officer very much in the new mould of thrusting careerists. Sharing best practice was a principle in Police Scotland, which meant that senior officers moved regularly – fine in theory, but it spread around other practices too. Wilson had got a lot more cocky since then and there were too many incidents lately that left her uneasy.

Today, for instance. Before Johnston could fold up his letter she'd seen enough to recognise what it was: a speeding fine. There was only one reason for him to show it to Wilson and Wilson to say, 'No problem, pal.' And there was no doubt Hammond was in on it too.

Graham was just finishing off the report when the inspector came over. 'You're down for a conference in Edinburgh tomorrow, aren't you?'

'Yes, sir. About using children as mules to get drugs out into the Borders. Actually, I was going to speak to you about kids here hanging round the bus shelter where Felix Trentham was found. I've seen them there several times and I don't recognise any of them. I wondered if we could have a problem.'

He considered that. 'It's always possible, I suppose. The trouble is we can't just grab them by the scruff of the neck the way they could back in the day. I'll keep an eye on it.' He smiled. 'Maybe you'll get all the answers to the problem tomorrow. They know everything in Edinburgh.'

Graham smiled back, though she always thought he was unusual in looking less pleasant when he smiled than when he didn't. She went back to file her report with a stifled sigh. Hammond was flavour of the month with the District Commander; he was adept at massaging the statistics so that it looked as if he was doing a terrific job – in Graham's view, to the point where they were downright lies – so they weren't likely to get rid of him unless he decided to go for promotion and that could take a while.

Cassie woke and squinted at the clock, astonished to see that it was quarter to nine. She'd slept so badly of late that she was usually ready to get up by six, despite the winter darkness.

She made an irritated noise as she jumped out of bed. She had wanted to be at her desk well before Gil came in at nine-thirty to find out from Jess, her PA, what had been going on in the last couple of weeks.

She looked out of the window at the weather. The wind had dropped overnight, the sleety rain had stopped and with the sun just coming up over the valley the sky was clear, streaked with amber and gold – a bright, chilly winter's day. Cassie always preferred to cycle down if possible and it didn't look as if showers were imminent. It would save time too if she just put on her Lycra now and had a shower when she arrived; she kept everything necessary to produce the finished product that was the Chair of the Foundation down there in her office. She dressed, buckled on her helmet and went round to the shed at the side to fetch her bike.

The road was clear though the snow was still lying in the fields and hills – a picture-postcard perfect view, with the stark outline of bare trees and the roofs and spires of the town below sharply etched against the morning sky, the old peel tower on the hill above starkly dramatic. The cold air was exhilarating and after a good night's sleep she was feeling better, more alive, after those terrible zombie days between Felix's death and the funeral. Getting back to work would do something towards making her feel she had turned a corner and freewheeling down the hill she felt a welcome surge of energy.

She was close to the junction with the main road when she heard a car coming down behind her. There wasn't much traffic on this little road but what there was tended to be of the rugged variety, demanding quite a lot of the space available. It made life less exciting if she tucked herself well in, almost on to the verge.

She only had time to think that it was coming far too close before she felt the impact. The bike spun away beneath her and she flew through the air, landing heavily in the ditch at the side of the road as the vehicle rushed on by. Then – nothing.

CHAPTER FOUR

Marta Morelli had barely slept. When she did doze off, she kept starting awake as if immediate danger threatened. Twice she had tiptoed through to Anna's room to see if she too was wakeful, but each time Anna was asleep and Marta had silently retreated, thankful that at least for a few hours Anna had respite from her problems. Perhaps the tranquillisers and too much wine hadn't been such a bad idea after all.

At five she had stopped trying to sleep. For well more than thirty years she had been Anna's dragon guardian and above all her friend, smoothing away every bump in the path. Their lives had been so intertwined for so long that she could barely have articulated her own interests. They had never counted for much; it was her joy and privilege to serve a genius she believed in with all her heart. She felt that yesterday she had failed.

How could she sleep, when she was failing?

Anyway, Anna would need cosseting today. There was a sweet Italian bread she particularly loved and if Marta put it to rise it would be ready for her breakfast.

The brilliant lighting in the kitchen had hurt her eyes, gritty from lack of sleep, as she mixed the dough. It wouldn't start getting light for hours yet and it made her uneasy that to anyone looking in she would be spotlit, as if on a stage. She cupped her hands against one of the windows to peer into the car park. It was empty and at any sign of movement the outside lights would come on. She must stop being paranoid.

She made herself bustle around, collected a bowl, flour, eggs – anything to take her mind off what had happened. They had made sure of state-of-the-art security – but yesterday someone had effortlessly breached it.

It was easy to explain. With the reception going on, there had been no security at all; any of the caterers could have put the envelope on the table, or any of the guests – or even a watchful someone who could have seen the open gates and the front door unguarded and taken his chance. And had he left, once he'd delivered it?

They had both felt something close to panic. 'What if he's here – right here in the house, still?' Anna's voice was trembling. 'I suppose we can look at the security film, but I'm scared to go out into the hall.'

With her own voice unsteady, Marta had taken charge. 'I'm getting Davy,' she said and went to the phone.

Davy Armstrong was whippet-thin and wiry with

dark brown hair and a long, narrow face. He had worked for Anna ever since she moved in, acting as gardener, driver or Mr Fixit as required and living with his wife in a grace-and-favour cottage two minutes away.

Anna got up to greet him, somehow managing to look calm, even faintly amused. 'I'm sorry to disturb you, Davy. I thought I heard the sound of movement from upstairs but it's probably just that I have an overactive imagination.'

'Well now, that's your job, isn't it?' He was slow-spoken, with that soft Borders accent. 'And it's no wonder if you're a bit jumpy. It's been a hard day for you, with that rubbish lot and their cameras. Me and Elspeth, we've been thinking about you the whole time. She says to give you her love.'

For the first time that day Anna's eyes brimmed with tears. 'Thank you – that's kind,' she said.

Davy nodded. 'Right. I'll just away round the house. I'll check all the rooms, and the cupboards as well, so you can be sure.'

He disappeared, and they heard his footsteps going along the gallery and doors opening and shutting. Neither of them spoke until he put his head round the door.

'No sign of anything. Now you just put on the security once I leave and you can go off to your bed with a quiet mind.'

'Thanks, Davy. I'm very grateful.'

'Och, no bother.'

As he left, Anna turned to Marta. 'There are good,

kind people, you know. In our world we don't see too many of those.'

'The Armstrongs like you, *cara*.'

'There aren't too many of those either.' She sank back into the corner of the sofa with an exhausted sigh.

Marta gave her a worried look. 'We don't have to sit here, waiting for the next one,' she said. 'We could go away. It would be natural. Have a break before the launch at our hotel. When you're stressed this always eases your mind. If we are not here, he could do nothing.'

'It's the Writers' Retreat week, remember – I have to be here for that. Anyway, he'd still be here when we got back and the last thing I want is to have him to follow us there where we'd be more exposed. No, Marta. All we can do is wait for his next move.'

Then Anna had paused. 'Payback time. Does that mean it's coming – or that there has been payback already?'

Kneading the dough, Marta shuddered. Surely it couldn't mean that Felix—No, no, she had told Anna, there had been no sign of violence. No one had forced Felix to take the overdose that killed him. Anna had nodded, but Marta had known she was thinking the same as she was – with Felix you wouldn't have to force, you'd only have to offer.

There had been no more anonymous notes after his death, until now. Indeed, though she had never said so, Marta was sure Anna had wondered if the letters had come from Felix himself. As she had. But his name was cleared now, poor boy.

So who could it be? The words had rung in her head all night; even now as she took the finished bread out of the oven she couldn't stop thinking about it. There was a monster lurking in the back of her mind, the monster that she couldn't forget and she didn't want Anna to remember – not that even Anna knew the full truth about that.

And despite the seductive fragrance of spice and orange peel that was flooding the house Anna, when she came down to breakfast, had no appetite for Marta's golden loaf.

DCS Jane Borthwick was frowning over the file that was open on her desk when DCI Kelso Strang came in. She looked up and smiled.

'Oh good! Morning, Kelso. I wasn't sure if you'd be working in the building on a Saturday.'

She was a serious-looking woman and her appearance, well-groomed but understated, played into that. She had a reputation, well deserved, for being formidable but there was warmth there when she smiled. She'd placed a lot of trust in him and Strang liked to think he was delivering for her. He took his place in the chair opposite.

'I'm involved in a small conference here this afternoon – a consciousness-raising exercise for the rural divisions. I've just been checking out the speakers. I wanted to get up to speed on this county lines problem before it actually blows up in our faces.'

She nodded, tapping the file. 'It's at the top of my

agenda. It's the hot favourite with the press at the moment: urban drug dealers setting up distribution lines out from the wicked cities into the innocent counties. Really gives them something juicy to sink their teeth into, doesn't it?'

Strang grimaced. 'It's happening, right enough. We're starting to get trouble in areas where there's never been a problem before. But getting a handle on it – that's a whole other question. We can't exactly board the country buses at the Elder Street station before they set out and frisk any suspicious-looking kids for mobile phones on speed dial to one of the known players.'

'If only! No, we need to have at least one end of the string before we do anything. But there's something I've homed in on. Did you see the media reports last week about Anna Harper's son?'

'Yes, poor kid. The old story – too much money, too few constraints.'

'Hard to handle wisely, certainly. I'm a big fan of her writing, particularly *Stolen Fire*. The triumph of the human spirit – it's one of the most inspiring books I've ever read.'

'The film came out when I was a teenager and I got hooked after that. I can't think of anyone else who has a genius like hers for tackling the great themes and still producing totally compulsive reading.'

'She's kept me up till two in the morning sometimes,' Borthwick agreed. 'So I had a little bit of a dig into the story about the ill-named Felix. He'd been living here in Edinburgh, on the streets much of the time. Came up on a minor drugs rap and then went back home to the sister, Cassandra, in Halliburgh – decent little town in the Borders, no major problems noted there before. I'd be interested to know whether the stuff he OD'd on came from his old contacts or from new ones. According to the report from the Family Liaison Officer, Cassandra was convinced he was clean, in which case it's very possible he got it on the spot. I saw her name on the conference list, PC Kate Graham – it might be worth seeking her out for a chat.'

'Kate Graham?' he said. 'There was a Kate Graham on my training course at Tulliallan after I left the army. Bright girl, I remember – I'd be surprised if she's still only a PC.'

'Common enough name. Anyway, seek her out today, will you? Halliburgh is exactly the sort of place that could be a target for a bit of private enterprise. See if you can find an excuse to go and check it out.' She paused. 'It's such a filthy trade. He was brought back to the sister's house, you know. She had to watch him die.'

'See what I can do, boss.' Strang went back to his desk, sickened at the thought. A fatal overdose was common enough in the cities yet the dealers in death, it seemed, were all but untouchable. If Halliburgh's problem was of recent date it might have less firmly established lines of supply.

Anna Harper's books had sold across the world and won every prize going because their message was that, however hideous the blows of fate, you could find a strength within that was unquenchable. Yet her own son had not managed to find it.

Strang had reread *Stolen Fire* during the dreadful days after Alexa died. It had helped, a little. He owed Anna for that.

Water was dripping across her forehead, which seemed an odd thing – something to do with the headache, perhaps. Cassie Trentham surfaced slowly, trying to make sense of what she saw as she opened her eyes.

She was lying on her side in a muddy ditch that was now a small running burn after the recent rain and snow. Her cheek hurt, her hip hurt, her knee hurt and her cycling helmet was pressing into her head. It was icy cold and she was shivering convulsively.

Was anything broken? She moved experimentally and everything worked, even if painfully, and she dragged herself into a sitting position, then on to her knees, giving a cry of pain as the bruised left one took the strain. Her cycling tights were ripped from knee to thigh and when she put her hand up to release the chin strap on her helmet and relieve the pressure on her head it came away bloodied from a gash on her cheek. She patted her head gingerly but though she could feel a bump the skin wasn't broken. The helmet itself was stoved in on that side but thankfully it had done its job.

Cassie stood up shakily. There was snow clinging to the verge and she slipped twice before she managed to climb back on to the road. Her bicycle was lying further down the road, its back wheel completely buckled. She looked up and down the road but there was no sign of the vehicle that had knocked her down, or of any other, for that matter.

What to do now? Cassie looked at her watch, fortunately unscathed, and to her surprise it was only quarter past nine. How long had she been unconscious then? A couple of minutes, if that. She'd just been briefly stunned. Her head was pounding and she hurt all over, though at least she could walk. But which way to go?

Retreating to Burnside was appealing but it was a long trudge back up the hill. On the other hand, the Foundation was in sight, and downhill at that. Jess would sort her out, tend her wounds and provide paracetamol, then she could have a shower, change her clothes and be driven home if she didn't feel up to staying.

Yes, that made sense. She limped off in that direction, feeling the stiffness easing off a little as she walked. It was only then she began to feel rage boiling up over what had happened. The bastard who clipped her bike must have known what he'd done yet he'd driven on – for all he knew she could be dead. Or worse, lying there dying from lack of attention. There wouldn't be any point in reporting it; she hadn't caught so much as a glimpse of what hit her. It wasn't even the first time she'd had a near miss – motorists seemed either to be ignorant of how much space they had to leave for the hapless cyclist or couldn't care less. The latter, probably.

She'd have to get someone to remove her poor battered bike from the road. She wouldn't be buying another one. This had put her right off the whole idea.

Richard Sansom finished a late and leisurely breakfast and went up to his room to prepare for the day ahead. He was in a good mood. The White Hart had been a pleasant surprise, with a busy bar, and if the food wasn't exactly fine dining, it was well cooked and pleasantly served. He could have done a lot worse, stuck here for the next couple of weeks.

He had worked out his schedule carefully. It certainly featured making his number with Anna Harper to assure her that he was hers to command, but perhaps not first. He could start with a visit to the Foundation and check out the situation this morning.

He could make it his business, too, to see how effectively they were handling this Retreat Week. With Anna being so determinedly reclusive, Harrington's had suggested these as a way of keeping her name in the public eye. The generous support for struggling writers was excellent PR and the one week when she agreed to take a masterclass attracted a very gratifying amount of press attention. It would be interesting to check out the criteria for being offered a place – this one, in particular, was always wildly oversubscribed. The release of *Jacob's Angel* a week later was no coincidence.

He set off along the Halliburgh high street. For someone living in central London, this seemed like stepping back into the past – there were still individual butchers, greengrocers and bakeries alongside the Spar supermarket. It had a slightly run-down feel, with several buildings standing empty and far too many sad-looking charity shops, but the town was busy on this Saturday morning and it was noticeable how many people greeted each other or stopped to chat. A place with a real sense of community.

The Harper Foundation building, big, white and modernistic, gave the same impression as Anna's house: here was someone showing contemptuous indifference to the community Sansom had been observing in the high street a few minutes earlier.

It was no secret that Anna was an autocrat. Her generosity with funding for local causes was well directed and well publicised – Harrington's saw to that – but given entirely on her own terms. It wasn't hard to be generous when you had her sort of money. In return she expected that if she wanted something, she would get it.

From the conversation round the bar the previous night Sansom had gathered that it hadn't made her popular. He'd got chatting with some of the locals and they were ready enough to take her money, but they'd spit on the ground afterwards with a clear resentment at Being Done Good To, suspecting they were being exploited at the same time. Anna's aloofness was a big PR problem, but she wasn't going to be persuaded to change her ways.

The reception area was minimalist, like the house, with a streamlined desk to one side made of some dark tropical hardwood but there was no one behind it. On the other side of the room beside a seating area with cream leather sofas and glass and chrome coffee tables a small group had gathered, clustered round a woman lying on one of the sofas. He stopped dead, staring.

First one head turned as he opened the door and now the others were turning too, and the woman struggled to sit up. She was wearing black Lycra; it was covered in mud and the tights had a tear down the left side. There was a bloodied cut on her cheek and the battered cycling helmet at her feet told the story. She was holding a glass of what could have been brandy and there was a woman sitting beside her dabbing at her face with a cloth.

A younger woman in a pencil skirt and a silky cowl-neck top detached herself from the group and came over to greet him. 'Sorry, sir. There's been a bit of an accident. What can I do for you?'

'Looks like I've come at a bad time,' he said. 'No problem. I'll come back later.'

The injured woman swung her feet to the floor. 'No, no,' she called. 'I'm fine, really. Surface damage only.' With her creamy skin, golden brown hair and that classic profile she was very like her mother; very pale, though, probably from shock.

Sansom smiled and went over to her. 'Looks as if you've been in the wars! I didn't manage to speak to you yesterday, Cassandra, but we have spoken on the phone. I'm Richard Sansom.'

'Oh yes, yes of course. I'm sorry – this is so stupid! Jess, leave that now. I'm going to go and clean up – this'll all come off in the shower. And take away the brandy – I'm feeling woozy enough without it.

'Richard, just give me time to get myself respectable and we can have a chat, if you don't mind waiting. Someone will fetch you coffee.'

'Of course I don't mind,' he assured her. 'Though I can always come back later . . .'

'I'll be absolutely fine. See you shortly.' She gave him a bright smile as she limped off towards the stairs.

It was an impressive performance; Anna's daughter obviously had the steely self-discipline as well as the looks. A tough cookie.

Gil Paton, who had only come in himself five minutes before and was still wearing his parka, had been narrowly observing the new arrival. Cassie had welcomed him as if he was in some sense important, so how come he'd never heard of him? He went over with his hand outstretched. 'Gil Paton. I'm Cassie's deputy. Richard Sansom, you said?'

'That's right. I'm in charge of Anna's PR. Normally I wouldn't have come until the end of the week to start preparations for the launch, but having come for the funeral I can take the chance of checking over the set-up for the Retreat, making sure we get as much good publicity as possible—'

Paton felt his hackles rise. 'Oh, I can assure you I have everything in hand. I've sharpened up on a few things that – well, not to criticise Cassie or anything, but she had to keep so many balls in the air before I arrived that it's not surprising there were some possibilities she missed. But I've covered all those now.'

'I'm sure. Locally,' Sansom said smoothly. 'I do more wide-angle stuff, you know? Glasgow, Edinburgh, Dundee – I've appointments set up with the buyers in the bookshops to check they've got everything in hand.'

Patronising bastard, Paton thought. 'Oh, I'm sure—' he began but Sansom cut across him.

'I'd like to have a look round. You're probably a busy man – I can just explore. Is the Retreat accommodation through there?'

'It's not a problem,' Paton said through gritted teeth. 'I'll take you. I can explain how it's set up. This way.' He stalked ahead through an arch in the further wall and down a short corridor.

In another echo of Anna's own house, the huge room at the end of the building had a wall of windows only broken by the entrance from the street. A staircase led up to a wide, gracefully curved gallery with half a dozen doors along it and against the back wall there was a long table with mugs, a box of tea bags and vacuum jugs of coffee, hot milk and hot water along with a plate of home-made biscuits. Underneath the gallery, spaced well apart, there were half a dozen individual workstations with large, black leather office chairs. Three were occupied.

Sascha Silverton was at one of them, her desk surface bare apart from a state-of-the-art hybrid laptop. Next to her Marion Hutton was working in deep litter, loose papers and books piled up as she tapped away on her iPad while Jason Jackson had placed himself at the end nearest the windows.

As the door opened and the two men came in Sascha glanced round. Gil Paton she had met and had a late coffee with the previous night; yes, she'd been keen to pump him about Anna's background story and the set-up at the Foundation but distinctly less keen to hear how he was planning to reshape it and how much he resented Cassandra Trentham coming in tomorrow when he, Gil, was perfectly able to cope on his own. His companion definitely looked more interesting – tall, fair-haired and quite a sharp dresser.

She tossed back her hair and stood up. 'Morning, Gil.' She had a low, husky voice. 'We're bright and early at our desks today, aren't we, Marion?'

Marion looked flustered, half got up and knocked one of the tottering piles of paper to the floor, then dropped to her knees to pick them up. Gil stepped forward to help her while Sascha turned to meet the other man with an encouraging smile.

But he had walked on past her towards the farthest desk and was greeting Jason Jackson as if he was a mate. That surprised her: her fellow writer hadn't made a good impression. He'd been helping himself to coffee and biscuits when she came in after breakfast and when she'd introduced herself had responded with a surly sort of grunt. He looked scruffy too – unshaven and wearing builder's-bum baggy jeans, with a sneery expression – so maybe the new guy wasn't as classy as he looked.

'Well, hi there,' he was saying. 'I didn't realise last night that you were a writer.'

Jackson looked up from his laptop, surprised. 'Didn't know you were something to do with the Foundation. You never said.'

'I'm not really. I work for Anna's publishers and I'm to be up here for a bit doing PR for her.'

Jackson's lip curled. 'Oh, of course. Nothing but the best for our Anna, eh?'

Gil, being thanked profusely by a blushing Marion, stood up frowning. 'Not the sort of remark you'd expect from someone who I see has made free with her hospitality already,' he said to Sascha in an undertone, eyeing the coffee mug and biscuit crumbs on Jackson's desk. 'Local, of course. I think it's just as well he won't actually be staying here.'

Sansom was smiling, saying easily, 'Well, that figures, doesn't it? Will I see you down the pub again tonight, or will you be socialising here?'

Jackson flickered a contemptuous glance at his companions. 'What do you think? Oh, I'll be there all right. We'll get them in for you and you can dish us the dirt on the real Anna Harper – the one behind the perfect public image.'

Sansom dealt with the question with practised skill. 'You're coming to the wrong person,' he was saying smoothly when the door behind him opened and Cassie Trentham came in. She'd been impressively quick; she was very much looking the part of Chair of the Foundation now, her silver silk shirt open at the neck to show a heavy gold chain and a pale grey cashmere jacket picking up the tones in her soft tweed skirt. The only jarring note was the cut on her cheek, beginning to bruise, and a bandage on her leg but she seemed perfectly poised.

'Richard, do forgive me. At least it's given you a chance to see the set-up.' She glanced round at the others, smiling. 'Hello, I'm Cassie Trentham. Welcome to the Harper Foundation. I hope you're settling in all right?'

Jason said nothing. Marion nodded shyly and Sascha came forward holding out both hands. 'I'm so glad to meet you. I promise you I'm absolutely your mother's greatest fan.'

Cassie's coolly polite thank you as she submitted to the double handshake suggested that she'd heard that before and Sascha was annoyed with herself. You don't make your mark if you go round bleating clichés. She opened her mouth to say, 'Oh God, how gauche! Sorry that slipped out,' but Cassie had turned back to Sansom.

'Richard, why don't you come up to my office and we can have a proper talk?'

'Good idea,' he said. 'The only thing is, I wondered if I should go up and at least leave a message for your mother to see if there's anything she wants me to do. Would that be appropriate?'

CHAPTER FIVE

After Richard Sansom had gone, Anna Harper turned to Marta Morelli, allowing herself to shudder at last. 'I need a drink,' she said.

For once Marta didn't point out that it was early in the day to start hitting the bottle. 'Cognac?'

'Scotch.'

She went to the drinks cupboard and poured that, then cognac for herself, her shaking hand making the crystal ring as the decanter's edge caught its rim. She didn't trust herself to manage a tray; with one glass in each hand she said, 'Come, we will go through to your study.'

They had seen Sansom in the big sitting room but more and more just now they were using the study: towards the back of the house with its smaller window it made them feel less exposed. It had two walls of bookcases behind Anna's work area with a desk and filing cabinets and in front of the fireplace on the opposite wall there were comfortable chairs and a huge square coffee table piled high with books and magazines. As Anna sank into her customary seat Marta set down the glasses and bent to put a match to the fire laid ready in the grate.

'We will feel better with a fire,' she said almost as if she meant it, glancing anxiously at Anna huddling now over her glass. 'You did well. I don't know how you could look calm while he told us.'

'You did too. We've had practice now – we've been waiting for something to happen for weeks now.'

'Not this, though.' Marta sat down opposite, putting her hand to her head. 'This . . .'

When Anna spoke there was a hysterical note in her voice. 'She might have died, like Felix. One after the other, he's stalking us down. I can hear the rustling in the bushes – there's a tiger there, waiting to strike. We just don't know where or when.'

Fighting down her own fears, Marta said, 'But we must not panic.' Anna was always volatile; it was her role to be the steadying influence and she added with a conviction she didn't feel, 'We don't know it was anything bad – just a minor accident, like Richard said. Maybe this could be – it is a narrow road.'

'Oh Marta, you don't think it was, any more than I do. And we don't believe he won't try again. What can we do now? We have to protect her. And ourselves.'

There was a long pause. The fire, starting to catch,

gave a sudden crackle and a spark flew up. They both jumped; Anna's whisky slopped on to her skirt. She dabbed at it as Marta said, 'We call the police.'

Anna looked up, startled. 'But what do we tell them? We believe someone wants my children dead, but we can't give them a reason? If we say there have been threats, they'll want to see them, question us about why and when. Otherwise they won't take it seriously – they'll just say what Richard said, it was only cuts and bruises. And Felix – dying from an overdose was an accident that had been waiting to happen to him, as far as they were concerned.'

'We don't say this. We say there is a person who drove dangerously. Your daughter could have been killed. You want to know who this person was and you are an important person here. They will have to pay attention. Maybe they can do the work for us, to find out who he is.'

Anna sat up slowly. 'Yes – yes, that could work. Oh, you are so good for me, Marta – I can't imagine where I would be without you. Of course that's what we can do. I'll ask to speak to that inspector who came about Felix – he seemed competent enough. And Cassie can come and live here meantime where we can see to it that she is safe. I'll send Davy to fetch her from work.'

The conference at Police Scotland, Fettes Avenue in Edinburgh, aimed at stations in the Borders division, was well attended. The latest twist in the war against drugs that Scotland was so comprehensively losing was a hot topic: even areas that had previously suffered only minor problems were seeing the epidemic spreading like Ebola.

After the horror of Felix Trentham's death, PC Graham had felt a particularly personal interest. She had lived in Halliburgh all her life and it sickened her to see evil like this taking root in her own neighbourhood, such a peaceful backwater before.

Of course, what the speakers had to say wasn't news to anyone: underage kids with no satisfactory home background – and there seemed to be increasing numbers of these – were being seduced into gangs. Taking orders on mobile phones, they were actually doing doorstep deliveries of substances that got more powerful and more dangerous by the month.

With the Human Rights legislation and the restrictions on stop and search, there was little the police could do about it. The lectures were interesting in themselves but at the end of it there wasn't really any sort of answer, just a lot of hand-wringing.

Not that she had actually thought there would be. Feeling depressed, Kate joined the queue making their way out of the room, thinking that such new information as there was could have been circulated by email, without the cost of bringing them all in here. Still, Police Scotland was so far in the red that saving a few hundred would be a drop in the ocean – and at least she could put a tick in her 'professional development' box, which would mean she wouldn't be threatened with the 'Equality Impact Assessment' training module next month.

She was just reaching the door when a voice hailed her. 'Kate! It *is* you! I saw your name on the list and wondered if it was the Kate Graham I knew in Tulliallan days.' She turned round to see DCI Kelso Strang making his way between the rows towards her. 'Good gracious, Kelso!' she said. 'I suppose I shouldn't be surprised – I knew this was where you were based.'

Yes, she knew; she'd seen the coverage there had been of his cases and read his sad history in a background piece too. The accompanying photo had shown the left side of his face – perhaps purposely? – so she was unprepared for the heavy scar that ran down the right-hand side. He wasn't quite the hunk he'd been back then.

'I move around a lot but I have a sort of broom cupboard here in HQ – it's not much, but I call it home. You're still in Halliburgh, I see?'

She could hear the surprise in his voice and she coloured. She'd done well on the training course, better than many contemporaries who were in much more senior positions now. 'Yes. I was encouraged to work towards promotion but then I'd have had to move. And – well, my mother was ill for a long time and after she died my dad was just really lost. He was a lot older and now he can't manage for himself.'

'I'm sorry about that.'

He sounded as if he meant it, sounded too as if he regretted for her the career she might have had. 'I'm sorry about your wife, too,' she said. 'I read about it in the papers.'

Strang's face darkened. 'Yes. It was . . . hard.' Then he gave a stiff sort of smile. 'But we have to play with the hand we're dealt, don't we?'

The room was emptying. He looked at his watch. 'It would be good to catch up. How are you placed for time?'

'Oh, it's no problem now with the Borders Railway. There's a good service to Tweedbank, so no more long scary journeys when the weather's bad.'

'That's good. They're threatening us with something nasty before very long. Why don't we go and have a drink—' Then he stopped and groaned. 'Oh no! I'm on bedtime story duty again tonight.'

Graham tried not to look surprised. A new girlfriend – or new wife even – with a kid, presumably. 'Oh, don't worry,' she said at once. 'You certainly can't break a bedtime story promise.'

'It's my niece,' he said. 'My sister's had marital problems and they're staying with me meantime. Betsy is not someone to be trifled with and Peppa Pig is the current obsession, heaven help me. Look, why not come back with me and when I've done that we can grab a bite to eat – there's a decent pub nearby, and then I can drop you off at the station if it won't make you too late.'

'That's a tempting offer. Dad always makes jokes about me having a late pass when the carer's covering, but he doesn't mind.'

She followed him through the corridors to his office – minuscule indeed – and then to the car park. As she got into the car she gave a sudden laugh and he looked at her quizzically.

'I was just thinking, the last time I saw you was the final night of the course in Tulliallan. Mayhem! No one would believe graduating police officers could behave like that. I remember you leading a group of other savages down the stairs bellowing in triumph at having got a senior instructor's car up on to the top landing.'

Strang looked abashed. 'Well, yes. But that's what an army training does for you – it was quite a feat of engineering, I'd have you know. And as I remember it, you weren't sitting primly in a corner somewhere.'

'Not exactly,' she admitted. 'Anyway, it's tradition to trash the place on the final night of the course. One last hurrah before we have to spend the rest of our lives being law-abiding.'

'Pretty much,' he agreed. 'At least we try, mostly. Right, I'll take you back to meet Betsy. She's very cute but she's an absolute minx.'

At half past five Sascha Silverton closed her laptop and looked around. Jason had packed it in a little earlier then disappeared through the door to the street in his usual graceless fashion without a goodbye.

Marion had irritated Sascha all day by her constant fluttering, getting up to make a cup of tea, leafing through the papers on her desk, giving tiny sighs when she couldn't find what she wanted, making little excursions up to her room, stopping for a chat at Sascha's desk as she passed.

The remaining retreaters had arrived but they weren't a lot more promising: a sullen, ratty little man called Mick McNab who worked, he told her over lunch, in the gig economy so that he had time to write the hard-boiled crime that would make his name. When she said she wrote full-time, he scowled. 'All right for some.'

She'd actually heard of the other one, Elena Jankowski, who was dark and intense, with very pale skin and hooded grey eyes; it was hard to say what age she was. There had been a little stir about her first book, a slim volume that had been nominated for one of the big prizes – Sascha couldn't remember which one – but that had been a year or two ago and when Sascha googled her there didn't seem to have been anything since. She had gone straight to her room, emerged briefly for lunch where she said the bare minimum politeness required and then retreated again.

The evening meal would be at seven, Gil had said, and there would be wine and beer put out for a happy hour at six. 'See you then,' he had said to Sascha.

So that settled it. She stood up. 'I'm just going for a walk. Check out where the hot nightspots are in Halliburgh.'

Marion looked alarmed at the very idea and Mick said, 'Don't think you'll find there is much.'

'No, I didn't actually mean I thought there would be,' Sascha said with elaborate patience. 'There must be a pub or two.'

'You'll get it free here in half an hour,' Mick pointed out.

'Mmm,' she said from halfway up the staircase on her way to fetch her coat. She came back down after a few minutes in which she'd brushed her hair and renewed her make-up – you never knew who you might meet – and with an airy 'See you later,' went out into the street.

It had been a long, hard winter with little sign of spring as yet and tonight it was bitterly cold with a sort of crystalline chill that even seemed to have stilled the wind. It was getting dark; there was a thumbnail of moon low in the sky and one star showing above the roofs and spires of the town. Sascha turned up the faux-fur collar of her tweed coat and stopped to put on her gloves.

Further down the street there was a large, expensive-looking BMW SUV parked immediately outside the door to the Harper Foundation and as she looked a small man, thin and wiry, came out and held it open for Cassie Trentham. He closed it behind her then hurried to hold the car door for her, though she had opened it already herself and Sascha heard her saying, 'Oh for goodness' sake, Davy,' as he shut it behind her and went round to the driver's side.

Sascha watched her being driven off and her mouth twisted in envy. It was all right for some; Cassie Trentham had been given everything on a plate, while

Sascha Silverton had grafted hard for every penny she had. The childish cry, 'It's not fair!' was ringing in her head as she set off down the hill into the town.

Cassie Trentham sank into her bath with a groan of relief. The warmth was comforting to her aching muscles and she had hopefully tipped in an excessive amount of her favourite Jo Malone Pomegranate Noir bath oil and lit the matching candle, as if she thought relaxation could be bought over the counter. It couldn't, of course, not with her brain humming with the events of the day.

Davy Armstrong had brought her home. He'd appeared at the Foundation at half past five, asking to see her. When she came downstairs, a little surprised, he'd said bluntly, 'I'm to take you home, Cassie.'

'Take me home? What for? Is there a problem?'

'Your mother's not happy about you being away out there on your own, after what happened this morning.'

Cassie swore, then apologised. 'Sorry, Davy. Oh, it was only a minor bump – she wasn't meant to know. Who told her – oh no, don't tell me. It was Richard Sansom, wasn't it? Lying toad – he said he wouldn't.'

'She'd have found out anyhow,' Davy pointed out. 'It's all over the town already.'

Cassie pulled a face. 'Oh, it would be, of course, but Ma doesn't exactly hang round gossiping in the street, does she? Anyway, it doesn't make any difference. I'm not going back to be incarcerated in the ice palace.'

'I'm to bring you. That's what she said.'

'Oh, a kidnapping?' Cassie laughed. 'I tell you what, as a special concession you can run me home and report to her that I'm safely there. But attempt to take me back to Highfield and I start screaming out of the window that you're abducting me.'

There was a lot of head-shaking but she won, of course, and Davy drove her back to Burnside. 'I promise I'll tell her you did your best, Davy,' she'd said as she got out of the car.

'It's not that. She's worried about you, lass. Could you not just—'

Cassie's voice had hardened. 'No, Davy, I couldn't "just". I've spent too much of my life already "just" doing what my mother wants, not what I want myself. Thanks for the lift.'

'You'll be going in tomorrow with the Writers' Retreat being on, won't you? What time in the morning?'

'*What?*'

'I'm to chauffeur you. Boss's orders.'

'For heaven's sake, Davy, I've got a car of my own!'

'She just feels you need a wee bit of looking after. And it's no problem for me.'

For a moment she had thought of opening up the argument again but she was, quite honestly, too tired. It didn't really matter and if her mother would settle for that it would save trouble. She submitted with bad grace.

The more she thought about it, the angrier she got with Richard Sansom. She'd got on very well with him over lunch. He was easy to talk to, on general things at first, drawing her out to talk about life in the Harper family. Normally she shifted away from that sort of discussion for fear it might damage the sacred Brand, but since his job was promoting it anyway, she didn't have to worry.

He'd asked interested questions too about the whole creative thing, questions that Cassie had often asked herself too. Like where *did* genius like Anna's come from, for instance.

'What were her parents like?' Richard asked. 'Any sort of literary background?'

'No idea,' Cassie said. 'They were dead before I was born and she never talks about them. Out of sight is out of mind for my mother. My father left when I was four, but we never talk about him either. The only person she does talk to is Marta.'

Richard picked up on that immediately. 'They obviously go back a long way. How did they meet?'

'Oh, at least I can answer that. Ma's always loved Italy and she spent some time there just after she left school, I think. That's when she began writing *Stolen Fire* and she got to know Marta at that time. Marta told me that she'd let her read it as it was being written and she knew then that Anna was a genius, and it had been her privilege to make it easier for her to give her gift to the world. That's what she said, anyway.'

'Fascinating. So, is she paid as a housekeeper or something?'

'No idea. She always seems to have money – she likes good clothes, expensive perfume, that sort of stuff. But we don't talk about things like that in our family, Richard. We don't talk about much, as a matter of fact.'

'We've tried to persuade Anna that if she was a bit more accessible it would actually defuse the interest in her background. There's always someone digging, but even we don't know if Harper is her real name or where she came from.'

'Well, all I can tell you is that it's the one on her passport. But Felix and I . . .' her voice faltered for a second, but she went on, 'We reckoned she changed it by deed poll sometime. Don't know why – we used to invent reasons, like a prison record or a personal scandal that would reflect badly on "The Brand".' Cassie indicated quotation marks. 'High-class call girl was Felix's bet. She'd hardly need the money now, but we've always known she takes lovers in London.'

Richard nodded. 'Yes, we have too. Risky, when she has such a sanitised public image. But – "The Brand"? I can hear the capital letters as you say that. What is it?'

'It's the sort of thing you lot talk about, isn't it – establishing a personal brand for an author? It's what Anna is to the rest of the world and everything has to be in keeping with it. It was held over us like an iron rod. "Don't do that," Marta would say, "It will be bad for The Brand." She was even hotter on it than Ma would be.'

A waitress appeared with another glass of wine. 'I didn't—' she protested, but Richard nodded to the girl to set it down. 'I've got the car so I can't drink, but that's no reason why you should sit there with an empty glass.'

Cassie looked down. He was right; her glass was indeed empty, though she hadn't finished her main course. 'Oh dear – I hadn't realised. I'm talking too much.' She'd felt uneasy, at that point. She hadn't eaten breakfast and wine on an empty stomach, combined with shock, was not a good recipe.

But Richard said smoothly, 'Not at all. It's very helpful background for us. Tell me about the retreat set-up – how does that work?'

Relieved to have moved away from personal subjects, she said readily, 'Oh yes. Actually, it works very satisfactorily. The retreats cost money, obviously, but in PR terms it's small change, and then it's often in use for Harper Foundation business meetings and if people have flown in from abroad, we can offer hospitality since we're dragging them away out here. The rest of the time it's available for local events – concerts, lectures and that sort of thing. It's popular for small conferences that are based nearby too – we have an excellent firm of caterers who know the ropes and it makes it all very easy. Now with Gil here I can travel more.'

'Oh yes, Gil,' Richard said with a sly smile. 'Am I right that the more you travel, the happier he will be?'

Cassie laughed. 'Definitely! He's developed a very possessive attitude to the Foundation, and of course that shows loyalty, but to be honest I do find it a difficult relationship. He behaves as if he's trying to elbow me out

– he even wanted to co-sign my Christmas cards! Either that or he's being a bit too friendly.' She stopped. 'Oh dear, what a bitchy thing to say. I've had too much to drink and it's loosened my tongue. I must be getting back.'

'No pudding? I'll get the bill, then.' He didn't try to detain her, but as they waited for it to come he said, 'So – what has it been like, being Anna Harper's daughter?'

She hadn't weighed her words. 'Tough,' she said. 'You had to take a lot of things on trust, you know? Like, she was our mother, so she loved us – that was axiomatic, even if you didn't see many signs of it. Mostly she was somewhere else, mentally or physically. I could take it, but Felix—' she broke off, tears coming to her eyes. 'Let's say I wouldn't recommend it, OK?'

That had been the wine talking. She'd regretted it afterwards, especially now she'd had evidence of Richard's treachery. Certainly her mother's PR was his job, but people move on; she couldn't know what he was planning to do with what she'd told him, and if he was as two-faced as that his next move might be to sell the story. What might that do to The Brand, she found herself thinking? Automatically, guilt kicked in and her stomach lurched. She gave a little wail of frustration. She was still feeling guilt about possibly damaging The Brand? *Guilt?* After all that had happened?

Cassie had kept herself so busy today that she'd hardly had time to think about Felix, but now the grief came flooding back. If Anna's work hadn't been so all-important she might have given her son the love he needed, might have pitched in to protect him after it all went wrong, instead of leaving it to Cassie. Admittedly she'd said herself that she didn't think it would help, but Anna had agreed readily enough. She seemed to be trying to protect Cassie now, though – was being overprotective, indeed. All the accident had resulted in was a cut and a bruise and she'd come off her bike before. So why—?

The slimy worm of an idea crept into her mind. What was it that had made Anna so jumpy? Cassie had said to Kate Graham that the person who had given Felix the drugs was a murderer; had Anna, perhaps, silently thought that too? Was she afraid that this was an attempt on her remaining child? The bath had cooled and suddenly she was shivering with a cold that came from within. She climbed out and huddled into her fluffy towelling robe.

It was pitch-dark outside now. The wind had dropped and it was very still, with that deep silence that seems unbreakable, almost oppressive. Cassie went through to her bedroom, aware in a way she had never been before of her own isolation. The robe was damp and when she took it off to change into lounging pyjamas her nakedness made her feel even more vulnerable. Someone could be out there, moving silently beyond the drawn curtains . . .

Oh, this was ridiculous! She was frightening herself in the most stupid way. An idiot driving a car had come too close to her on her bike this morning, just like all the other idiots who had come too close to her in the past on a regular basis, only this one had got it wrong and then had driven on because he was scared at what he had done. If it had been one of the huge 4x4s that were so common about here, it was possible he – or she, for that matter – might not even have noticed. It made perfect sense.

She went through to the kitchen to make herself a cup of coffee. For a moment she actually hesitated on the threshold; here, open to the hillside, there were no curtains and anyone could look in. And she could look out, she reminded herself firmly. She could look out and see that there was no one there, as indeed there wasn't.

Feeling a ridiculous sense of pride at her own common sense, she carried her drink triumphantly through to the sitting room. Here she had drawn the curtains and switched on the lights before she went to have her bath and it looked inviting. She switched on the TV and flicked through to find a box set to watch. Something absorbing enough to stop her sitting here thinking about Felix, thinking about the darkness swathing itself around the cottage.

Game of Thrones was doing its work. Cassie had stopped listening for footsteps and the background music was loud enough to drown the sound of a car drawing up outside, so when the knock came on the front door, it came as a shock. She froze, her heart pounding till she thought her chest might actually explode. What should she do?

CHAPTER SIX

Kelso Strang only had misgivings about the wisdom of his plan when he arrived at his cottage in Newhaven and observed the reaction of the females in his family. Finella's look of surprise was replaced by one of delight as she came forward to welcome her brother's guest; Betsy, after giving Kate a narrow look came over to hold her uncle's hand in a very proprietorial way.

'You're going to read me my bedtime story now,' she said, in case this strange woman might have distracted him from his duty.

'Yes, Betsy, that's why I'm here,' he said, then turned to Finella. 'Kate and I were mates at Tulliallan but I hadn't seen her since until she turned up at a conference today. I'll do the story bit but I'm going to take Kate round the pub for a bite before she catches her train. Hope you haven't planned anything?' As if she would, he added silently. Fin wasn't very good at thinking ahead about food if there was a ready meal in the freezer; doing anything more interesting usually fell to him.

'Of *course* not,' she said. 'That's a splendid idea.'

Kelso could see Kate shifting uncomfortably. 'Yeah, fine. Now, Betsy—'

Betsy was standing waiting for him, holding an album of Peppa Pig stories. He sat down and took her on his knee, rolling his eyes at the two women above her head.

He opened the book with some revulsion. Then he looked at Betsy, then back at the book. 'Do you know,' he said, 'I've noticed something. When you're listening to a Peppa Pig story, you have this sort of Peppa Pig face' – he illustrated with a screwed-up expression and a snuffle – 'and it's like having a little pig for a niece instead of a little girl.'

Betsy frowned. 'I don't want to look like a pig.'

Kelso shrugged. 'Well . . .'

She was already scrambling down from his lap and putting Peppa Pig back on the shelf. He saw the two women exchanging smiles.

'You're a natural,' Kate was saying, as Betsy came back bearing a book whose cover illustration showed Disney princesses of the most synthetic sort.

'I want this instead. And the stories are longer too.' She looked a little put out as the adults laughed, but didn't let herself be diverted. 'And you always do two now if I've been good and I was good, wasn't I, Mummy?'

'Oh, *very* good,' Finella said basely as Kelso, with a resigned groan, hoisted his niece back on to his knee and began reading.

The White Hart in Halliburgh high street had smart paint and gleaming brasswork as well as a board chalked with the evening menu; it was the only pub Sascha Silverton had seen that looked the sort of place Richard Sansom might frequent. She pushed open the door and went in.

It was early but there were half a dozen people standing at the bar already, as well as couples at two tables beside the open fire. There was no sign of Richard Sansom, but Jason Jackson was there talking to two men, one with light red hair, pale skin, freckles and a beer belly, the other taller, quite thickset, with dark, curly hair cut short, and he was listening with a sardonic expression. They were turned away from the bar and she hesitated for a moment; she had no great wish to further her acquaintance with Jason but having overheard them talking this morning she guessed Richard Sansom would join him if he did come in.

She stepped up to the bar. 'Gin and tonic,' she said to the barman, then, 'Oh, hello, Jason – fancy seeing you here!'

He stopped in mid sentence, looking startled as he turned. 'Oh – yeah, hello,' he said, sounding irritated, and was about to turn back when the shorter man who had been eyeing her said, 'Who's your pal, Jason?' He moved round to stand a little too close to her so that she took an involuntary step backwards.

The taller man said coolly, 'Stop slavering, Grant. Show a bit of couth, can't you? Give the lady room to breathe. Hello, I'm Steve.'

'Sascha,' she said. She didn't really take to him much, but at least he wasn't as squalid as his companions and it had given her an in to the group.

'Visiting, Sascha?' Steve asked.

Jason answered for her. 'Oh, she's one of Anna's little toadies. Here for a chance to suck up to the great genius.'

'Look here—' Sascha protested, but he spoke across her, 'Not that it will do any good, you know. Show the tiniest bit of promise – always supposing there's any possibility of promise in a chick-lit writer – and she'll screw you into the ground. She's a bitch of the first order and her lezzie pal is worse.' His face had gone red and there was even a fleck of spittle at the corner of his mouth as he went into a tirade.

Sascha didn't shock easily but she did gasp as it got more and more obscene, and she was grateful when Steve said with unmistakable authority, 'Shut it, Jason. You're in a public place.'

To her surprise Jason subsided, only muttering, 'And I suppose you'll arrest me if I don't?'

'Quite possibly, yes. Or I'll get Grant to do it. It's a bit beneath me to go round feeling collars. Have another drink and calm down.'

'You're police officers?' Sascha asked.

It was the shorter man who answered. 'That's right. DC Grant Wilson and the guy who's a bit up himself is

DI Steve Hammond. Apart from that he's almost normal. So you won't be bothered by the rougher element while you're drinking here.' He grinned at her, exposing a mouth full of teeth that were crooked and stained, as he rested an arm along the bar in a way that more or less trapped her at one end.

The rougher element might be preferable but Sascha wasn't quite ready to beat a retreat to one of the tables. Leaning round Grant, she said to Jason, 'OK, you've got a pick at Anna. But what do you know about her that I don't know? The lezzie bit, for instance? I never heard that.'

She was aware it might set him off again, but she did want to know, and in fact Jason didn't return to the abuse. 'Well, you wouldn't. You never hear anything about her, but it sticks out a mile, doesn't it? Best chums like that – what else would it be? And Morelli – she's the one that does the nasty business. Listen, have you ever heard of a devil's garden?'

'Devil's garden? No.'

'You find them up the Amazon. There'll be this tree with dead ground all about it, no other plants, because there's a kind of ant that lives on this tree and poisons any plant that encroaches. Anna's the tree and Morelli's the ant, see? She's the parasite and the protector as well.'

It was, Sascha had to admit, a telling analogy. She'd heard rumours before that Anna was pretty ruthless. 'But why would she need to do that? She's got the world at her feet already. What has she got to be afraid of?'

'She's got a secret.'

They all looked at him. 'What is it?' Sacha said.

'Wish I knew.'

'How do you know she's got one, then?' Steve asked.

'Stands to reason. What do you know about her background? Nothing, right? There's something she's scared of. I need to know what it is and then I can get her off my back. Until I do, I'm wasting my time writing the next book.'

'Sounds like blackmail to me,' Steve said severely. 'I don't think I heard you saying that. Blackmailers are the ones who end up with a tag round their big toe in the morgue. Talk to me about it before you run yourself into trouble.' He downed the remains of his drink. 'Anyway, I'm off. Got a hot date tonight.'

'Oh?' Grant was immediately interested. 'You've kept that one to yourself.'

'Joke, Grant,' Steve said with elaborate weariness. 'Do keep up. It's work.' Turning to Sascha, he said, 'Nice to meet you. See you again, maybe?'

'Oh, probably,' she said. She'd certainly got useful information but there had been no sign of Richard Sansom and now Grant was moving in closer.

'Want another drink, pet?' he said.

She was just about to make an excuse about getting back for the evening meal when the door opened and there, at last, was Sansom. 'Thanks. Just a quick one,' she said.

* * *

'It's nothing grand,' Kelso Strang said as he held open the door of his local for Kate Graham. 'It's got a nice view out over the Forth, though, if we're early enough to get one of the tables by the window – oh good, there is one.'

Kate went over and took a seat as Kelso went up to the bar. There were two or three of the regulars there who greeted him warmly, as did the barman.

'Your usual, Kelso?'

'Not tonight, thanks, Jacky. I'm going to be driving so it's a Beck's Blue, I'm afraid. Glass of wine for you, Kate?' As she nodded, he became aware that every eye was turned on her. Idiot! he said to himself savagely. It had seemed the ideal opportunity to carry out JB's request that he pump her for information about Halliburgh but he hadn't calculated on the assumptions that were likely to be made by his sister and his friends. He could only hope that Kate herself wasn't under any illusions.

He came back with a menu. 'I can recommend the fish. Down here it more or less leaps out of the water and on to your plate.'

'You've convinced me,' she said. 'That's a problem in the Borders – since the supermarkets arrived the fishmongers have closed. There's a fish van comes round, but you can't always get to it. Fish and chips sounds great.'

'Good choice. Make that two, Jacky,' he said, collecting the glasses and sitting down. 'Now tell me, how's life in Halliburgh?'

Kate shrugged. 'Well, it's home. Never lived anywhere else, so I can't see it dispassionately, but it's a nice wee place to live in. Good community. It's been a bit rough of late, though – you probably read about Anna Harper's son?' Her round, pleasant face darkened at the memory.

Kelso nodded sombrely. 'I hear you were right in the middle of that.'

'Yes. It was quite awful, being totally helpless as the kid died. I try not to think about it. The great Anna is a cold fish, but his sister, Cassie – she's really hurting.'

'Mmm. Any idea where he got the stuff from?'

'Locally, if you ask me. There's definitely more of it around, just like they were saying today.'

He'd meant to chat about more personal things before he broached the topic he'd been commissioned to raise, but they'd got there rather sooner than expected. It was obviously preying on Kate's mind, but he didn't want to seem to be interrogating her.

'It's difficult, isn't it?' he said carefully. 'What are you noticing?'

'Hard to pin down. But what they were talking about today – you know, the county lines stuff? Well, there's always been some drug taking but I've got the feeling that there's more of it in the community now and it's not just weed, either. And too often I'm seeing kids I don't know, sometimes hanging around the bus shelter where they found Felix Trentham. A few of them are locals and I've stopped to have a word once or twice but they just say the others are their pals. The thing is, they're not actually doing any harm and some of the older ones are pretty savvy about their rights. There are the usual signs, though – expensive trainers, smartphones, that sort of thing, but I can't just seize a phone and check out the address book, more's the pity. I've mentioned it to DI Hammond and he said he'd keep an eye.'

Kelso considered that. 'How would they get to Felix, though?'

Kate pulled a face. 'The truth is, Felix would have got to them, given half a chance. But poor Cassie was convinced he'd turned over a new leaf and that someone who knew about his problems had slipped it to him deliberately. Murder, she was claiming. Wanted it investigated.'

'Murder? You wouldn't have much to go on.'

'I know. Nothing, really. But the family always wants to believe it when an addict says he's clean.'

'Can you see any line you could pursue? Is your DI following that up?'

There was a long, long pause. Then she said, 'Can I talk to you in confidence? I'm worried, and I don't know who I could talk to without losing my job, but we go back a long way . . .'

The arrival of the food gave him a moment to consider what to say. He wasn't going to lie to her and say he wouldn't tell anyone when he would be reporting back to JB, but on the other hand it sounded as if this was something he really needed to hear.

Once the niceties of vinegar or sauce had been settled, he said, 'I promise you that your name will never be mentioned, but if there's something that has to be tackled

I can't brush it under the carpet, can I? I suspect you wouldn't want me to.'

Kate bit her lip. 'I know. It's a big risk, but I trust you. You were the one who almost came to blows after the ethics lecture with that guy who said you were a fool if you fought clean when the other side were fighting dirty.'

Kelso sighed ruefully. 'Oh yes, I remember. He's done very well for himself – I saw he'd got promotion the other day. So . . . ?'

Her hands twisted together. 'Right. Here goes. We got a new DI a couple of months ago – Steve Hammond. Very sharp, very able – impresses the Divisional Commander no end. Gets things done and has the stats to prove it, but – well, we all know they're fake.'

'You'd have to say there's a lot of that about.'

'OK, given the bureaucracy everyone's struggling with you can understand it. But this is more than that – claims to have investigated when nothing's been done, doesn't allocate a crime number when there's a complaint so that a failure won't show up, that sort of thing. Doesn't want to open up any sort of scandal that might tarnish his reputation for efficiency. And though I hate to say this, there's what the English guys call blue curtain stuff going on – though I suppose, given the colour of our uniforms it should be black curtain here.'

Kelso was concerned. 'That's bad news. Are you sure?'

'Do I have proof, do you mean? No. They take good care that nothing comes my way but there's a lot of sniggering conspiratorial stuff going on in a little group that centres round Hammond – his satellites, really. I do know that one of them got a speeding ticket recently – I heard them talking about it, and it was obvious it was just going to be dropped. One of the young PCs told me she thought they did that for pals as well if the money was right.

'Then there was a complaint from one of our habitual problems – a nasty drunk, violent and abusive with a mouth like a sewer. Claimed he'd got beaten up when he was arrested for starting a brawl in one of the pubs, and quite honestly, he'd asked for it so often it wouldn't be surprising if someone snapped. But no fewer than three officers just happened to be around to swear that he'd been staggering and fell and hit his head.'

Kelso grimaced. 'It's sickening, that. When you're meant to be fighting crime and it's right here in the centre spreading corruption from the inside out.'

'The worst of it is that whenever we get someone new, like the PC who told me about the speeding points stuff, they get drawn in before very long. They don't try it with me, or a couple of the other oldies—'

'Oh, come on, Kate!' he protested. 'You're not an oldie – or if you are, what does that make me? Prime of life, we're talking here.'

She laughed and agreed, but there was a look on her face that suggested she felt that time had passed. 'Anyway, being left out is hard if you're a new officer when you have to find your mates in the force. And I know the idea that moving officers around is officially to spread good practice, but that cuts both ways. Grant Wilson – he's a DS – was always a creep, but since Hammond came he's got a lot more cocky.'

'Mmm. You are in a difficult position, aren't you?' Kelso said with considerable sympathy. 'But to go back to the Felix business – I know Detective Chief Superintendent Borthwick was taking an interest. Is there anything, anything at all that you think might be worth following up?'

'I'm not CID,' she pointed out. 'I can't muscle in and start investigating if Hammond is just brushing it aside. And I can't afford to lose my job. Dad needs me at home.'

Jacky came over to clear the plates. They waved away the dessert menu and ordered coffee.

'How are you coping, Kate?' Kelso asked. 'With all that responsibility you're not getting the chance to use your talents. Are you happy with that?'

Her blue eyes filled with tears, which she rapidly blinked away. 'A lot happier than I'd be if Dad was in a home dwindling away and I was off somewhere pursuing some grand dream of a career. I'm all right. But do you think there's anything you can do about what I've told you?'

'Leave it with me,' he said. 'Give me your mobile number and I'll come back to you. I promise we won't come in with hobnailed boots.'

Kate smiled at him. 'It's a load off my mind, actually. I can just keep my head down and leave it to you.'

* * *

Betsy was in bed and Finella was watching a game show when her brother came in, but she switched it off immediately. '*Well!*' she said with heavy emphasis. 'What a nice girl! I'm so happy—'

Kelso looked at her in horror. 'For goodness' sake, Fin! Kate is a colleague. We had things to discuss – professional things, if you're interested – and since I knew her way back, I thought we could talk over a meal. And it was very useful.'

Finella smiled. 'You don't have to make excuses to me – or even to yourself, come to that. Time's passing and Alexa would want you to move on.'

He looked at her coolly. 'Yes, that's what they always say, isn't it? But would she, really? We'll never know.'

'Of course she would!' Finella protested. 'She was so warm and generous. She wouldn't want a life of mourning for you.'

'No,' he said. 'Perhaps not.' He went to the fridge and took out a beer.

'Now, Kate seems really nice. And you'd have a lot in common—'

Kelso flipped the lid off the bottle and chucked it in the bin with a violent gesture. 'Yes, Kate's a nice woman. But do you remember Alexa?' He compressed his lips and when he spoke again his voice was hoarse. 'The first time I met her, the world went crazy. I couldn't believe anyone so perfect existed. It was the middle of the night but suddenly the sun was shining. We used to say, a nightingale sang in Charlotte Square.' He cleared his throat. 'Now, if you'll excuse me, I've got some work to do.'

He paused on the way to his bedroom that acted as a study as well. 'And I don't want to have to meet even one more of your divorced girlfriends. All right?'

Finella switched the TV back on but she wasn't hearing the inane remarks and the canned laughter. She did, indeed, remember Alexa. She was unforgettable – so lovely, so brimming with life that it was all but impossible to believe she was dead. And she'd seen Kate – sweet-faced, with round blue eyes and pink cheeks, a little on the plump side. Kelso was good at covering up, but she knew he was still suffering badly and she hated to see it, but he clearly wasn't ready to move on. She just hoped that Kate, who had looked at him so admiringly, hadn't read too much into their 'professional' evening.

Whoever was out there would have heard the TV so she couldn't pretend she wasn't in and she couldn't pretend she was asleep. Getting up on to shaky legs, Cassandra went to the door. It wasn't late; normally she'd have opened it without a second thought, but there was a peephole and she peered through it.

She could make out that it was a man who stood on the doorstep, but it was too dark to see his face properly. As if he had realised what she was doing, he called, 'Don't worry, miss – police. DI Hammond,' just as she switched on the outside light and recognised him. He'd spoken to her a couple of times about Felix; he'd said all the right police-type things, with practised coolness, which wasn't comforting when you were falling apart. Thank God for Kate, she thought as she let him in.

He waited politely to be offered a seat, then settled on the sofa opposite. She felt awkward in her lounging pyjamas, perfectly modest though they were, and even more awkward when she noticed the sex scene that was playing out in lurid detail on her big-screen TV. She snapped it off hurriedly.

'Sorry,' she muttered, 'I wasn't expecting visitors.' She gestured to her clothes. 'Not very appropriate for a police interview.'

He laughed easily. 'No, you're all right. It's just a chat, really.' He leant forward to look more closely at her. 'You've had a nasty knock, haven't you?'

Just for a moment there she'd let herself hope that he'd come to say they'd found the bastard who had killed her brother, but of course they hadn't; she could tell from the way Kate had spoken that they weren't even planning to look.

'Oh!' Cassie put her hand up to her cheek. 'I'd almost forgotten about it. Is – is that why you're here?'

'A complaint has been made—'

'Oh. My mother. Right?'

'Not at liberty to confirm or deny.' He made a joke of it. 'I just need to get an idea of how that happened from you. This morning, was it?'

While she gave him the details, he listened in silence, never taking his eyes from her face. She showed him the bandage on her leg and a small graze on her hand.

'That's the sum total of my injuries,' she said. 'Oh, and one mangled bike. Not really enough to make a fuss about.'

'You were very lucky,' he said. 'It's not thanks to the driver that it wasn't a lot worse. Now, I need to take you through this. You were cycling down to Halliburgh, at around the usual time for going in to work, riding on the left-hand side, yes? When did you become aware of the car behind you?'

Cassie frowned. 'Oh, a moment or two, I suppose. I heard the engine.'

He pounced. 'What sort? Big car, small car?'

'I . . . I don't know. I didn't think about it. Just, someone was coming so I tucked in as far as I could, like I always do. I've had a few close shaves before now. I sort of supposed it would have been one of those big 4x4s since they take up so much of the road, but I haven't any evidence.'

'Can you think? None at all? Not a glimpse, not a smell?'

She shook her head. 'Sorry.'

'It could even have been a small car?'

'Yes, I suppose so. I'm sorry, I haven't been much help.'

'Don't worry about it. We picked up your bike and I'll get someone to check it for paint flakes, anything like that. Had you been passed by any other cars before?'

'No. It's a very quiet road.'

'Any afterwards?'

'No. I could have used one – it was a long way limping down to the Foundation.'

'Right,' he said, and stood up. 'If we find we have something to go on, I'll get someone to take a proper statement. Thanks for your time. I'm sorry to have butted in on your evening.'

'That's all right. Thanks for looking into it. I wouldn't mind getting someone to pay for the damage they did to the bike.'

'Do you have another one? If you're planning to go on—'

'I know, I know, be very careful,' she finished for him. 'It's rather put me off, and as it happens my mother's insisting her driver takes me to and fro.'

'Very sensible,' he approved.

It had all been so down to earth that she was feeling better as she showed him to the door. Then just as he went out he turned and said unexpectedly, 'I should ask, really – there isn't anyone at the Foundation, say, who might have a grudge against you, is there?'

Her shock probably showed in her face but she managed to say lightly, 'Not enough to try to kill me, I hope!' and he nodded and went off down the path. But she was feeling cold all over again.

CHAPTER SEVEN

Just as Sascha Silverton had assumed he would, Richard Sansom came over to speak to Jason Jackson, though without any obvious enthusiasm. She heard Jason say, 'Let me buy you a drink and you can come clean about Anna Harper.' She saw Sansom stiffen and she stepped away from Wilson, who was ordering their drinks, to take the opportunity to say hello.

She was gratified by his reaction. Clearly he hadn't noticed her that morning; his eyes widened in appreciation as she smiled up at him. 'We almost met earlier at the Foundation. I'm one of the writers – Sascha.'

'Yes of course,' he said quickly. 'You looked hard at work when I came in. Are you finding it useful?'

'It's such a luxury, not having to do anything except write. It's a wonderful facility—'

She was rudely interrupted by Jason. 'Do you want that drink or not, Richard?'

'Thanks, but I'm just going to have supper. I'll get a drink at the table.' He turned back to Sascha. 'Are you heading off back to the Foundation? I gather the evening meal is part of the package.'

'Oh yes, it's very generous. But I end up eating more than I really want to and I noticed they've got a smoked salmon starter here that would suit me better.'

'Why not join me, then?' Sansom said. 'From a professional point of view, I'd be interested to hear how you heard about the week and what you think of the show so far.'

'Well, that would be nice. Thank you very much,' she said, ignoring Wilson's scowl and muttered, 'Hey!' as she took the drink he handed to her. What did the man think – that he'd bought her along with the drink?

They had just taken their seats at a table when a woman came in. She was slim and slight, and pretty in a sharp-featured way with a dark ponytail. She was looking round and then saw Jackson.

'Hi Jas,' she said. 'Thought you'd be here. You coming home for supper tonight?'

He looked at her coldly. 'Let me think, Kayleigh. Chef cooking three courses with free booze – going home to fish fingers that you'll probably burn anyway? Tough choice.'

Kayleigh coloured, but held her ground. 'If you're not coming home, can you give me some money now? Danny needs new trainers and I'm skint.'

Wilson stopped glaring at Sascha. 'Hello there,' he said. 'Jason's girlfriend, right?'

She barely glanced at him, her attention focused on Jackson who was fishing in his pocket with bad grace.

Wilson tried again, stepping closer. 'You work for Anna Harper, don't you? What's she like?'

Sascha had been listening but Sansom had been looking at the menu. His attention caught, he turned to look over his shoulder.

Kayleigh's eyes flicked briefly to Wilson's face. 'All right,' she said. 'Jason—'

Jackson had stopped hunting for his wallet. He was looking at her as if he'd never noticed her before and then he said, 'Come on, I'll walk you home.' He finished his pint and put down the glass then ushered her out.

Wilson, abandoned, finished his own drink and with a resentful glance at Sascha left the pub. Sascha and Sansom looked at each other and then laughed.

'Quite a little vignette there,' Sansom said.

'Oh, I love pubs! All human life is here.'

'Is that where you get your ideas? I'm sure there's a story there.'

'Definitely. I'm just mentally writing the dialogue as Jason and his lady go off home. He's definitely the bad guy. After about twenty pages a decent guy would come along and by the end of the book she'd have dumped Jason and been set up for happy ever after with the new one. His book would totally bomb as well. The nice thing about writing is you can make people pay for their sins.'

Sansom was amused. 'I can see that must be very gratifying.'

The drinks arrived. She held up her glass, saying '*Slainte!*' and gave him a long look under her eyelashes. 'But it's not what I want to do, really. It's shallow. I've been given a talent for writing and I want to write the sort of book that changes people's lives, like Anna Harper has.'

'A tall order.'

'Yes. But I'm sure she could help me, inspire me. I just need to catch her attention. You know her. Tell me all about her.'

'You can't expect me to dish the dirt on her, you know,' he warned.

'There's dirt?' Sascha said brightly. 'I've always had the impression she's squeaky clean.'

For a moment she thought he was tempted. But he only laughed and said, 'Is it the smoked salmon? I'll go across and order it.'

Sascha settled back in her chair. She hadn't got much out of him yet, but the evening was young.

'There's a problem in Halliburgh,' DCI Strang said to DCS Borthwick on Sunday morning. He hadn't been sure she would be in, but she was frowning over a pile of files on her desk as she scribbled on a comment; now she put down her pen and looked up at him.

'Why does no one ever come in and say there isn't a problem somewhere?' she asked with a sigh. 'That's a rhetorical question. So, what sort of problem? The sort we can handle or the sort that's going to be on the front page of the tabloids tomorrow?'

'Hope not. It's under wraps at the moment, but if it came out it would go big. I had a long talk with Kate Graham yesterday.'

'She was the one you remembered, then?'

'Yes. I was surprised she was still a constable because she was considered one of the high-flyers. She's had family problems – mother ill then died, father needing care – so she's stuck in the family home. It was lucky I talked to her. She's been very worried about what's going on in Halliburgh. Do you know anything about DI Steve Hammond?'

Borthwick shook her head. 'What's he been doing?'

He repeated what Kate had told him and Borthwick's expression grew more and more grim.

'So hard to handle,' she said. 'We can't just dump the woman in it, so we'd have to have some excuse to investigate. If they're up to all that there'll be more going on than even she knows about.'

'Something struck me at the conference. I think Kate was the only officer on the list who wasn't CID. There were quite a number of inspectors, in fact – a couple of them were speaking about their own local problems. I sort of assumed that the reason Halliburgh had sent low-level representation was that they had no particular problem. But after what she said about him, I suspect he's the kind that's not too keen on finding that something's less than perfect on his patch.'

'That's all we need,' Borthwick said. 'We'll have to think about it and hope to come up with something. Can I leave it with you?'

'Actually,' Strang said, 'I thought about it a lot last night and I have an idea.'

Borthwick brightened. 'I like it when you say you have an idea. Tell.'

Strang explained and she listened intently. 'I could certainly swing that. Everyone's short of staff. Have you someone in mind?'

He told her and she laughed. 'Well, well, Kelso. Come round to my way of thinking, have you?'

'It's always wise, boss,' he said. But he was smiling too.

It was a grey day even for late February in Edinburgh, heavily overcast, and a few flakes of snow were drifting down past the windows of the Fettes Avenue police station. Depressing stuff, and DC Livvy Murray always hated to be assigned to Sunday duty anyway, but she'd made the best of it by finding a desk in the farther corner of the CID room, a large filing cabinet shielding her from the line of sight of anyone opening the door to find a constable who could be saved from the mischief Satan found for idle hands to do. She'd never have got away with it with her former sarge, an eagle-eyed and grizzled veteran, but his successor was still wet behind the ears.

She needed all the free time she could snatch if she

wasn't going to have to miss out on a social life altogether. She was working for her sergeant's exams and it was tough, really tough. She'd bunked off too often at school to have acquired any habit of studying and she could think of a few teachers who'd get a good laugh out of seeing her now, with her face screwed up and muttering under her breath as she tried to persuade the facts to stay in her head. She had the nasty feeling that there wasn't anything between her ears to stop them going in one and straight out through the other.

She heard the door open, but didn't bend forward to see who it was. A couple of detectives were working at other terminals and they'd be spotted first if there was some random task to be allocated. Then she heard Angie Andrews' voice saying, 'Hi! Anyone seen Livvy Murray?'

She was hoping the others might not have registered that she was there but when one said, 'Oh yes, she's—' she leant forward into view hastily, as if she'd been going to answer all along.

'Hi, Angie. Something you want?'

Angie, the Force Civilian Assistant allocated to the Serious Rural Crime Squad for admin, made her way across. 'Skulking, are you?'

'Hard at work,' Murray said with perfect, if misleading, truthfulness. 'Ooh, like the hair!'

Angie was sporting a new hair colour, a sort of deep mahogany that was only a shade away from purple. 'I really fancied magenta but I compromised. Not sure the

DCI was taken with it, even so. Gave me a bit of an odd look, but since #MeToo we've got them too scared even to raise an eyebrow. Anyway, he wants to see you.'

'Oh, right!' She got up with some alacrity. 'Something on?'

'Not as far as I know. He's in his office.'

Murray followed her out. She'd hardly set eyes on Strang since the case in Caithness; ordinarily their paths didn't cross. CID at Fettes Avenue was a big department and with Strang's SRCS job he was quite often away in any case.

She was feeling more settled in Edinburgh now and she'd found a few party-minded mates. She still missed her native Glasgow with its cheerful friendliness – no one in Edinburgh ever asked, 'Are you all right, hen?' if you were looking a bit down – but the pull to get back had diminished since her schoolfriends had started having kids and babysitters that meant the evening had to stop at eleven, eleven-thirty if they were going completely wild, and they were all falling asleep into their drinks anyway. With the Glasgow force, too, she had previous, while here she was starting to get a bit of respect.

Like any daily job, though, it wasn't exciting. The two investigations she'd been on with Strang had left her with an addiction to the rush of adrenaline that came with high-profile cases. If he was sending for her, could it be another major one? He'd seemed relatively pleased with her last time, apart from a few occasions when she'd overstepped the mark, and it would be a real feather in her cap if he actually wanted to work with her again. When she worked with him she learnt a lot, and Murray had ambitions.

Certainly he greeted her warmly enough. 'Good to see you, Livvy! How's it going?'

She'd never been in his office before. If you were into cat-swinging it would present a serious problem and the chair she sat down on was so near the desk that she had to sit sideways.

'Fine thanks, sir. I'm just starting to work towards my sergeant's exams.'

'Glad to hear it. Are you managing to find time for your studies? It's hard to settle in to work again when you come home from a long shift.'

'It certainly is,' Murray said without a blush. There was a pile of papers on his desk and she tried discreetly to read the top one upside down for a clue about what might be going on, but the heading 'Crime and Justice Statistics' didn't look promising.

'I think I might have a job for you,' Strang said. 'It would be highly confidential, with a lot of working on your own in quite a tricky situation.'

To her surprise, she felt a bit of a pang at the thought that they wouldn't be working together but it sounded like an interesting assignment. 'Undercover work, sir?'

He laughed. 'I hadn't really thought of it in those terms but yes, I suppose it is. Would you be up for that?'

'Absolutely, boss,' she said with a beaming smile. 'Where would it be?'

'The Borders. A place called Halliburgh – do you know it?' She shook her head and he went on, 'The thing is, you'd be undercover in the police force. We have reason to believe that there are some problems there. I'm going to give you the details, but I'm not going to tell you who supplied them. There's a lot at stake.'

'Is it an officer?'

'Yes, and the position they're in means they can't afford to be a whistle-blower. I'll be relying on you to gather evidence that lets us take action. The super is very keen to root it out before there's some sort of scandal.'

Murray listened carefully while he told her what she needed to know. On the face of it, it didn't sound as if it would be hard to blend in. Rural CIDs were notoriously understaffed and with all the fuss there was at the moment about county lines, they wouldn't be surprised if they were allocated extra manpower. Or even woman power.

'So what am I tasked to do, sir?'

'Well, I hesitate to say this, Livvy, but you'll have to use your initiative.'

She grinned. 'Never thought I'd live to hear you say that, boss.'

'Within reason,' he said, showing definite signs of alarm. 'Keep it low-key, remember. At the moment we're only talking about fairly low-level corruption and for that all you have to do is keep your eyes and ears open and your mouth shut and log everything. But there are one or two things that suggest they may be turning a blind eye to the drugs situation to keep their slate clean so don't go stirring up that particular hornet's nest. A murdered DC might be convincing evidence that there was a serious problem, but it seems to me rather too high a price to pay.'

'Can't argue with that. Will I need to stay there, boss?'

'I don't think so. It's just a little over an hour's drive and I can allocate you a car. Weather's the only problem and they're muttering about a nasty system coming in, but we can arrange that you stay there if it comes to that.'

'That's fine. When do I start?'

'I'm sending out a general email to the Borders forces as a follow-up to the conference, saying extra manpower is being allocated and the super has just spoken to the Borders District Commander who actually suggested Halliburgh off his own bat – he thinks he has a hotshot DI there who might make a difference with a bit more backup. Ironic, really.

'So I'll sort out the formal side so you can pick up a car tomorrow and get down there on Tuesday. They'll have been in direct touch with Hammond by then. I think that's all. Good luck! I'm on the end of a phone, remember.' He paused. 'Have you any special assignments today?'

'Not at the moment, sir.'

'Well, tell your sergeant I've approved letting you off your shift since you'll be having a long commute for the next while. You can use the extra time for studying.'

He had kept his face straight but she had a feeling that he knew perfectly well that the minute she left the room she'd be on the phone to see what she could arrange as a farewell if she might be going to get stuck out there in the sticks.

'I'm taking you up to Highfield,' Davy Armstrong said as he drove Cassie Trentham away from her cottage. 'Your mum wants to have a word.'

'Davy!' Cassie was outraged. 'I have a job, remember? I agreed to be driven to and fro but I never agreed to being transported anywhere on my mother's orders. Just stop when you reach the Foundation and let me out and then you can go and tell my mother that she can reach me in the normal way, by telephone, and we can make a mutually satisfactory arrangement. I'm all grown-up now – *Davy!*'

She gave a shriek of annoyance as the car swept smoothly on downhill into the town and past the Foundation. Davy gave her an apologetic glance.

'I know, I know. You're all like that when you get a wee bit older. You don't think you're a child any more, but you have to remember that your mum thinks you are and she's worried about you. I know what my Elspeth would be like. What does it cost you to let her see with her own eyes that you're all right? It'll not take long and

I'll be waiting to whisk you back whenever you're ready.'

'I'm ready right now,' Cassie muttered, but there was no point in arguing about her mother's sensibilities. Inspector Hammond hadn't denied that it was Anna who'd reported her accident and that was characteristic: when her children had a problem Anna's reaction had always been to call in appropriate experts – even if, in Felix's case, they'd been worse than useless. She accepted that Anna would want to know that her daughter was all right, but it was hard to believe that she was feeling maternal enough to want the reassurance of seeing her. Elspeth Armstrong she wasn't.

When the car stopped in front of Highfield's door, Cassie got out saying witheringly, 'You'll notice I'm not saying thank you, Davy,' but he only laughed.

The alarm was usually off at this time of day, but she had to punch in the code to open the door. There was a woman crossing the hall who looked startled as Cassie came in.

Cassie didn't recognise her – fairly new, probably. With Marta's demanding standards, cleaners tended to come and go. 'Morning!' she said. 'Do you know where my mother is?'

It was clear that the cleaner hadn't known who she was either. She said, a little hesitantly, 'I haven't seen anyone, but I've cleared the breakfast.'

'Probably the study, then. Thanks.'

Cassie walked through the hall, and under the gallery, to reach Anna's study and opened the door.

The two women were sitting by the fire. 'Oh!' exclaimed Anna, her hand going to her throat, and Marta jumped visibly. 'Good gracious, you gave me a fright!'

'Who did you think it was? You sent for me, after all. Did you expect me to ring the bell and wait?'

'No, no of course not,' Marta said. 'This is always your home, *cara*, you know that.'

'I have a home, Marta. My own cottage. Burnside – remember? And I have a job, Mother, and I don't appreciate being forced to come here instead of doing it.'

Anna said tartly, 'Oh, don't be silly. I don't believe for a moment that Davy actually strong-armed you though the door. Come and sit down. Do you want some coffee?' She indicated the Nespresso machine in the corner of the room.

'No, thank you.' Cassie sat down. Her mother had seen her now, if that truly was what she wanted, but she didn't seem much interested in the scar and the bruising. On the other hand, when she looked at Anna, and Marta too, there were more visible signs of stress than she'd ever seen before – heavy eyes, and dark circles underneath. There was a little bloody line on Marta's lip that looked as if she'd been biting at it. Perhaps she'd been too quick to judge her mother for showing so little emotion about Felix. Emoting had never been Anna's style.

'So – why did you want to see me?'

'I'm sure Davy explained that I'd be happier if you came and stayed here, just for a bit. I know you turned it down, but I—'

'Why?'

The two women exchanged glances. Marta spoke first. 'The weather, Cassie. It worries your mother. You would be safer here.'

Surely that was nonsense. This morning she'd managed to shake off the worries of the previous night but now the bad feeling was creeping back. 'Look, I've agreed to let Davy drive me, so I don't see what the weather has to do with it. And I take it that it was you who told the inspector about what happened? Richard Sansom told you, I suppose.'

Anna was swift to seize the moral high ground. 'I think I might be entitled to have heard it from you first, don't you? Naturally I was concerned, and I didn't want whoever did that to you to get away with it.'

'Neither do I, but I can't remember anything helpful so there doesn't seem a lot of point in making a fuss, especially since I won't be cycling.' Intercepting another look between the two of them, she said sharply, 'This isn't adding up. There's more to this, isn't there? Have there been death threats again?' Being a celebrity meant that these were commonplace but Anna had people to handle them and had never seemed rattled before.

And she wasn't now, apparently. After a second she threw back her head and laughed. 'Oh dear, now I'm scaring you. No, there's nothing out of the ordinary. It's when they lose interest that you have to worry. It's just with the forecast for bad weather ahead I wouldn't want you to be cut off there on your own. But if you're determined, I know there's no point in arguing.

'Now, tell me about the writers. Any promising talent?'

Despite being able to see that Marta was digging her nails into the palm of her hand, Cassie found herself sidetracked.

'I haven't really met them properly. I'd a full programme on Saturday and Richard took me out to lunch – as you presumably know.'

The barbed remark was ignored. 'He seems to be a cut above the usual publicity type,' Anna said. 'We've had some horrors in our time, haven't we Marta?'

'Oh yes, we have.' Marta sounded like someone reluctantly forced to play charades. 'There was that girl with the purple hair—'

'Oh, goodness, I'd forgotten her. And the piercings!'

Cassie got up. 'I really don't have time to waste listening to you reminisce. If you'll excuse me . . .'

Again, a glance passed between Anna and Marta and Cassie had the strong sense of words unspoken. She couldn't guess what they were, and Anna only gave a tiny shrug as she said goodbye.

Kayleigh Burns was just finishing doing the hall when the daughter came out and went straight out of the front door. She hadn't stayed long and she wasn't looking best pleased. Kayleigh hadn't heard any raised voices, but maybe posh people didn't make a lot of noise when they'd a row. She'd been in the wars somewhere, though, with that nasty bruise on her cheek. But she didn't spare much time thinking about that. She'd too much other stuff on her mind.

More than ever now she was regretting getting in tow with Jason. He'd been so rude to her on Saturday night in front of his pals – even if it was true enough that she'd had the packet of fish fingers lying out waiting beside the cooker. And worse, he could really dump her in it now, even if he swore he wouldn't.

They'd argued yesterday and she'd managed to drive up the price – he'd given her more than she'd have thought he could possibly have in his possession. Kayleigh had been able to say to Danny, 'If you want Converse trainers that much, I'll get them for you.'

He'd been going on and on about them; all his mates had them, and smartphones as well, but when she asked where they got them, he turned evasive. From their parents, he'd said, but she knew some of them and they hadn't the money any more than she did. She knew where the money for all the gear was coming from and it made her feel sick. The trainers might keep Danny happy for a week or two, but it wouldn't be enough. She couldn't keep up with that sort of spending and Danny wouldn't want to be left out. She could see where he was drifting, and she felt sick at the thought.

She'd mentioned it again to Jason last night and he'd scoffed at her, told her she was a neurotic mother.

'Every kid wants stuff,' he'd said, 'and then they nag at their parents till they get it. Just like Danny did.'

But she didn't know where Jason was getting his money from either. When she'd challenged him he'd muttered something about a lucky bet, but she'd never seen signs of him being a gambler before. She had a nasty feeling that she knew.

And his latest idea was worse. She'd tried to say no, but he'd reacted so violently that she'd given in. She'd never been scared of him before, but she was now.

CHAPTER EIGHT

Gil Paton was silently seething this morning. He'd been irritated yesterday by Richard Sansom's attitude in the first place and then when he'd gone to see Cassie after she got back from her lunch with him for a debrief, she'd been less than communicative.

'Oh, we just chatted,' she'd said. 'He seems pretty much on the ball.'

He'd made the mistake of saying, 'I thought it was a bit odd that he'd carry you off for lunch when we could have got lunch here and I could have contributed,' and she'd stared at him.

'Gil, it wasn't a business meeting. It was just a getting-to-know-you session.'

'Right. It's just, well, to be honest, I sometimes feel you're trying to exclude me.'

There was no mistaking her irritation. 'Gil, I'm

grateful for the help and support you give me, but I have my job and you have yours. They're not the same; your job is running the Foundation here and it's a big enough responsibility for you not to feel you have to take on aspects of mine.'

Then she'd changed the subject by asking him how the writers were settling in. He'd given her a fairly terse reply and then gone off to nurse his grievance. This had been the job of his dreams, the job he deserved, but it wasn't, really. Cassie used her privileged position to block him constantly. It was his right to be involved in all the big decisions, an important part of the public face of the Foundation; instead she got all the invitations to the parties and premieres while he was expected to sort out the plumbing problems in the cloakrooms and keep the cleaners up to scratch.

He'd thought, too, that he would get to know Anna, gain her respect so that she would take an interest in him, but that hadn't worked at all – she'd never actually bothered to come and meet him. Marta hadn't either. The unfairness of it cut deep; he felt entitled to much more than that.

This morning had been even worse. Even though he'd still been feeling annoyed, he'd made the effort to go in and be pleasant and cheerful at their usual meeting. Then, quite by chance, he'd said, 'I wonder if they'll be wanting to make *Jacob's Angel* into a film.'

Cassie had laughed. 'Oh yes. We've been in negotiations for some time. Terribly hush-hush, of course, but I know I can rely on you not to say anything.'

Rage was almost choking him, but he managed to say stiffly, 'Naturally.' Then he'd got up, saying rather pointedly that he supposed he'd better get back to his duties downstairs. He even thought he'd heard her sigh as he went out. Yet another example of her rubbing it in that he was just the hired hand.

When he reached the Hub, Sascha, Marion and Mick were all working at their desks. There was no sign of Elena; he'd hardly set eyes on her since she arrived. She was the one with real literary class, Gil reckoned, the sort the Foundation ought to be supporting instead of people like Jason Jackson, who was right at this moment making free with coffee from the flask on the refreshment table.

He turned round as Gil came in. 'Ah! Just the very man.' He walked across, holding out his mug. 'What do you call this?'

Gil looked. It did, admittedly, look a bit weak this morning. 'Coffee,' he snapped. 'What do you call it?' He was smarting already and now his hackles rose at being treated like a waiter.

Jason contemplated it, as if he was seeing it for the first time. 'Hard to say, really. Bilge water springs to mind, but perhaps that's a rather clichéd comparison for someone who's a writer. Still, never knock a cliché until you can offer something better and it's such a good description that I have to admit I've failed.'

'Yes, I heard that you had.' Gil delivered the putdown with vicious satisfaction.

Jason's eyes darkened. 'I suppose I shouldn't be surprised by that. Someone told me once that rabbits have a rather nasty bite. But I was talking about the coffee. Surely Anna Harper can afford to provide something better than watery Nescafé?'

To everyone's surprise, before Gil could point out coldly that it was filter, Marion spoke up. 'I think it's very nice. It's very generous of Ms Harper to do all this for us and it's rude and ungrateful to complain.'

Jason stared at her for a moment, then burst out laughing. 'Oooh, I bet the kids in Primary 3 were terrified of you! Sorry, miss. Don't smack my fingers or I'll cry.'

There was something odd about him this morning, Gil thought. He'd heard him being disrespectful of Anna more or less regularly and he'd treated Gil himself with careless contempt to the point where he'd had to walk away before he gave way to unprofessional rage, but just now Jason seemed almost high, as if he'd taken something. Which could well be the explanation.

Marion contented herself with a withering glance. Mick gave a short laugh, then went back to typing. Sascha got up and came over.

'I want to dissociate myself from what Jason's saying too. He doesn't speak for any of the rest of us, Gil.' She turned to Jason. 'Sneering at Anna Harper while you grab whatever's going with both hands is pretty low – just sponging, really. This is meant to be an opportunity for a writer, and I doubt if you're even that. Your publisher doesn't seem to be rushing out a follow-up.'

A look of black temper crossed Jason's face and for a moment Gil thought he was going to hit Sascha. 'You watch what you say, woman,' he snarled, but controlled himself enough to add with an unpleasant smile, 'And what about you? I looked you up on Amazon, but oddly enough I couldn't find a chick-lit author by the name of Sascha Silverton.'

Sascha's face flooded with dark colour. 'You really are a vile little man! I don't write chick-lit under my own name. I'm saving that for the sort of book I really want to write, the kind I'm lucky enough to have been given the opportunity to work on now, which is why I'm grateful to the Foundation.'

Gil, alarmed by the escalating row, said hastily, 'Look, I think—' but he was ignored. Jason cut across him saying, 'Oh really? Judging by the puerile drivel that I read on your laptop when you were out of the room, even your pals at Mills and Boon wouldn't take it.'

Sascha's big brown eyes were murderous slits. 'You'll regret making an enemy of me, Jason Jackson. I have useful friends. Wait and see.'

For a moment he hesitated. Then he laughed. 'Ooh, I'm scared! But don't we all?' He walked away, back to his desk to pick up his laptop and his coat. 'I've had enough of this place. The stink of incense being burnt on the altar of the great Anna Harper is turning me sick.

She's fooled you all, but she hasn't fooled me. Goodbye, suckers.' He pushed open the door to the street and slammed it as he left.

The sound echoed in the huge room. In the silence that followed Gil could hear Sascha still breathing fast but it was Marion who broke it. She was trembling a little, but her voice was determinedly bright as she said, 'Well, that wasn't very edifying, was it? He really is a very unpleasant young man. I hope that's the last we're going to see of him here. Are you all right, Sascha?'

Mick, who had been a silent observer, said, 'Oh, I reckon Sascha can look after herself. You gave as good as you got, girl.'

'I'm sorry, everyone,' Sascha said stiffly. 'I'm mortified that I allowed him to get under my skin. I suppose we're all just ridiculously sensitive when it comes to someone criticising what we write.'

'Of course. I can understand that,' Gil said. 'I'm sorry too that you've been exposed to such a nasty little scene. This is meant to provide a tranquil haven for you to get on with your work.'

As if it was a signal, they all moved back towards their workstations, though Mick said drily, 'Oh, don't apologise. Sure brightened up my morning.'

Looking at Sascha's face, set in frigid lines, Gil didn't think she'd go along with that. He would have said he yielded to no one in his loathing for Jason Jackson, but he might even have to give her best.

* * *

When Gil left her office, Cassie Trentham sat back in her chair, her shoulders sagging in weariness. She really was very tired; she'd forced herself to keep going just as if her head and her cuts and bruises weren't sore and her heart didn't ache. Grief was very debilitating; the energy you needed to keep it at bay sapped your strength.

What she didn't need was other people creating more problems for her. People like Gil. He'd been a mistake and she had no one to blame but herself. The demands on her time grew every year and appointing a deputy who could take over running the Hub made a lot of sense. She'd had a good field when she advertised – Anna's name was a big draw – but too many of the candidates seemed overqualified: bright young graduates who were looking for more than she was prepared to offer.

Gil had far and away the least glamorous CV. He'd moved about in various jobs, but he had good references and he'd really done his homework on the Foundation and Anna too; it was his enthusiasm that had won her over. One or two of the applicants had made it obvious that they were disappointed by the job specification but he would have no reason to think that the job she appointed him to do was beneath him.

Reason clearly had nothing to do with it. He'd started encroaching almost from the start and she found it hard to deal with his sulking when an impractical suggestion he made wasn't taken up. She couldn't really figure him out; sometimes he seemed to be trying to chat her up and put her down at the same time. There was no doubt that he bitterly resented her superior position. As he saw it, he had beaten a whole lot of strong candidates to get his job whereas she had sailed into hers by virtue of being her mother's daughter.

Cassie did actually feel a little guilty over not telling him about the negotiations for the filming rights to *Jacob's Angel*. It was their London lawyers who were handling this, of course, so in a way it was nothing to do with the work here, but if she'd had a deputy who wasn't suffering from delusions of grandeur she'd have talked to him about it. If she'd told Gil, though, he'd have wanted to come along the next time she went up for a meeting and if she told him that wasn't appropriate she'd have had another hissy fit to deal with.

It couldn't go on like this. She had a slight hope that he might flounce out when he realised she wasn't going to let him elbow her aside, but she had a nasty feeling that he wouldn't abandon the ground he felt he had gained. Sooner or later she'd have to sack the man, but please, not now. Not with everything else she was having to cope with at the moment.

Like Anna. What was going on there? It might seem natural enough for a mother to look drawn and haggard when she'd just lost her only son, but Cassie had never seen Anna looking like that, not when Felix died, not even at the funeral. She hadn't started on the possessive, protective stuff until after Cassie's own accident.

It was so obvious that there was something they weren't telling her. She couldn't understand why not; if it was a threat to her own safety, she had a right to know what it was. Then she could decide whether or not she wanted to be taken into protective custody at Highfield.

Anna and Marta had always had their secrets. When they were young, she and Felix had known that but never really questioned it – children tend to accept whatever is familiar and it was just the way things were. But talking to Richard Sansom had brought home to her how little, how very little she actually knew about her mother. She'd said, almost casually, that she and Felix had reckoned Anna had changed the name she'd started out with, as if that was just something people did. It wasn't what normal people did, but if you were Anna's child 'normal' sort of didn't apply.

There was a lot subsumed under 'The Brand'. It had been dinned into them that nothing must tarnish Anna's image as someone so dedicated to her art that it left her no energy for commonplace activities like giving interviews and going to literary festivals; part of the mystique was that her past was a sealed book. Now her daughter was starting to wonder in earnest what that book contained.

She was rubbing her brow to try to smooth out the furrows when there was a knock on the door. She had no appointments this morning. Oh lord, she thought, please not Gil again!

But when she said, 'Come in,' it was Sascha Silverton who opened the door, peering tentatively round it.

'Look, I'm sorry to interrupt you. I hope you don't mind – I won't keep you long.'

Why, she wondered, when someone says, 'I hope you don't mind?' is it a reflex to say, 'No, of course not,' even when you do mind, quite a lot?

Cassie forced a smile. 'No, of course not. Take a seat.'

She saw Sascha's eyes scan the room and could read her thoughts as she registered Mies van der Rohe chairs and Cassie's le Corbusier desk. It was certainly a very elegant office but then it was an important part of the package for the Foundation's office, and the Foundation's Chair as well, to look the part as the front office for The Brand. As with Gil, Sascha's envy was unmistakable.

She was, however, smiling at Cassie in a nervous sort of way, her eyes modestly lowered. 'Look, this is a bit embarrassing. I've come to apologise.'

'Good gracious! Whatever for?'

'I'm afraid there was a bit of a scene this morning in the Hub. I'm sure Gil will tell you all about it and I wanted to say sorry before you heard.'

It wasn't hard to recognise this as a pre-emptive apology that would allow Sascha to get her retaliation in first and the last thing Cassie wanted was to be drawn into a petty squabble. She said lightly, 'Oh, I'm sure there's no need. It certainly wasn't loud enough to disturb me and I daresay there weren't any windows broken.'

'No, no, of course not.' This clearly wasn't the reaction Sascha had been expecting and she sounded a little tetchy as she went on, 'It's just it seemed so awful that with all the Foundation is doing for us I couldn't rise above stupid comments by one of the other writers and let myself down by responding in kind.'

Clearly, Cassie was now meant to ask which one. She said, 'I suppose it's inevitable that creative people do have volatile temperaments. I'm sure it will all blow over. But tell me, are you finding this is going to be a useful week for you?'

To be fair to Sascha, she was quick to recognise defeat. She clasped her hands together and said, 'Oh, I can't tell you how much! It's – it's inspirational, just being here. I know I sounded gauche when we spoke before but actually meeting Ms Harper's daughter threw me a bit and I blurted out the "greatest fan" rubbish. But I've really studied her work, read everything I could about her and I feel if I could actually talk to her she would reach out to me as a kindred spirit.'

Somehow Cassie didn't think Anna would see it quite like that. 'You'll have the chance to talk to her at the end of the week when she takes the masterclass, you know.'

'Of course, and I'm thrilled about that. But sitting in the group with other writers isn't the same as a one-to-one would be. You're her daughter – you must know how I could approach her.'

Cassie laughed, shaking her head. 'Sascha, I can't think of any approach that would be likely to meet with success. She pours her energy into her work and she must necessarily restrict her other activities. I'm sorry. I know it disappoints a lot of people.'

'I see. And of course I understand.' There was that hint of annoyance in her voice again, but then she smiled. 'It's wonderful that she used precious time to set this up for people like me – I'm fascinated by the whole idea of the Foundation. Look, I know you're very busy, but could I take you out for lunch sometime this week? I'd really enjoy getting to know you a bit better. You must have such a fascinating life!'

'That's a very kind offer,' Cassie said. 'But I'm sure you'll understand that just at the moment I simply haven't the time, with the launch of *Jacob's Angel* imminent. In fact . . .' She turned her wrist as if to look at her watch.

Sascha did take the cue and stood up saying, 'Of course. Well, thanks for seeing me, anyway.'

Cassie looked after her very thoughtfully as she went to the door. And just as Sascha turned away she had caught a look on her face that meant she wasn't too surprised that when Gil did indeed come to report on the fracas he said, 'She looks all sugar and spice, you know, but my goodness, she has an ugly temper. She gave Jason Jackson a look that was positively evil.'

Towards two o'clock in the morning the clear sky darkened as a great mass of purplish cloud blotted out the stars. A snow squall started, great soft flakes that fell thicker and faster until the ground was covered and the air was a mass of swirling whirling white, the street lamps no more than balls of sodium orange light.

Half suffocated by the feathery stuff clinging to his face, Jason Jackson swore as he struggled up the hill towards Highfield, taking two steps forward and sliding one step back. Perhaps he should have waited, but the forecast was for worse to come later and he was too impatient anyway to postpone it till better weather came.

He couldn't think why he hadn't thought of it before. Of course he should have known that Kayleigh had the code to take off the security alarms – she went in at seven to have everything ready for their breakfast – but it was only on Saturday evening that it had suddenly clicked. He'd had to come on heavy before she would give it to him and she'd driven a hard bargain once she did, but now he had the Open Sesame to the treasure cave of Anna's past.

The house was in darkness so his worst problem would be the security lights, and as he punched in the gate code and walked into the garden they flashed on immediately. But Kayleigh had said that they slept at the back, and at this hour surely they would be asleep. He went on, crossing his fingers.

Now the snow was his friend: the great plate glass windows were obscured by it if anyone did look out and it muffled sound too. He was making footprints, admittedly, but it was so wet underfoot that he was confident the evidence wouldn't be there in the morning. Now he was shivering, not with the cold but with excitement, like a dog.

In the eerie snow-stillness he took off his shoes, leaving them on the step under the arch above the front door, then keyed in the other code and tried the handle cautiously. Well maintained, like everything in this house, it swung open smoothly and the only sound was the click as he shut it again. He winced and stood still in the shadow until he could be sure there was no reaction.

It was pitch-dark inside. Jackson took out his phone and shone it round the great yawning space and along the gallery above until he saw a passage underneath that must lead towards the back of the house – and, he hoped, to the answers to all his questions. Across the hall and under the stairs, Kayleigh had said, for Anna's study.

A few yards down the passage, the beam of light picked out a flat-panelled door in some heavy pale wood; that should be it. Again, it opened easily and quietly; he closed it over but didn't risk shutting it in case anyone was listening, disturbed by the faint click of the front door.

This was the right place. She did herself well, did Anna. The torchlight picked out expensive-looking modern rugs, comfortable chairs, a fireplace where embers were still faintly glowing. At the other end there was a wall of books readily accessible from her desk with its dark red leather office chair and its flashy computer equipment and there, yes, right there, was a bank of three filing cabinets. They were made of light wood and each had a card slot showing numbers and letters – some sort of office code, presumably.

Jackson drew a deep breath. His hands were shaking as he went towards them, afraid now that even in this inner sanctum they might be locked against any unauthorised access. He tugged at the first one; it slid out with only a tiny sigh of movement and he punched the air in triumph.

Where to start, though? He didn't have unlimited time and there were literally hundreds of documents in each of the cabinets. He looked at them helplessly for a moment, then noticed a lever-arch file lying on the top of one of them. When he picked it up, there was a whole index showing everything they contained and he gave a wolfish grin as he played the torch down the pages. He did admire efficiency! And here was what he was looking for: Personal. The cabinet nearest the window, then.

It took only a moment to find the drawer and he took out the files – four of them – and laid them on the desk. There was a shaded lamp; he paused again for a moment listening intently for any stir of movement on the air, then switched it on.

It gave him a real kick to sit on Anna's literary throne and open up the story of her intimate life – all the ammunition he needed to make sure that his next book would be given kid-glove treatment, maybe even a cover puff from Anna herself. Not to mention compensation for what she'd done to the last one as well.

Marta had fallen into bed exhausted at midnight. Now she was simply too tired to get properly to sleep, just dropping off for a few minutes and then jerking awake again.

She and Anna had talked endlessly about the problem of Cassie. Since she was a teenager she'd wanted to rebel – touch of her mother there – but with careful manipulation she could usually be talked round. Felix's death had changed all that and now she seemed actively hostile. How could you protect someone who was determined not to be protected?

Marta had tried to look on the bright side – 'At least she's agreed to being driven. Davy will see to it that she's all right' – but Anna wasn't ready to be reassured.

'And then he drops her at the cottage, out there all on its own. She's so vulnerable, Marta, but she won't accept it. And I can't think what we can say to persuade her. We could have played up the death threats scenario after she mentioned it, but she'd want to know why the usual protection stuff wasn't swinging into action.'

There was really no answer to that but they went round and round, stressed already and getting more stressed the longer they talked. It was almost midnight when Marta said, 'I could get Davy to go round there tomorrow and put in some extra security – a panic button, say. We'll think of something to tell her tomorrow,' and at last Anna had been prepared to go to bed.

Now Marta was moving restlessly to try to find the position that might court sleep. Perhaps her eyelids were beginning to get heavy . . . Then she heard a click – soft but heavy, like a big door shutting. The front door?

The house should be completely silent. She sat up, listening. She'd slept with her door open lately in case Anna was wakeful and her room was the one nearest the stairs. As she listened, barely breathing, a trace of light swept across the opening. Someone was inside the house!

She slipped out of bed and tiptoed on to the landing. The light was now pointing down the passage under the stairs and leaning over the gallery she could see it being played on the door to Anna's study. She heard the tiny sound as it was opened and caught the outline of a male figure before he went inside and shut the door behind him.

Only pausing to pick up the fob key from her bedside table, Marta crept along to the security control room next to her bedroom, its door sliding silently open as she pressed the fob. She closed it behind her before she switched on the light.

There was a panic button, but she ignored it meantime. There was a desk with a terminal on it, showing roving CCTV pictures of every room in the house in turn and she sat down, looking for the right button to press. Click! And the monotone pictures of the dark, empty house gave way to colour and movement as it homed in on Anna's lighted study. She pressed again to lock it on position.

There was a man sitting at Anna's desk with a pile of files from one of the cabinets in front of him. He had opened one and was reading through it, but he was frowning, flicking over the pages. Then he laid it aside and opened another one.

Marta studied him intently. He was wearing a hoodie so his face was in shadow and all she could make out was that he had the two-day stubble look that was so fashionable nowadays and heavily marked dark brows so his hair was probably dark too. It was difficult to say what age he was or what height, but he didn't look very tall. How could he have got hold of the security code?

Then she realised: the cleaner, of course. What was her name – Kayleigh? Well, she'd be looking for a new job tomorrow. She didn't know who he was but with pictures like these someone else would, and he wasn't wearing gloves either.

He was getting impatient now, flipping over pages faster and faster and moving on to the next file. When he'd gone through the last one, evidently without finding what he was looking for, he brought his fists down on the desk in a gesture of rage, then froze as he listened for any reaction to the sound he had made. At last, satisfied that it was safe he stood up and gathered all the files together neatly. She could see his mouth moving – swearing under his breath, probably.

He slotted them back into their places and shut the cabinet again. Marta tensed, waiting to see what he would do now; this might be the moment for the panic button after all. But he shook his head as if in frustration, then moved towards the door as Marta switched cameras to view the hall. If he made for the stairs . . .

But he didn't. In his stockinged feet, she noticed, he padded across to the hall to let himself out. One of the panels in front of her lit up as he reactivated the code before he left, presumably thinking that would conceal his intrusion. After a pause – as he put on his shoes? – the outside lights came on then went off a minute later. He had gone.

There was a small, grim smile on Marta's face as she went back to her bedroom. At least they had a reason to give Cassie for stepping up the security at Burnside.

CHAPTER NINE

It was still dark when DC Kate Graham got up to hurry through her preparations for work and set out everything ready for her father's carer. She was on the early shift and DCI Strang had phoned her the night before to tell her that an officer from Edinburgh had been seconded to Halliburgh CID on the suggestion of the District Commander, as a result of discussions after the county lines conference.

'Well, that was a coincidence,' she'd said brightly and he had cleared his throat.

'Er, yes, in a manner of speaking. Anyway, she's DC Livvy Murray. I've briefed her on our discussion and she knows that there's someone who thinks there's a problem but she doesn't know it's you and there's no need for you to tell her. I've worked with her before and she's young and very bright, if a bit headstrong – she might benefit from your sound common sense, if something came up.'

Kate hadn't been sure how much she liked being designated as the voice of common sense as opposed to young and very bright, but she'd said, 'Yes, of course. I'll take it as it comes.'

'Thanks, Kate. I know I can rely on you. Keep me in the picture – you've got my number – and I'll let you know if there are other developments.'

Her father, sitting in his wheelchair by the fire in the big, comfortable sitting room, was ostensibly reading his newspaper but when she ended the call and said, 'That was Kelso Strang,' he raised one eyebrow.

'Oh aye?' he said.

'Oh, for goodness' sake, Dad! That was a professional call to tell me a new DC is arriving tomorrow. Just like our meeting the other night was a professional one too.' She was bitterly regretting telling him about it, especially when he said 'Oh aye?' again. She'd been painfully aware of Kelso's discomfort when his sister was far too welcoming and his embarrassment when the regulars in his pub were far too interested; she had no illusions. After all, she was full of sound common sense, wasn't she?

And it was only common sense to be wary this morning. She was by nature a truthful person and she needed to work out her lines for the part she had to play ahead of time. She must be mildly surprised by the arrival of the new DC; she must be friendly to her as a newcomer but nothing more. And she'd have to be on the watch to see how Hammond and Wilson greeted the arrival of someone tasked with looking at the drugs situation in Halliburgh who might find out something that would mess up Hammond's carefully constructed reputation for efficiency. She had butterflies in her stomach as she parked the car and went into the police station.

But this morning there was something of a fuss going on. The previous night, apparently, had seen a knife fight between a couple of teenage boys and though it had fortunately been stopped with no more than surface damage, the boys, their parents and their briefs were all milling around demanding immediate attention from a harassed DS Wilson. There was no sign as yet of the new DC but with all this no one would even notice Kate's efforts at amateur theatricals.

It was bad news, though. She knew both boys by sight; they were in the bus shelter group she'd noticed before. Halliburgh had never been troubled by knife crime and this was unwelcome confirmation that the problems she'd guessed at were very real. Perhaps the new, young, very bright DC might be able to make sure it couldn't be airbrushed out of existence for the sake of a clean reputation.

Kayleigh Burns was feeling sick as she drove up to Highfield at seven o'clock. She was heavy-eyed from lack of sleep too, since she hadn't been able to settle until Jason came back from his mission. And he'd been in a bad temper; he was tight-lipped, but it was clear things hadn't gone the way he wanted. When she'd asked what had happened he'd given her a good swearing, but she'd persisted.

'Oh, for God's sake! No one knew I was there, and I've reset the codes. All right? Now leave me alone.'

She wasn't sure she trusted him but the gate code worked and the door code too, and she let herself into the kitchen with a little 'phew!' of relief. There were no signs of any unusual activity overnight there or when she went through to Anna's study to lay the fire.

Kayleigh went back to the kitchen and then set the breakfast table in the little morning room that gave on to the garden. Last night's snow had disappeared; it was raining now with a dreary determination and even though it looked as if Jason had been right, she was still twitching with nerves. Marta Morelli was scary at the best of times and Kayleigh gave a little shudder as she thought of what would happen if she somehow discovered what Jason had done.

When she heard Marta's footsteps on the stairs she busied herself running the tap and wiping the already immaculately clean sink with a cloth. Marta said, 'Good morning,' as she came in and Kayleigh had to bite her lip to keep her teeth from chattering.

'Morning,' she muttered over her shoulder, still wiping.

'Kayleigh, I need you to help me with something when you've finished there.'

Marta's voice sounded pleasant enough, but this

morning anything out of the ordinary was enough to make her knees tremble. 'Yes, fine,' she managed, and with one more swill around the sink she wrung out the cloth and turned, wiping her hands on her apron.

Marta looked pained. 'There is a towel for that, as you know.'

'Oh yes. Sorry.' She went across to the hook where it hung and dried her hands properly. That was standard for Marta, which reassured Kayleigh a little as she followed her out, across the hall and up the stairs. But when she stopped outside the flat door inset into the wall and took out a fob, Kayleigh could feel the blood draining from her face and her head felt light, like a balloon that could float away. She had never been inside, but she knew what that room contained.

'Come in,' Marta said and sat down herself at the desk in front of a screen. She pressed a button and there was Jason, sitting at Anna's desk on Anna's chair reading a piece of paper. One drawer of a filing cabinet was pulled out. Kayleigh gave a gasp of horror, swaying on her feet.

'Oh, useless girl, don't faint!' Marta's voice wasn't pleasant now. 'There's a seat there – sit down if you have to. Who is he?'

For a wild moment she thought of saying she'd never seen him before in her life, but Marta seemed to have heard what she was thinking. 'Don't say something stupid. It's plain how he got the codes to come in. Your boyfriend, is he?'

'Yes,' she whispered.

'Name?'

'Jason Jackson.'

'Ah!' His name seemed to mean something to her; maybe she'd seen it on the list of writers at the Hub. 'And what did he want, when he broke into Ms Harper's house?'

She found her voice. '*I don't know!* He didn't tell me. And whatever it was, I don't think he got it because he was angry when he came home.'

'Yes,' Marta said. 'And why did you give him the codes?'

She could be honest about that, at least. 'I'm . . . I'm scared of him. He's got a wicked temper when he's crossed.'

Strangely enough, Marta's face softened a little. She even gave a little, humourless laugh. 'The old story! Women never learn, do they?'

Emboldened, Kayleigh went on, 'I was beginning to think anyway that I'd had enough. He's living in my flat and he's not paying his way. And now I suppose he's lost me my job and I don't know what I'll do.' She sniffed, feeling the tears coming to her eyes.

Marta paused, looking at her with a penetrating stare. Then she said slowly, 'Maybe it is all right. You're a good worker and I don't want to have to look just now for someone else. I shall be telling the police and you will be required to tell what has happened. Don't warn him. That is clear?'

Kayleigh's eyes widened. 'Do you mean it? Oh, I'm

not going to tip him off. He bloody dropped me right in it with this and I don't owe him anything – he treats me like scum, anyway.'

Marta stood up. 'Then we can agree. Now, Ms Harper will be down soon looking for her breakfast so you can go and see everything is ready. I will talk to you about it later.'

Kayleigh, with the alacrity of a rabbit that has, against the odds, escaped from a stoat, was halfway out of the door when Marta said, 'Oh, by the way, what age is he?'

'I'm not exactly sure, but he's older than me. I'm thirty.'

For some odd reason she got the impression that Marta was pleased, but she didn't give it any more thought than that as she scurried downstairs breathing a prayer of thankfulness.

DC Livvy Murray had never been to the Borders. She'd always had the impression that it was just countryside with fields and stuff, which was fine for people who liked that sort of thing but not worth giving up free time for when you could spend it in town where there was plenty to do.

As far as she could see through the driving rain and the mud thrown up by the wheels of other vehicles, she'd been pretty much right. There were towns, of course – Peebles (wee grey place), Galashiels (wee grey place) and Selkirk (wee grey place). Halliburgh was another of the same; as she drove slowly along the high street past where the old police station had been and on to the outskirts where the new one had been built around ten years before, she felt depressed already. She'd be all right if she could commute but the forecast was getting more and more alarming about this new weather system coming in and she could end up sticking straws in her hair if she got snowed in down here.

Still, what did the forecasters know? She'd checked last night and it hadn't said anything about persistent rain and when she parked the car and hurried into the station it looked as if it was on for the day.

It was a dismal-looking place, showing its age already with chipped paintwork and even a front door that had warped and resisted at the first attempt at pushing it open. Built on the cheap, no doubt, and no money for maintenance these days.

There were quite a few people sitting around waiting in reception – a surprising number for such a small place, Murray thought. It looked like separate family groups, centred round a couple of youths looking sulky, and she eyed them with some interest, considering what Strang had told her about Halliburgh's problems. When she reported at the desk asking for DS Wilson, she was told he was tied up and directed to the canteen to wait.

With a cup of coffee in the corner, Murray had a good observation point as officers came and went for their breaks. She hadn't really thought of herself as a spy until now, but she became uncomfortably aware that in a small place like this she was marked out as a stranger.

The reactions were varied. Some smiled and said hello, some looked faintly wary and a couple introduced themselves. One of them, PS Colin Johnston, even told her what the current fuss was about.

'Don't know what got into them – young idiots!' he said. 'Nothing wrong with the families – they just see all this stuff about gangs in the media and then they send away for a knife "for protection" and this is what happens.'

'If there's knives, you might think drugs,' Murray said. 'Have you had any bother with the drugs coming out from the city? I've come from Edinburgh and that's a big thing at the moment.'

She sensed a withdrawal. 'No, not much. We're lucky here – quiet wee town, you know, and DI Hammond runs a tight ship. That pair'll get twitched back into line easy enough.' He got up. 'Well, I'd better get back to the coalface. See you around.'

He was heading towards the door just as it opened and a man in plain clothes came in. Murray did the usual observation check – mid forties, reddish hair, pale blue eyes, sharp-featured apart from a rather fleshy mouth. He was looking flustered. 'Colin, get upstairs and start taking statements from the parents – keep them happy till I get back to speak to the lads. They're getting restive and there's another problem. There's been a complaint about Jason Jackson and Steve wants me with him.'

Johnston looked shocked. 'Jason? What's he done, for God's sake?'

'Only broken into Anna Harper's house, the bampot. Caught on CCTV. We'll see what we can do to smooth things over. It's all we need. There's a DC arrived from Edinburgh too—'

Murray stood up. 'That's me, sir. DC Livvy Murray. Can I be of any help?'

He looked at her with what she thought could only be described as revulsion. 'Oh. I see. No, not right now. You'll need someone to get you up to speed. Col, you arrange that first, right?' He barely waited for the other man's answer.

'No problem.' Johnston turned to Murray. 'Sorry about that. Just a minor nuisance, but it'll keep DS Wilson tied up. I'll find a constable to show you round.'

He was trying to sound offhand but she had no doubt that he was worried. Jason Jackson – a pal in trouble? She'd have to make it her business to find out who he was.

She followed Johnston down a corridor and opened the door on to a room where there were three uniforms working at desks and terminals. 'Ah, Kate – you'll do,' he said to a pleasant-looking woman Murray guessed was in her early thirties. He beckoned her out into the corridor. 'This is PC Kate Graham, Livvy. Kate, DC Livvy Murray. She's been seconded from Edinburgh.'

'Oh! Goodness!' Graham said. 'Well, that's nice. We can always do with a bit more manpower – well, womanpower, I suppose.' She gave a nervous laugh.

Murray had to smother a grin. It wasn't hard to

work out who Strang's informant had been; the strain of pretending this was a surprise showed all over her honest face. Johnston didn't notice, fortunately; he was moving away already saying, 'Show her round, Kate. Fill her in on how we operate. OK?'

'Yes of course, boss.' Graham turned to Murray with an attempt at a welcoming smile that wavered slightly at the corners. 'From – from Edinburgh, did he say? Had you a good drive down?'

'Wet, but no problems.' Murray was making a lightning calculation; she could let Graham struggle on, or she could say something she'd always wanted to say. With a quick glance up and down the empty corridor, she leant closer and said, 'Your secret is safe with me.'

Graham's face flared scarlet. 'Oh! Did – did Kelso tell you?'

'No,' Murray said. 'You did. You're a hopeless liar.'

Graham bit her lip. 'I know,' she said humbly. 'I'm out of practice. My parents always caught me out and then I felt rotten at having deceived them, so I gave up. Honesty was easier.'

'Well, I admire you for it, but it doesn't make adult life any easier. If my mother caught me out, I got a good clattering and it made me an expert at making sure she didn't. I can safely promise you that you can be sure I won't dump you in it. It's a bit of luck that you've been asked to give me the scenic tour. We can talk as we walk, then, and if there's anyone tries to join us you can just say, "Oh, I forgot to show you the women's toilet," and then we can lose them and go back.'

'I feel guilty that I wasn't courageous enough to be a whistle-blower.' Graham had begun to relax a little as they walked on. 'But my dad's frail and he needs me here and even if the top brass backed me, once people knew, I wouldn't be able to stay. There are too many officers happy to go along with Hammond and Wilson, so—'

'Don't worry about it. I'll make the waves if necessary. And it's not only Strang that's stirring it – DCS Borthwick's pushing this too. And she'd be one scary lady to have on your case. She wants us to take another look at what happened to Felix Harper.'

Graham was looking brighter every minute. 'I've got good gen on that. Look, I'm due a break in ten minutes. I'll whiz you round the rest of the station and fill you in on the personnel – oh, and that is the Ladies', by the way – and I know a quiet caff where they do a good ham roll and we can talk properly.'

'Done,' Murray said, following her up the stairs. Strang might have thought she should have restrained her impulse to charge in, but it looked as if it was paying off. He had told her to use her initiative, after all.

Marta Morelli sat down at the desk in the security room and pressed the button to play back the images of Jason Jackson's activities the previous night while DI Hammond and DS Wilson stood beside her watching.

Hammond's face was professionally impassive but there was a little pulse beating at his temple and the other officer, the red-haired one, was scowling.

'Of all the headbangers!' he burst out at last. 'Sorry, madam. But everyone knows you've got a lot of security – he can't have expected to get away with it.'

Hammond quelled his sergeant with a glance. When he spoke, he was much more measured. 'Do you know what he was hoping to find?'

'I?' Marta shrugged. 'I don't know – something he could sell to the gutter press? I can assure you he won't have found anything. But we have been deeply threatened by this. He is someone who may be planning to harm Anna. He would not be the first.'

'Do you know him, Ms Morelli? I believe he has one of the places on the Writers' Week at the Foundation.'

'Not by sight, though I knew who he is. We always try to help local people, as you know, and Ms Harper knew that he had little success with his first book so she wanted to help him. This was a mistake, perhaps.'

'Was this how he managed to get into the house?'

Marta shook her head. 'No. It was the girlfriend. Kayleigh Burns. She is our cleaner, so she has to have the codes to get in. She told me who this was and she is ready to talk to you. I think this man is a bad person, Inspector, and I want you to treat this very seriously.'

'Of course,' Hammond said. 'Do we go downstairs?'

'Along the gallery to the sitting room.'

As Marta waited to close the door, Wilson paused.

'Since he didn't actually do any harm,' he said, 'maybe we could just have a strong word with him—'

She gave him a blistering stare and he stopped almost in mid word.

With the overcast sky and rain beating on the windows, the room was flooded with cold grey light. Sitting on one of the oversized white sofas, Kayleigh Burns looked very small and scared. She stood up as they came in.

Waving the officers to the chairs opposite, Marta nodded to Kayleigh to sit down again and sat beside her. The woman was unconsciously twisting her hands as she glanced at the detectives.

'Tell the police, Kayleigh,' Marta prompted.

She licked her lips. 'Well, you know he's my boyfriend. On Saturday night after I saw you in the pub' – she gestured at Wilson – 'he came home with me and he said I'd to give him the codes to get in here.'

'And it didn't occur to you that perhaps you should say no?' Hammond's voice was stern.

'It did!' she protested. 'I told him I wouldn't. But he was angry and I was scared.'

'Scared? What of?' Wilson asked, a sneer in his voice.

Kayleigh glared at him. 'He's hit me before and I didn't want him to hit me again. All right?' Wilson subsided.

'Tell the policemen what he did then, Kayleigh,' Marta prompted. It had taken her a while to get the full story out of the girl and she was determined that the police should hear it.

She hung her head. 'He said he would give me money. Quite a lot.'

Marta waited for the officers to ask where he had got it from, but when they didn't, she asked the question herself.

'I don't know,' Kayleigh said. 'He told me it was a lucky win gambling, but I didn't believe him. There's people he hangs around with I don't like. And I'm worried about my boy – his mates have too much money as well. Where are they getting it from, that's what I want to know?' She was losing her nervousness. 'What are you going to do about it, now I've told you?'

Hammond sighed. 'I can see that you're worried, Kayleigh. Needlessly, I think, because we do keep an eagle eye on that sort of thing – believe me, we know it's everywhere nowadays, but we won't let it take root here. But is there anything you can tell us that would link Jason to it?'

'Just . . . what I've told you.'

'And why do you think he wanted to break into the house, anyway?'

'I don't know! He's just obsessed with Ms Harper – blames her for his book not selling. He really hates her.'

Marta stiffened. 'You hear what she says, Inspector? This is a man who found his way right into our home last night, a man who has a grudge against Ms Harper. What do you know about him?'

DS Wilson bristled. 'We're asking the questions . . .' he began but again Hammond cut in. 'He frequents our local, but he hasn't come our way professionally, madam.

I would say this is just a sort of stupid stunt—'

Marta's eyebrows arched almost to her hairline. 'Would you? I am sorry, I would not, and Ms Harper has been very upset. And the other thing you should be looking at is the source of this man's money. If it was a bet you can find out who made it. If it was not, you would be asking yourself about drugs, would you not?'

There was a glance between the two men. Then Hammond said, 'We're very conscious, of course, of the recent tragedy with Felix Trentham—'

'Yes, you would be, I think. So you are doing – what?'

Kayleigh shifted uneasily in her seat, as if aware that the temperature in the room had dropped to something well south of zero. Wilson was visibly twitching and even Hammond looked ruffled.

'We couldn't find any witnesses, madam, and with Mr Trentham's known problems there was nothing to suggest anything other than that he took the overdose himself.'

'Poor Felix,' Marta said. She paused for a moment as if she was weighing something up, then she drew a deep breath. 'He would be likely to, you see, if someone offered it to him. Deliberately, perhaps. And his sister too – almost killed in an accident by a car that did not stop. Then this man with a grudge – this man who breaks into Ms Harper's house. We must ask ourselves why all these things have happened, must we not?'

This was a high-risk strategy but it was worth it to see the effect on the officers. Wilson seemed too shocked to speak and even though Hammond managed to sound calm, he was obviously on the defensive.

'I hear what you say, Ms Morelli, and of course we will look into all of that. I've taken it upon myself to head the investigation into Ms Trentham's accident – the bicycle will be undergoing forensic testing as we speak, though in all honesty I'm not sure it will tell us much. I've spoken to her, of course, and she was unable to help me.

'As far as the drugs situation is concerned, we are on top of the problem, as I said. We even have a new officer specially charged with increasing our vigilance—'

'That is good,' Marta said. 'She can come to speak to me. At once. To reassure me and Ms Harper that though you did not see it before, you now see that this is very serious. And that this man is not free to have a vendetta because he is not such a good writer.' She got up. 'That is excellent. Thank you very much, Inspector Hammond and Sergeant Wilson.'

Wilson barely waited till the front door was shut behind them before he burst out, 'Why did you let that old bat from hell run off at the mouth like that? Why didn't you tell her we make the decisions? You won't actually do any of that, will you?'

'Oh yes,' Hammond said as they got into the car and drove off. 'I'm going to make sure she sees we're doing stuff. It won't have much effect, but it will keep her happy.'

'And we care – why?'

'We care, Dumbo, because the District Commissioner likes getting asked to receptions there and meeting people he's read about in the papers and coming away with a fat cheque for the benevolent fund. And he thinks I'm walking on water and I want him to keep thinking that way.'

'So what happens about Jason?'

'He apologises profusely. He proves he couldn't have knocked down Cassie Trentham and that he wouldn't even know where to find dope for Felix.'

Wilson sniggered. 'And he'll do that – how?'

'Oh, he'll do that. Trust me. Meantime, you have to brief the woman from Edinburgh. What's she like?'

'Just a wee totty. I'll feed her the party line and tell her what to say. Those women are paranoid, with all this rubbish about a vendetta. Jase would just be looking for something juicy to sell to the tabloids.'

'Lucky he didn't find anything,' Hammond said. 'He was talking about blackmail the other night and he'd be just daft enough to try. Let's go and pick him up so I can wring the stupid bastard's neck.'

When Richard Sansom came into Cassie Trentham's office with only the most perfunctory of knocks on the door and demanded, 'What the hell is going on?' he didn't sound like his usual suave self. He had obviously been out in the rain; his jacket was wet and his fair hair ruffled as if he'd been running a hand through it.

Cassie looked up from her laptop with a sigh. 'Richard, you probably know more than I do. All I know is that I got a call from Marta saying that Jason Jackson had broken into Highfield House last night and that there wasn't any damage but they've changed the entry codes and she's sending Davy out to my cottage to put in an alarm. Have you seen them?'

'No, and it's stressing me out. She told me about the break-in and that she'd informed the police but when I said I'd be right over she told me Anna was upset and wouldn't want to see anyone today. How do they expect me to do my job if they keep me in the dark? They should have called me before they did anything. Now the police are involved it'll leak to the press and the last thing we want at the moment is a distraction from the main event.

'What was the man doing, anyway? He's always seemed to me far too interested in Anna in a very unhealthy way.'

Cassie shrugged. 'Just looking through some papers, she said.'

Sansom went very still. 'What papers?'

'How would I know? Richard, why don't you sit down? You're looming over me and it doesn't help.'

'No. Sorry.' He sat down. 'It's just – this is going to have to be a major presentation problem now. If only they'd called me, I'd have gone round and talked to the man myself, discovered what he'd found out and threatened to inform the police – a threat's always the best way to shut someone's mouth. What leverage have

I got now to make him tell me what I need to know and stop him telling everyone else? Now it's out of my hands and God only knows where this will go.'

He was sounding distraught. Cassie looked at him with some surprise. 'I wouldn't get so worked up about it, Richard. Marta's pretty savvy herself and she'll certainly have discussed it with my mother. If a scandal was likely to erupt because of something Jackson found they wouldn't have gone public. She'll have her reasons for what she did. She always does.'

'She's not telling me, though,' he said bitterly. 'I have to know all the details so I'm ready for an ambush. The press would love a juicy story to link to the *Jacob's Angel* launch.'

Cassie frowned. It was odd that he should be getting quite so upset about all this. 'Richard, what do you know that I don't know? What do you think Jackson could have discovered that would be so detrimental? Nothing's ever emerged before. Whatever secrets Anna may have are pretty well hidden, I would say.'

'Well, yes. Yes, I suppose so.' It looked as if he was making a considerable effort to calm down. 'You're probably right. Thanks.' He got up. 'You'll tell me if anything else comes your way?'

'Of course,' she said. 'Try not to worry too much.'

'Thanks.' At the door he paused. 'I think I'll just go anyway and see if I can have a word with Jackson. See if we can keep the lid on this. You'll have his address on file, won't you?'

'Yes, ask Gil. He'll be able to help you.'

It was strange, Cassie thought, that he should be quite so upset. Then she suddenly remembered – of course, he was a relatively new boy in the PR job. The poor man was probably terrified he'd lose it if something mucked up the launch. She was tolerably certain that nothing would. The Brand always managed somehow.

He could have told them what he wanted, threatened them, even crept upstairs with a knife—no, she mustn't let herself think about that.

She hadn't been sure that bringing it all out into the open was wise but Marta's judgement was usually sound and she'd seemed almost exhilarated after her encounter with the police, as if it had solved something, and she was busy now with work about the house, leaving Anna alone in the study. Alone with her torment.

The fear was blotting out everything else – fear for herself, yes, but more for the daughter who refused to let her mother protect her without being told why she should need to. And Anna simply couldn't do it – not that, not now. It was all just too sordid. She knew Cassie blamed her already for Felix's death. If she confessed that she had been aware of danger without putting them on their guard too, her daughter would consider her a murderer, no less. And perhaps she was right, at that. They had fled from those first notes sent to the London address and imprisoned themselves behind the state-of-the-art security system while leaving her children vulnerable.

A sudden squall of icy rain beat against the windows and Anna, with a shiver, pulled her chair closer to the fire. It was burning sullenly and every so often there was a hiss and a puff of smoke as some rain found its way down the chimney. She picked up a magazine from the coffee table and tried to read it – anything for distraction – but after a moment she put it down on her lap.

When what everyone called the real world brought

ugly problems, it had been her habit to withdraw into that alternative world, her world, to talk with the people who were certainly as real to her as the ones she met every day – more real, in some ways. But *Jacob's Angel* was long finished now; the characters had melted into thin air, leaving not a rack behind. This was her fallow period, when an idea would whisper to her and gradually, gradually, her new world would people itself. It hadn't, as yet. She was alone in her head, with her fears.

Marta was being naive, though. She seemed to think the police would lock Jackson up for their protection, on her say-so. But what harm had he actually done? Oh perhaps, with the influence they had, they could push to have him charged with house-breaking, but if it ever got to court there would be no more than a token punishment. All she had to rely on now was the security system that had been so contemptuously bypassed last night – and she would even have to step out of it on Friday when her masterclass was scheduled. She couldn't cancel without drawing more unwelcome attention.

Anna had looked at last night's footage for a long time, at the man whose literary 'career' Marta had so swiftly arranged to sabotage. It hadn't been necessary; Anna had read the book then herself and it was clear it was going nowhere. Marta's reaction, though, had been what it always was: Anna Harper, Genius, The Brand, had to be unique. She had to be. Otherwise what justification could there be for what they had done?

* * *

DC Livvy Murray and PC Kate Graham came back from their break just as a man in a hoodie and jeans was leaving the police station. He barged past them, scowling.

'Oh dear! Somebody isn't happy,' Graham said.

'You don't know who he is?' As Graham shook her head Murray went on, 'I wonder – could he be the Jason Jackson that DS Wilson said was a bampot for breaking into Anna Harper's house?'

'He did *what*? That'll be big trouble. The District Commander loves our local celebrity. It'll be all round the town.' They had paused in reception. 'What are you going to do now?'

'I think I'd better try to report to DS Wilson,' Murray said.

She went over to identify herself to the FCA on the desk and was told that Inspector Hammond, not DS Wilson, wanted to see her. As she made her way along the corridor to his office she was wondering what that signified. There was a chain of command; she'd have expected any orders to come through her sergeant, not directly from on high. He couldn't possibly have sensed something odd in her arriving, could he? No, of course not, she told herself firmly.

When she opened the door of the office DS Wilson was there as well as the man behind the desk – Hammond, obviously. Wilson got up to introduce her and she was very aware of being assessed as Hammond shook her hand. She assessed him in her turn: dark-complexioned, dark curly hair cut short, brown eyes, thin-lipped. Smart casual clothes that said sharp operator.

'Take a seat, DC Murray. Now, you've been seconded here to assist in the Borders operation to counter this county lines business. Have you been involved with it in Edinburgh?'

'Not really, sir. Heard about it, of course, but no direct experience.'

'Right, right. Well, not a problem.'

Had she imagined he looked pleased? 'Anyway,' he was going on, 'we're on top of things here, as far as anyone can be, these days.'

It was smug, very smug. With deliberate malice she said, 'PC Johnston was telling me there was a knife fight last night. Is there a lot of that, sir?'

Both men were taken aback. After a moment Hammond said, 'Oh no, absolutely not – just a couple of silly lads, was all. Spend too much time on the Internet, that's the trouble. We've given them a fright and got the parents on side.

'Now, I've got a task for you. You may have heard of Anna Harper, the author, who lives here?'

Murray nodded, though she'd known nothing about her before researching the famous writer's son's overdose after DCI Strang had spoken to her.

'She and her companion, Ms Morelli, are upset about a stupid stunt by a local writer who broke into her house last night. We've just spoken to him and he didn't mean any harm, just being far too nosey. Probably had an eye on getting something to sell to the tabloids. But she's trying to link it now to Ms Harper's son's death – you know?'

'Yes, sir.'

'Tragedy, of course, but hardly surprising, given his problem. Now they're claiming that this, and a minor cycling accident the daughter had, were the result of deliberate murder attempts. Nonsense, of course – we've investigated thoroughly and there's not a shred of evidence in either case. But they are very influential and they need convincing that we've done everything possible. I mentioned to Ms Morelli that you were part of our increasing vigilance and she was very keen to speak to you. Italian – a bit emotional, you know? Can we rely on you to make sure she doesn't feel she's being fobbed off?'

Murray made a lightning judgement. Needle them by asking them to explain exactly what had been done – next to nothing, according to Kate – or play dumb and get the chance to quiz someone at the heart of the Felix Trentham tragedy? No-brainer.

'Right, sir. Natural they'd be upset after what's happened and then a break-in. I'll do my best to reassure the poor ladies.'

That was the right answer. Hammond gave a nod of satisfaction, asked an avuncular question about how she was settling in and dismissed her. She went back to the CID room.

It still showed the signs of former glories when it had been a fully staffed department, with several computers now shrouded in plastic sheeting. It was empty at the moment and Murray chose a corner with a working terminal, hoping that Wilson wasn't planning to follow her in. Kate had given her the reference for the Felix Trentham case and she speed-read through the reports.

They had, admittedly, appealed for witnesses. They had spoken to the man who had found Felix in the bus shelter and to the other three men who had carried him up to Cassandra Trentham's cottage, Burnside. They had interviewed Cassandra herself, and Anna Harper. There were a couple of brief reports from Graham, acting as family liaison officer. And then – nothing. Just a copy of the death certificate.

Murray closed it down and was leaving the room as DS Wilson came along the corridor. He frowned. 'Don't hang about, Murray. She's a difficult woman and it's your job to keep her sweet.'

'On my way, sir,' she said. 'Just finding directions.'

In the car she thought about what she had been told. There wasn't a drugs problem, there wasn't a knife crime problem, a housebreaker was just a harmless idiot. Either they were determined not to see what was going on under their noses or they were very stupid indeed. And she didn't think Hammond was stupid.

Jason Jackson was in a dangerous mood as he packed up his things: humiliated, betrayed, angry, even more than a little worried. Kayleigh was kicking him out. She'd phoned to tell him, had the nerve to say, 'I want you out before I get back,' the cow. He'd have stayed to argue the toss when she finished work only Hammond had said that really wasn't a smart idea.

What got to him most was that Anna Harper had won. Again. The Anna Harpers always did, sailing through life cushioned by money, success and self-satisfaction. For a heady moment he'd thought he was on to something that would level the playing field, something that would force her to come begging to him.

And what use had his mates in the polis been? He could almost hear the sound of running water, with the way they were washing their hands of him as he told them what had happened. The best he could hope for was that those two old witches could be talked down from actually linking him to Felix Trentham's death and his sister's accident.

He didn't need Hammond to remind him to be careful what he said. He knew the sort of reminder he was likely to get if he forgot that 'They' weren't keen on publicity. It was uppermost in his mind when the doorbell rang.

For a moment he was tempted not to answer but not answering the door was no solution if you were dealing with people who would simply kick it in, and he didn't need that kind of hassle either. He swallowed hard and opened it.

It was Richard Sansom who stood there. 'Jackson, I need a word with you.'

Jackson swore at him, trying to shut the door again, but Sansom put his shoulder to it and shoved. Caught off balance Jackson staggered back and Sansom strode in, slamming the door behind him. In the dark narrow lobby he towered over the other man, taller, heavier, stronger. Definitely threatening.

Jackson had never been pugnacious. Truculent, yes, petulant more or less constantly, but self-preservation ranked high in his list of priorities and he'd had a lifetime of ducking confrontation.

'Look, cool it, OK? What's all this about?'

Grim-faced, Sansom stared him down, then walked past him through the open door of the sitting room, where stuff was piled waiting to be put in a couple of cardboard boxes. Jackson hesitated for a moment, then followed.

'Sit down.'

He could have refused, but somehow he didn't. He swallowed nervously as he sat down on one of the easy chairs by the coffee table. Sansom brought over an upright chair and placed it so that Jackson had to look up at him.

'What did you think you were doing last night? And how did you get in, anyway?'

'Girlfriend,' he muttered. 'Gave me the code.'

'So what was it about?'

'Look, Harper saw to it that my book was rubbished. She's got it in for me and I wanted something to get her off my back. You've no idea what it's like to put everything you have into a book and just have it trashed—'

'I'm happy to say I don't, and I don't care either. What did you do?'

'All I did was go to her study. There are filing cabinets there. I know she has secrets—'

He seized on that. 'What secrets? How do you know?'

'If I knew I wouldn't have had to break in, would I?' he whined. 'I just know she has to have. I've read every interview she's ever given and every question about her past gets killed off. I reckon they have to give her final approval before they even talk to her.'

Sansom gave a small, cold smile. 'She's not stupid.'

'I didn't say she was. She's clever, very clever. And she's got her attack dog to do the dirty work. Something should be done—'

'Never mind that. Filing cabinets. What did you find?'

'Nothing!' That came out as a howl of rage. 'Absolutely sodding nothing!'

Sansom stared. 'I don't believe you.'

'Suit yourself. Oh, I can quote you letters of appreciation. I can tell you her national insurance number and the name of the shoemaker who keeps her details for her handmade bloody shoes. The most sensational information was that she takes medication for blood pressure. It was as if they'd expected someone to break in and purged the files just in case.'

'That's really true?'

'Oh yes, it's true. And because of that I'm in trouble with the law, which I've kept clear of up till now. My girlfriend's throwing me out on to the street. My next book's going to get strangled at birth too, if I ever find a publisher to take it. And now I'm even scared to open the door.'

His sense of grievance had overwhelmed him and that had slipped out. Fortunately, Sansom seemed to be attributing it to his own intrusion and he was visibly relaxing. 'Should have thought of that sooner,' he said brutally and got up.

'It's my job to manage Anna's publicity and keep everything positive. Perhaps you could claim you were drunk at the time and such a great fan that you had the crazy idea that you had to speak to her. I want this kept as low-key as possible, which is distinctly to your advantage. And I have connections. If you try to get smart over this, I can see to it that there isn't a publishing house in the land that would touch your next book with a ten-foot pole. Got it?'

Slumped in his chair, Jackson said nothing as Sansom went out. And when, a while later, there was another knock on the door he gave a little whimper of fright and his knees were shaking as he got up to answer it.

It really was some house, DC Murray thought as she drove up to Highfield House. It must have cost a bomb but on a day like this it didn't look glamorous, just sort of bleak and forbidding. Days like this weren't exactly unusual and if she'd that sort of money she wouldn't have splashed out on something that made you feel depressed just looking at it.

She got out to speak into the intercom at the gates and waited shivering for a response. It was a few minutes before a voice with a foreign accent agreed to admit her and she could jump back into the car, wiping her wet face with her hand. It was ridiculous to feel that there was something faintly sinister in the way the gates swung silently open. That was just what electric gates did.

The front door had been opened by the time she got there and there was a woman waiting for her. She wasn't tall – about Murray's own height – but she had a dignity of carriage that made her look somehow imposing, even though with her olive skin and black clothes she seemed to be rocking some sort of Mediterranean peasant vibe. The top and skirt screamed designer, though, and the heavy gold chain at her neck would have kept a peasant in pasta and Chianti for a year.

She glanced at Murray's warrant card, then took her upstairs to a sitting room that would have been sort of stunning on a good day, Murray thought, but with the wind moaning and rain clattering against the huge windowpanes it was just grim.

'So,' Ms Morelli said, 'you have been sent here because the local police are not coping with the drug problem in this little town?'

Thrown by the directness of the attack, Murray found herself flannelling. 'Er . . . I don't think that was quite—'

'No? Then why have you been sent here?'

'There has been a problem everywhere with gangs from the big towns trying to infiltrate rural areas and we're trying to make sure it doesn't take hold here,' she bleated, then encountered Marta's coolly contemptuous stare.

'This is something you believe? Or this is something you have been told to say?'

Murray blushed. She'd let herself be flustered into some sort of defence of Hammond and Co when it was really her job to bust wide open the fiction that Halliburgh, thanks to his vigilance, was a haven of peace and good order.

She took a deep breath. 'No, I don't believe it. I think that Mr Trentham's death was clear proof that there is a problem and the source of the drugs he took has not been fully investigated.'

They had been standing in the middle of the room. Marta gave her a long, hard look, then gestured to one end of a long sofa. 'You sit there. I will sit here, beside you, and you will tell me what is going to be done about this man – this Jackson creature.'

She'd never had such an uncomfortable interview in her life. Ms Morelli was past scary and she needed to think very carefully about what she was going to say. 'I know you've spoken to Inspector Hammond and he's in charge, of course.'

'You know what I told him, then?'

'Not really.'

'I told him that there has been an attempt on Ms Harper's daughter's life by knocking her off her bicycle and that her son died because he was offered drugs here. I told him that this man, who broke in last night, has a lot of money, which he says came from a bet he made but I believe he is lying. My cleaner says he is their friend and they think he should just be told he is a bad boy and must not do this again. They will not find out what he is doing. "Investigating", they will tell me – they like this word. It means, doing nothing.

'This is why I wanted to see you, because you come from somewhere else, not this place. So can you do something? Get him locked up, so he does not harm any of us?'

'It's not up to me,' Murray said. 'But tell me the full details and I'll see what I can do.'

Again Marta appraised her. Then, 'Yes,' she said. 'But you must understand that there is very serious crime here, but your inspector does not believe it.'

It was when she said the words 'very serious crime' that the idea came to her. As Murray listened to the long story that Marta was telling her, her mind was working at fever pitch. Surely attempted murder here could be classed as serious rural crime, the sort of thing that should involve the SRCS? She thought Marta's argument was far-fetched to say the least, but she was certain that there was, just as Kate Graham had said, some very unhealthy stuff going on in Halliburgh – and if drugs and kickbacks didn't feature in it, she would be very surprised. There certainly had been no attempt at all to find out where Felix had got the drugs that killed him. That wasn't direct proof, but she was sure that if she could find a way of getting Strang to look at it, the proof would be there all right.

She had permission to use her initiative. Yes, but within reason, the boss had said. He'd also said that DCS Borthwick was taking an interest in Felix Trentham's death. Would it count as being within reason if she told this 'very influential' woman that the SRCS existed?

'So you see, I must insist that proper action should be taken,' Marta finished, her piercing eyes fixed on the detective's face.

Murray cleared her throat. 'I expect you know that there is a special squad that investigates serious crime in rural areas?' she said untruthfully.

DS Wilson was alone in the CID room when Murray got back. He pounced on her. 'Well? How did you get on with the Morelli woman?'

Murray, her face schooled into an expression of limpid innocence, said, 'Oh, all right, I think. She's concerned, though. She's heard of the SRCS and I think she may be going to contact someone.'

'She's *what*? For God's sake, you were meant to calm her down, Murray!' He was looking horrified.

'Oh, she wasn't upset or anything. I told her what you said, about there being a drug problem everywhere and that we weren't going to let it take root here, but she wasn't really interested. She just thinks it would be better to find out a bit more.'

Wilson's face was turning an alarming shade of puce. 'What are we supposed to do now? Do you have any idea of what you've dropped us in, Murray? Did you try to talk her down?'

Murray did her best to look surprised. 'Not really. Didn't know that would be a problem.'

'Well, not exactly, just, well, difficult,' Wilson spluttered. 'I don't know what DI Hammond will say, though – someone going over his head like that.'

'Well, I'm sorry if I did the wrong thing, Sarge,' she said, with a faintly huffy note in her voice. 'I couldn't really tell her she wasn't to, could I?'

'No, of course not. It's just that . . .' His voice trailed away.

'What do you want me to do now?'

'Oh, I think you've done enough already. I'll see you tomorrow after I've spoken to DI Hammond. You've let us down badly over this, Murray. Not a good start for a new officer.'

'No, sir. Sorry, sir.'

She managed to avoid grinning until she was out in the corridor. If she set off back to Edinburgh now, she might even manage to catch Strang before he went off duty. She didn't know how he would take it and using her initiative hadn't always been popular. It would be better to tell him straight away. Bless me, Father, for I have sinned . . .

He mustn't let go. He must stay icy calm, however hard it was when you were daily being subjected to ritual humiliation.

It was only when Gil Paton came in to see the writers at their evening meal that he heard about the break-in, and even they only knew because Sascha Silverton had been gossiping to the waitress.

'It's all over the town,' she said. 'Jason Jackson arrested – well, that's hardly a surprise, is it? But Gil, what on earth has been going on?'

It was the loss of face that got to him. With four people sitting looking at him hopefully he was being forced to admit he knew less than they did and he couldn't stop the bitterness showing through as she told him how it had happened – the cleaner had told Jackson the codes and he'd actually broken in.

'I suppose they'll have to change them all now and everything,' Sascha said. 'I'd have thought they'd have had to let you know the new one by now.' He didn't like her as much as he had at first – there was something very sly about the look she gave him.

That rankled too. 'Yes, you would, wouldn't you?' he said. 'Just, I suppose, they've been busy, with the police there and everything. And as you say, Jason Jackson was plainly a big mistake all round. Now, how are you enjoying your supper? That chicken looks good.'

When he escaped, he phoned Cassandra. Twice. But she didn't pick up. It was all of a piece, making sure he knew his place as she saw it.

When they give you lemons, make lemonade. This could be his chance for the meeting he had worked so hard to engineer. He could go round to the house and say he'd been so sorry to hear Anna had had such an upsetting experience and he'd come to see if there was anything he could do. Cassie couldn't stop him this time.

It was quite possible he'd got it all wrong; Anna might not be the one who was cold and hostile. It might be her daughter, who'd just spelt out his lowly place in the pecking order. He went straight out to his car and drove round to Highfield.

The gates, of course, were closed and he had to press the buzzer. He'd never been trusted with the original code anyway. Of course he should have known that it would be the housekeeper's disembodied voice that would answer. 'I was hoping to see Anna,' he said. 'It's Gil Paton.'

'Who?' the voice said sharply.

Writhing, he said again, 'Gil Paton. Cassandra's deputy.'

'Oh – at the Hub? So what did you want?'

'I was hoping to see Anna,' he repeated, 'just to say how sorry I was about last night.'

'Last night?'

Was the woman stupid, or being obstructionist? 'The break-in.'

'Oh yes. The police have this all in hand. I will pass on your message to Ms Harper. Thank you.'

The 'Ms Harper' was a definite reproach. 'Anna' was not for the likes of him. He gave it one last try. 'I'd really like to speak to her myself—'

'She is not seeing anyone today. Goodbye.'

The speaker went dead. He could have screamed his frustration as he got back into his car, but he pushed it down, banking the anger for future use. It would only give him temporary relief and, he often told himself, revenge was a dish best eaten cold.

DCI Strang was just finishing off the report on his last SRCS case when DC Murray knocked at his door. He was surprised to see her, and then alarmed.

'Livvy! I didn't expect to see you back so soon. Please tell me they haven't rumbled you.'

Murray laughed. 'Oh no! I've no problem conning people. They're not just awful pleased with me at the moment, though, and if I'm honest I'm not sure if you'll be pleased or not.'

Regretting his folly in ever using the word 'initiative', however carefully fenced about it might have been, Strang said, 'Break it to me gently. Misdemeanour or gross misconduct?'

Murray looked sheepish. 'I'd better tell you how it happened. When I arrived there were a couple of boys in that'd had a knife fight so they were busy and I got handed over to Kate Graham first.'

'Oh yes?' he said warily. 'Was she helpful?'

'You don't need to worry. I know it's her.'

'She told you?'

'She didn't need to. I never saw anyone who was so pants at acting innocent. Lucky no one else noticed. I thought of kidding on that I hadn't guessed but it just seemed kind of cruel to make her go on trying. And I'm sure she's right – Hammond might as well be carrying a pot of whitewash around with him. He's not tried at all to find out where Felix Trentham got the stuff.'

'That's what the super is interested in. Did you see a line to follow?'

'Better than that.'

Strang listened, fascinated, as she recounted what Marta Morelli had said. He saw Murray take a deep breath. 'Then she said "very serious crime" and I thought of the SRCS. I explained what it was for and I think she'll be on the phone to you.'

She was looking nervous and he didn't know himself what he thought about it. 'Do you believe what she was saying?'

'Nuh. Not even sure she does. She's reaching – don't know why.'

He thought for a moment. 'It does give me an excuse to go there and have a poke around, anyway, but I don't know how the super will see it. We can't start taking direction from manipulative ladies. Leave it with me and I'll speak to her tomorrow. Are you quite happy to go back? Not finding it too uncomfortable?'

Murray grinned broadly. 'Oh, I'm having a fine time. See me – see Mata Hari!'

He smiled at that, a little ruefully, as she left. This could be a very clever move. On the other hand, it could be a disaster. That was the trouble with Livvy; you could never be sure which way it would go.

As it happened, he was in a position to go immediately if JB okayed it – and then an unworthy thought struck him. He couldn't tell Finella how much he sometimes longed for personal space, even if it only meant a quiet evening with a good book and a dram, but here was a perfect excuse. There was no way Police Scotland would pay for accommodation so close to Edinburgh, but if he paid himself he could find a decent pub and stay over for a night or two. Bliss!

CHAPTER ELEVEN

'Fin? Just letting you know I'm going off on an assignment today,' Kelso Strang said.

'Oh,' Finella said. 'Is it . . . is it a long way away?' Her voice had gone flat.

'No, not really. Down in the Borders.'

She brightened immediately. 'Oh, that's good. So you'll be commuting, then?'

He almost groaned. Fin was becoming much too dependent on having him there to share nursery runs, read stories, thwart tantrums and babysit sometimes so she could keep up with her friends. That quiet pub was calling him, promising a break from the never-ending demands of childcare, but he had heard how her voice changed and he hadn't the heart to go ahead with his escape plan.

'Yes, I think so. Weather permitting.'

'Oh, they're all talking about this Beast from the East, of course. But you know how they exaggerate these things and I've never known you bothered about driving in snow! I'm glad I won't have to break it to Betsy that Unkie was going to be away. You know what she's like.'

'Indeed I do.' Then, in a small bid for freedom, he said, 'It does mean I won't be back for bedtime stories.'

Fin laughed. 'Not to worry. She'll just pile them up for you when you get back.'

'Right,' he said hollowly. 'See you later.'

He had gone in to report to Detective Chief Superintendent Jane Borthwick promptly that morning feeling distinctly nervous, finishing with, 'I did say that, given the situation, Murray might have to use her initiative, within reason, but I'm not entirely sure whether that covers it.'

'Well, well,' Borthwick said, 'she has been stirring things up, hasn't she? And this woman – Morelli? – has been in touch already?'

'First thing this morning. Very insistent. Claiming there have been two attempted murders and that the local CID has done nothing about it.'

'Could she be right?'

'Murray thinks it's very unlikely. Cassandra Trentham's accident looks like just that, and for all the claims about Felix being clean it would be entirely consistent for him to seek out drugs wherever he could get them. But Murray's quite sure that Hammond made no attempt to track where that might have been, and that their friend Jackson seems to have more money than he was likely to have come by honestly.'

'Hmm.' Borthwick thought for a moment. 'Does Murray think Hammond's just trying to protect his glittering reputation or is he in it too?'

'Kickbacks, in her opinion. Not getting his hands dirty, but not actually averse to a brown envelope or two.'

'So, we have an interesting situation. It might well be overkill to send you in because a woman trying to pull strings has some pet theory that may have no basis in fact, but it would let you check out what is going on in Halliburgh CID without calling for a formal investigation, which would undoubtedly leak and bring the press gathering like vultures.'

Strang winced. He always hated it that decisions were so often made on PR grounds rather than for operational reasons, but bad press did always have serious repercussions. 'I suppose that's right. According to Murray, Hammond was very keen on placating Ms Morelli, so her request would let me say that's just what we're doing, even if we don't believe there's anything in it. He can't stop me digging a bit deeper than he has done so far. Jason Jackson's another line I can follow.'

'Right,' Borthwick said. 'I'd better clear it with the District Commissioner but if he agrees, can you get down there today? Once they know you might be coming there's no point in hanging about and giving them time to tidy away the dirty linen.'

'A couple of loose ends to tie up first, but I can certainly get down there later on.'

From his office, he phoned Murray to put her in the picture. He considered phoning Kate Graham too, but considering what Murray had said about her inability to lie convincingly he thought the better of it, and smiled. Nice woman, Kate.

It was all DI Steve Hammond could do to hold on to his reputation for omniscience. DS Wilson was well on the way to doubting him, almost quivering this morning as he stood there to be briefed on what they were going to do now.

'Look, come on. It's fine. I've worked out a couple of tweaks – things we can do to beef up the enquiries that stupid woman's making a fuss about, and once the SRCS have made a token visit and seen that there's nothing in it, they'll go away again. Granted, they'll speak to Jason too, but he knows the score. I think one of the guys was going to have a little chat with him just to go over his lines. There's no need for them to look anywhere else. And if they did, they wouldn't find anything.'

'You're sure?'

'Course I'm sure. We've been careful. Arm's length, we always said, and that's how it's been.'

Wilson took a deep breath. 'I want to believe you, and you're usually right.'

'What's with "usually"? Always, more like. Now, what we need to do . . .'

At the end of the meeting Wilson went away reassured, Hammond thought. He was on edge himself; he'd had to spend time persuading the District Commander that he had everything in hand and welcomed a visit from the SRCS that should convince Ms Harper that they were taking her concerns seriously, even if there was no substance to them, and he seemed to be satisfied with that. Hammond prided himself on his talent for dealing with superior officers that had served him well in the past.

He'd just have to employ it when it came to dealing with Strang, the DCI at the head of SRCS. It was a fairly new organisation but it had got quite a bit of publicity in a couple of big murder cases and it had given Strang something of a reputation, but as long as he was focused on what Jackson had done, it would be fine. They just needed to make sure he didn't poke his nose into what didn't concern him.

On an impulse, he googled DCI Kelso Strang – know your enemy was always a good principle. A number of entries came up and he clicked on a newspaper report of the case in Caithness. It had given him a good write-up; the top brass must be pleased with him. He was just about to close it to click on an entry that mentioned 'profile' instead, when something caught his eye. He froze.

DC Livvy Murray was the other officer named. Murray – that was what Wilson had said when he'd introduced the new officer from Edinburgh. He hadn't mentioned 'Livvy' but Hammond had little doubt that this was the same person. And the implications were horrifying.

She had been sent down here before Marta Morelli had made any contact with Edinburgh. He'd be willing to bet that the reason the woman had heard of the SRCS was because Murray had told her. Murray had seized on this as a way to open the door for them to investigate something else – what?

He'd been set up. He'd taken her at face value – the hennaed hair, the cheap clothes, the accent – and he'd handed the chance to her on a plate with a wee frilly doily and a cake fork. He picked up the phone and pressed the number for the CID room – Wilson should be there.

The first thing to do was to neutralise her, get her out of the way. The next thing was how to neutralise Strang. That wouldn't be quite so easy.

There seemed to be a lot going on in Halliburgh police station when DC Murray reported for duty. Had word got round already? She saw Kate Graham hurrying along the corridor and said hello, but since Graham just smiled and said hello back rather than giving her a painfully obvious conspiratorial look, Murray guessed Strang hadn't told her anything.

When she reached the CID room, a constable was there with a mangled-looking bicycle and DS Wilson was filling out a form and looking harassed. As she came in, he said, 'Now see that gets sent off for testing immediately. Clear?'

'Yes, sir.' The constable took the form and carted the bike away.

Wilson turned, looking at her with undisguised loathing. 'I hope you're satisfied that you're involving us all in a lot of totally unnecessary work.'

'Am I, sir?' She was definitely getting good at innocent. 'What's happened?'

'Your friend has managed to wangle it so that the SRCS is to be sent down to tell us we've done everything wrong. Can't think how the woman knew anything about it.'

'Read something somewhere, I suppose.'

'Anyway, you're not flavour of the month with the boss, so you'd better keep out of his way. There's a report to be written up after that fight on Monday. You'll get the reference number from the duty file. And if you finish that, there's a backlog of filing that needs doing.'

She was tempted to point out that this wasn't really a job for a detective, but knowing what was coming to him she decided to be merciful and said, 'Yes, sir,' as meekly as she could.

The phone on the desk buzzed and he picked it up. As Murray watched, his face changed. 'Right, boss,' he said and hurried out.

So what was that about? she wondered as she sat down to access the interviews. Had they just heard that Strang was actually on his way, or was this some new development? She'd been interested that Wilson was stressing the urgency of sending off the damaged bike – Cassandra's, she reckoned – which had presumably been sitting through the back somewhere since it happened. The best you could expect from forensic tests was paint flakes from the car that had hit it – if there were any – but it could take months to get the results and even then all it would do was give you some idea of the make of car. Since Cassandra had come to no harm, they were unlikely to commit manpower to following it through. So it was most likely window-dressing for Strang's benefit.

And Felix's death? Was there something they were doing about that too, to beef up that investigation, so-called? She'd certainly be watching out for that. Meantime, she could get on with reading the file.

The interviews with the boys were unexpectedly fascinating:

Wilson: So where did you get the knife from then, Johnny? The Internet?
Johnny: Yes, sir.
Wilson: Why were you carrying it? Had you heard that people say you need it for protection?
Johnny: Yes, sir.
Wilson: And when did you buy it? Recently?
Johnny: Yes, sir. Someone said Olly was out to get me, so I needed it.

Wilson: But Olly's one of your mates, isn't he? Do you realise how stupid that was?
Johnny: Yes, sir. Sorry, sir.

And so it went on, leading question after leading question. No attempt to ask about gang mentality, nor what the quarrel had been about, nor whether there were others involved. The interview with Olly followed exactly the same pattern, and the bland summary stated that the knives had been confiscated and they had been given a warning.

Scotland takes knife crime very seriously. According to the guidelines, carrying a knife means arrest and prosecution. These kids were minors, but even so you don't just take away the knife and tell them they've been bad and not to do it again. At the very least, you'd be expecting referrals to youth workers. If this was meant to keep her busy and stop her causing more trouble, it had spectacularly misfired. This would give Strang the perfect place to start digging.

At that moment the door burst open again and DS Wilson appeared.

'Leave that, Murray,' he snarled. 'I need you to go now to take a statement from this woman – someone's stolen garden equipment from her garage. You'll get details of the complaint from the desk.'

'Yes, sir. I'll just—'

'No, don't "just" anything. Close down that file and get on your way now.'

He stood over her as she logged out and picked up her bag. 'And take your time,' he said. 'The less I see of you the happier I'll be. It might be smart to stop trying to be clever. For your own good.'

There was no mistaking the threat in his voice and Murray's stomach lurched. She'd thought she was doing well, but somehow they had discovered what she was and the joke about Mata Hari felt a little flat now. 'Yes, sir,' she mumbled and hurried out.

As she took down directions for finding the house – some miles out in the country – she kept hearing Strang's voice saying, 'A murdered DC might be convincing evidence that there was a serious problem.'

Strang had told her that he wouldn't admit he knew her. If they really had somehow found out, that could land him in it. Should she phone to warn him about what had happened? She cringed at the thought; after boasting about her talents for deception this would be dead humiliating. Maybe she should wait for evidence that they had found out and that it wasn't just Wilson being in a bad temper because the boss had bawled him out about something.

Or maybe she should phone him. She still hadn't made up her mind as she drove off to check out the theft which, she noted, had been reported three weeks ago.

PC Kate Graham had been tasked, along with PS Colin Johnston, with questioning some of the local boys she had seen hanging around the bus shelter. She'd been taken aback when he asked her for a list, since when she'd talked about this in the wake of Felix's death there had been a marked lack of interest. Today, though, there was a definite atmosphere of tension and DS Wilson was doing a lot of uncharacteristic chivvying.

He was obviously in a bad mood and Graham had a terrible feeling she knew why. Murray hadn't said anything to her, but something was clearly going on and the butterflies in her stomach had returned wearing tackety boots.

She had gone up to see Cassie Trentham the previous evening after she heard about Jason Jackson's arrest, worried that this might have upset her again, but she was mainly puzzled.

'I don't know what it was all about. I phoned to ask my mother, but Marta said she was lying down with a headache – no idea whether that was true or not. And all she said was that she didn't think the police were taking things as seriously as they should and she was "taking steps".'

'What did she mean?' Kate asked.

Cassandra gave a short laugh. 'If I were the police, I'd be distinctly worried. Marta is entirely ruthless about anything that affects Anna and she's supremely efficient. She's also got Davy to have security stuff installed here – look at that great ugly panic button.' She pointed. 'Ruins the look of the sitting room. And they've made a mess of the paintwork putting in the alarms.'

Kate looked and there was indeed some damage.

'Oh dear, I suppose you'll need to get someone to touch it up.'

'Oh, Marta has that in hand already. They're coming tomorrow. Supremely efficient, like I said.'

'Well, an alarm system isn't a bad idea. Just as long as you use it.'

Cassandra had looked at her very seriously. 'Do you think I need it, Kate? My mother's scaring me with all this. She won't tell me what's behind this sudden desire to wrap me in cotton wool. And I suppose knocking someone off their bike could be a good way to kill them.' Then she gave a little laugh. 'Oh, I don't really think that. I think this is some sort of weird fantasy my mother and Marta have concocted between them. The penalty for having a mother with an overdeveloped imagination.'

She spoke lightly but Kate could see the anxiety and she considered her words carefully. 'Looking at it as objectively as I can, I can't see any reason for it not being just a careless motorist who clipped your bike. On the other hand, it won't do you any harm to be careful if it keeps your mother happy.'

'Oh, I suppose so. It's bloody irritating, that's all. Still, as you say . . .'

Cassie had shrugged her shoulders and changed the subject. What she had said was still very much on Kate's mind as they drove to the school.

There were five boys on Graham's list. PS Johnston took the lead in questioning them: stock questions, and he got stock replies. No, they didn't know anything about drugs. Or knives either, since he'd mentioned that. Any gear they had, they'd got from their parents – or, in one case, an indulgent uncle.

The fifth boy, Danny Burns, was the youngest and much the least adept at deflecting questions. When Johnston asked if he had a smartphone, Danny's response was bitter. 'No, I don't. Everyone else does, but not me.'

'And why's that?' Johnston asked.

'Mum doesn't have any money, I s'pose.'

Graham noticed his shoes. 'Nice pair of Converse trainers, though, Danny. Where'd you get the money for those?'

He hesitated. 'Mum got it from her boyfriend.'

'Generous man, is he?' Johnston asked.

Danny glowered at him. 'Nuh. He's a mean bastard.'

'Maybe he doesn't have much to give you,' Graham suggested.

'Rolling in it,' he said with a disgusted sniff.

She waited a moment for Johnston to ask the follow-up question, but he didn't. He said, 'Now,' as if he was going back to the routine questions. She cut in, 'Where does he get all this money from, Danny?'

He opened his mouth as if he was going to tell her, then shut it again. 'Dunno,' he mumbled.

Johnston moved very quickly on and she didn't get a chance to follow it up. Graham was more convinced than ever that Halliburgh had a problem with officers who were far too keen not to find out anything about the drugs problem on their patch. She'd find a quiet moment and let Livvy Murray know what she'd found out.

When the desk buzzed to say that DCI Strang had arrived, DI Hammond went down to greet him. The man was tall, with something of an army bearing, but it was the scar that ran down the right-hand side of his face that caught the attention first; perhaps it was that that made him look somehow daunting – that and the level brows above cool hazel eyes. He advanced on him with his hand outstretched.

'DCI Strang? I'm Steve Hammond. Glad to meet you, sir. Very grateful you've been able to come down to help us with this problem. Come to my office and I'll arrange for coffee. Reasonable journey down from Edinburgh?'

Strang's response seemed wary, but he shook hands and followed along the corridor with some anodyne remark about the traffic. Hammond was pretty sure he had the upper hand; there was no way Strang could know they'd sussed out his plant.

'Ms Morelli has no doubt given you her take on what has happened?' he said. 'I'm sorry for the ladies – it's been a very stressful time for them recently.'

'Yes indeed,' Strang said. 'And your take is . . . ?'

Hammond sighed. 'It's a case of *post hoc ergo propter hoc*, I'm afraid. That means—'

'Yes,' Strang said, 'I do know. After something, therefore because of it. You're suggesting that Ms Morelli is assuming that because Jackson burgled Anna Harper's house after her son died and her daughter had an accident, he was responsible for those?'

He wasn't sure how to take this. Did that mean Strang accepted the idea, or he didn't? 'I'm afraid so, yes. And it's awkward because Anna Harper has a lot of clout around here. We can't just say we've investigated thoroughly and leave it at that.'

'I see. Then we have to check it all out and reassure her, don't we?'

'Absolutely,' Hammond said heartily. 'I can talk you right through it now, if you like.'

'No need to take up your time. I can get the details later. Can you brief me on this Jason Jackson, though?'

Hammond was beginning to feel that perhaps he didn't have the upper hand after all. He still had the Murray hand-grenade though; it would be a serious embarrassment for Strang to admit she'd been planted in his team without his knowledge. But he'd need to deploy it when it was most damaging. He certainly mustn't waste it.

He sighed. 'Oh yes, Jason! He's one of the regulars at the pub I go to myself. Talks as if he's the big man but he's a pussycat. His problem is he's got a thing about Anna Harper wrecking his future as a writer. He told me he thought she must have secrets that he could use to stop her trashing the next one and I gave him a stern warning at the time about blackmail. He was dumb enough to break into the house and got the reward he deserved –

found nothing. So now he's got himself in big trouble.'

He was watching Strang to see how he was reacting, but he couldn't read him. Oh well, if all else fails, try flattery. 'I've heard about your reputation and I have to say I'm grateful for your help in sorting out this mess.'

There was no visible reaction to that either. But Strang said, 'Does he have some connection with the drugs problem here? Any known link with Felix Trentham?'

Was this the moment to take him on, say, 'I suppose your little spy suggested that?' No, not yet – play along until you could make a proper assessment of the damage.

'I don't know of any connection at all, sir. If I had, of course I'd have followed it up.'

'Of course,' Strang said with a deadly politeness that suggested he didn't believe a word of it. He went on, 'I believe you have an officer here, recently seconded from Edinburgh? I've actually worked with her before, so if you can manage without her, I could use her in the enquiry down here. It'll save bringing someone else down.'

Hammond had got it wrong. The grenade hadn't been in his hands at all, but the chief inspector's and he'd just taken the pin out and thrown it, to deadly effect. He had a hollow feeling in his stomach and while he said, 'Yes, of course,' he was frantically trying to convince himself that all the firewalls he had put in place were still there.

'There's someone over there at that cottage again, Duncan.' It was starting to get dark and Edna

McNaughton had gone to draw the curtains. 'They must have got it rented out at last.'

It was a shabby-looking single-storey building with grey pebble-dash cladding, across the valley and halfway up the hill opposite their own bungalow.

Her husband didn't look up from his Sudoku. 'It'll be in a bit of a state. It's years since the last lot moved out.'

'I saw a man carrying in some stuff earlier. I wonder when they'll be moving in?'

He only grunted and she raised her voice.

'I said, I wonder when they'll be moving in?'

'I heard you. How would I know?'

'Maybe you could go across, just say hello, Duncan.'

He looked up and out of the window at the pouring rain. 'Are you daft, woman? Go out on a night like this and tramp half an hour across there to bother complete strangers just because my wife's a nosey besom?'

'It's just being neighbourly,' Edna protested. 'There's no one else around here and they might like to know that we're happy to help them while they're doing it up. They might want a cuppa sometimes.'

'How do you know they're doing it up?'

'I saw him carrying in some hardboard, that's how. But if you're determined to be unfriendly—'

'I'm not unfriendly! I just like keeping ourselves to ourselves, that's all. If I'd wanted neighbours popping in to borrow a cup of sugar, I'd have bought a house on an estate.'

'Wish you had. At least I'd have had someone to talk

to who didn't think that conversation was a dirty word.'

Duncan grunted again and went back to his Sudoku. Edna heaved a sigh, then with a last look over at the cottage drew the curtains across.

CHAPTER TWELVE

DS Wilson was badly shaken. He'd allowed DI Hammond's assurance to liberate him from the inconvenience of personal scruples: if you didn't take what was offered, with no questions asked, you were a mug. If you were daft enough to ask questions yourself, you were inviting trouble. Wilson liked money and he didn't like trouble.

He'd always done as he was told because Hammond obviously knew what he was doing and could handle any problems, but of course so far there hadn't really been any. Sure, there were some guys around who were a bit old-fashioned, but most of them reckoned there wasn't any harm in doing a favour or two for your mates. No one else was going to do you any, that was for sure – everyone had a down on the polis.

He had felt a bit uncomfortable with the brown

envelopes. That was distinctly further than he'd gone before Hammond came. And it still wasn't anything to do with him, really. He was savvy enough to know how dangerous the guys who provided them were and the less he knew about them the better. All Wilson had to do was keep his mouth shut and not turn over any stones to see what was squirming underneath while Hammond, cool and confident, did the dirty work with Jason.

But Hammond wasn't cool and confident this morning. The little bitch they'd sent down from Edinburgh to spy on them had rattled him, and Strang had rattled him a lot more. Hammond had looked almost hesitant beside him when they came into the CID room looking for Murray; Strang had just come right out and said he'd worked with her before and wanted her assigned to him now. When Wilson had told him she was investigating a break-in some distance away and wouldn't be back for some time, he'd smiled and said, 'Ah, I thought she might be. Don't worry – I'll contact her myself.' Which didn't make him feel any better.

Strang had wanted to interview Jason first and when Hammond offered to accompany him, he'd said, 'No thanks. I won't take up your time. I'm sure there's a lot of chasing up to do here.'

In the silence after Strang had gone, Wilson had said, 'What do we do now?'

Hammond was looking grim. 'Chase things up, like the man said. Anything you can think of, never mind what, so long as it's down as having been covered. Change the password so that Murray can't go playing herself with the records.'

He said, 'OK, boss,' but he knew he wasn't sounding confident and Hammond looked at him sharply.

'It'll be all right. Jason isn't a weak link. He knows the score and he's not stupid. He's in deeper than any of us. I'm just going to tip him off.'

Wilson nodded and Hammond left. As he watched the inspector's retreating back the thought came to him: *He's not the weak link. I am.*

As DCI Strang walked along the corridor to the main entrance, PC Graham came towards him with another uniform. He saw her eyes go uncertainly to his face, but he met her look with a blank stare. Even so, she looked guilty. Oh dear, he thought, Murray had been right – she was pants at acting. Luckily the other officer had been looking at him not his companion, otherwise he'd have been asking her what the problem was.

He phoned Murray once he got back to his car. 'Good call to let me know they were on to you, Livvy – you're learning! It let me say directly that I knew you and wanted to co-opt you to this investigation – rather took the feet from Hammond.'

She was obviously pleased. 'Thanks, sir. That's great.'

'Where are you?'

'Half an hour out of Halliburgh – theft of garden stuff three weeks ago. The householder was surprised – said she'd been told they'd just log it for the insurance.'

Strang laughed. 'Oh yes, they're running scared. Always useful – that's when mistakes are made.' Then he said more seriously, 'Be careful, Livvy. See if you can have a quiet chat with Kate. She gave me some useful feedback from an interview with Kayleigh Burns' son. I'm on my way to see Jackson now and when I tweak his tail about the kid saying he'd a lot of cash, they'll know the Harper stuff isn't actually our main concern and it could get nasty.'

He drove on to park off the high street outside Kayleigh's flat. Hammond had warned him that Jackson was being kicked out by the girlfriend and might have left already. He'd certainly have let Jackson know by now what was heading his way and it would be interesting to see if he was still there. If he was smart, he would be.

The door opened promptly and the man who stood in the dark hall was managing to act surprised as he said, 'Yes?' He was better at it than Kate Graham.

'Jason Jackson?' He produced his warrant card. 'DCI Strang. Did DI Hammond tell you to expect me?'

'No. Should he have?'

That didn't sound quite so convincing. 'No, not at all. Could I have a word?'

Jackson groaned. 'I suppose it's about this bloody housebreaking. You'd better come in. Don't trip over the cases. I was such a fool – you shouldn't get drunk, you know that?'

'Yes, Mr Jackson, I had worked that out.'

There were, indeed, a number of suitcases stacked around the sitting room and Strang weaved his way through them to a chair with its back to the window – always a position of advantage. As Jackson sat down opposite him, Strang noticed a bruise on his left cheek, just below the eye.

'Been in the wars?' he said.

'Wars? Oh, this.' Jackson rubbed at it. 'That's why I warned you – I tripped over one of the cases and fell against a doorpost. All I needed, on top of the hangover.'

'You'd been drinking? Before or after you broke into Highfield?'

'Oh before, obviously. I'd never have done it sober.'

'Why did you do it drunk?'

Jackson shrugged. 'Released my inhibitions, I suppose. I'd been upset Anna Harper had got someone to rubbish my book so no one bought it. I suppose I sort of got the idea I could go in and speak to her, ask her to promise not to do that to the next one. Not that she would've.'

The heartfelt bitterness of the last phrase showed up the insincerity of what went before. Jackson had a yarn about the break-in all ready to spin and Strang had no interest in hearing it. Instead, he said, 'What were your movements last Saturday morning?'

That took him aback. 'Saturday morning? I can't remember, offhand. What time?'

'First thing – 8.30, 9.00.'

'Saturday – oh, of course. That was the day the

writers' thing started at the Hub. I'd have been here, getting ready to go up. I got there probably around 9.30.'

'Any witnesses?'

'Kayleigh was here. It's her day off and she was going shopping in Gala.'

'Do you have two cars?'

'One. Hers. Don't even get to use it while she's at work,' he said morosely.

Jackson knowing Cassandra Trentham's movements in advance had been unlikely, anyway. Strang moved on.

'You seem to have a lot of spare cash, Mr Jackson. I hear Danny Burns has some very nice trainers.'

Jackson looked at him sharply. 'Who told you that?'

Strang raised his brows and said nothing.

'Oh, that'll be Kayleigh trying to cause trouble, I suppose. Last time I do her a favour. The little bugger kept whinging on about not having any of the gear the other kids have – I'd had a bit of luck on the gee-gees so I gave her a sub. All right?'

'What was the bet?'

'Got a hot tip on Home and Dry at Lingfield a couple of weeks ago. 40/1. Nice little earner, that one.'

Jackson had been all prepared for that question, anyway. 'Still got the betting slip?'

'The betting slip? I probably threw it away. It might be in my wallet. Let me check.' He went over to go through the pockets of a leather jacket that had been slung over a chair.

No, acting wasn't his strong suit either. Strang

would be astonished if he came back without it.

'Well, that's lucky. Here it is.'

Strang looked at the slip, which did indeed show a handsome payout on Home and Dry. 'A Glasgow bookmaker? Not a local one?'

The reply was glib. 'Happened to be in Glasgow at the time. It's a mate there that gives me tips from time to time.'

'Right.' He handed back the slip and stood up. 'Let DI Hammond know where you're moving to. I'll leave you to get on with your packing. Thanks for your time.'

'That all you wanted?' Jackson looked confused by the abruptness. 'Well – that's good, then. Watch the boxes on your way out.'

Back in his car, Strang took out a notebook and wrote down the details of the betting slip. He could pass that on to the Glasgow force and get them to go through the extensive records all bookmakers have to keep – and the CCTV – with a fine toothcomb. He reminded himself that he needed to keep an open mind; it could be true. But if it wasn't, what it told him was that the money must have come from a highly professional outfit, to have produced a cover story so slickly. And perhaps it was also true that Jackson had hurt his face falling over a case, but it was also possible that the visitor who had brought the betting slip hadn't been amused by what Jackson had done.

Then he took out his phone to call Murray. There was no answer; she was probably driving back, so he left a message.

'Livvy, I want you to take Kate and go to the school again and lean on Danny Burns – see if you can get anything out of him about where Jason gets his money from. Ask the head to get him out of class for you on another excuse – you don't want the other kids to know.'

Richard Sansom came into Cassandra Trentham's office carrying a bunch of daffodils. She took them, looking surprised.

'Thank you, Richard – a nice little touch of spring. But what do I owe this to?'

He sat down opposite her. 'It's an apology. I ranted at you yesterday when Marta had brought the police in without warning me and I should really have gone and ranted at her instead.'

Cassie laughed. 'Oh, I don't think you should have, you know. I'm a much less dangerous person to rant at. Have there been any problems?'

Sansom mimed wiping his brow. 'Mercifully, not so far. I had a word with Inspector Hammond and he seemed to think it would all just fade away. Jackson didn't actually cause any damage and they've no interest in prosecuting. Just a police caution, probably, and the press don't seem to have got hold of it.'

'What did he do it for?'

'He's obsessed with digging up dirt on Anna. I went round to see him and he said he hadn't found any so I came the heavy, put the frighteners on him and told him if anyone asked he was to say he was just a fan who got drunk and confused.'

'Oooh, I didn't realise issuing threats formed part of the PR duties,' Cassie said in shocked tones. 'You look much too civilised.'

'I'll have you know I played a useful game of rugby in my day, so threats and violence come naturally to me. He caved immediately – a bit of a pathetic specimen, actually.'

'I have to say I didn't take to him myself. So – any further plans?'

'If everything's quiet here, I'll probably go off to Dundee. Haven't touched base with Waterstones there yet.' He got up. 'I'll let you get on with your day. I hope I'm forgiven.'

She smiled up at him. She couldn't help liking Richard; he was certainly very charming, and he'd amused her. There wasn't much that did, right at the moment.

The door through to her secretary's office opened and Jess put her head in. 'There's a DCI Strang waiting downstairs to speak to you. Do you want me to send him up?'

Cassie and Richard exchanged glances. 'Yes, show him up,' she said slowly. 'That's escalation, isn't it – a DCI?'

'It's a disaster,' he said, looking agitated. 'It means there's something they're taking seriously. What the hell have they homed in on?'

She tried to soothe him. 'It's probably just because of

Anna. They always pull out the stops whenever anything happens to her – Marta makes sure of that.'

Jess appeared again, with a tall man following her. 'Detective Chief Inspector Strang,' she said, and retreated.

Cassie got up and went forward. 'I'm Cassandra Trentham. This is Richard Sansom, who's head of publicity for my mother.'

They shook hands and Strang said to Sansom, 'You'll be busy, then, with the new book coming out shortly.'

Surprised, Sansom said, 'You know about that?'

'Got it on order at my local bookshop.'

'Excellent! It's good to know we have a cultured police force,' Sansom said. 'Well, I'll get out of your way.'

'Just a small question to ask before you go – it'll save bothering you later. Can you tell me your movements last Saturday morning?'

Cassie could see that Sansom was working out what that implied, just as she was, and she was pretty sure they were coming to the same conclusion. He looked as horrified as she felt, but he only said, 'That's straightforward enough. Got up late, had breakfast at the hotel, came up here and found poor Cassie had been knocked off her bike. She was being terribly brave.' He gave her a fleeting smile. 'Anything else I can help you with?'

'No, that's all for the moment, sir, thank you.'

As Sansom shut the door behind him, Cassie said, in a small voice, 'Does that mean you think someone did it deliberately?'

* * *

Gil Paton was hanging round the hall when Richard Sansom, scowling, came down the stairs and headed for the front door. He hurried after him and grabbed his arm.

'What's going on? What is all this about?'

Sansom stopped, then without turning took hold of Paton's sleeve between two fingers, lifted it off his arm and dropped it. 'Shall we start again? You wanted to ask me something?'

Paton took a step back. 'Sorry, sorry. It's just you've been closeted with Cassie – and now a senior police officer! What has he come about? As Cassie's deputy I need to know what's going on. It's important – there may be repercussions, you see.'

Sansom looked down at him from his superior height. 'I feel sure that if Cassie wants your input, she'll ask for it. Now if you'll excuse me, I've work to do.'

He walked out, leaving Paton speechless. He ought to have a ready reply for rudeness like that but somehow he'd never been able to stand up to bullies, despite plenty of practice. The scars were burnt deep into his soul.

'Gil!'

Sascha was coming along the corridor from the Hub and he turned to greet her with little enthusiasm. He hadn't forgiven her for needling him.

'Oh – Sascha. What can I do for you?'

'It was just to ask you to tell the caterers I won't be in for—' She broke off, looking at him sharply. 'Are you all right? You're looking a bit agitated.'

'Oh – no, not agitated. It's just with everything that's going on, the Jason Jackson business—'

'Oh yes, I heard! The receptionist is through in the Hub having a cup of coffee and she said we have a chief inspector, no less. That looks like overkill, doesn't it, just for a break-in when nothing was taken?'

He said stiffly, 'You must know more about it than I do.'

'Oh, I have my sources! How is Anna taking it? I expect you'll have been round to see her?'

The woman was pure poison. Paton could feel one of his tension headaches coming on. 'She's all right. And of course I'll tell the caterers. Out for supper, did you say? Again? Somewhere nice?'

For once, he seemed to have got to her. 'Oh – well, yes, I suppose so,' she said. 'Thanks, Gil – I'd better get back to my desk. It's flowing quite well this morning.'

'That's good. See you later.'

He wondered idly where she was going, but he had other things on his mind. And he should have a word with the receptionist – Polly, a nice enough girl but not a mental giant – about not gossiping.

'I'm sorry if this is alarming for you,' DCI Strang said.

Cassie Trentham was looking pale and tired and so vulnerable that he really felt for her. Watching her brother's death had been one of the most horrible experiences you could imagine and to be living now under what could be a death threat must be pushing her close to the edge.

She was brave, though. 'I can cope,' she said.

'Look, there's actually no reason to suppose your accident was anything more than just that – careless motorist, happens all the time.'

She was no fool, either. She gave a him a cool look as she said, 'Yes, Inspector Hammond said that. But, correct me if I'm wrong, they don't usually send out chief inspectors for a minor traffic accident, do they?'

Strang smiled. 'No, you're right of course. You'd normally get a detective constable to take a statement, but there are a couple of factors here. This isn't an interview, just a chat. As you probably know, your mother wields a lot of influence and a big part of my brief is to reassure her. In the second place, I head up the Serious Rural Crime Squad, which is a bit of a maverick outfit where the roles are much more blurred, so don't read too much into it.

'I agree with Inspector Hammond. Can I ask you first if you always cycle to work at that particular time?'

Cassie shook her head. 'No. I like to cycle if I can but I'm definitely a fair-weather cyclist. And on Saturday I slept later than I meant to – I'd usually aim to be at the Foundation by nine o'clock and it was almost quarter past when it happened.'

'So it would be hard to arrange for someone to be in exactly the right place at the right time. Was there anyone who might have known your plans?'

'Not really. Well, Gil, I suppose, Gil Paton who runs the Hub for us. He knew I was planning to come in quite early, but he wouldn't have known I would take the bike. Anyway, I really can't see Gil doing that.'

'I'll have a chat with him after this. Let me stress that I still think this was an unfortunate accident, but I want to be able to tell your mother and Ms Morelli that we've checked it all out thoroughly.'

Cassie nodded, then said, 'And Felix's death?'

Strang sighed. 'I'm sorry for your loss and sorry too that this should have happened in a place that until recently wouldn't have had a real drug problem, but there's been an orchestrated attempt by the dealers to expand into the countryside and it looks as if he fell victim to that. We're working on it right now, but unless you have evidence that someone forced it on your brother, there's not much we can do.'

Tears stood in Cassie's eyes but she blinked them away. 'He was still . . . struggling,' she admitted. 'Kate Graham – she's the liaison officer – has been very tactful, but I could tell she thought that too. It's just – if you did want to kill Felix, it would be a really good way to do it. I don't know why anyone would want to kill Felix, though – or me, for that matter. But "accidentally" knocking me off my bike would be a good way to do it too, wouldn't it?'

He was taken aback. They had all assumed that the imperious Ms Morelli was overreacting and had used her demand as a cover to get him access to the inner workings of Halliburgh police station, but when Cassie put it like that . . . He said slowly, 'Can you think of any reason – any reason at all – why it should be deliberate?'

'Oh, I've thought and thought, but I can't come up with anything. I only know that my mother and Marta are really strung up about it and there's something they're not telling me, but they just deny it and make up silly reasons for why they're fussing. It could be something to do with The Brand.'

'The Brand?'

'The Anna Harper Brand. It's what we were always told when they said we couldn't do something – it would reflect badly on The Brand.'

'I see. Anyway, you're not cycling now, are you?'

'My mother's driver, Davy Armstrong, is behaving like a nanny, taking me to and fro, usually with a lecture thrown in. And I can hardly move in my cottage without setting off alarms. It's quite ridiculous,' she said petulantly.

Strang smiled. 'Too much security is never a bad thing.' He got up. 'And try not to worry. It's still very much more likely than not that your accident was just that.'

But was it? he was thinking as he went downstairs. The big question was why – why would anyone want to kill Anna Harper's children? And if there was something she knew, why wouldn't she tell her daughter, even if she wasn't keen to tell the police?

As he reached the hall, a man came forward and accosted him – a thickset man with dark hair and a pasty, rather flat face, framed by a dark beard.

'DCI Strang, I'm Ms Trentham's deputy, Gil Paton. If there's some problem here, I really ought to know about it.'

He seemed very uptight. Strang said mildly, 'We have everything in hand and I'm sure Ms Trentham will be able to tell you anything you want to know.'

The reply had clearly riled him. 'Oh yes, I'm not to be told anything, is that right? Despite the fact that if something goes wrong it will all land on my shoulders and it won't be Cassie who gets the blame. What are you here for?'

There was a young woman behind the reception desk who was taking an obvious interest and Strang said, 'Why don't we find somewhere to sit down? I've a couple of questions to ask you, anyway.'

Paton took fright. 'Questions? Why should you have questions for me? What sort of questions?'

Strang indicated the reception area at the further end of the hall. 'Let's go over there.' He walked ahead and sat down on one of the cream leather seats. Paton followed him, then noticed the receptionist watching him.

'What are you staring at, Polly? Why don't you go through to the Hub and gossip for a bit, like you usually do?'

Polly gave him a killer look, then flounced off down the corridor. As Paton sat down beside him Strang noticed that the man was shaking – temper, or nerves?

'I'm doing routine enquiries about the morning when Ms Trentham had her cycling accident – last Saturday. Can you tell me your movements?'

'My movements?' He was immediately defensive. 'When Cassie was knocked off her bike? Are you accusing me of having something to do with that?'

'I'm not accusing anyone of anything, Mr Paton.'

'Oh no? You're not picking on me? But did you challenge Richard Sansom? I don't think so!'

'You're quite wrong. I did indeed. Now, Saturday morning?'

Paton gulped visibly. 'I didn't do anything out of the ordinary. Got up, had my breakfast, walked up here and arrived to see Cassie lying right here on the sofa. That was it. All right?'

'Any witnesses?'

'When I live alone? If I'd arranged to have one, that really would be suspicious. And there's nothing more I can say.' He folded his arms, as if he was erecting a barricade.

'You know where Ms Trentham lives, and you knew she was planning to come in on Saturday morning?'

'I suppose she told you that. Yes, I did! Is it a crime?' he said wildly. He had gone very pale. 'So somehow, I'm the person who wanted to knock her off her bike and kill her? What proof do you have? I demand that you tell me.'

'Mr Paton, this is merely a routine interview. You're not being accused of anything. It would be helpful if you kept calm. Can I ask if you told anyone about Ms Trentham's plans?'

For a moment he looked confused. 'Told anyone . . . ?' Then his face brightened. 'Yes, yes I did, in fact. I told Sascha Silverton – she's one of the writers here for the week. You should go and ask her about her movements too.'

Strang glanced at his watch and got up. 'We will, yes, but I'm afraid I haven't time now.'

Paton's face darkened again. 'They always say that the police make up their minds and then distort the facts to suit. Well, I won't stay quiet while you lot fit me up.'

'I'm sure you won't, sir.'

As Strang left on his way up to Highfield he was beginning to think that what he had thought of as the cover story might, after all, be the bigger problem.

DC Murray would have claimed that she wasn't oversensitive, but the atmosphere when she got back to Halliburgh police station was chilly, to say the least. Word of her treachery had obviously got about and when she went in to report to DS Wilson, it was downright arctic.

'Oh, back then, are you?'

Well, two could play at that game. 'Yes, I've interviewed the homeowner and I'll file the report,' she said just as coldly. 'Now I have an interview to do for DS Strang and I want to take PC Graham with me. I take it that's all right?'

Wilson's eyes narrowed. 'Why her?'

Murray smiled. 'Because she's polite. It goes a long way.'

She was prepared for a row – would rather enjoy it – but to her surprise he hesitated, then backed off.

'Fine,' he said, then added, awkwardly, 'we're all on the same side, after all.'

Oh, how wrong you are, sweetheart, she thought. Yet as she went to find Graham she found herself wondering what he'd meant with that remark – could it be a clumsy attempt to get back on the right side of the fence? If you were happy enough to do the dirty in one way, you might not find it too hard to do it in another, if the stakes were high enough.

CHAPTER THIRTEEN

The reply when DCI Strang buzzed for entrance to Highfield was distinctly hostile and seemed only marginally less so when he identified himself. It was all of a piece with the aggressive architecture of the house, but the gates swung open anyway and when he drove in and parked at the front door it was open already.

The dark-haired woman who stood on the threshold could only be Marta Morelli. She was wearing black – mourning, perhaps? – and she invited him in politely enough but her body language, with shoulders tense and arms clasped across her body, sent out an antagonistic message even as she said, 'I will take you to the sitting room and explain to you what has been happening.'

She headed off without waiting to see if he was following her, so she was climbing the stairs when he said, 'Thank you, but there's no need for that, Ms Morelli. I've been given a very full report already. I'm here to speak to Ms Harper.'

Marta turned, giving him a look that would have curdled milk. 'Ms Harper is seeing no one today. She has been very much shaken by what has happened.'

'Of course. I can appreciate that, but I'm afraid I must insist.'

She drew a sharp breath, as if no one had ever dared to say anything like that to her before. 'But this is an outrageous intrusion—'

'Merely routine practice, I assure you,' Strang said soothingly. 'I'm sure Ms Harper will understand. Where is she?'

Marta said nothing, only glaring at him defiantly.

He hadn't planned on getting aggressive himself, but she was playing games and he didn't have time to join in. He hardened his voice. 'Ms Morelli, perhaps you aren't aware that obstructing the police in the course of their duties is a criminal offence. You can take me to Ms Harper or I can arrest you.'

She was a hard woman. For a moment she tried to stare him down, then with her mouth pursed she came down and took him along a passage under the stairs and tapped on the door.

Anna Harper was sitting in front of the computer on her desk, though it didn't seem to Strang as if she had been doing anything – listening, perhaps, to the discussion in the hall. She wasn't in black; she was wearing a thick white cowl-necked sweater that looked like cashmere with pale grey trousers.

'Anna, this is a very rude policeman who will be arresting me if I do not permit that he interrogate you,' Marta said. Her Italian accent seemed much more pronounced than it had been before.

Anna stood up. She was very pale and with the blue circles of tiredness round her eyes she did indeed look as if she was, as her dragon lady had said, very much shaken. He went over and introduced himself.

'I apologise, Ms Harper. I don't want to cause either of you any distress but if we are to find out what may be behind all this, I must be able to pursue my investigation.'

She gave him a weary smile. 'Yes of course, Chief Inspector. Marta always tries to protect me but naturally I'm ready to cooperate in any way I can. Do come over here and sit down.'

There was a cheerful blaze in the fireplace, and they sat down in the chairs at that end. Marta made to join them and Strang's heart sank; he'd have to send her away and that would no doubt provoke more hostility.

'I'm sorry, Ms Morelli. I really need to speak to Ms Harper on her own.'

Marta flared up. 'Surely you police cannot stop someone from having a friend to support them—'

'Marta,' Anna said, 'I'm perfectly happy to do as the inspector asks. We have nothing to hide, after all.'

A look passed between them and Strang thought he could read the message it was meant to convey: that they did indeed have something to hide but she could hold the line.

'If you are happy, *cara*, then that is all right,' Marta said stiffly and walked out, her back rigid.

Anna pulled a little face as the door closed. 'I'm sorry about that. The thing is, if I am to have time for my work, Marta has to screen out the demands that are made and at the moment when we have had such a traumatic time she is probably more than usually protective.

'What did you want to ask me, then? I'm afraid I know nothing about the break-in. I slept through it. You'd have to talk to Marta to get the details.'

'I have those. Someone will come round later to give her the statement to sign. This isn't a formal on-the-record interview. I know what Ms Morelli thinks about what has happened and I just want to hear your version.'

'We agree, of course,' she said sharply.

'Ms Morelli feels we should have taken the culprit into custody but I'm sure you know as well as I do that this is unfeasible.'

She sighed. 'Yes, of course I do. But you have to understand that as an Italian Marta is more familiar with the inquisitorial system where the presiding judge will lock up the suspect until evidence emerges.'

He let a small silence emerge, then said, 'Evidence – of what, Ms Harper?'

On the face of it, a simple enough question. But Anna gave a little gasp and looked nervously about her before she said awkwardly, 'Evidence, well, evidence of what he's done, this man. My son is dead, my daughter was attacked, my house was broken into. I think it's your job to find it.'

Strang said, very gently, 'The problem is, I can understand why he broke into the house – he had a grudge against you and perhaps he thought he might find information that would discredit you. But I would need you to tell me why you believe that he would have wanted to kill your children. If he had a murderous resentment towards you, why wouldn't he have seized the opportunity to attack you once he was inside your house?'

'How should I know?' she protested. 'Perhaps he thought he could pile pressure on me that way—'

'Has he communicated with you, then?'

A logical enough question, he thought. But her reaction was astonishing: she shrank back in her chair, her face flared red and she stammered as she said, 'No, no, of course he didn't! We'd have told you at once, naturally. That man, Jackson – he was very angry, perhaps saw an opportunity with my poor Felix and took it by way of revenge.'

'And your daughter's accident?'

She was gripping her hands tightly together as if she was trying to hold on to something – the thread of the story she was so clumsily constructing, perhaps. With her skills she should be better at it than this and almost as if she had overheard his thought she visibly pulled herself together and said, with an unconvincing laugh, 'Oh dear! I'm sounding like some sort of crazy conspiracy theorist! I know that the view of the police was that Felix's death was tragic but not suspicious and that Cassie's accident was just that, so perhaps you are right and Marta and I are just a pair of hysterical women.'

'It's been a very difficult spell for you. It's hardly surprising that you should be feeling confused.' He paused for a moment, then surprised her by standing up. 'I think I'll leave it there for the moment. This is my number – you can contact me at any time. And I can see you are well protected by security here, but if you do have doubts about your safety and your daughter's, please think very seriously about what more you can tell me. Secrets are dangerous things.'

Anna didn't move as he thanked her and left the room, but he was aware of her eyes following him. He didn't see Marta again as he left.

It was embarrassingly obvious that Anna was hiding something. Something in her past so damaging that she seemed prepared to risk Cassie's life and even her own by obstructing the investigation? And someone had indeed communicated with her, judging by her reaction.

Blackmail, then? He could rule out Jackson, who wouldn't have needed to make his ill-judged raid if he'd had the information already. Who, then – and why?

Perhaps he should have challenged her, pushed her to see if she would crack. It was always possible she might have, but in his experience victims did not readily open up about their own past sins – and putting undue pressure on a recently bereaved mother wasn't smart, whoever she was. Anyway, if he thought he might get any sort of useful admission he'd want to be on an official footing first.

Anna had a global reputation to protect, of course, but surely she wouldn't behave like this for the sake of a bit of bad publicity? He had to ask himself what secret could be so terrible that it must be concealed, whatever the cost.

Upstairs in the security room Marta was watching the interview. She couldn't hear what was said but she saw with dismay that this policeman had asked Anna something that had left her flustered and nervous. He had noticed that, of course he had, but Anna had pulled herself together in the way she always did when she took a blow: squared her shoulders, tossed her head and managed to stay calm.

When the man had left, though, she saw Anna sag forward, putting her hand to her brow and she jumped up to hurry downstairs. She put a hand on her shoulder.

'What did he ask, Anna?'

She sat up with a little shudder. 'We should have been prepared for this. He asked me about communication – he'll be thinking about blackmail now. Dear God, if only it was! I would pay whatever they wanted, to make this go away.'

Marta sat down heavily in her usual chair. Comforting Anna, finding the answers for her was her role in life, but just at the moment she couldn't think of anything to say. Whoever it was who was their enemy was looking not for money but revenge.

* * *

DC Murray was amused at the way Danny Burns looked coming into the headteacher's office – the picture of injured innocence, but with just a touch of anxiety that suggested that while he might not be guilty of any recent offence, his conscience wasn't entirely clear. She'd looked like that many a time herself.

He looked surprised to see the two women, then, recognising PC Graham, definitely wary.

'There were one or two questions DC Murray wanted to ask you following on from our talk this morning when we were asking about the gear you and the other kids have, remember? All right?' She placed herself to one side and quietly got out a notebook.

'S'pose so.' His eyes were firmly fixed on the floor.

'Great trainers, Danny,' Murray said.

He flared up. 'Why's everyone on about my trainers? All the guys have them! Why don't you talk to them?'

'Maybe we will. But you're a bright boy, Danny. You know as well as I do who the guys have got the money from – guys who get them to run errands for them. Just errands, that's all, like anyone would. Right?'

The boy looked away. 'Dunno. Better ask them.'

'The thing is, what's interesting is that you didn't have trainers, until Jason gave you the money. So – you don't run errands?'

'No!' There was definitely resentment there.

'But you'd like to?'

'Well, it's just errands, like you said. Nothing wrong with that, is there?' He looked at her defiantly.

'So, why don't you, then?'

'*He* won't let me! Jason – he goes, "Your mum wouldn't like it," and so I wasn't allowed. They didn't want me.'

Murray pounced. '*They*, Danny?'

She let the pause lengthen when he didn't reply. Eventually he muttered sullenly, 'I dunno. No one really knows.'

'Jason's pals with them, though, is he? They'd do him a favour?' Danny shrugged. 'Do you think that's where he gets his money from, Danny?'

He shrugged again, biting his lip, and Murray said more gently, 'I know it's hard for you. You're not stupid and we all know what these "errands" are, don't we? You've kept out of it so far, so you're not in any trouble, but you're worried about dobbing in your mates. Look at it this way: the police know what's going on and before long they'll be picked up. They'll have a record and we'll be on their backs from then on. If you want to be a real friend, tell them that. Tell them to come and talk to us.'

She didn't think he would, and he certainly wouldn't give names. But the kids in the school with noticeably expensive gear would be an easy place for the drug squad to start once they were called in. Then a thought occurred to her.

'Do you know about that man who died, Felix Trentham?'

Danny looked uncomfortable. 'Yeah, I guess.'

Murray leant closer and fixed her eyes on him. 'He

died, Danny. Died because someone got him drugs. Do you know anything about it, anything at all? It really wouldn't be clever not to tell us.'

He was still very young. His eyes dropped and his chin wobbled. 'I didn't know anything, honest! Just, like, that the errands stopped after that. I heard the lads saying they were like laying off for a bit.'

Murray sat back in her chair and looked at him. It wouldn't be right to push him any harder and in fact she didn't think he knew much more than that.

'Right, Danny, that's fine for now. And don't worry, no one will know we've spoken to you. But sometime you'll have to quietly come round to the police station with your mum and go through what you've said and make a statement. OK?'

He didn't look happy but the tears hadn't come and that hint of defiance was back as he went to the door. 'Haven't told you anything, really,' he said.

'That's right. You didn't, really,' Murray said, and as the door shut she added to Graham, 'Better if he can tell himself that. It'll be easier for him to lie if anyone challenges him.'

Graham nodded, closing over her notebook. 'Is Jason running the operation on the ground, do you think?'

'Seems likely. We'd better get back and I'll try to find the boss. I hope he's annexed an office.'

DCI Strang had indeed found an office, before he set out to interview Anna Harper. The CID operation in Halliburgh having been scaled down there was no lack of space and DS Wilson had been obsequiously eager to help him.

'This one's a bit dusty I'm afraid, sir, but there's not too much litter lying around. I'll put someone in to clean up and it'll be ready by the time you get back. I can find a kettle and a coffee tray, if you like.'

'Thanks, Sergeant. That will be very helpful,' he had said, and when he returned Wilson was hovering to show him what had been done. There was a computer set up on the desk, all the surfaces were shining, the promised coffee tray was on a side table and there was even a coat stand in one corner.

'There's a list of codes for the computer there. And if there's anything else you want, you've only to let me know, sir,' Wilson said as he left. 'Only too happy to help.'

Strang raised his eyebrows. Running scared, indeed! Was DI Hammond going to find himself isolated, like someone with a nasty case of plague? He took his laptop out of his case and set it up; he didn't fancy using the station computer system, though having access at least to the files that weren't specially protected would be useful. He settled down to recording notes from his interview with Anna.

There was a knock on the door and Wilson appeared again. Was all this eagerness going to become a nuisance, he wondered, but he wronged the man; this was to ask whether he would see someone called Sascha Silverton who had arrived asking to speak to him.

'She's one of the lady writers up at the Foundation this week,' Wilson said. 'Says she heard you wanted to speak to her.'

Strang frowned. Yes, he had said that, but it had been well down his priority list. 'Get her to make an appointment,' he was saying, when the woman herself appeared at Wilson's shoulder; a good-looking woman certainly, but one who had a heavy hand with the slap.

'Here! I told you to wait,' Wilson said, but she gave him a gleaming smile.

'Oh sorry! I just thought if I could be a help I ought to take the first opportunity. I'd hate to be a bother' – the gleaming smile was directed at Strang now – 'but I know in these situations getting all the evidence in quickly is of such importance.'

Strang rose reluctantly. 'In that case, Ms Silverton, perhaps we should get on with it at once. What do you have to tell me?' He waved her to one of the chairs on the other side of his desk and nodded to Wilson to leave.

She settled into it, looking around. 'Do you know, I've never been in a DCI's office before! What a pity I don't write crime! I'd be fascinated – well, I'm fascinated anyway. It's a job that must be a constant challenge! You must tell me, how have you begun on this case?'

Was that really a dimple? She fluttered her eyelashes too; was she for real? Perhaps winsomeness came readily to 'lady writers' – though not if you were Anna Harper!

'Just in the normal way, Ms Silverton. Now, what was it that you wanted to tell me?'

'Well Gil – you know, Gil Paton, up at the Hub? – he said you were looking into poor Cassie's accident. Do you have a theory about it?'

'No. I prefer facts.'

'Of course. Now, I know it was in the morning she was knocked off her bike – I saw her limping around at the Foundation not long afterwards. So do you think that someone knew when she was going to be coming in and actually seized the opportunity to make an attempt on her life?'

He was beginning to have a very unwelcome suspicion about this woman. 'I have no reason to think that. What do you know about it?' Then, very deliberately, he added, 'Of course, I believe you were told that she was going to come in to the Foundation that day, despite her recent loss?'

Sascha hadn't expected the question and for a moment she lost her poise. 'Only in the vaguest possible way. No idea of time, no idea she would be cycling. Nothing to do with me, Inspector.'

'You weren't out in a car at the time it happened?'

'Of course not! I was having breakfast in the Hub – anyone will tell you.'

'So you can't shed any light on what happened?'

'I'm afraid not.'

'Then perhaps I can ask you what the evidence was that you were so anxious to give me immediately?'

She seemed to have prepared for that question and now they had stopped talking about her own movements, she seemed more confident.

'If you can tell me what line you're going on, who you are looking at particularly, I'm sure I can help you. I've met almost everyone who could be involved – except Anna Harper, of course. She's absolutely my icon, you know, but she keeps herself very much to herself – but perhaps she's opened up more to you? She must be very anxious,' she said with an encouraging smile.

Strang gave her a long, steady look and she hesitated, but carried on, 'And of course I can tell you about Jason Jackson. He has a bone to pick with Anna, of course – I expect you know that? He's a nasty bit of work and I'm only astonished that he apparently confined himself to hunting through her papers. Do you know what he was looking for?'

She looked at him enquiringly, wide-eyed.

Strang got to his feet. 'You know, I'm getting a very odd feeling about this. For some reason you seem to be interviewing me, not the other way round.'

'I . . . I don't know what you mean! I came here so you could ask me any questions you like.'

'Which paper, Sascha?'

The smile had gone and temper showed in her face. She jumped up. 'I don't like your tone. If you don't want to question me, I'm entitled to leave, aren't I?'

'And I don't like journalists who don't declare themselves and try to trap people into giving them useful material – not very competently, in your case. I asked you, which newspaper? I shall be making a complaint to the editor.'

She looked as if she was thinking about brazening it out, but then her shoulders sagged. 'Oh, for God's sake! I don't have a newspaper – I want to get a job with one. I thought if I could manage to wangle an interview with Anna Harper it would be my calling card, because she never normally talks to anyone, but she's too high and mighty, locked away in her million-pound mansion keeping her secrets safe.'

'You think she has secrets?'

'I've followed up every scrap of information I could dig up and got nothing – she's covered her tracks too well. Why would she do that if she didn't?'

'You seem to have taken a lot of trouble for no result at all. Why focus on her?'

Sascha had no ready answer. 'Just . . . I was interested. And I was bloody fed up with churning out soft porn for stupid women who wanted a new romance every week to make up for the ineffable dreariness of their lives.'

'And you thought it would be a scoop to get the inside story of what, as far as I know, is nothing more than a minor case of attempted burglary? It's not exactly hold-the-presses stuff.'

'No, I suppose not,' she said sulkily. 'So, thanks for nothing.'

On the way out she turned and said, 'You do understand it was just that I was interested in Anna, like anyone might be?'

It was an odd thing to say and even as Strang said, 'Yes, of course,' he was trying to work out what she had meant. Covering her back, for some reason? Anna would inevitably attract interest, and if he'd been her PR advisor he'd have suggested she should be a bit more open – the suggestion of secrets was enough to make that interest more obsessive. It was no accident that the word 'fan' was short for fanatic.

Jackson had his own declared reason for stalking her – but was Sascha another stalker? If it hadn't been for that final remark, he'd have written her down as just another journalist raking for whatever muck they could find, but it had him wondering now. There were so many weird currents swirling around this case that you couldn't be sure who was and who wasn't involved.

Strang glanced at his watch and yawned. It had been a long day, he'd only had an energy bar since breakfast and there was still a debriefing to have with Murray before he could set out on the long drive home. It would be interesting to see what she'd come up with, and not just about the county lines problem. The Harper case seemed to be expanding in all sorts of unexpected directions.

With the alarm screaming, Cassie Trentham opened her front door and went into the cottage fumbling for the fob. It was such a hideous noise, such an unwelcoming way to return home. She didn't feel it was reassuring, more an invasion of her sanctuary.

Her ears were still ringing as she went to the window to wave to Davy, who was lurking outside as he always did, 'to see her safe in', as he said. As if Marta wouldn't have made sure it was linked to the Highfield system! They'd have been on to it instantly if anyone had broken in.

She went back to shut the door, hesitated, then locked it. She'd never locked herself in before and in a way she felt it was foolishly neurotic. On the other hand – well, it had been an unsettling day. She'd been spooked by the way Anna and Marta were acting anyway, trying to scare her one minute and then pretending there was nothing wrong the next. As children she and Felix had been conditioned to accept an unexplained directive from Anna with a shrug of their shoulders, but she wasn't a child now and if there really was some threat to her she had a right to know what and why.

Cassie had tried telling herself that they were imagining it. Anna could be neurotic and Marta sometimes got swept along with her. She'd almost managed, until the interview today with that nice policeman. He'd been trying not to worry her, but she had spotted the moment when he had suddenly realised there might be something in what she had said and taken it seriously. She'd wanted him to tell her politely that she was being silly and he definitely hadn't done that.

But standing here agonising wasn't going to do any good. She went through to the kitchen and got a bottle of white wine out of the fridge and sat down in the sitting room with her glass. She picked up the remote and turned on the television.

It was halfway through the news and there was a big

story about the snow that was, apparently, planning to sweep in from Russia in the next day or two with devastating effect. The Beast from the East, they were calling it.

Davy had been on about it too, all the way back to Burnside, using it as another excuse to get her to move back to Highfield House, but she'd pooh-poohed it.

'Come on, Davy, we're hardy people, us Borderers! We're used to snow. It's the city folk get their knickers in a twist and make a great big fuss – and it's the end of the world if a couple of snowflakes fall in London. If you're scared of driving just stay at home. I'll manage.'

Davy had protested at this slight to his manhood, but she'd only laughed and got out of the car.

Now as she watched the report, she began to have some qualms. They were saying this wasn't like anything they'd seen for years and it was true, she was very isolated out here. Perhaps she might think of staying at Highfield, just for a few days until it was over.

If there was one thing she hated, though, it was giving in. It looked all right at the moment – she could take stock tomorrow and make her decision then.

CHAPTER FOURTEEN

It was half past seven by the time Kelso Strang arrived back in Newhaven – well after Betsy's bedtime so at least he would be spared a story-reading session tonight. But even so, with the alternative of withdrawing into his bedroom or watching Fin's choice of television – or worse, listening to her worries over her daughter's latest misdemeanour at nursery – returning home wasn't an appealing prospect.

He suddenly remembered that it was jazz night at the pub – just what he needed, to unwind over a pint with undemanding company. And it was ridiculous to be feeling guilty for parking the car outside the house and walking along to the pub instead of going in.

At home now all too often he felt like a cat being stroked the wrong way, spiky and irritable; it dismayed him, rather, that for all his good intentions in offering a home to Fin and Betsy, he couldn't stop himself impatiently wondering how long it might be before they moved out. On the gloomy days, he wondered if it would ever happen. He took a seat in one corner and sat back, soothed by the familiar atmosphere and the easy chat and feeling tension seeping out of him.

The band started up and as the music made satisfying patterns in his head, he found his mind drifting back over the events of the day. Somehow it always liberated his thoughts, as if it cleared space for the workings of the subconscious to make themselves known.

As he drove back, he had been thinking about the case they could mount against Steve Hammond. There was plenty to work on, he reckoned, with what Livvy had said about the schoolkids and the Glasgow connection with Jackson, along with the evidence Kate could give once they got under way, particularly since Wilson seemed to be keen to get onside. He could speak to JB about the politics of getting in the drug squad at once.

But now it was Anna Harper who was at the centre of his freewheeling thoughts, vague ideas that came up and vanished again. Was she right about a plot against her and her family – or had she such a guilty conscience that she had constructed one out of random events? She believed it, anyway. And Marta Morelli did too.

He let his mind drift on to her, the strange, forbidding woman whose life was so closely interwoven with – what, her employer? Her friend? Her lover? Somehow that last didn't fit with their interaction. She had been more like a protective older sister, at once admiring and convinced that the younger was incapable of managing on her own. Fin had been like that, he acknowledged with a rueful smile, until her own world had fallen apart.

They were certainly in it together, Harper and Morelli. Whatever Anna had done, she had been, and would be, supported. But what could it be? His mind ran over the possibilities.

If they weren't prepared to give the police information that could protect them, it had to be something illegal. Something that would have the sort of tariff that would ensure a jail sentence – with Anna's money she could pay any sort of fine and still have plenty to retire on quietly if it had turned her public against her. Kate had said that Cassie believed she'd changed her name once before; she could do it again – and that was something he should look into. There was no official register for Deed Poll name changes but that might be somewhere to start.

Murder – you'd go to any lengths to conceal that. The victim certainly couldn't strike back, but a son? A daughter? Anna herself had used the word 'revenge'.

Drug-dealing? With her own son dead of an overdose, evidence of that would certainly ruin her relationship with her daughter and kill her career. The motive for a dealer was usually money but with Anna's success she would hardly need that. Then it struck him – she hadn't always been wealthy, had she? The struggling author, trying to buy time to write her masterpiece? And living in Italy, he seemed to remember. It would be more than far-fetched to link Anna with the Mafia, but that was another reason to root about in her early life.

Those were the obvious ones, but human sins take many different forms. Fruitless, really, to speculate, but somehow he felt he'd made progress and had new avenues he could explore.

It was getting late and he wanted to make an early start tomorrow. The band was taking a break and the TV above the bar was switched back on in time for an item about the storm they'd all been talking about so he paused on his way out to watch it. As the doom-laden prophecies were churned out he gave a mental punch in the air. Yes! Here was his excuse for booking in at that peaceful pub he'd wistfully imagined.

The light was still on in the sitting room, so Finella hadn't gone to bed and when he reached the door he could hear voices. There was another woman with her, a member of the support group that Fin had joined: Michelle, an angular divorcee with light brown eyes like a hawk's, who always made Kelso feel like a vole being assessed for nutritional value.

'Goodness, you're late!' Fin said. 'I thought you'd be home to have supper with us.'

'Oh, poor soul! They do work you hard, don't they?' Michelle said, oozing sympathy.

'No sympathy needed. I just fancied the jazz night at the pub so that's where I was. Did you have a nice evening?'

He hadn't said sorry. Both women looked put out, and Michelle said pointedly, 'Yes, what a shame you missed it. Fin made us a lovely supper. We put some in the fridge for you.'

He refused to let them make him feel like an errant husband. Fin hadn't told him her plans – largely, he suspected, because he'd told her before that he didn't want any more threesomes with her chums – and if he wanted to justify himself, he could point that out. On the other hand, he could just say, 'Thanks very much, but I'm good.'

He did, adding, 'If you'll excuse me, I'm just going to get my head down. I'm making an early start for work tomorrow. And Fin, given the forecast I'll be staying down there for the next few days until it's blown through. All right?'

'Of course,' Fin said, a little stiffly. 'See you in the morning.'

As Kelso closed his bedroom door he heard a, '*Well!*' from Michelle and Fin saying, 'I'm sorry about that.' And now he was feeling guilty again, dammit!

But as he checked the bag he always kept packed in case he had a sudden call to head off, he felt a reprehensible lifting of the heart at the thought of getting away.

DC Livvy Murray too had been watching the news, but the thought of being trapped in Halliburgh wasn't nearly as appealing to her. Police Scotland wasn't famous for the generosity of its provision for officers' accommodation and she could see herself stuck in some dismal B&B, which was probably grudging with its heating.

The meeting with Strang had given her plenty of food for thought. She'd told him about Danny and he'd filled her in on the information that had come his way. A bit to her surprise, he'd seemed to her to be a lot more open to believing there was something to Marta Morelli's claims than she'd been herself, but then he'd spoken to Anna Harper and she hadn't. He'd wanted to hear what she was thinking, though, which gave her a little kick of pride.

She had paused for a moment to collect her thoughts, then said carefully, 'OK. I want to kill Cassie Trentham, right? Never mind why – I just do. Maybe knocking her off her bike won't kill her, but then it could, and it'd look like an accident. Fine. But how'd I find out she'd be cycling or what time? I could get spotted if I hung around waiting for her to appear and, anyway, she could decide not to.

'And Felix Trentham – I wouldn't be able to stand over him to get him to take the stuff – I'd be out in the open then and he might talk. If I was just being hopeful and arranged for it to be offered to him, he might really be clean and not take it. So . . .'

Strang had sighed. 'Yes, I don't disagree. That's a very fair summary. But there's something very wrong here, more than just that and Jackson's silly attempt. Those two women are terrified and I'd bet my next month's pay that someone has directly threatened them. Could this be opportunistic rather than accidental?'

Murray had been struck by that. 'Better just hope

another chance doesn't come his way, then,' she'd said and Strang had agreed, with some feeling.

The next morning as she drove down from Edinburgh she was thinking again about how much she'd enjoyed their discussion. She knew she tended to be prickly and far too ready to resent any hint of a slight on her abilities, but she couldn't fault him yesterday. She was starting to get the message that clubbing him round the head with what he'd once described as one of her 'Ta-da!' moments wasn't the way to earn professional respect. Lesson learnt?

The sky was heavy today, with purplish clouds and a light rain falling. The radio was full of dire warnings about what was to come and she'd reluctantly packed spare knickers and T-shirts and her toothbrush. She certainly didn't want to find herself in Edinburgh and cut off from what was going on in Halliburgh; a dismal B&B was a price worth paying.

However, PC Kate Graham appeared as she walked into the police station. 'Livvy! I've been looking out for you. Are you still planning to commute to Edinburgh? The forecast's bad.'

'I'll have to check with the boss, but I think I'll be staying here. It's probably all exaggerated but it's daft to ignore the sort of warnings they're giving.'

'I was going to say, why don't you stay with me? We've got plenty of room and my dad always enjoys visitors. I did a big shop yesterday so the freezer's full – and I got another battery for the camping light in case there's a power cut. Oh, and I got candles in Asda too – the last packet, actually.'

Murray brightened. 'That's really kind! I bet you have a proper fire too, right? Perfect! If there was a cut in Edinburgh I'd just have to die of hypothermia in the dark.'

'That's fine. I'll take you along when you're clocking out. Are you coming to the briefing? Hammond's going to be spelling out the action plan.'

Murray hesitated. 'I'll go and see what the boss wants first. Thanks again, Kate.'

Cassie Trentham's meeting with the organisers of a charity convention wanting to use the Hub for their programme of talks in July had been cancelled, which made sense.

'They were going to be driving over from Glasgow,' she said to Gil Paton. 'Given the forecast it would be asking for trouble. Even if the weather doesn't actually hit until tomorrow, the traffic will be crazy by this afternoon, with everybody getting back home to sit it out. Anyway, I can use the time.'

Gil, though, wasn't pleased. 'It seems a bit panicky, if you ask me. And cancelling at the last moment like this – well, it's frankly disrespectful. And if you were short of time, I could easily have handled it myself.'

Cassie choked back a tart reply. She knew he loved it when he was able to take centre stage and explain, in what Cassie usually felt was unnecessary detail, how everything worked and what would and wouldn't be provided. Usually she'd just have handed it over to him, but this charity was looking for sponsorship as well, which was her business.

Gil resented that. In fact, Gil seemed to resent everything these days. He was getting more and more openly hostile and she was starting to feel it couldn't go on much longer. Once the Writers' Week was over they would need to have a long, serious talk – not that she imagined that was likely to change anything. He was really working his ticket and, in the end, she thought, there would have to be a showdown. She'd pay whatever it took to make him go.

She was just getting back to trying to clear her emails when there was a knock on the door and Richard Sansom appeared.

'Hope I'm not interrupting you? I bumped into Gil downstairs and he said you'd had a meeting cancelled so I thought I'd pop up and see if you could spare me five minutes.'

He was looking a bit agitated. 'Of course,' she said. 'Any excuse for a break. Coffee?'

As she went across to the machine in the corner of the office, Sansom said as he sat down, 'Gil seemed a bit out of sorts. Muttering away quite nastily – you know?'

She pulled a face. 'Oh yes, I know. He's not happy, but then he does make things difficult for himself. So – what can I do for you?'

'It's the situation at Highfield. Is Marta keeping Anna prisoner?'

'*Prisoner?*' Cassie was so startled that she slopped the coffee she was pouring out. 'Why on earth should you think that?'

'It's just that every time I phone to speak to her, Marta says she's unavailable. I even went to the house this morning and some girl answered the buzzer and said no one was available. Do you know what's going on?'

Cassie handed him a mug and sat down. 'If they're saying Anna's unavailable it'll be because she doesn't want to see anyone. I can assure you that she makes all the decisions.'

'Fine, fine. Then I need to see her, OK? I need to know if she's going to appear for the masterclass, and you know she agreed to a brief interview with a carefully vetted journalist. If she's changed her mind and is going to pull up the drawbridge because some moron broke into the house, I have to know, so I can do the damage limitation bit. There's a lot involved here, Cassie, with this being the springboard for the new book.'

He was getting very worked up and she could understand it: this was going to be his first launch and if it was messed up it wasn't Anna who'd get the blame. She said soothingly, 'Look, Anna's an old hand. She has a good understanding of the bottom line and I'm sure it will work out all right. I do believe they were shaken by the housebreaking on top of everything else and she just needs a day or two to recover—'

'But don't you understand! I can't leave it – I need to get to her now! Look, can you take me in? You need to see to it that I can speak to Anna directly.'

Cassie stiffened. He sounded angry and she didn't appreciate being given orders.

'Sorry, Richard. If my mother wants peace and quiet at the moment, I'm not going to barge in. Why don't you discuss it with Marta when she answers the phone? She'll know the best way to deal with it.'

Sansom put his mug down on the table with a bang and got up. He was scowling and his mouth was compressed with temper. 'Fine!' he said. 'I won't waste your time or mine. Thanks for the coffee.'

Cassie stared after him. She'd rather liked Richard, but they always said you couldn't judge a man until you'd seen what he was like when he lost his temper. What a shame! She went back to her emails, wondering what she'd done to have two disgruntled men inflicted on her in one morning.

When DC Livvy Murray arrived, the emergency briefing had started. She found a seat in one corner as DI Hammond took to the stage while Strang stood at the back.

They were preparing for considerable disruption. There was a report from the traffic police on the likely trouble spots, which, by the time they were finished, more or less covered the whole area. Gritters might be out already but they were expecting to fight a losing battle in the next thirty-six hours. Provision had to be made for vulnerable adults and they were advising that schools should close. Commercial helicopters were on stand-by to take out food for farm animals if the situation got worse . . . And on, and on.

Murray had to admit that Hammond was good at this sort of stuff. He was crisp and efficient and he'd got together a crisis team, each with an area of responsibility so that everyone knew who to contact when things, inevitably, went wrong. When he had finished, she saw Strang go forward and say something to him that must be a compliment because Hammond looked gratified.

They were obviously going to be on hand if needed but she had her own commission to work at today. Strang had told her his idea about playing the woman instead of the ball and he was going to retreat to his office after this to talk to JB about whether she felt they should move on Hammond. Her own first job was to find out more about Anna Harper – where did she come from, what did she do before she became famous? Then she had to liaise with Glasgow to check the bookies who had issued the betting slip.

And on her own initiative she decided to try chatting up DS Wilson. She'd been watching him, standing well away from Hammond – noticed, too, that as the meeting broke up and Hammond came across towards him he looked awkward, then made to go.

Murray moved forward as unobtrusively as she could and heard Hammond say, 'Hang on, Grant. Maybe we should have a chat in my office?'

'Oh, sure. A bit later? I've said to DCI Strang that I'll

get him organised for somewhere to stay.' He scuttled off.

Hammond reacted as if he'd been struck in the face without warning. For a fleeting moment, Murray saw a look of alarm cross his face, then as someone came up to ask him a question, he gave his head a little shake and the professional mask slipped back into place.

That briefing had proved Hammond wasn't a stupid man. Had he figured out the threat? And what was he going to do about it? Whatever it was, he'd better make it quick. Strang was at this moment making the case for action right now.

DCI Strang had been marshalling his arguments before he called DCS Jane Borthwick. He wasn't sure she'd be happy about the idea of digging up Anna Harper's past, and he wasn't at all sure that she'd favour taking visible action right away.

He'd great respect for JB but being an intelligent and effective officer didn't get you to the top of the ladder if you weren't political as well. She would balance up the pros and cons of immediate action: would it look as if they were on top of a problem or would it merely highlight a problem that at the moment no one knew you had?

She listened – she was good at that – and then she said she had reservations. He sighed quietly.

'You think this – Wilson? – could be persuaded to give us solid evidence if we did him a deal?'

'I'm getting that impression, boss. He'll be reluctant,

of course, but he's running round me in circles wagging his tail. It'll be quite easy to talk to him on his own and hint that trouble is on the way and I'll be surprised if the pressure doesn't get to him.'

'Then I think that's what we do. Come back to me when you've got what we need from him and I'll authorise a raid. Are you going to lean on Hammond?'

'I don't want to spook him. And frankly I'd prefer to move sooner. We're here officially to look into the Anna Harper case but there isn't much more we can investigate directly there. If he realises we're actually focusing on the drugs situation there won't be anything for a raid to find.'

Borthwick hesitated, then said, 'Anyway, tell me about Harper.'

'Difficult. The housebreaking's neither here nor there. The son's death and the daughter's accident – could be nothing, but Harper and her friend are both terrified and she's concealing something she's determined not to disclose, despite what's happened. So it could be blackmail, but it's certainly not over something trivial.'

She was intrigued, but wary. 'Where do you start with that? For goodness' sake, don't get out the thumbscrews. She's the complainant, after all. The Hammond situation is bad enough but "Police Bully Anna Harper" would be worse.'

'I know, I know. I could only work on her anxiety about their own safety and she brushed that aside. We can sniff around but I can't see there's anything more we can do on the spot.' And he repeated, 'So unless we're going to move quickly on Hammond we can't stay down here.'

There was a long pause and he knew what she was going to say before she said it. She was always risk-averse and this was going to have serious repercussions for the reputation of Police Scotland.

'I hear what you say. Just give it a day or so, then I'll agree if you think you've enough to go on. With the weather that's blowing in, Hammond will have too much to do to think about his own problems.'

He agreed, of course, but he could only hope she was right.

DC Murray settled down with her laptop in the corner of the CID room. There was a lot of coming and going; when DS Wilson came in, she looked up at him with an encouraging smile, but he looked through her as if she wasn't there and went out again. Bummer.

Liaising with Glasgow only took minutes, but when DCI Strang called her to his office, she had little progress to report on Anna Harper.

'There's no trace of her before 1987 when her first book was published but I suppose all that means is she wasn't in the public eye before that. There wasn't Twitter and Facebook in those days – you really could live under the radar.'

Strang considered that. 'Or I suppose that could just be a pen name. Plenty of authors do that. And officially changing your name is just a civil matter with no official record so it'd need a lot of digging to find out what the real name was.

'Let me give it some thought. Anyway, the boss isn't going to bring in the drug squad till we've had a chance to get something out of Wilson.'

She was just opening her mouth to say she was planning to chat him up when he went on, 'The important thing is to let him come of his own accord, thinking that confessing before we've found out anything will give him a bargaining chip. If we approach him, he'll know we're on to them and he could decide it was safer to clam up.'

Phew! She breathed an inward sigh of relief. She could really have screwed up there, just when she was doing so well. 'Right, boss,' she murmured.

'The snow's in our favour, in fact,' he said. 'We haven't much excuse to stay on if we've nothing more we can do on Anna Harper, but it looks as if no one's likely to be going anywhere in the next couple of days. Are you fixed up for somewhere to stay?'

'Kate's offered me a bed, bless her cotton socks. What about you?'

'Wilson's found me a pub. I'll ask him if he'd like a drink later. Though I think we're all going to be busy quite soon. The temperature's risen a little bit and that's always what happens when the snow's on its way.'

'Here we are,' Kate Graham said, leading the way up the garden path with Livvy Murray at her heels. As she opened the front door, she called out, 'Hello, Dad! We've got a visitor.'

It was a pleasant-looking house, very much in the local style, built in pinkish-grey stone with fretwork along the roof and round the little porch. Inside, the hall was spacious, with a settle along the wall under the staircase and a polished oak table with a bowl of spring flowers. Livvy Murray could smell hyacinth and furniture polish and just a faint hint of woodsmoke.

She went through to the comfortable, old-fashioned living room with its deep sofas and armchairs where the fire was burning and the lamps were lit, and an old man with a shock of white hair sat in a wheelchair. He looked round at her beaming and said, 'Well, who have we here?'

She was suddenly struck by a pang of bitter envy. Lucky, lucky Kate – did she realise how lucky she was? She'd have died rather than bring a colleague back to the bleak flat that had been her own home, where there had never been a father at all, and where her mother would more than likely have been drunk amid the squalor of dirty dishes and the smell of unwashed clothes.

She went over to shake hands. 'How do you do, Mr Graham. I'm Livvy.'

'No, no, call me Hugh. My goodness, your hands are cold. Come in to the fire and Kate will find you something to warm you up.'

Kate went over to an old-fashioned cocktail cabinet

in one corner. 'He's only saying that because his tongue's hanging out for a Scotch. What about you, Livvy?'

'Sounds good to me,' she said, sitting down and holding her hands out to the blaze.

'So – to what do we owe this pleasure?' Hugh said. 'I don't get about as much as I used to so it's quite a treat.'

'I stay in Edinburgh but I'm on secondment down here and Kate said I could come here till the storm passes.' She smiled across at her hostess. 'Was she always bringing back homeless kittens as well?'

'Tchah! Nonsense,' Kate said but Hugh nodded. 'You've obviously got the measure of her. Now, tell me about yourself.'

Kate brought over the drinks. 'I'm going to take my glass of wine through to the kitchen and get the supper started. No, Livvy, I'm fine,' she said as Livvy got up. 'You stay and amuse Dad. But be careful – he'll get all your secrets out of you without you even noticing.'

And somehow, with the whisky, the heat of the fire and the warm interest in the man's blue eyes, so like Kate's own, she found herself telling him more about herself than she'd ever told anyone else.

Then Hugh said, 'Now tell me about your boss, this Kelso Strang. Good man, is he? Kate's talked a lot about him. They were great pals when they were at Tulliallan. Sad business, his wife dying like that, but of course, life must go on.'

It was obvious what he was doing, and why. Even

as she gave him all the assurances a careful father could wish, she was struggling with a sense of shock. Kelso was a widower, a still-sorrowing widower, she was sure, and she hadn't for a minute thought of him taking up with his old mate.

Kate came back just at that moment and said sharply, 'Dad! What are you up to? Don't embarrass me.'

As Hugh protested Livvy was thinking, 'Kate? I can't believe that.' And then, to her horror, a thought crossed her mind. She'd been feeling envious of her kind hostess. Surely she couldn't be even the slightest, teeniest bit jealous, as well?

Davy Armstrong's warnings, as he dropped her home, had been even more lurid today, but Cassie held firm. She'd wait and see, she told him. It was raining and she got quite wet just coming in from the car, but it looked as if she wouldn't need to make a final decision before the next morning.

The glass of wine with the weather forecast was becoming a habit. As she fetched it and sat down to listen she pulled a face; she'd better pack a bag tonight and give in. It wouldn't be all bad; if she was at Highfield it might even give her a chance to find out what was going on with her mother.

Cassie had only taken a couple of sips of her wine when there was a knock at the door. She frowned; she hadn't heard a car, but then the TV had been on. She was cautious now, after all the warnings, and she peered

CHAPTER FIFTEEN

'Cassie! Cassie!' She had heard his voice as if it had come from a long way off, as if it was bringing pain with it. She didn't want the pain; she kept her eyes tight shut, trying to stay in the quiet place where it wasn't.

'Come on, snap out of it! It was just a little tap – I didn't hit you that hard, for God's sake!'

Despite her efforts, the pain had arrived in her head now. The pain, and the memory. They had been on her doorstep; there had been a gun – *a gun!* – and then, nothing. And they weren't on her doorstep now; she was lying down. She wanted to open her eyes, to see where she was, but some instinct was telling her to keep them shut. Lie still, ignore the panic building inside, pretend she was still in the quiet place even while her tormented brain was trying to work things out.

'Cassie!' He was yelling now at a painful level,

but she mustn't flinch. She mustn't react, must make herself go limp even when he picked up her arm and dropped it. He groaned. 'Cassie! All I want is the code. You can hear me, can't you? Tell me the code and then everything'll be all right.'

Code? For a moment she wondered if she was dreaming after all, in some spy movie where the code would disarm the nuclear weapon that would annihilate the world.

'The code for Highfield. What is it?'

He had been talking as if he knew she could hear him, but she schooled herself not to react, to breathe regularly. The Highfield code – Marta had told her, but she was useless with numbers; she'd scribbled it down in her diary somewhere, but she couldn't remember what it was. And if she could, she wasn't going to give it to him. Not after what he had done to her.

He didn't say anything more, but Cassie could sense his presence, hear his small, impatient sighs and movements. She began drifting in and out of sleep with no idea of time; she had a dream about a door slamming but she was too tired to open her eyes.

The peaceful little pub of DCI Strang's imagination wasn't anything like this. The bar looked as if it hadn't been renovated in the last twenty years and there was a heavy, beery smell as if the stained floral carpet hadn't been cleaned in that time either. The group of elderly men sitting hunched over at the bar looked as if they'd always been part of the fixtures and fittings.

DS Wilson had escorted him in. 'I'm afraid it's a bit old-fashioned, sir, but Halliburgh's a wee place and there's not too much choice. They say you get a good breakfast here, though.' Then he said to the barman, 'Ron, this is DCI Strang – I told you about him.'

Ron was bald, overweight and supremely uninterested. 'Oh aye.' He turned to pick up a key from the shelf at the back. 'There's only the two rooms. This is the big one at the front. You've your own shower. If you're wanting something to eat, we've pizzas and that.' He indicated a laminated menu that looked like a list of microwaveable food.

Perhaps the gods were punishing him for his churlish behaviour last night. Glumly, Strang thanked him and picked up the key and his bag.

'You all right then, sir?' Wilson asked.

'Thanks very much, Sergeant. I was going to say, do you fancy a drink, or are you hurrying off home?'

He saw calculation on the man's face. Then he said, 'Well, never known to refuse, me! Just a quick one. Thanks very much, sir.'

'Give me a moment to dump my stuff upstairs. I'll set up a slate – order what you want. Mine's a Scotch. Famous Grouse, if they have it.'

He spoke to the barman, then went upstairs. The room was immediately above the bar but so far it didn't look as if he'd be kept awake late into the night by the regulars whooping it up. It was large, certainly, even with the partitioned en suite in one corner, and the saleroom brown furniture – bed, wardrobe and matching chest of drawers – looked slightly at a loss for how to fill the space. He hadn't seen a candlewick bedspread for years and there was an obvious dip in the mattress, but after Afghanistan all he looked for in a bed was that it was flat enough to lie on and when he checked the sheets were clean. Then he rooted about in his bag and took out a tiny voice recorder, activated it and slipped it into his pocket.

When he came downstairs again, Wilson was sitting at a table by the window with the drinks in front of him. 'Is the room OK, sir?' He was looking anxious.

'Oh, it'll do. Cheers! Now, tell me your first name – I can't go on calling you Sergeant. Grant? Fine. Have you been in Halliburgh long?'

Wilson was only too ready to tell him the story of his life, not that there was much to tell. He'd started off in Dundee, was posted down here when he got his sergeant's stripes and like everyone else, he'd resented the downgrading of the local CID.

Strang made soothing noises, then said casually, 'And DI Hammond – how long has he been here?'

'Oh, eighteen months, or so.'

It was a very cautious reply. Strang said, 'Good boss, I guess? I was impressed with his efficiency this morning.'

Again, that calculating look. 'Yes, of course. He's good, but . . .'

'But?'

'Of course I don't really know him, if you see what I mean, except just as a colleague, and the last thing I'd want to be is disloyal, but I don't always quite see eye to eye with him about some things.'

Strang had once seen a dog walking out on to the ice on a pond performing the same manoeuvre, testing each step before it committed. 'I'm interested. What sort of things?'

'Just – oh, I don't know. Maybe I just mean a different sort of emphasis. As a sergeant you can't just tell the DI what he should be doing. You see' – he leant forward, lowering his voice – 'I'm really worried about the drugs problem now. County lines stuff, you know?'

'Yes, I know.'

'Well Steve – DI Hammond – he just sort of doesn't seem to notice. There's kids like a couple we'd in the other day having a knife fight.' He gave Strang a sly look. 'Like your DC Murray said, it'd make you think maybe drugs – she's smart, isn't she? Steve just brushed it off, though. But I'm worried. I don't know why you'd do that.'

'You're not suggesting he's deliberately turning a blind eye?'

'No, no, of course not. Just hasn't thought about it properly, I expect. But . . .'

Strang let the silence develop and Wilson went on, 'Just between ourselves, off the record, I'm a wee bit worried that maybe—no, that's daft. Like you said, Steve's a good officer. I don't believe for a minute he'd get mixed up in anything he shouldn't.'

He looked at his watch, gave an artificial start, then jumped to his feet. 'Oh damn, I didn't realise it was that time. Sorry – I've got to meet someone. Can I buy you the second half tomorrow?'

'I'll look forward to it,' Strang said gravely. 'See you in the morning.'

As Wilson went out, Strang reached into his pocket to switch off the recorder. It wouldn't constitute evidence, but it might serve to remind Wilson of what he'd said already if he decided to clam up. In fact, he was pretty sure this was only the first instalment. The man had clearly gone away convinced he'd laid the groundwork that could put him in the clear if things began to unravel.

Strang finished his drink and glanced around. The bar had an atmosphere of settled gloom – indeed, he half wondered if the old boy in the corner of the bar had actually died but no one had noticed. He'd be better in his own room with the emergency bottle he always packed, but surely even a small place like this must have somewhere better. He certainly wasn't going to settle for a reheated Forfar bridie and beans for his supper and he went out into the street.

It was cold and the dark and sullen sky seemed nearly to be skimming the roofs of the buildings. It had been raining earlier; it had gone off, but the still air was laden with moisture, oppressive, and as Strang walked along the almost-deserted street past darkened shops and office buildings, it gave him that uneasy sense of something waiting to happen. The forecasts had been talking apocalypse for days now, but even allowing for exaggeration it sounded as if the Beast from the East really was going to be nasty.

Further along the street he saw a building with light streaming out from the windows – a pub, with a sign reading The White Hart. It was smart-looking, with gleaming windows and even window boxes with a gallant show of crocuses, and there was a promising-looking menu on the board outside – much more what he had in mind. His spirits rising, he stopped to read it, wondering why on earth Wilson wouldn't have directed him here.

He was pushing open the door when he saw a group of men at the far end of the bar – Wilson, Hammond and another younger man he recognised as one of the uniformed sergeants. So this was why he was to be kept away: Wilson had been trying to stress that his relationship with Hammond was purely professional, and fairly distant at that. Strang backed out, closing the door again quietly.

This was all very well, but he'd be seriously pissed off if it meant his only option for supper was a greasy bridie. However, it seemed that the gods now felt they had punished him enough: further along there was an Indian restaurant, which proved to be every bit as good as the one he usually favoured in Edinburgh.

The snow started falling in the early evening. It hadn't been cold enough for the ground to freeze so at first the little flecks that were almost rain landed and disappeared. The bigger flakes were sleety, falling faster now so the first slippery slushy layer was laid for the bigger ones, the ones like cotton wool balls, to begin the build-up that would create morning rush-hour chaos despite the gritter trucks working through the night.

'For God's sake, woman, are you coming?' Duncan McNaughton shouted. 'We don't want to get stuck here.' He was waiting in the hall of their cottage with the front door standing open and the car was right outside. Already it was getting a covering of snow.

Edna's voice came from upstairs. 'Won't be a minute. I'm just closing the suitcase. Did you turn off the water?'

He gave an impatient sigh. 'Yes, of course I bloody did. Hurry up!'

Edna appeared on the stairs. 'I'm coming. And don't you swear at me, Duncan McNaughton.'

Duncan grabbed the case from her hand and went out to sling it in the car. As she followed him, she looked across the valley to the house up on the hill. 'Well, goodness me! That's that car back there again! You wouldn't think anyone would drive out here now with the weather closing in.'

Locking the front door, he said, 'Maybe they're back just to switch off the water.' He got in and started the car.

Edna was looking over her shoulder as they drove off. 'Oh, the car's got its lights on now so maybe you're right. What time did you tell your sister we'd be coming?'

* * *

Davy Armstrong looked at the clock on the wall in the kitchen and got up from the breakfast table. 'I'd better be a wee bit early this morning,' he said to his wife. 'Folk always get their knickers in a twist when there's snow and the high street'll just be crawling along.'

His wife looked up. 'Will you manage to persuade Cassie to come in from Burnside? The way it's looking she could get cut off there, easily.'

Davy shook his head. 'Don't know. She's thrawn, that one – once she's made up her mind, she digs her toes in.'

'She'd be more likely to come in to stay at Highfield House if you told her you think she'd better just stay where she is,' she pointed out.

He laughed, shrugging on his oilskin jacket. 'Right enough.' He went out.

There was quite a covering on the little road up to Cassie's cottage. It wasn't a problem in the SUV at the moment, but the weather wasn't letting up and there was at least a chance the argument would be made for him when it was impossible to get back later.

Usually Cassie was on the lookout for him and she'd appear at the door before he could turn off the engine. There was no sign of her this morning, so after waiting for a few minutes he gave a tactful toot on the horn. Still no movement.

Maybe she'd slept in. He grabbed his hat from a side pocket and went up the path to the front door to ring the bell. It was only when there was no reply that he began to worry. What if she was ill? He rang the bell again, a longer peal this time, waited, and then he tried the handle.

The door should have been locked. Cassie had said to him just the other day that she'd started locking it, even though it seemed a bit silly. But it opened and he went in, calling her name.

The alarm wasn't set. The lamps were burning in the sitting room and the television was on, showing some breakfast news programme. There was a glass of wine sitting on the coffee table and when he went through to her bedroom, his heart in his mouth, it was obvious the bed hadn't been slept in.

He'd seen her go inside last night, before he drove off. There was no sign of any sort of struggle but the unlocked door, the abandoned glass of wine and the TV left running told a story that left him feeling sick with dismay.

The police – but then perhaps it would be best to report to his boss first. Davy took the key from the inside and locked up. He drove back down the road trying to work out how best to tell Anna, who was already looking like a pale ghost of her former self, what had happened.

DC Murray arrived at the Halliburgh police station just before nine o'clock. PC Graham was technically on the late shift but she was on stand-by if needed and judging by the activity already it was likely that she'd get a summons before very long. There had been a good snow covering overnight; so far transport was running, with only a few local difficulties, but now the snow was steadily falling with a quiet, sinister efficiency.

DCI Strang was in before her, the receptionist told her, and she went to his office.

'Good morning, boss,' she said brightly. 'Was the pub all right?'

He shrugged. 'Not quite what I had in mind, but not to worry. I've had good thinking time. You all right with Kate?'

Murray beamed. 'Oh yes. They've this lovely house and her dad's the old-fashioned kind – a real charmer. She's got everything really nice – like, you know, a wee bunch of flowers in my bedroom and stuff. And then she's a great cook.' She realised she was on the brink of saying, 'She'll make someone a lovely wife,' and stopped herself in time.

He didn't seem much interested. 'Fallen on your feet, then. Couple of things now. I'd a drink with Wilson after work that turned into what he obviously thought was a subtle first move in opening a negotiation to shop Hammond, all the "I'm sure he couldn't" stuff. He said he was in a hurry and he'd buy me the second half tonight, and no doubt he'll work round to saying, "You know I said I was sure he wouldn't but now I've started thinking about it . . ."

'Very keen to stress they were colleagues not friends – which is why, if you please, I've ended up in a dismal, dingy apology for a pub instead of the rather nice one further along the high street, because that's where he goes with his drinking buddy DI Hammond.'

There was no mistaking the bitterness in his tone so she probably shouldn't have laughed, but she couldn't help it. He looked taken aback for a moment, then gave a reluctant grin. 'Oh, laugh if you like, but if you say that worse things happen at sea, I won't be responsible for my actions.

'Now, I'll give you the tape I took of the conversation to listen to – jot down any observations you have. I'm going to go and speak to Hammond – tell him there's still a few checks I need to make on the Harper case, to give us a reason for staying on till Wilson gives me enough to persuade DCS Borthwick to act on the drugs. Meanwhile, I want you to get on to the passport office. I did a bit more research on name change regulations and that's an area that requires disclosure of the original name. They've well-automated systems now with all the border checks, so it should be easy enough to find it once we get round the data protection problems. If necessary, I can pull strings to get someone to lean on them, but you never know – have a friendly chat with the people in Glasgow and they just might cut us a bit of slack. OK?'

'Sure.'

He was frowning; then he said slowly, 'Though I suppose it's possible she just went on using the one she had – it would only have been seen at border checks. Supposing that was what Jason Jackson was actually looking for in her files, what he failed to find. I've been ready to believe what Hammond said, about him just generally looking for some dirt to dig, but maybe there's more to it than that. He's been told he has to report his new address, so I'll get that from Hammond and have another little word with him. And it's a good excuse for hanging around, anyway.'

He stood up and just at that moment the phone rang. He reached across to pick it up. 'Strang here,' he said.

Then Murray watched him as his face turned pale.

At Highfield House the gates swung open as DCI Strang's car approached. There was another car and a badged 4x4 there already and as Strang and DC Murray reached the front door it was opened by PS Johnston.

'DI Hammond and DS Wilson are up with the family, sir. Mum's in a bit of a state.'

'Natural enough,' Strang said grimly. 'Upstairs, did you say?'

'That's right, sir. I'll take you up.'

Knocking the snow off their shoes they followed him upstairs to the great white room that was bathed in a sort of eerie brightness. With the snow settling on the huge windows and blotting out the view, it looked as if they were a fourth wall imprisoning the occupants in icy misery.

As they came in Murray hung back. There was a man in an oilskin jacket standing near the back wall, twisting his hat in his hand and looking as if he wanted the floor to open and swallow him and she went to join him. He gave her a despairing look and she nodded to him with a straight-lipped smile.

Strang had gone forward to where Anna Harper was sitting on one of the sofas near the blank windows. She was ashen-faced, with tears on her cheeks that she hardly seemed to notice. Sitting beside her like a guardian dragon, Marta Morelli was grey and gaunt, but tearless, and she was ranting at Hammond and Wilson who were standing with their backs to the dead fire, doggedly studying their feet. She broke off as Strang appeared and glared at him.

Strang said, 'Ms Harper, I'm very sorry indeed that this should have happened.'

Anna nodded dumbly, but Marta turned on him. 'Sorry! Sorry is no good! We told you we were in danger, and you did nothing, nothing! None of you did anything! What has happened to Cassie?'

'I'm afraid I don't know, as yet,' Strang said quietly. 'I'm not clear about the circumstances.'

Hammond cleared his throat. 'Davy Armstrong here called us to say she wasn't there when he went to pick her up this morning. He said it looked as if she'd been sitting with a glass of wine watching the TV last night and left the house unexpectedly.'

Strang glanced towards him. 'Anything out of place, Mr Armstrong?'

Davy shook his head. 'Just – she wasn't there.'

'No footprints, car tracks?'

'No. It was snowing all night.'

'He's given me the key and I've sent a car up there now,' Hammond said. 'I was going to tell the ladies we'd go and check whether she's got her phone with her, her handbag, that sort of thing. There's no proof as yet that she didn't leave of her own accord.'

The two women stared at him with what Murray could recognise as blank disbelief. Marta hissed, 'Go, then, stupid man! You stay here.' She stabbed her finger at Strang and then, noticing Murray, added, 'And her. She said you would help us.'

Hammond and Wilson were making their way to the door with unseemly haste. Davy Armstrong cast a piteous look at Murray and she murmured, 'I'd just go if I were you,' as she went forward.

Murray joined Strang and they sat down opposite the two women without waiting to be asked. Marta looked annoyed, Murray thought. She'd been expecting them to stand there like naughty children to be harangued.

With tightened lips Marta said, 'So, now you tell us what you are going to do.'

'No, Ms Morelli,' Strang said. 'I'm going to ask you some questions, Ms Harper. Have you spoken to your daughter on the phone since last night?'

Anna had been sitting like a statue, her hands folded in her lap, her eyes wide and tragic. Now she fixed them on his face. 'We . . . we tried this morning, after Davy came. It was just on voicemail. I . . . I haven't spoken to her for a day or two.'

'You don't know if she might have had plans to go out?'

Marta cut in. 'At night, in the snow? What stupidness is this?'

Anna said wearily, 'Marta, please . . .' She put a hand on Marta's arm and she subsided. 'Inspector, I know that isn't the answer and I think you know too. Something has happened to Cassie. You know I was afraid of this—'

'Yes, Ms Harper, I know. And you know that I said there was something you weren't telling me – something you are both deliberately concealing.'

Murray, watching intently, saw that the women didn't look at each other. They so obviously didn't look at each other that it was screamingly obvious that they wanted to.

Neither of them spoke and Strang went on, 'As I said, we have to bear in mind that there has been no sign of a struggle that would suggest violence was involved, so there may be an innocent explanation. We will naturally proceed with the standard investigations we do in circumstances like this, but these will be slow and difficult with so little to go on.

'I'm going to ask you again, Ms Harper. Your daughter, for whatever reason, is missing. What can you tell me that would give us a pointer to where to look for her?'

Anna had been sitting so still that both Murray and Strang jumped when she leapt to her feet and screamed, 'I don't know! I don't know who has done this! If I did, do you really think I wouldn't tell you?' She ran out of the room.

Marta got up, holding her arms wide in a demonstration of outrage. 'Now you see what you have done? She has had enough already, and you bully her!'

'No, Ms Morelli, I did not. I asked her a simple question and I will ask you the same. If you are genuinely worried about the welfare of your friend and her daughter, tell me what it is that you both know and I do not.'

For a moment she held the pose but suddenly her arms fell to her sides and her shoulders slumped, as if she had no more strength to go on fighting. 'I can't help you. Just – the man who came in this house – you let him go. You arrest him again, perhaps, and he tells you why he did it. Then you will know.'

Strang sighed. 'Just one more question – can you tell me if Anna Harper is a pen name?'

Marta went very still. Then she said flatly, 'No. It is her real name.'

Murray didn't believe her and she could see that Strang didn't either. His frustration was obvious, but he said only, 'Thank you, Ms Morelli. I have noted what you said and we'll leave it there for the moment. Perhaps you could talk to Ms Harper and explain to her that I will be coming back to ask the same questions again unless we find her daughter. I'll be arranging for your phone line to be tapped but if anyone does phone please contact me direct. Ms Harper has the number and I will be arranging for the panic button that links to the police station to have another link to my own phone, day or night.'

* * *

Marta Morelli came downstairs and listened. Where was Anna? Had she gone up to her bedroom? She heard the sound of faint sobs coming from the passage below the staircase and went along to the study.

Her friend was crumpled in a chair, her face buried in a cushion, and Marta perched on the arm, patting her back. 'Hush, *cara*, she may still be all right. He may be using this to tell us now what he wants – money, some sort of reparation, acknowledgement. Even if it hurts The Brand—'

Anna sat up, her face blotchy and swollen. 'The Brand! she cried wildly. 'Sod the bloody Brand. What are we to do now, Marta? Are the police still here?'

'No, they have gone for now.' Marta went across to slump in her chair. 'But he is going to come back, to ask us again.' She added, with heavy emphasis, 'He wanted to know if Anna Harper was your real name.'

'Marta! What did you say?'

'I said it was, of course. But whether he believed me . . .' She shrugged.

Anna gave another sob. 'But we can't help him! We don't know ourselves who this is. What we can tell him wouldn't take him any closer. Oh, he could dig into our lives, snare us in the law and I still wouldn't have my daughter back. He wouldn't find the murderer who killed Felix and tried to kill Cassie before.'

Grasping at straws, Marta said. 'There is to be a tap on our phone. If he wants money, they can trace where it comes from.'

'But is it money he wants? Surely he would have demanded it, before now.' She put her hand to her head. 'I think he is going to kill her. We will get another note then – another "payback time". And I think I would die myself.' She paused for a long moment, then she said slowly, 'Marta, do you think it is time we told the police everything? It is bad, but surely not *so* bad . . .'

Marta looked at her. She hadn't cried earlier; she began to cry now with great racking sobs. She'd never cried before in front of Anna, though God knew sometimes she'd wanted to.

'I'm sorry, I'm sorry,' she wept. 'Oh, if it would only be me, I would tell them. I always thought to pay for my sins. But they will never believe it was not you too.'

Anna was staring at her. 'Marta, you're frightening me! What are you talking about?'

She bowed her head, covering her face with her hands. 'I never told you what I did. And I don't know if you can forgive me.'

And then she confessed.

CHAPTER SIXTEEN

DCI Strang slammed the door with vigour as he got back into the car, then swore violently, bringing his clenched fists down on the steering wheel in an agony of frustration. Murray looked at him in surprise. She'd never known him react like that before.

'Sorry,' he said, 'sorry. But this is driving me mad. I can't stand feeling helpless. That woman really cares about her daughter – she's not faking it. Yet there the two of them are, taking refuge in denying that they know who did it. Clearly they don't believe that the big secret – whatever it is – could lead us to him. OK, that may well be true, but they've no idea of our capacity for investigation, if they'd give us somewhere to start. And because they won't trust us, we can only go through the motions of indiscriminate questioning while God knows what is happening to poor, nice Cassie Trentham, and we're just sitting round waiting for the next disaster to happen. And watch this space.'

She hardly knew what to say. He was always so self-controlled that it was a shock to hear such raw anger in his voice. 'I suppose we just go on doing the legwork. Something usually comes to the surface when you dig.'

Strang gave a deep sigh. 'You're right, of course. OK, let's head for the cottage. I feel sure Hammond will have covered the bases – whatever else, he's an effective operator – and after that we can head round to the Foundation and see what they have to say for themselves. Her very self-important deputy isn't too fond of her, for a start, and there may be other undercurrents we don't know about yet.'

Murray was relieved to hear him sounding a little more positive. 'Hope we can get up there all right. The snow's really beginning to lie now.'

But as they reached the side road, they could see that the plough had been along recently, opening a single lane through the piles it had thrown up on either side. 'You can't fault him on efficiency,' Strang said. 'With the current situation, it may be just as well the drug squad didn't dash in and suspend him.'

The snowplough had gone only a short distance beyond Burnside and the cars had parked in the space its turning circle had created. Murray gave an anxious look behind her as Strang manoeuvred the car to face downhill again.

'It's filling up again already,' she said. 'It'll be a real problem if there's a wind.'

'Pity that's the forecast, then.'

He stepped out of the car and walked across. Murray, on the nearside, had to climb out into a snowdrift that came up to her knees and followed him, squelching in her sodden socks and ankle boots, mentally snarling as she brushed off her trousers as best she could. She hadn't thought to bring wellingtons. Didn't have any, in fact. You didn't need them in the city. Good place to be, the city.

At least they'd cleared the path. Hammond opened the door for them and they went in, looking round at the scene he had described earlier. The TV had been switched off, but the glass of wine was still sitting on the coffee table.

'They're checking the house now, sir, but so far there's nothing to suggest any sort of trouble,' he said. 'But she didn't take her handbag or her phone. We've got them bagged up to take in for examination.'

Strang glanced round about. 'Looks as if there's good security and there's a peephole in the door. She must have seen who it was before she opened it. Someone she knew, then – she'd been warned to be careful.'

'Could even have gone with them of her own accord,' Hammond suggested. 'We don't necessarily know she was snatched.'

'Did she take a coat?'

Hammond looked put out, Murray thought, at not having thought of that. As he said defensively, 'Well, ladies have a lot of coats,' she went across to a row of pegs on the wall beside the door. There was a thick weatherproof jacket hanging there; the surface was dry but when she ran her hands over it, it was still damp underneath the sleeves.

'I guess if she had taken a coat, it would have been this one,' she said, and earned herself an approving nod from Strang and a cold look from the inspector.

DS Wilson appeared, carrying a wine bottle in a plastic bag. 'This was in the fridge, sir,' he said to Strang.

It was about half full and it was sealed with a silly, novelty stopper – a pair of stiletto heels. Murray felt a lump in her throat; Cassie, who loved pretty shoes and got jokey presents from her friends – where was she now?

The two uniforms who had been checking the rest of the house came back in, shaking their heads. The small room was getting crowded and Strang said, 'Right. We'll head off to the Foundation now.'

'Yes, sir,' Hammond said. 'We'll be getting back to the station. We can't put everything else on hold, unfortunately, and I don't see what else we can be doing at the moment.'

'You're right there,' Strang said grimly. 'Oh, by the way, did Jason Jackson get in touch with you about where he's staying? I wanted to have another little chat with him.'

Murray looked sharply at Wilson, and saw him twitch. Hammond, though, seemed perfectly calm as he said, 'No. Should he have?'

'Yes, he certainly should,' Strang said tartly. 'Can you find out for me and let me know?'

'Of course, sir. We'll chase him up.'

But as they left, Murray did think that if Jason Jackson had gone to ground, it might be very convenient for anyone who had reason to be nervous about what he might say if pressed.

The kitchen at the Hub had only a skeleton staff this morning, though it was hard to think of Chrissie in quite those terms. With her younger, slimmer colleague Joanne she had struggled up from the town with the morning rolls and she was in a complaining mood.

'Took me all my time to get up that hill,' she muttered. 'And how are we going to get down again, I'd like to know?'

Joanne giggled. 'Just sit on our bums and slide.'

'All right for you,' Chrissie said darkly. 'You're two stone lighter and twenty years younger. And we're going to be on our own by the looks of things. Can't see that Gil Paton struggling in to help.'

'Not a great walker, our Gil, you'd have to say.'

Chrissie snorted. 'Thinks the Good Lord equipped him with wheels instead of feet.'

Still, they had the breakfast ready by the time the first of the writers appeared – Marion Hutton, who brightened when she saw them.

'Oh, well done, ladies! I thought it was going to be do-it-yourself this morning. We'd be fine with coffee and toast, of course, but rolls are an unexpected bonus! Is there anything I can do to help?'

'That's real nice of you,' Chrissie said, 'but we'll warsle through. There'll be no problem now that guy that was aye moaning about something's gone.'

Elena Jankowski arrived, said a polite good morning, took an apple and a cup of coffee and went back upstairs. Marion sat down to her own breakfast, looking guilty. If she was a real writer she too would be hurrying back to her desk, instead of lingering in the hope of something to distract her. Fortunately, Mick McNab appeared and was happy to sit and exclaim about the Beast from the East, which was making a start on living up to its media billing.

It was much later when Sascha came downstairs. They'd cleared away the breakfast and the others were back at their desks by the time she appeared, and Marion jumped up in concern.

'Oh dear! Joanne has just cleared away, but I'm sure—'

'Don't bother,' Sascha said curtly. 'Coffee's fine.'

Marion withdrew, hurt. Mick looked up. 'Dearie me, someone got out of bed on the wrong side this morning.'

Saschia sent him a withering look. She wasn't looking at her best today, as if she hadn't slept well. With her coffee mug in hand, she looked round about her.

'Where's Gil?' she demanded of no one in particular.

'He isn't in yet,' Marion said.

'You may not have noticed – there's a bit of that weather stuff out there,' Mick added.

Sascha turned on him. 'Yes, I had noticed, funnily enough. What I want to know is, what does this mean for us? Will Anna Harper use this as an excuse for not doing her masterclass? That was the whole point of coming here – I'll be absolutely furious if it's cancelled. I've taken a week off work for this.'

Mick shrugged and went back to his work. Marion said soothingly, 'I'm sure she'll try, Sascha, but it's getting worse all the time.'

Sascha scowled. 'Gil should be here, keeping us in the picture. What's his phone number?'

Marion was looking blank when Gil himself appeared along the corridor from the Foundation reception hall. He was wearing a cagoule and leaving puddles on the floor as he stamped the snow off his boots.

'About time!' Sascha said aggressively. 'We all feel entitled to know what's going to happen.'

'Well, not all,' Marion bleated, while Gil gave Sascha a dirty look.

'Do you have the slightest idea what it's like out there? It took me half an hour to dig out the car and then it wasn't keen to start. You're lucky I've got a four-wheel drive or I wouldn't be here by now.'

'So what about Anna's masterclass?'

Gil shrugged. 'Have to see what the weather's doing by then, I suppose.'

Sascha had just embarked on her argument for getting Anna to do it whatever the weather, when Gil's phone buzzed.

'OK, I'll be right there.' He turned and said over his shoulder, 'That's the police back again,' as he went towards the corridor.

Cassie Trentham had no idea what time it was. Her head hurt, she still felt sick when she sat up and she had drifted to and fro between sleep and waking for what seemed like forever. She had no watch and the unvarying light of a light bulb hanging in the middle of the ceiling gave her no clue.

The room, a bedroom perhaps, had been ruthlessly stripped down – bare, damp-stained white walls and its window blocked by hardwood panels. There was nothing in it apart from the metal-framed fold-up bed she was lying on, a chemical toilet in the far corner, a small wooden table with a big bottle of water on it and a couple of rickety chairs.

Cassie tried to work out what that meant, but somehow with her poor sore head she couldn't think clearly. She eased herself to her feet and stood waiting for the dizziness to pass before she went to try the door – locked, of course. She went to the window and tried to get some purchase on the hardboard, but it was nailed down all round. There was nothing at all in the room that she could use as a lever. Her tongue felt thick in her mouth and she tipped up the bottle to drink from it, wincing as icy water splashed down her neck

She listened, straining her ears, but could hear nothing; it was deathly still. And it was bitterly, bitterly cold. At least there was a thick duvet on the bed and it was still warm from her body so she crept back under it and pulled it up over her head as she was swept by waves of panic.

She only realised she had gone to sleep again when the sound of the door opening woke her with a start. He was there, shutting the door behind him as she struggled to sit up. There was snow melting on his jacket.

She could almost smell his tension and his voice was rough as he said, 'That's better, Cassie. Now we can talk business. I'm in a hurry, so just get on with it. What's the new code for Highfield?'

She ignored that. 'Why have you kidnapped me? What are you going to do to me?'

His mouth tightened. 'We'll talk about that later. Code, Cassie.'

She didn't know it. She could remember Marta telling her, remember scribbling it somewhere – her pocket diary, probably? – reckoning she probably wouldn't need it anyway, not being in the habit of making unannounced visits. Should she tell him that, or lie? If only her head didn't feel so muzzy, she might be able to work out which was best. Then it came to her: if she said she knew but wouldn't tell him he would most likely hit her, and she didn't think she could bear that at the moment.

'Come on! I haven't time to waste.' He was getting angry. 'Code?'

'I-I can't remember just now,' Cassie said, putting

a hand to her head. 'Maybe I might, later, when I'm feeling better.'

His eyes were as cold as stones but again she could sense his anxiety. 'You've one more chance. Keep thinking. I'll come back and you can tell me then. Or else.'

'Or else – what? And what do you want it for, anyway?' As if she didn't know!

He made no attempt to answer, just turned his back and walked out. A gust of cold air swept in as the door was shut, and she heard the key turned in the lock and then the sound of a car driving away.

Cassie huddled into a ball under the duvet, too deeply scared even for tears. He was going to kill her, either before or after he killed her mother, depending on whether or not he could get into Highfield, and there was nothing she could do.

Surely they must be looking for her by now? Davy would have raised the alarm first thing – only when was that? Had she been here a day? Two days – more? And she kept drifting off, so she didn't even know now how long it was since he left.

DCI Strang and DC Murray were waiting by the desk where Cassie Trentham's secretary Jess was acting as receptionist. 'It's just me today – none of the other staff has managed to get in, except a couple of ladies in the kitchen,' she explained. 'But Gil Paton's just made it, so I've buzzed him – oh, here he is.'

Observing him approach, Strang could see the

defensive set of his shoulders even before the man reached them.

'So,' he said belligerently, 'what are you wanting this time?'

'Just one or two questions, sir, if you don't mind.'

'Doesn't matter if I do, does it?'

Was this carrying the fight to the enemy before war had been declared? 'I suppose not, sir. But I'll be wanting to speak to everyone anyway,' Strang said. 'Have either of you spoken to Ms Trentham since last night?'

Jess had been looking embarrassed by Gil's behaviour and she was quick to say, 'No, I haven't. We spoke before she left last night and she did say she might have to stay at Highfield tonight if it was getting any worse, but she certainly intended to be in this morning.'

'Haven't seen her since yesterday morning,' Gil said. 'Why – can't you find her?'

'She isn't at her house and we're anxious to trace her whereabouts,' Strang said carefully.

Gil seemed unmoved. 'Well, she's not here. As you can see. And being told what her plans are isn't for the likes of me. Her mother probably knows. Or *Marta* – she knows everything.'

Jess looked astonished at the bitterness in Gil's tone. 'Do you mean that she's actually *missing*?' she said.

Strang was just saying, 'We're not prepared to assume that at this stage but it would be helpful if anyone had any information they could help us with,' when he heard the tap-tap of heels and Sascha came hurrying along the corridor from the Hub. His heart sank; if his suspicions were correct, this was a story that was going to break any minute now. Caught up in the morning's problems he hadn't contacted JB and she had to be forewarned. The sooner they got out of here, the better.

'Constable, please could you take Mr Paton over there just to run through his movements last night and today,' he said to Murray. 'Good morning, Ms Silverton.'

Sascha's eyes were gleaming. 'Did you say "missing", Jess? Is someone missing, Inspector?'

'We're trying to establish the present whereabouts of Ms Trentham. Have you had any contact with her since last night?'

She brushed the question aside. 'Me? No. But Inspector, I have some questions I want to ask you about what has happened. Do you believe she has been abducted? I'm a journalist.'

'That isn't a surprise,' he said drily. 'But you're only a journalist if you have a press card.'

Sascha's face flushed. 'Well, I'll get one when I break this story.'

'If you say so. Until then, you're a member of the public, not the press. What did you do last night and this morning?'

Her big brown eyes filled with tears. 'I need this story! All I want is—'

'Ms Silverton – last night?'

For a moment she looked as if she was going to ignore him. Then she said sulkily, 'I walked into town to see if I could persuade Richard Sansom to have supper with me. I'm sure he knows a lot more about Anna Harper than he's told me so far and I'm sure I could have got more out of him if I'd another chance. But he wasn't there and now it looks as if Anna Harper won't do her masterclass either, and I've wasted time and money to come here . . .' She brought out a tissue and dabbed her eyes.

'And this morning?'

'Got up, about twenty minutes ago. That's it.'

Jess said coldly, 'It's been something of an abuse of hospitality, hasn't it, Sascha? Odd that you didn't mention your plans when you applied. If it's helpful, Chief Inspector, yesterday evening I went home to my family and left them this morning to come in here. Is . . . is Cassie in trouble?'

'We hope not,' Strang said. 'Thank you for that. The other writers – in the Hub? Right.'

Her eyes narrowed, Sascha stared after him as he went through and Murray joined him, leaving Gil sitting on one of the cream leather sofas. 'Swears he drove home last night, drove here this morning,' she muttered. 'Doesn't seem much bothered about Cassie.'

He paused. 'And?'

'Don't know. So full of his own grievances it would be hard to say.'

Mick McNab was cooperative but unhelpful. Given the free food and booze, along with the weather, he hadn't left the Hub since he arrived. Marion Hutton was the same, though she laid less emphasis on the booze and more on the worry about Cassie. Elena Jankowski, whose first novel Strang had seen reviewed but hadn't read, was patently disconnected from the world outside the four walls of her room.

Even in that short time the snow was noticeably deeper when they came out of the Foundation, but there was still enough traffic to keep the road passable.

'I'll have to call the boss,' Strang said. 'I'd like to have had some minor progress to report before I broke the news to her, but the wretched Silverton is going to bring the roof in.'

Murray fully shared in the general police antipathy to the ladies and gentlemen of the media, but she said, 'I was a bit sorry for her, mind. She'd obviously pinned a lot on this. I'd guess she's pretty skint.'

Strang gave a short laugh. 'Don't waste your sympathy! She'll be on the phone to the *Scottish Sun* this very minute. Look, I'm going back to the station. I want to put pressure on Hammond to find Jackson – he's a niggle at the back of my mind. I'll let you off at the White Hart and you can check up on Richard Sansom. OK?'

'Sure, boss.'

He pulled up and she got out, leaving him to drive on composing in his head the best way to present a very unpalatable report to Detective Chief Superintendent Jane Borthwick.

Richard Sansom wasn't at the White Hart. The woman behind the bar acted as receptionist as well and she was able to tell Murray that though she wasn't sure when he'd left the day before, he'd asked for his room to be kept for him.

'Do you know where he's gone?' Murray asked.

'No, he's been to and fro a lot. Nice gentleman – well set-up, you know? He said he had bookshops to visit and he'd some other contacts to see as well – all this Anna Harper stuff, I suppose. He said he'd be back tonight but with all this snow I can't see it.'

'Right,' Murray said thoughtfully. 'Don't have his phone number, do you?'

'No, sorry.'

'When he gets back, ask him to call this number.' Murray gave her a card, then paused on her way out. It was going to be a long walk along the snowy street to get to the police station and she was entitled to a break. 'Could you do me a cappuccino? And a biscuit or something?'

'Sure. Doughnut?'

'Oh yes!' The word she was looking for was 'No' but somehow it didn't come out that way. She took a table by the window and sat deep in thought.

She'd been really gratified that Strang had left her to interview Gil Paton, who had after all been in pole position as chief suspect when they arrived. He was treating her seriously at last and she was determined to prove her worth.

Gil, in her estimation, wasn't a starter. He was just too feeble, whinging and bleating away about unfairness, and quite frankly she couldn't see him having the guts to kidnap Cassie – plunging a knife into her and running away possibly, but not this. She hadn't met Richard Sansom yet, but 'well set-up' sounded more plausible.

And if you were planning to snatch Cassie, you'd have to prepare somewhere to put her. So what had Sansom been doing, these past few days? Unspecific visits were a perfect excuse. And, of course, Cassie would have had no hesitation in opening the door when she looked through her peephole. He was shaping up into a very promising suspect.

Strang had said something about Jackson too, but she didn't really go for that. He'd had his chance when he got into the house and he hadn't taken it, so why would he be a threat now?

No, there was definitely more mileage in Richard Sansom. Of course, Anna Harper must have his number – and now she thought about it, she had the Highfield number on her own phone. But when she dialled it and asked to speak to Ms Harper or Ms Morelli, a woman took her name and request, then came back and said they didn't have it. Foiled. The doughnut was delicious, though.

She'd better make the trek back to the station and get on to Anna Harper's publishers for the phone number and background checks. Strang would be busy sorting out the press statement with DCS Borthwick so she'd have time to build up a really professional case to present to him.

Strang was dead against looking for a motive before you got in the evidence, but with a kidnapping it was pretty obvious – money. No one would be more aware of the extent of the Harper fortune than Sansom. Not only that, he was in a good position to find out about Anna's backstory.

Yes, Murray was pretty sure she was on the right track as she licked the sugar off her lips and set out along the pavement, a muddy mess of slush. There weren't a lot of people about and the snow was still falling, infuriating fluffy flakes that kept clinging to her eyelashes. And her nose, come to that. Her favourite things – not!

Now she could definitely feel a breeze – just a slight one. So far. They'd been forecasting wind and if it really got up, there would be chaos.

Driving back from Brookside, DS Wilson couldn't quite control the tremor in his voice when he said to DI Hammond, 'What's Strang wanting to interview Jason about?'

Hammond didn't look at him. 'Crossing "t"s and dotting "i"s, I expect. That would be par for the course.'

'Do you know where he is?'

'Yes. But Strang doesn't, which is the main thing. And we'll keep it that way. Our enquiries are going to draw a blank – right?'

'Right,' Wilson echoed. 'And the Trentham business?'

Hammond shrugged. 'I'll hand in the bag and the laptop, but nothing's going to happen until all this blows through. You can check what's come in while we've been away and I'll check up with Traffic. And for God's sake don't start hyperventilating about Jason – everything's under control. OK?'

'Sure,' Wilson said, as easily as he could. He didn't believe it, though. He couldn't see DCI Strang just being fobbed off, and worse, he didn't think Hammond believed it either. He was whistling in the dark and there was a muscle jumping in his cheek. They were in serious trouble.

Tonight, when Wilson had the promised drink with Strang, he was going to have to pluck up courage and tell him the lot, if he wasn't to go down as well.

CHAPTER SEVENTEEN

DCI Strang had taken the precaution of working out a press statement before he phoned DCS Borthwick. An instructor at Tulliallan had told them once that if you had to present a superior officer with a problem, offering a solution – or anything that looked like a solution – at the same time would do wonders for your reputation. It was sound advice; JB was worried certainly, but she was definitely grateful to have something ready when the 'Famous Author's Daughter Missing' headline hit.

'We'll have a bit of respite, anyway, with the present conditions,' she said. 'How is it with you? The city's about at a standstill here and all the schools are closed. There's trouble with the trains too.'

'They seem a bit more robust about it down here, but I can hear the wind now and there's so much lying that if it brews up a gale we'll be immobilised. Even as it is, we can't do the usual thing of checking the few neighbours Cassie Trentham has – that road will be completely blocked by now.'

Borthwick said, 'I'm very concerned about the poor girl and I can't begin to imagine what her mother must be feeling. No ransom demand so far?'

'No. We've got a tap on their line and I've instructed that it's to come direct to me if there's any development. I have the clear impression they don't expect one and would be relieved if one came. They seem to believe quite genuinely that Anna's son was murdered and Cassie only escaped death by accident, but they still won't come clean about whatever it is that's haunting them.

'We have to assume that she's in mortal danger. I loathe feeling helpless while some evil bastard plays games, but there's little more we can do at the moment.' He gave a heavy sigh. 'Maybe Anna and her rather sinister friend will see it differently if there's still no news by tonight.'

'Keep me posted,' she said and rang off.

Strang sat back in his chair. He had been racking his brains, but they were stuck unless Murray came in with useful information about Sansom. He had to admit she was earning her keep in this operation when they were having to investigate while keeping the local force at arm's length, and her judgement was improving too, provided she didn't get seduced by a theory and go hurtling off at a tangent.

He emailed the press statement through to the desk and gave instructions that this was the only information to be given to the press and that no calls from them were to be put through to him. He buzzed Hammond to chase him up about Jason Jackson's address but had no joy there.

Could Jackson's disappearance be significant? On the face of it, this could be a simple precaution – go to earth, in Glasgow, probably, and keep out of the way until whatever fuss there was had died down and then the old, sordid business could creep back again, as it always did. On the other hand—

There was a tap on the door and Murray put her head round it. 'Are you busy?'

'Sadly, no. Come in. How did you get on with Sansom?'

She sat down opposite him. 'Not at all. He's missing too.'

She had loaded the remark with heavy significance and his eyebrows rose. 'Missing missing, or just not there missing?'

'Oh, we don't know yet, of course. He left sometime yesterday and told the hotel he'd be away last night but planned to be back again today. But it's funny it was just when Cassie disappeared, right? And if this is all about dirt on Anna, he'd be quite likely to know, wouldn't he? That was Sascha Silverton's take on it. And there's so much money, he could get the kind of payoff that would let him vanish to the Caribbean for the rest of his life.'

Strang recognised the signs of a pet theory. 'Don't you think there would have been a ransom demand, if that was what it was all about?' he said gently. 'And I doubt if famous authors make a habit of disclosing their most sensitive secrets to their PR man.'

Murray turned crimson. 'You think I'm running away with it, don't you?'

'Well, yes. Admittedly, when we have so little to go on and we're being pinned down and useless, it's tempting to try to reason back from the farther end. But all we can say with any certainty right now is that the person who came to the door wasn't a stranger. Cassie was aware she was in danger and she wouldn't have let in someone she didn't know. All right, she's lived in Halliburgh all her life and she knows lots of people, but at the moment, on the basis of what her mother believes, we're narrowing the field to those who have a direct connection to the Harper Brand, as they call it.

'But that's about it. Not much. Still, what we can do is focus more on the county lines problem – that's rather got eclipsed today. I'm hoping that stressing that I want to talk to Jackson will have heaped a bit more pressure on Wilson. I have to say I'm counting on a confessional session with him tonight.'

Murray looked out of the window. 'It's almost dark already,' she said, 'but I think the snow's more or less stopped.'

Strang turned to look. 'That's something. But listen to the wind.' There was a sudden gust even as he spoke and a flurry of fallen snow puffed up. 'That'll mean trouble. I wonder how Traffic's managing.'

'Rather them than me,' she was saying when her

phone rang. She took it out and looked at the number. 'Not recognised.'

'Take it, anyway.'

He listened as she said, 'Thanks for getting back to me,' then mouthed 'Sansom' to him.

It was a brief call. 'Well?' he said.

'He's still away. He called the hotel and they gave him my number. He says he's been over in Dundee seeing a buyer, but he was phoning to say he couldn't get back because of the weather. So he's still away.'

Strang looked at her provocatively. 'And what does that tell us?'

Murray gave him a demure smile. 'Nothing. We have to keep an open mind. As yet.'

Anna Harper was pretending to be asleep. After an hour of tears and regrets, once she had managed to assure Marta that whatever happened they were standing together – at least she hoped she had – there was nothing more to say and anyway she felt more comfortable with her swollen eyes shut.

Marta was slumped in the chair opposite, her hand under her cheek as she lay against a cushion. Risking a glance at her under her lashes, Anna reckoned she really was sleeping. Breaking so many years of silence had unleashed an emotional storm that had totally drained them both.

Not that Marta regretted what she had done; far from it. They'd been in daily contact all those years and she'd believed that they had shared the same views on most things; it was only now she realised that those views had been hers, not Marta's. A gulf had opened between them and she had to sort out her thinking. Marta was still her cherished friend. She owed her and she needed her too. If something happened to Cassie—the tears welled up again and she had to stifle a sob in case it woke Marta.

She couldn't blame her for being what she was born to be. In the grand scheme of morality her own sin was the greater. She had made a bad choice because of the gift that drove her – and sometimes she felt that she had never had a choice at all. On the odd occasion when she had reread one of her books, she found herself saying, 'Did I really write that?' But she hadn't regretted what she had done, either – not until now. Now her guilt was like a hard stone lodged in her chest.

She'd never been the maternal sort; she had found her children disorderly, individualistic, not easily directed in the way her other creations were, and she was eternally grateful to Marta for having made up for her deficiencies in that area.

Only she hadn't, had she? No one could. Anna's children had suffered from the lack of their mother; she had lost her son and now she might lose her daughter too.

What was he doing to Cassie, right now? Behind her closed eyelids terrible pictures flashed one after the other – Cassie pleading, hurt, raped even – or dead? She was going to be sick. Abandoning pretence, she leapt up and ran out of the room.

Marta, exhausted, slept on.

PC Kate Graham came into the main CID room, where DS Wilson was scowling over the big Ordnance Survey map fixed to the wall. At his side PS Johnston was pointing to one of the trunk roads.

'They've got a major problem there. Looks as if they're going to have to set up barriers across the blockage to stop the mental giants with a Discovery who think they can bulldoze through from getting stuck and then expect us to bail them out. It's blowing a gale out there now.'

'Total nightmare,' Wilson said heavily. 'OK, tell them to go ahead. Don't see what else they can do.' Johnston nodded and set off and then he noticed Graham. 'Want something, Kate?' He sounded irritable.

'I was really looking for DI Hammond,' she said. 'Do you know where he is? I got a call from one of the crews asking if they still need to keep the B6453 open.'

'The B6453? I shouldn't think so. We need every crew we've got on the major roads and that's a losing battle. We've got a dozen brain-dead members of the public trapped in their cars on the outskirts of the town – Steve's out there dealing with them now before they all start phoning their MPs.'

'So I'll tell them that, shall I?'

'Yeah, that's fine.'

'So where should they go instead?'

'Oh, for God's sake, how should I know?' he snapped.

Graham stood her ground. 'Sorry, sir. But I don't know who's in charge of this when DI Hammond's out, and the crews are waiting to be told.'

Wilson groaned. 'Oh, right, right, I suppose they are. It's just I've got far too much on my plate.'

He was losing it – twitching, even. They were treating this as a major emergency; the phone lines were jammed with frantic calls and admittedly this storm was a serious weather event, but even so, they were used to snow disruption in these parts and it surely wasn't enough reason for Wilson to go to pieces. It wouldn't help anything.

'Shall I ask them where they think they should go?' she suggested gently. 'They know the situation on the ground, after all.'

He jumped at the suggestion. 'Good idea. Just get them off my back. I'm going to be stuck here all night unless the ploughs abandon the struggle. Sooner the better.'

Just as Graham was leaving, the door opened and DCI Strang came in. He smiled at Kate and said to Wilson, 'How's it going? You don't look too happy.'

The man's face was so pale it was almost grey. 'It's chaos out there – chaos! They've never seen anything like it. The forecast's getting worse by the minute.'

'Anything I can do?' Strang offered.

'Thanks, but not really, sir.' He had a prominent Adam's apple; Graham noticed it bounce up and down as he gave a gulp and went on, 'About that drink, sir—'

Strang laughed. 'Not to worry. I guess you'll be pretty tied up here.'

'Yes, but I really wanted a chat with you, sir.' Was that a tone of desperation in his voice, Graham wondered? It was intriguing – but she really had no business still to be listening.

She was going to slip away just as Wilson's phone rang. With a muttered apology he listened, then said, 'I'll be right there.' He turned to Strang. 'Sorry, sir – I'm needed downstairs. Can we make it tomorrow?'

'Sure,' Strang said easily. As the door shut, he said to Graham, 'Well, what did you make of that, Kate?'

She pulled a face. 'There was a snowplough being diverted to clear one of the minor roads instead of trying to keep the main road clear and he didn't know what to do. He's completely losing it. But it sounds as if you're being cast in the role of Father Confessor.'

'That's what I'm hoping. He's giving all the signs. It's just painfully frustrating that there's so little we can do right at the moment. Well, I suppose I might as well go back to the pub. Are you having to stay on duty?'

'No. I'm off more or less now. Livvy's gone back to my house already.' She hesitated. 'By the way, she told me where you were staying – it's awful, that place! If you'd like to come to us for supper instead, I've got plenty for four. Plenty for several days, to be honest – I'm well used to stocking up in winter.'

Strang laughed. 'Let's hope it won't come to that! But

that's very kind, if you're sure. Your cooking got a terrific write-up from Livvy.'

She went pink. 'Oh dear – now you'll have raised expectations. Just very old-fashioned stuff – my father hasn't really caught up with the vegan revolution.'

'Sensible man. I'll go back to fetch my coat and then maybe you could sherpa me across. It's looking like a white-out now.'

DC Livvy Murray was installed already in front of the fire in the Grahams' sitting room with a glass of whisky in her hand. Even traversing the relatively short distance from the police station had proved something of an ordeal. Unlike the delicate flakes that she had muttered about before, what was viciously stinging her face now had fallen earlier and was being whipped up by a merciless and rising wind. The gritting that had been done was now no more than a blurred stain of salt and sand and no one was about to tread the snow to slush on the pavements. It was piling high against walls and into doorways and turning the cars into snowy mounds.

When she reached the Grahams' house she could see that someone – Hugh's carer, perhaps? – had made an earlier attempt at clearing a path but it was filling in again already. In the vestibule she took off her shoes, thickened into wedgies with impacted snow, and looked mournfully at the saltwater stains on her ankle boots from the gritting mixture. They'd been an investment, she had told herself at the time, but it was a market where the bottom had fallen out. The uppers weren't looking good, either.

Hugh Graham had been pleased to see her. 'Come on in, Livvy! Pull the chair right up to the fire – you look absolutely perished. What you need is a drink – you know where to get it.'

'You're not fooling me, Hugh – that's just an excuse. You're only pleased to see me because it's a good half-hour before the usual time. I'm sure Kate would say we should wait till she gets back.'

'Ah, but as Kate's father, I can overrule her. You look to me like a woman badly in need of a medicinal Scotch. What's it like out there?'

Livvy shook her head at him as she went to oblige. 'You're a bad influence! It is mind-blowing, though – like one of these wildlife films about the Arctic. You'd think there could maybe be a polar bear behind one of the parked cars that look like icebergs.'

She gave him a report on the situation round about, then said, 'Now, I've got instructions for you from Kate. She's going to see if Kelso Strang would like to come over for supper. He's staying at The Sun – apparently it's pants—'

'Indeed it is. Poor man, poor man!' Hugh was looking delighted. 'Of course she should bring him, an old friend like that. Maybe he'd prefer to stay here – we've another bedroom . . .'

Livvy gave him a warning look. 'Now that's exactly

what Kate's afraid of. If he comes, it's no big deal, right? He's a senior colleague, that's all.'

'Of course, of course, but they were really good pals, and with him being a widower now . . .'

'Are you really that desperate to get rid of your daughter?' she said teasingly. 'Kate's not on the hunt for a man, you know.'

To her horror, Hugh's eyes filled with tears. 'Oh, I'm not saying she is. It's just she doesn't get to meet folk down here and she's getting older. She gave up what would have been a good career to look after her mum and then when she might have had a chance to move on I became an old crock and she won't leave me, even though I've told her she should.'

Livvy was dismayed. 'Oh dear, I'm sorry I joked about it. But to be honest, I don't reckon she minds. This is her home, she's got friends here and you're very good company. We all make our own decisions, and this is hers – you have to respect that.'

'It's the guilt, that she's given up her life for her mother and me. If she could just find the right guy . . .'

Livvy shook her head at him. 'All I can do is repeat what Kate told me to tell you – that if you say anything to Kelso that makes her feel embarrassed, it'll be a very long time before you see another apple crumble.'

At least that made him smile. 'She's bringing out the big guns, is she? I tell you what, I'll be thoroughly rude to the bloke, shall I?'

'Don't think you could be, actually. You'd find yourself

slipping into being nice after three minutes. Oh, I think I hear someone now.' She got up to look out of the window. 'Yes, that's them both. I'll go and open the door.'

He hadn't really thought it through. Faced with the prospect of the cheerless pub on an evening like this, when experience told Kelso that a power cut might well be on the cards, supper at the Grahams' house as described by Livvy Murray sounded very tempting. It was only when Kate's father greeted him with a warm handshake and, 'Come away in – I've heard a lot about you,' that he remembered his sister's reaction when he'd brought Kate back to his house. There was a very similar look on Hugh Graham's face.

'Oh dear,' he said lightly, 'I hate to think what that might be. Kate knows where all the bodies are buried.'

'Oh, we always brought her up not to be a clype. I think your secrets are safe enough with her. What happens in Tulliallan stays in Tulliallan, is that right?'

'Yes, Dad.' There was a warning note in Kate's voice. 'It was all a very long time ago.'

'Of course, of course,' Hugh said hastily, then with a rapid change of subject, 'Now tell me, is there any news about this poor girl?'

'I'm afraid not. We're trapped by the weather, of course, and from the latest reports it may even be worse by the morning.'

The conversation became more general. Kate's cooking lived up to its billing with a cracking fish pie and the company was good. He'd never seen Livvy in a relaxed situation like this and she was very funny, playing off Hugh who was relishing the craic.

He'd been on tenterhooks all evening, though, and when his phone rang, he jumped, as did they all. He got up and said, 'Sorry. I'll have to take this.'

'There's the study next door,' Kate said, and he went out. You could always hope that this would be the call that said they'd found Cassie and that she was fine, even if you really knew it wouldn't be.

It was the desk at the police station. 'Will you speak to Jason Jackson, sir? He said you'd want to talk to him because it was very important and he wouldn't talk to anyone else.'

'Fine,' he said. 'Jackson? Strang here. You wanted to speak to me?'

'Yes,' Jackson said. He sounded agitated. 'Look, I've just heard about Cassie Trentham and knowing the way your minds work I reckoned I'd be right at the head of the suspects list. I just wanted to tell you that I know absolutely nothing about this. I'm in Glasgow, dossing down with friends here and we've been together all of last night and this morning – I've got four witnesses.'

'Sounds like a powerful alibi. At least, on the face of it, it does, depending on the company you're keeping. Someone will come round to take a statement. Where are you staying? We should know – I instructed you to keep us up to date with your movements.'

'I did!' Jackson sounded aggrieved. 'The minute I

knew I could stay here, I clocked in with DI Hammond.'

He didn't want to scare him off. 'Did you? Oh, right. Tell the desk again now, will you? Thanks.'

Even if Wilson didn't come across with the goods it was getting to be time they got moving on Hammond. If he knew to lie about Jackson's whereabouts, he knew they were on to him and Strang didn't want him to slip through their fingers and disappear. Yet again, he cursed the weather as he went back to the brightly lit room and the ring of interested faces.

He shook his head. 'Routine stuff. Anyway, it's time I set out on the trek to the pub. I may be some time . . .'

In a way, it had been easier when she was still concussed, as she now realised she had been. Cassie wasn't so sleepy now and there was nothing she could do in this bleak prison to distract herself from the terrors that prowled around her. She fought them off – with poems she remembered, songs that she sang as loudly as she could, marching up and down swinging her arms to generate some heat, but when her guard slipped they were back at her throat, shortening her breath into panic attacks. She'd cried a bit, but it didn't help. It just made her feel worse and she sagged into a sort of listless grey nothingness.

She was hungry now too, hungry and cold. She'd set the bottle of water on the floor beside her so that she didn't squander the precious heat under the duvet when she wanted a drink – and she would have to ration it. There was no way of knowing how long she'd been here and even less of knowing how long she would be here. She was afraid of him, but perhaps she was more afraid that he would never come back and she would be left to starve to death. How could anyone find her?

Now she could hear the wind howling and roaring like some savage animal and she remembered – the Beast from the East, of course. Perhaps he couldn't get here anyway, even if he wanted to.

Then she heard a sound – the bang of a car door. She sat bolt upright, wrapping the duvet round her as her teeth chattered partly with cold and partly with fear. A moment later, there was a sound outside – he was stamping his feet and swearing. He was angry – with the weather, with her? What would he do?

He unlocked the door and opened it, a dark silhouette with snow on his coat and his boots. A cold breath came in with him and in her fevered thoughts it seemed unearthly, like the chill they say accompanies an apparition.

Before he could say anything, she cried, 'What are you going to do to me?'

It was as if she hadn't spoken. 'The code, Cassie,' he said. 'I'm in a hurry. Time's up.'

CHAPTER EIGHTEEN

Kelso Strang couldn't get to sleep. It was unusual for him; his years in the army had taught him not to waste the precious resource of time available for sleeping, and not to be fussy about where or what on. Admittedly The Sun's mattress was the kind that had received unremitting punishment over the last twenty years at least, but that wasn't what was making him toss, turn and try to beat the lumpy pillows into a more user-friendly shape.

Where was Cassie tonight? He couldn't get her out of his mind. Was she still alive, even? Was there something more he could have done today? And there was, too, something that was niggling at him, some connection that had prompted a brief thought, which he couldn't pin down now. He wasn't even sure it was particularly relevant, just some little quirk that for some reason was bothering him now. It wasn't the first time he'd been aware of frustration at the block between conscious and unconscious thought; he'd never worked out a way to join them up and access what was in there, so what was the point of agonising now?

Rational argument, unfortunately, was no kind of remedy for sleeplessness and at last he got up and fetched his laptop. If the wind didn't drop soon – and it showed no signs that this was the plan – tomorrow would be another day of forced inactivity. He began with a list of in-depth background checks he could commission tomorrow; he could ask JB to fast-action them, but even so it would take days for the reports to come through, especially if the disruption meant that office staff couldn't get in to work.

The police check on Hammond would be easier, though – just a question of accessing the records. They would know where he'd come from and there'd be a string of contacts, which might tell their own story. But he had a gut feeling now that they couldn't afford to wait for that if they wanted to nail him; any evidence would disappear and, he was afraid, so would he. There were always jobs for the bent coppers if they moved in the right circles. His lie about Jackson's address ought to be enough to convince JB they had to move immediately.

Research on Gil Paton and Richard Sansom could take longer. He wasn't about to play Livvy's game of spot-the-villain: was a smooth, intelligent man more plausible than a lumpish whinger with his grievance against Cassie blatantly on display? He'd seen too many cases in his time to think that they wore an 'It's me!' badge that you could see if you looked hard enough. And, of course, there was always the possibility of some outside agency, as yet unidentified.

There was a sudden bellow of wind, then a slipping sound, and a crash. Kelso got out of bed and padded over to the window, rubbing at the condensation to see out. He could see a roof tile rapidly sinking into the snowdrift below. There would be a lot of damage done tonight.

He gave a huge yawn as he went back to bed. That was more promising. But as he started drifting into sleep a thought struck him and suddenly he was wide awake again. He'd made the connection. But there was nothing he could do now, except lie down seething with frustration and listen to the wind howling and whipping up the hardened snow to thrash against the window.

'But I can't remember it!' Cassie Trentham said. 'Marta told me, but I didn't pay any attention at the time. I was busy, and I knew I'd only have to ring the bell and they'd let me in.'

'You're lying,' he said.

She was. How did he know that? Perhaps policemen got special training for when they were interrogating suspects. Part of it was true, though; she must concentrate on that bit if she wanted to be convincing.

'I'm hopeless with numbers. I can't even remember my car registration or my mobile number without checking.'

Hammond stared at her for a moment, a stare that was an assault in itself. Then he said, 'So – you write them down. That's what you do, isn't it?'

She had made a trap for herself. 'No. Well, sometimes I don't. I didn't this time—'

'Don't waste my time, Cassie. You're a pathetic liar.' He was moving from foot to foot, as if he was on an adrenaline high, too psyched up to stand still. 'You wrote it down. Where?'

Then as she licked her dry lips, seeking for something to say, he burst out, 'Your diary – you'd write it in the diary you keep in your handbag. Beside your bunch of keys. And I kept those.' She knew her face was confirmation of what he'd just said, but she couldn't do anything about that. He was ranting on, 'I can't believe it – I had the sodding thing right there in my hands and I didn't know.

'Right – I'm going back, while I can still get out.'

'What are you going to do?'

He went to the door. 'I'm going to kill our mother,' he said in what was almost a conversational tone.

'*What?* What do you mean? And – what about me? Are you going to kill me too, or just leave me here to die?'

It did at least make him pause. 'Do you know, I haven't quite decided,' he said. 'Blood should be thicker than water, shouldn't it? But I'm not entirely sure that it is.'

Then he was gone, turning the key in the lock as he left.

Marta Morelli woke feeling cramped and stiff. She moved, easing herself painfully upright in the chair, her face tight and sore with the tears she had shed. The fire was out and when she looked round there was no sign of Anna.

She looked at the clock on the mantelpiece: half past one. She must have slept for hours, slept through Anna getting up and leaving. She must have gone up to bed.

Marta's mouth was dry and she felt sticky and unclean. Still feeling groggy, she stumbled through to the kitchen and drank water while her coffee brewed, then poured herself a double espresso. It would wake her up, help her to order her chaotic thoughts.

Anna had not turned against her, thank God. It had taken a lot to convince her, but she believed it now. She had offered to leave, to confess, even to kill herself, but the friendship that was the most important thing in her life had held fast. They had been too emotional to make decisions; that would have to wait for the morning once this long dark night was over.

Anna had been shocked. She had known she would be, which was why she had never told her. Anna had been brought up with very different values; Marta's own were of a more primitive sort. More natural, she had often told herself, even as she paid lip service to those that Anna seemed to hold dear. Her religion, a faded thing now for all those early years of going to Mass, inclined more to the Old Testament than to the New: payment for sins, revenge for evil done, was simple justice. At least, it had seemed that way at the time. Now, when payment was being called in on your own, it felt different.

Now, they were in a dark, dark place. Even if they told the police every last detail of their past, they had taken so much care to cover their tracks all those years ago, there would be no way to trace anything back. Yet someone had found them now – and they both knew who he was, or even she: they just didn't know anything else – except that whoever it was had views more like Marta's than Anna's.

She finished her coffee, washed and dried the cup and saucer and put them away so that the kitchen was pristine, as always, when she left. Upstairs, the door to Anna's room wasn't quite shut and she pushed it open cautiously. It was in darkness, apart from the pool of light from the lamp at the side of her bed. Had she fallen asleep reading – or was this more like the night light a child would have in their room to keep night-fears at bay? There was no sign of an abandoned book and Anna's face, relaxed in sleep, still showed the tracks of dried tears. As she watched, Anna muttered something, moving her head uneasily. She was suffering, even in her dreams.

Marta had felt helpless, fearful, guilty – oh yes, guilty above all. But now she was angry, with the burning rage of helplessness. She went back to her own room and went to the chest in the corner, the one that had a special drawer with a false back, where she could keep her jewellery safe from casual theft.

And not just her jewellery. Beside their padded boxes lay the gleaming, silvery knife. She picked it up, smoothed her thumb across it, then touched the flick switch and the wicked stiletto blade sprang out – long, razor-sharp, but dull and mottled with use and age. Marta looked at it for a moment with an odd, tight little smile. Then she flicked it away again and slipped it into the pocket of her skirt.

She had lost faith in the protective alarms and she had slept enough. She was going to mount guard through the dangerous hours of darkness and in the morning she and Anna would have to make up their minds about what to tell the police.

Cassie heard the outer door slam, then a car door, then an engine starting, coughing a little, restarting and then catching. He was going away, leaving her alone again with the tearing wind that sounded more savage than ever, rattling the windowpanes behind the hardboard as if it was determined to shatter them and let the snow have its way inside as well.

Her mind was reeling. *Our* mother – that's what he had said. And that comment about blood being thicker than water? What could it conceivably mean?

Anna had never told them anything about her past. Cassie and Felix had speculated about it occasionally, had asked Marta once or twice, but when the question was deftly brushed aside, they hadn't persisted; children have very little curiosity about anything that took place before their own important arrival on the planet. What had happened, that this man who claimed he was her son had wanted to kill her? And she was totally useless, unable to do anything to warn Anna that soon he would have what he needed to creep into the house on his deadly mission.

Suddenly, through the noise of the storm, Cassie heard another sound – the outer door opening again and closing, someone moving, the key being turned in the lock. The door of the room was flung open violently so that it bounced on its hinges and Hammond stood there again. Did this mean that he had decided to come back and kill her first? With an animal instinct, she cowered under the duvet – as if that could be any sort of protection!

She'd thought he was angry before; now he was in a towering rage, screaming a flood of obscenities about the snowploughs, which had not, as he had instructed, kept the road from here to Halliburgh clear.

'Haven't been able to get the car out of here, let alone back on to the road. Even if they send a plough out now, I doubt if they'll get it open.'

He had taken a phone out of his pocket and a moment later was venting his anger to some probably blameless subordinate. 'Well, who did cancel the order? Why don't you know? I know it's a small road, but I gave the order that it was to be kept clear. Get a plough on to it right now, top priority, and—What do you mean, they're stood down? When will they get going again?' He listened briefly, then said, 'Right. Not a lot I can do, then. You have my order – at first light, right?'

The energy of rage seemed to have evaporated. His shoulders slumped and he sat down on one of the ramshackle chairs, which creaked alarmingly, then leant forward on the table putting his head in his hands. He looked, she thought, defeated.

Something had gone badly wrong with his plans. Cassie sat up, her brain working furiously. Surely she could use this to her own advantage? They always said that in a hostage situation you should get them talking, get them to think of you as a real person, not a pawn. She said what she judged would be the most likely thing to catch his attention. 'Are you . . . are you really my brother?'

And then the light went out.

Marta wasn't asleep when she was plunged into darkness. She was sitting on her bed, propped up against the pillows and she tensed – she knew what would happen next. She groped for the landline, but that took a moment and it rang twice before she could pick it up to hear the disembodied voice of the security recording warning that there had been an interruption to the circuit and that the system was down. She heard Anna stirring even as she punched in the number to confirm that she was aware.

'Marta – was that . . .?'

'No,' she called back. 'Just security, because of the power cut.'

'Oh. I couldn't think what had happened. I'm just coming—'

'Torch – in your bedside drawer.' Marta felt for

her own and switched it on as the bobbing light from Anna's approached.

Anna trailed in, looking almost ghostly, with a white cashmere robe draped round her shoulders and her hair disordered round her white face.

'I'd forgotten there was always one there. I couldn't think what had happened when I woke up.' She still sounded fuddled with sleep. 'When I heard the phone, I thought—'

'I was afraid you would. I didn't get to it soon enough. Go back to bed, *cara* – you're worn out.'

'But now the alarm is down, we're unprotected,' Anna said. 'That's all we had to rely on—'

'I'm not tired. I would hear, if anyone came. You sleep.'

Anna sat down on the end of the bed. 'I don't think I can now. I'm scared to take a pill – I don't want to lay myself out in case something does happen.'

'Then we should phone the police station. They are there for our protection. They should do something, send someone.'

Anna sighed. 'Marta, they wouldn't, unless someone had actually broken in. With the snow and a power cut, they'll be getting hundreds of calls. It won't even go to the local station – some central switchboard will answer it.'

'The policeman gave me his number.' She got off the bed and walked across the room, swinging the beam to show where she had left her handbag.

‘It’s the middle of the night! You can’t . . .’ Anna said, but it was too late. Marta had found her phone and was dialling already.

When his mobile rang, he jerked awake. For a second he thought it could be part of a dream because opening his eyes didn’t make any difference. It was pitch-dark; no light at all coming in from the street lamps outside. He groped across the bedside table for the phone.

‘Strang,’ he said thickly, trying to summon his wits. ‘Who’s speaking?’

When the caller announced herself, he was suddenly wide awake. Contact, at last? But no; when he listened, it was Marta at her most *grande dame*, demanding immediate protection.

He could hear the storm still blowing outside. He said soothingly, ‘Even if the alarm isn’t set, your doors will be locked anyway, and use the deadbolts to make sure. Given the conditions, though, no one is moving about – in fact the road up to Highfield House must be blocked. You have a panic room, yes? If you have any reason to be worried, you can retreat there to be safe.’

‘But—’ he heard Marta say, then Anna spoke, ‘Inspector Strang, I’m sorry. You’re right, of course. My friend is very upset just now but there’s obviously nothing that can be done at the moment. We shouldn’t have disturbed you.’

‘That’s all right.’ Then seizing the moment, Strang

said, 'I wonder, though, if you have given thought to answering the questions I was asking you?'

There was a silence at the other end. Then Anna said, 'Oh yes. We've thought of little else. Tomorrow we will call you, if there's still no news.'

He had to settle for that. He peered at the time on his phone – quarter to two. It felt as if he'd been asleep for a very long time but he'd probably just been in that early deep sleep cycle. He still felt disorientated, particularly with the sort of deep darkness he didn't experience in his city life. He was just turning over to go back to sleep when he thought of turning on his bedside lamp. It didn't work, of course, but it meant that when the power was restored he would know – *if* the power was restored before morning.

Plunged so suddenly into darkness, Cassie gave a little scream of fright. She heard Hammond mutter, 'What the—' as she realised: of course, a power cut. You more or less expected that in this area when there was a big storm and the question was only whether the power would be restored in a few hours or a few days.

Her own house was well stocked with torches and candles – Marta, of course, had seen to that, and she even had a little camping stove to heat up a tin of soup if necessary. Here, there was nothing. She didn't know where the house was; it sounded as if it was out in the country, though, and even if you were a police officer who could issue instructions about getting your road cleared it wouldn't necessarily be possible immediately. They could be here for a very long time, trapped together in the dark. They would have to talk now – and it sounded as if they would have plenty to talk about. She was just trying to work out what to say when she realised he was crying – passionate, angry sobs.

'Am I owed nothing, nothing?' he said. 'The gods have been my enemies. From the day I was born I've had to fight alone.'

Cassie was glad now of the concealing dark. She wouldn't have been able to mask her astonishment that this man who had most likely killed her brother, had tried to kill her, had kidnapped her and planned to kill her mother, somehow seemed to see himself as a victim. Was there even any point in trying to express false sympathy? As he had pointed out, she was a pathetic liar and he'd hear the insincerity in her voice.

She didn't try, only said what was uppermost in her thoughts. 'Are you going to kill me?'

The sobbing stopped. Then, '*What?*' he said, as if he was irritated by such an irrelevance.

'Are you going to kill me?' she repeated. 'You tried before.'

'For God's sake!' Hammond was angry again. 'I didn't! It was the last thing I wanted at the time! I was playing Anna along so nicely until that spooked her, and then that idiot broke in and mucked everything up completely. I told you at the time it was just some fool who came too close to you and didn't stop.'

'But you asked me if anyone had a grudge against me,' she protested. 'That really scared me.'

He laughed. 'You should have seen the look on your face! I enjoyed that.'

It was a chilling insight. This was some sort of game to him. Her throat constricted as she said, 'And . . . Felix?'

'Ah, Felix.' His tone changed. 'He was my rival. He stole the childhood I should have had – and he threw away all my advantages. Our brother was a useless junkie dropout, Cassie.'

She didn't want him to have the satisfaction of knowing he had made her cry. She kept her voice level. '"Our" brother? "Our" mother? What do you mean? Who are you?'

'Oh, that's a good question. It's one I often ask myself.'

'And what do you reply?'

'I'm my father's son. At least I know that, and I know *he* loved me, even if things didn't work out as they should have.'

She recognised a bitter defensiveness. Anna, clearly, hadn't loved him, hadn't wanted him; that had disfigured his life and twisted him into the monster he was now. Could she encourage him to talk, play for time, hoping that by some miracle the search that must be going on would find her?

'How do you know Anna was your mother?' she asked.

He didn't answer immediately, and she softened her voice, cajoling him. 'Look, we could be here, just the two of us in the dark for a long time. Why don't you tell me about it?'

There was a long, long silence. Then he startled her with a sharp crack of harsh laughter. 'Why not? Though I may have to kill you afterwards.'

CHAPTER NINETEEN

Hammond didn't know why he'd agreed. Was it the darkness, that gave him a sort of cloak of invisibility? Or was it the gentle voice that seemed to promise a sympathy no one had ever given him? Or was it simply because the silence and secrecy had festered for so long that it was a suppurating boil and had to burst? It certainly wasn't to make excuses for himself; a just revenge needed no defence.

He'd recited the story to himself a hundred, a thousand times, like a ritual used to keep his anger smouldering. It would be good to say it out loud, to another person. There would be satisfaction in painting his pain on the darkness.

'He left, you see – my father. The day after my tenth birthday. Somehow they often seemed to have fights that spoilt my birthdays and I'd heard them screaming the night before. I knew it must be my fault. It only happened because I was a naughty boy – my mother was always telling me that. I tried hard not to be, but they still had rows anyway and this one was a humdinger. There was a crash, like they'd broken something – they'd never done that before. They had nice things, precious things. I heard her screaming something then – couldn't make it out. I just pulled the covers over my head and they were still at it when I fell asleep.

'I'm not sure why I woke up early – I know I used to get a worry pain in the pit of my stomach so it could have been that, or maybe there was some sound. Anyway, I lay very still, wondering if they were still yelling or if things would be back to what I called "normal" then.' He gave a short laugh. 'Armed neutrality, I suppose I'd call it now.

'The shouting had stopped but there was someone moving very quietly downstairs. Then right under my window the front door opened and I went to look. It wasn't fully light, but my father was walking to his car, carrying a suitcase. He often went away for a few days, for work. I hated that, but it wasn't unusual so I didn't run down in my pyjamas and throw my arms round his legs to beg him to take me with him and not leave me with her, like I would have done if I'd known.

'I'd never admitted I didn't love my mother. Well, I knew I had to, because that was what she was, even if I didn't think she loved me. Did you love yours?' He threw out the challenge suddenly and Cassie took a moment to reply.

'Yes, I did, in a slightly distant way. Like you said, you have to, because you're sort of imprinted. She was always quite cool, not touchy-feely, and sometimes I don't much like her. But I've cut her a bit of slack because she's not just the same as ordinary people. And I think she loves me, as much as she can with her nature.'

'Oh, well done you!' Hammond said sarcastically. 'Didn't you think it was your fault that you didn't get hugs and kisses like other kids? I did. She'd convinced me it was because I was a bad person. But my dad loved me, and I really, really loved him. She loved him too; he was a very loveable man.

'When his car drove off, I went back to bed. The worry pain was still there but if Dad was away there probably wouldn't be any dramatics and I'd mostly be out at school, so I went back to sleep. When I woke up again I could hear my mother moving about downstairs – half past seven, time to get up and get ready for school. I knew she'd probably be in a bad mood after the row last night, so I did everything properly– neat hair, tidy room, no dawdling, straight down to be in good time. Nothing to get her started, but I was still nervous when I went into the kitchen.

'Dirty dishes piled on the worktop, no sign of breakfast. A glass bowl lying in pieces on the floor – a beautiful thing, Venetian glass with blues and greens swirled through it – and she was sitting at the table crying, and she looked as if she'd been doing that for a long time. Her face was all blubbery with tears and her eyes were swollen almost shut. There was this little pile of torn-up paper on the table in front of her. As I edged my way into the room she looked up. I was only young but I couldn't mistake the look she gave me – pure hatred. It was like she'd hit me in the face. Then she said, "So you're what I'm left with, are you? He's dumped you on me and gone."

'My knees started shaking so I nearly fell. I sat down on the chair furthest away from her while she told me my father had walked out, then she said, "Didn't take you with him, did he?"

'It hurt so much that I could hardly breathe, could hardly understand what she was saying. She went on, raving away about was she meant to look after me now? I said, "But you're my mother. That's what mothers do." God, I was naive! And then she started to laugh, so hard she started to choke, and I could hardly make out that what she was saying was, "That's a joke!"

'I actually wondered if she'd suddenly gone mad. Could you go mad with rage? And if she had, what could I do about it? I just stood there, and suddenly she stopped laughing. She'd stopped crying too and her face was so ugly, blotchy and cruel.

'Then she said, "Oh, you're so stupid. You're not my child."'

Hammond heard a little gasp from Cassie. 'Nice, wasn't it?' he said.

'That's so unbelievably cruel,' Cassie sounded horrified. 'What a wicked way to tell you that!'

He smiled sardonically. 'Oh yes, there are whole treatises on how a child can be damaged if they're told the wrong way, aren't there? Well, I can assure you my evil stepmother tore up the rule book. Do you know, even then I could recognise that there was a sort of disgusting satisfaction in the way she said it.

'What she didn't realise was that what I felt at that moment was relief. If she wasn't my mother, I didn't have to pretend any more, I didn't have to feel guilty. Those thoughts I'd always believed were so naughty that I had to deny them even to myself – now I could admit that I hated her. I hated her, I hated her, I hated her. I always had. But I was scared now too. I asked whose I was, then.

'Thank God, thank God, what she said was, "Oh yes, you're your father's."' His voice thickened. 'At least I've got that. I think I'd have killed myself if he wasn't. But then she went on, "He bought you from her, you see." I couldn't work that out. I just said, "But who is my mother?"

'She sneered, "Some floozy who wanted money more than she wanted you, that's for sure." I suppose I looked bewildered – I knew you couldn't buy babies – and she started laughing again. "I'd better explain. You remember how you wanted a puppy and your father went out and bought you one? The one that got knocked down on the road?"

'Of course I remembered. That was the worst thing that had ever happened to me and even talking about it still made me want to cry. She was going on, "It was just like that. He wanted a child to play with just like you wanted a puppy and I couldn't give him one so he went to this woman and said, 'How much?' and she told him and he paid her and she handed you over and he gave you to me. I didn't want you, but I wanted him because without a child he would have gone. But now he's left anyway, and I'm stuck with you. An 'unwanted gift' – that's what they call it when things get sold off after Christmas, don't they? I could put you up for sale – only who would want *you*?"

'I probably flinched at that but I know I was persistent. I asked her again who my mother was. She shrugged. "I don't know. I never wanted to know and your father's probably forgotten. He's good at forgetting." She began to cry again.

'I got up on to my wobbly legs and walked out. When lightning strikes it can leave a fractal pattern tattooed into the ground and I was a whole different person from the kid that had walked in a quarter of an hour before. My stepmother – oh, she was just standard stuff – a poisonous woman like they'd all been in the fairy stories my dad had read to me when I was little. I didn't need to waste my energy on her. My father – the important thing was that he was my real father and once he was settled, he'd send for me.'

Hammond stopped and drew a deep breath. His voice was hard when he went on. 'Only, of course, he didn't. His new wife didn't want me any more than the last one had. It was only after he'd walked out on that one as well that we got close. Even then, he wouldn't tell me who my real mother was – wouldn't even talk about it – and it wasn't until he died that I found he'd kept all the papers and I discovered her name. But of course she'd changed it and it took me years to find out who she was now.

'I'm not stupid. My father was to blame too – for what he did in the first place and for his neglect afterwards. But the hatred that has shaped me is for the woman who had seen me as no more than a puppy to be sold to the highest bidder. There's a name for puppies' mothers, and it's been my life's mission to find that bitch and kill her. I claim my right to revenge and even this setback isn't going to stop me. Nothing's going to stop me. I'll find a way.'

He waited for a response but Cassie didn't speak and he snapped, 'Cat got your tongue? I've wasted half my life, tracking her down. I bought private detectives, who failed. I only joined the police to get access to the records I needed. There's been nothing more – it's sucked me dry until all I am is a hollow shell, and I can't be anything else until she's paid for what she did. You've heard it all. Now's your chance to give me a reason why I shouldn't kill her.'

He heard Cassie take a long breath. 'Because of what it will do to you. Look what this sick desire for revenge has done already – you said yourself it's made you a hollow shell. Killing my – *our* mother won't give you "closure", as they say. Nothing ever does. However hard it is, accepting it, putting it behind you and getting on with your life – that's the only thing that helps. An eye for an eye and a tooth for a tooth only creates more misery, not less.'

Hammond burst out laughing. 'You think so? How sweet and touching! Yes, it creates more misery – but for your enemies, and that balances the books. It would give me deep and lasting satisfaction. That's my prize.'

She didn't reply. They sat in silence for a long time. He was aware of her crying softly at one point but lost in his own complex calculations he was indifferent: she could cry if she liked. At last he realised that the wind was easing off, dropping right back and there was even a slow drip, drip of melting snow.

It was six o'clock; he could see a faint line of daylight round the edge of the hardboard panels. Any time now, the snowploughs would be starting their work. Providing they came, he could get in, go to the office, retrieve Cassie's handbag and then get into the house – and they'd be less vigilant during the day. His spirits rose. He'd had his defeatist moment but now he was back on track.

When he heard the grinding of the snowplough's engine, he sprang up. The room was still very dark and he headed towards the door with hands outstretched feeling for the handle. As he took the key out of his pocket, Cassie said in a small voice, 'So what happens to me?'

Hammond wasn't ready to answer that, so he didn't. He walked out, shutting and locking the door again behind him.

* * *

When Kelso Strang woke, it was just light but the power still hadn't come back on again. It was quarter to seven, and he jumped out of bed, annoyed with himself for not setting his alarm. He was habitually an early riser but the interruption in the middle of the night must have put his internal clock out and spoilt his plan for getting along to the police station the moment it was light enough to see the way.

He jumped out of bed and realised that the buffeting of the storm had stopped and the sun was coming up. Not only that, he heard a sudden rush as snow slid off the roof; the thaw had begun. The problems today would be not only getting all the roads open but dealing with the flooding that would inevitably follow.

He showered, shaved and dressed at speed, then went out into the street. There was a light wind but it had veered to the south and the great piles of snow were starting to collapse like so many failed soufflés. The street and the pavement were awash with slush and all but deserted; the odd car making its way gingerly along sent up bow waves of water. Strang concentrated on diving into shop doorways when one passed but even so he was caught and drenched twice so that he arrived dripping at the police station.

The civilian assistant at the desk looked horrified. 'Oh dear, you're awful wet! And with the power being down the heating's not come on.'

'Oh, I'll live,' Strang said. 'I expect I'll find a towel in the cloakroom. Tell me, is DI Hammond in?'

It was the crunch question. If she said, 'Oh yes, he's in his office, I'll buzz him,' he'd got it wrong.

'No,' she said, and he was already mentally framing the question for Kate about snowploughs and minor roads when she went on, 'You've just missed him, sir. He came in briefly a wee while ago and went out again.'

'Did he say where he was going?'

'Just, something about problems with the main road. Shall I call his mobile for you?'

'Yes, do that.'

He waited on tenterhooks as she listened, then said, 'Sorry, it's gone to voicemail. Do you want to leave a message?'

'No thanks,' he said. 'I'll just go and find that towel – my hair's dripping into my eyes.'

As he walked along the corridor he took out his phone. 'Livvy? How are things with you?'

'OK, except there's no power. Kate's just brewing up coffee on a camping stove and I'm lighting the fire.'

'Forget breakfast. Ask Kate which minor road it was that the snowplough was being directed to and get in here immediately. Ask her about a back way – I got soaked getting along the high street.'

Strang checked out the car park and was relieved to find that they'd cleared the worst of the drifts already and once Murray got there they could drive straight out to see whether his idea was a genuine breakthrough or a wild goose chase. He went back into the station to wait. But first, he had something else to do. He should have thought of it sooner and he went off to find the duty sergeant.

When Murray arrived, he met her in reception and marched her straight out. His face was grim. 'Let's get going. Badged car, blues and twos. He's checked out a Glock.'

Hammond had driven very cautiously along the high street, curbing his impulse to put his foot down to get there sooner. There was hardly any traffic and the thawing snow made the road surface like an ice rink; one small skid into a parked car would finish everything.

He patted his pocket to hear Cassie's keys jingling reassuringly – he'd taken those from Burnside long before – and he had the code number written down, just as if the numbers weren't seared on his mind! Getting hold of the handbag hadn't been difficult and he put back the diary afterwards and resealed the evidence bag. No point in leaving traces you didn't need to, even if you planned to be long gone before anyone would look.

The slope up to Highfield House was trickier still and the wheels lost grip a couple of times, but he was used to winter driving. And there were the gates now. Hammond drove on up until the SUV would be out of sight, then parked it with its nose in a snowdrift as if it had been abandoned.

There was no one about. He could hurry now and his heart was beating faster as he reached the tall gates.

There was still snow six inches deep piled up behind them, but he reckoned it was soft enough for the force of the opening gates to sweep it to one side. He keyed in the code. Nothing happened.

He tried again. Still no reaction. Had those bitches changed the code again? Or – then it struck him. The power cut! Had the security gone down? He could probably open the gate by brute force, but how could he be sure there wasn't some sort of trip switch still operating? It would be crazy to stake everything on a gamble like that.

And now he could see headlights coming up the hill. He couldn't afford to be spotted; moments later, with his car screening him from the road, he was crouching in the slushy snow as someone drove up to the electronic gates and got out.

The Armstrongs had been up early too, listening to their battery radio as they got dressed. Elspeth had slept badly and Davy was anxious to get across to Highfield. They were forecasting a major thaw, but there was no word when the power would be back on; most of the Scottish Borders had been affected.

'I just couldn't get that poor lass out of my head, wondering if she was all right,' she said as she stirred the porridge on their solid fuel stove. 'And I'm worried about the ladies' breakfast – I don't know what they have that isn't electric.'

'Oh, Marta will have made sure they're all right. You

know what she's like. I'm just wondering if there's been a phone call or anything. It'll have been a long night if they haven't heard anything.'

'At least the police'll be able to do a bit more today. I doubt they were able to do anything at all yesterday.'

Davy gave a heavy sigh. 'I wish I thought there was something they *could* do today. Where do you start looking, with something like that?'

'Don't you go over there with a face like that on you! You have to look on the bright side.' She set the bowl of porridge in front of him. 'You just eat that up and get across to see if there's anything you can do.'

When he reached Highfield House there was snow heaped up behind the gates and when he keyed in the code nothing happened – of course, the system would be down. He got out of the car and pushed, hoping the snow would be soft enough to shift; there was certainly meltwater pouring down the drive now. He had to put his shoulder to it, but he managed and was able to drive the car up towards the front of the house. The biggest problem was round about it where what had been on the roof had slid off to form banks around the base; it came up to his knees as he waded through to the front door and rang the bell.

It was a few minutes before he heard bolts being drawn back on the other side and Marta Morelli, looking bleak, appeared. 'I'm sorry, Davy, I had to check who it was. The alarm system—'

'Oh aye, I know. It's an awful nuisance, this. Elspeth

was wondering if you were all right for your breakfast.'

She gave a wintry smile. 'Oh, we're all right. Not very hungry, though, I think.'

Obviously no news, then. He was heart-sorry for them, but there wasn't much he could do. He said awkwardly, 'Just thought I'd come and see if there was anything you were needing.'

'Thank you very much. Anna will appreciate your concern.'

'Well, you know where we are.'

Davy nodded and went back to his car. Maybe, as Elspeth had said, the police would be able to do something once things got back to normal. It was all they could hope for. He drove back home.

Leaving the gates standing wide open.

The rhythmic dripping of the melting snow ticked like a metronome getting faster and faster in the silence after Hammond left. There was a little light now filtering through round the hardboard on the windows but if there was sunshine outside it wasn't doing anything to warm the air and Cassie retreated under the duvet. As he had told his story she had sat up, fascinated and appalled by what he had said; now she was very, very cold and very, very hungry. She picked up the bottle of water by the side of the bed and allowed herself a drink but there wasn't much left. She had no confidence that he would even bother to come back to kill her. Without water, you could die in a couple of days.

He was going to kill Anna first, though. He would find the code she'd scribbled down and sneak in on them while they thought they were secure. It was horrible to know what would happen but be unable to warn them. He'd wait till night-time, probably, when they were asleep. And Marta? Would he kill her too?

It just felt unreal, as if she'd stepped into a nightmare she couldn't wake up from. His story – did she believe it? That Anna would be so wicked as to agree to have a child she would sell on? The terrible thing was that from what she knew of Anna, there was that splinter of ice in her heart that all good writers are supposed to have, along with a ruthless dedication to her work. Did she care about anything else at all? Cassie herself, and darling, lost Felix, had come far behind that.

Yes, she'd loved her mother, she'd told Hammond – if that was his name, which it probably wasn't. She'd added that she didn't like her much, and that was true as well – but she admired her talent immensely. She didn't need the global razzamatazz to tell her that Anna had some odd, inexplicable gift that let her speak directly to people's hearts and make a difference, and that applied to her daughter's as well. Whatever she'd done, the world would be poorer if Hammond succeeded in carrying out his mission.

She was helpless to stop him, or to save herself. With the duvet right over her head she was warming up and she was tired, so tired. Despite the hunger pangs and the headache she still hadn't managed to shake, she fell asleep.

* * *

DC Livvy Murray had experienced DCI Strang's driving before when they were in a hurry, but the last time they hadn't been virtually aquaplaning. The water was running off the fields on either side and the piles built up by the snowploughs were spreading slippery slush right across the road. She tried not to gasp as they came up behind a cautious car that didn't move out of the way quickly enough, but he somehow manoeuvred round it and fortunately there was very little other traffic.

'It came to me in the middle of the night,' Strang told her. 'I went to the CID room yesterday afternoon to offer my services and Wilson was in a bit of a state, trying to deal with a worsening situation and he dashed off. Kate was there and mentioned there'd been a mix-up with snowploughs having been directed to keep open a minor road and I thought at the time that was odd – Hammond was coordinating the deployment and it was uncharacteristically inefficient. But I was focused on Wilson being ready to grass and it was annoying that he wouldn't be able to meet me last night – I was pretty sure Hammond had realised we were on to him when he lied about Jackson's address and I'd have liked more than that to convince the boss to act immediately.

'Then of course I was at the Grahams' and it was only after I went to bed that it came back to me about that road – and of course then it was a sort of "duh!" moment. We know Hammond was involved in some very dirty stuff already, so the profile fits. I've put out an

APB on his car, so we may get him that way – he won't realise we're looking for him yet.'

Murray could see what he was saying, but she was still not completely convinced. 'If he was planning to do a runner, it's plain dumb. He'd know that kidnapping Cassie would bring the roof in. What reason could he possibly have?'

'His motive, do you mean?' There was an ironic emphasis on the word and she winced as he went on, 'We can't possibly know. Maybe it'll become clear if we get him, maybe it won't. I still don't know that I'm right. Oh, that's the side road now.'

As he turned on to it, he said, 'Our job is simply to try to piece his actions together and hope we can get to Cassie before something happens to her.'

The snowplough had certainly been there, but while it had packed down the snow there hadn't been enough passing traffic to clear it and the surface was treacherous. To Murray's relief Strang slowed down; there was no need for sirens either. They passed a farm and then a few houses where there was no sign of life. They scanned them as they passed.

'Quite a few folk would get out when they knew this was coming in,' Murray said. 'They wouldn't be expecting the road to be passable so quickly.'

'We can get teams out to talk to them later, but the chances are there won't be witnesses. Some may even be second homes – it's a nice valley, this.' Then he slowed right down. 'Look up there – see the house on that slope? Somebody's driven out since the plough came through. Let's take a look.'

As they tackled the drive they slipped back once or twice and it was slow progress. Murray's stomach lurched; in policing you never knew when you'd find yourself looking down the barrel of a gun. Hammond could be lurking inside with his Glock – they could do very nasty damage, those – but his car wasn't there so he must surely have left. But even if Strang had guessed right and this was where he'd taken Cassie, what might they find then? The sick feeling in her stomach got worse so she tried telling herself that maybe the place just belonged to an innocent householder as they parked outside.

Strang reached the door first. While he knocked on it, she walked round the outside, looking in the windows at the empty rooms of what looked like an abandoned property. Then she turned the corner and saw the windows that had been blanked out.

'She could be here!' she yelled and instantly Strang hammered on the door yelling 'Police', then kicked up at the handle to shatter the lock.

Cassie woke in total confusion. The hammering, the voices – was this some new threat? Then 'Police!' and splintering wood.

And there was the sound of someone charging at the door of her prison. At the second onslaught it gave way and she recognised the chief inspector who had interviewed her as he burst in with a woman following at his heels who hurried over to her.

'Are you all right?'

She tried to collect her wits. 'Yes . . . I think so. But never mind that. It was him – your inspector. He's gone off to kill my mother.'

CHAPTER TWENTY

Detective Chief Superintendent Borthwick put down the phone, leant her head on the desk and groaned. There were good days and bad days, and any day when you had to issue a statement warning that a police officer – armed with a weapon he was perfectly entitled to carry, under Police Scotland rules – had gone rogue and was a death threat to one of the best-known authors in the country was most definitely a bad day.

DCI Strang had done a sort of good news/bad news presentation: Cassie Trentham was now safe in hospital recovering from a mild concussion and shock – good – before he told her about the threat to Anna Harper – bad.

Protection was the key issue. Strang was at the house with Anna Harper and her friend now, armed himself, and when the armed response unit that she was just about to action reached them – not much more than an hour, with sirens – Anna would be as safe as the Queen in Buckingham Palace. It was unfortunate that as she made the mental analogy, she remembered that the Queen had once woken up to find an intruder sitting on her bed and had to force away the thought.

With the order given, she turned her mind to briefing the media relations officer. Armed and dangerous, do not approach, the press release would have to say. A very, very bad day.

The good part of the day for DCI Strang had been when Marta Morelli opened the Highfield front door and he was able to tell her that Cassie Trentham was safe. Leaving him and DC Murray on the doorstep, she ran ahead to tell Anna Harper the good news. When they followed her to the study, the woman who had always seemed icily cold to him, and her friend who had channelled anxiety into aggression, were both reacting with uninhibited floods of tears and fervent expressions of gratitude. They were both looking so haggard that he doubted if they'd eaten at all, or slept, for the past couple of days.

That was the good bit over. The rest was downhill all the way, beginning with telling them that the person who was behind it was one of his own colleagues. The tears stopped, and the expressions of gratitude too. He could see Marta starting to bridle.

'But – a police officer? How could this be?'

He took refuge in the old cliché. 'I'm afraid there are bad apples in every barrel. My unit was despatched here because we had reason to believe that there were irregularities in DI Hammond's department—'

'The inspector?' Anna said sharply.

He saw a meaningful look pass between the two of them. Murray had obviously noticed it too; did she have any more idea than he did what it signified?

'Yes, I'm afraid so,' he said, as Murray caught his eye. He gave her a nod and she leant forward.

'Ms Harper, did he look as if he could be your son?'

Both women looked shocked. 'What-what do you mean?' Anna stammered.

It wasn't the question he would have asked but it certainly had shock value. Sometimes chucking in a hand grenade with the pin out was the answer and Murray was good at that. She went on, 'You see, he told your daughter his life story in some detail and that's what he claimed to be.'

Marta seemed more collected. 'And what was this "life story" that he told her?'

Strang said, 'I think we'll deal with it the other way round – you tell us the story. I asked you some questions before. Perhaps you will see reason and answer them now.'

The two women looked at each other again, then Anna said with her usual hauteur, 'Perhaps you will excuse us while we discuss what you have told us?'

Marta added, 'The maid in the kitchen will give you a cup of tea.'

Reluctantly Strang agreed. They weren't accused of any crime; this whole thing was a kid-gloves job and given that he had more bad news to give them he couldn't afford to make things worse. As directed, they went through to the kitchen.

The 'maid' was a woman in her thirties, slight and sharp-featured with dark hair pulled back in a ponytail. She looked startled to see them and seemed the anxious type; her hands were shaking as she wiped up something spilt on the floor and fetched mugs from a cupboard. When she told Strang her name was Kayleigh Burns it explained the nerves. If you were Jason Jackson's girlfriend and had helped him break into the house, it was understandable that you wouldn't really see the police as your friends. It was surprising she was still there; she must be good at her job. Help wouldn't be that easy to find in Halliburgh.

When he told her the good news about Cassie, she made the correct responses, but he got the impression that it hadn't been in the forefront of her mind. He glanced at his watch; he'd said they would return in ten minutes and he'd hoped for a quiet word with Murray over their cuppa but Kayleigh had just begun very busily clearing out a cupboard so he didn't really feel he could ask her to abandon it. They could have a quick word in the hall on their way back instead.

'What can he have said?' Anna's voice was hollow.

Marta was clenching and unclenching her hands.

'We must quickly work out what he could possibly know. And then we must tell them that. No need for anything more.'

Anna's face spoke of an agony of indecision. 'What we agreed last night, then?'

'We have Cassie back, safe. What do we gain, if we say anything more?'

Anna didn't reply immediately. Then she said, 'I know he came here a couple of times but I was so stressed I didn't pay much attention at the time and I can't conjure him up now. What is he like?'

Marta shrugged. 'Like anyone else. The evil does not show in his face, if that's what you mean.'

It wasn't quite what Anna meant and Marta knew that. She was just being cool-headed, as she always was. And as she had pointed out, with Cassie safe and her kidnapper identified, they could think about damage limitation.

Sitting on a ladder stool in the walk-in larder, Hammond was holding his breath. He had left the door open a crack so that Kayleigh could see that he was watching her, but though he could hear Strang's and Murray's voices he couldn't see the table where they were sitting. If she had the courage she could indicate, even with a flick of the head, that something was wrong, but he judged that she didn't.

He had walked through the open gates and approached the back door carefully, sticking close to the house and keeping below the level of the windows until he reached the kitchen door. It had a glass panel; standing back, he could look in at an angle and see most of it without being visible from inside – empty. He'd moved quickly then, tapping in the code just in case, choosing the most likely-looking key and getting it right first time. It turned smoothly in the lock – and the door didn't budge. He tried again, then realised – bolted on the inside.

Hammond leant back against the wall, beating his head against it. What was he to do? And now there was another car coming, skirting the house as it headed for the parking area where he was standing. Like an answer to prayer, he saw there were two other cars on the tarmac behind him, a large BMW and a smaller top-of-the-range Audi, and he had ducked behind them as Kayleigh's car appeared.

From his vantage point he watched her try to open the door, then knock, and saw Marta Morelli come to open it for her. They talked for a few minutes, then Marta left her getting busy about the kitchen. When he'd knocked on the door she'd looked surprised but not alarmed, then defensive when he said he wanted to talk to her about Jason.

'Chucked him out,' she said, as she let him in. 'Don't know where he is, don't want to know. Got me in enough trouble already—Oh!'

He'd got the little kick of pleasure he always got from the exercise of power at the look on her face as she saw the gun. 'Now shut up,' he said. 'I'm not here. You didn't let me in. You don't tell anyone anything, not with a word, not with a look. Got it?'

Her eyes wide with shock, she'd nodded. He'd quizzed her about the morning routine and made his plans – he wanted Anna on her own, so that he could tell her all the things he had been saving up to say to her; he wanted her crying, begging forgiveness. And he'd laugh in her face, and kill her. Vengeance his, justice done – a deep need satisfied. Then he would be gone, straight to the airport and to the little house in Spain that was waiting for him, with a quiet mind at last. When he didn't turn up for work, he had no doubt at all that Strang would pounce. Poor, dumb Wilson would have to take the flak but when they alerted Border Force they wouldn't be looking for a man with the name on his passport.

After breakfast, apparently, Anna always went to her study. That would be his moment; he'd settled down to wait. The doorbell ringing was an unwelcome interruption but of course the hunt for Cassie would still be going on. That might even be Strang, coming to pleat his feet. Making excuses for your failure was always painful. Shame he couldn't be a fly on the wall for that one!

He'd have to wait him out, but the footsteps coming towards the kitchen later caught him just as Kayleigh handed him the mug of coffee he'd asked for. With a menacing glance at her, he'd leapt back into the larder, slopping it as he went.

Then the roof caved in. He heard Strang say, 'Good

news – Cassie's all right.' It took an effort of will not to cry out at the unfairness of it all. What hope did he have, fighting against the brutal gods?

Anna Harper was sitting in one of the armchairs beside the fire when DCI Strang and DC Murray came back, with Marta Morelli in its counterpart on the other side, leaving a small sofa between them for the detectives to sit on. They were both looking much calmer now, Anna greeting them with a smile.

'Do sit down. First, I have to apologise to you if I've made things more difficult. I can only say that nothing we could have told you would have led you to your officer and I don't see even now that what I can tell you will help with a prosecution where there seems to be ample evidence of his guilt. Still, I feel I do have an obligation to explain.

'When I was very young, I worked as a secretary for a firm of engineers – I can give you the details if you want them later. And I'm afraid it was just the usual sordid story – drank too much at an office party and fell into bed with one of the managers. Oliver was a very attractive man – amusing and charming. I knew he was married but it didn't bother me, frankly – I wasn't looking for a relationship. I think we slept together another couple of times – maybe three or four, I suppose.

'Then I got pregnant. I was, quite honestly, horrified. I certainly wasn't ready to have children so I'd no hesitation in deciding to have an abortion – single mother on the breadline certainly wasn't for me. I had great plans. The affair had petered out, anyway, a while before that but I felt I ought to tell him what I planned to do – it was his child too, after all.

'I didn't expect an argument. Indeed, I thought that as a married man he'd give a sigh of relief. I certainly wasn't prepared for him to say he was overjoyed, that he'd divorce his wife and marry me and we'd bring up our baby together – the last thing I wanted, frankly. When I refused he began to cry. His wife couldn't have children and he'd always wanted a family.

'It was all very difficult. We argued for hours. Eventually he said if I would have the baby, he would pay me to do nothing until it was born and then he and his wife would adopt it.'

Anna paused, studying her fingernails as if she'd never seen them before. Marta was watching her anxiously and neither Strang nor Murray spoke, or even moved, until she went on. 'I'm not proud of this, you understand. I was very young, barely nineteen. I wanted to forget all about it, not find myself confronted years later by a child who had the right to know that I was its mother and could track me down. But what his offer represented was the time and freedom to write the book that had taken possession of me, the book I was getting up at five in the morning to write. It was going to take years to finish at that rate.

'So I accepted it, with one condition – that there should be no paper trail. I'd always loved Italy. I would go out there to write the book and have the baby, then claim I had an estranged husband who had gained custody and he would pick it up – I wouldn't even have to see him again, in that situation. His wife would have had to pretend to everyone at home that she was pregnant, but he didn't see a problem with it – they were desperate to have a child. Then I changed my name so that no one could ever find me – or so I thought.'

Anna lifted her head with a certain defiance. 'There you have it. You don't have to tell me that I've broken the law and now I'll be prosecuted. I've had to live with that fear all my life. But if I say that in my own mind my firstborn is the book not the baby, you may be prepared to accept that I believed that I would be a poor mother for it, and that a life where it would be brought up as a much-wanted child was better than no life at all.'

It was clear from the way Murray was shifting in her seat that she wasn't impressed with Anna's justification. Strang could feel Murray drawing breath to point out the result of this very convenient reasoning and turned to give her a warning glare.

As she subsided, he said, 'Thank you for telling us this, Ms Harper. Forgive me for pointing out that if you had been frank with us from the start, your daughter could have been spared an extremely distressing experience. For a start, you know the father's name. It might have been possible for us to trace the son, even if he too had changed his name – not Hammond, I take it?'

Anna said nothing, only shook her head, and he went on, 'You'll have to give a full and detailed statement. I'll send someone to do that. I can't make any comment about the likelihood of prosecution – that would be up to the procurator fiscal.' Then he turned to Marta. 'And can I ask where you come into this?'

Unlike Anna, Marta did not look down. She met his gaze squarely as she said, 'She came to my village. I needed work, she paid me for cleaning and I, *I* was the first person ever to read what Anna Harper wrote.' There was no mistaking her pride. 'She has changed people's lives with her wonderful books and I knew what she was even then, that there was no one like her, that she was truly important. I am not important, except that I am her friend.'

You couldn't possibly doubt her sincerity. 'Thank you, Ms Morelli. You will be asked to make a statement too and there are other questions I will have to ask – about communications I believe you were receiving from him, for instance. But there is something more I need to tell you now.' This time it was Strang who shifted uneasily. 'The story that Hammond told your daughter chimes with yours in many ways. We believe he has your entry code and I'm afraid he is armed and threatening to kill you, Ms Harper.'

The shock registered on the women's faces. Anna's hand went to her mouth to cover a gasp of horror; Marta froze, then looking at Anna she quite visibly pulled herself together and her voice was level as she said, 'Don't worry, *cara*. The system is down anyway, remember, and I bolted the doors last night. We have believed for a long time that he wants to kill Anna and we are safer than we have been before.' She directed a challenging look at Strang. 'We will have protection now, yes?'

'Certainly.' He took out his mobile to check for messages. 'Yes, an armed response unit has arrived from Edinburgh and is coming up here now. They may already have arrived. Constable, could you please go and check?'

Just as Murray left, a klaxon sounded. They all jumped with wild thoughts of a sudden attack, with the exception of Marta who said, 'Oh, this is good! That is to tell us that the power is back on. I will go now to set the system properly with a new code. We will be very safe now.'

Murray returned. 'Yes, they're just driving round to the back of the house.'

With some relief, Strang got to his feet. 'I'll go and have a word with them. Please try not to worry too much. I can understand that this is very alarming, but we have a task force arriving as well now the road is clear and there's a national alert for Hammond out. We'll have him before long.'

The van that had brought the armed response unit was in the parking area at the back, tucked into the farthest corner. The man commanding it was an old mate: Superintendent Andy Brown had fought to keep Strang in the unit after DCS Borthwick spotted his potential as a detective and his defeat was still a subject for wisecracks between them.

'Oh, you're quick enough calling in help when you get out of your depth, eh? Ever think you'd have been better to stay with the guys who really do the business?'

'Mornings like this, yes. You're simple souls, you lot,' Strang countered. 'No one asks you to explain why we've got a cop with an official gun running around trying to kill our leading novelist.'

Brown's cheerful smile faded. 'Hadn't heard that bit. They just told us the girl was safe but there was a threat to the mother.'

'There's a manhunt on now. He doesn't know we're on to him yet so that's a help. The kidnapping was all about getting the code so he could get access unnoticed, so it's likely he'll wait till dark. I daresay we can leave it to you lot to make sure he can't.'

'Trust me,' Brown said. 'What has he got?'

'A Glock. Pretty reliable, pretty accurate. I've signed out one as well.'

'Well, you were always the best. I'd back you if it came to a shoot-out,' Brown said. 'Wouldn't recommend it, though.'

'Not planning to have one, believe me. That's what you're there to stop. I'll leave you to it, then. There's a mountain of stuff waiting for me at the station.'

As they drove back into Halliburgh, DC Murray said, 'Just saying you likely wouldn't be a good mother isn't enough excuse for that carry-on. Her story checked out, though, and you could see all she'd been worried about was getting in trouble for not doing the adoption right. But to be fair, she wasn't to know the baby wasn't going to a good home.'

'I suppose the point is that if it had been done properly the authorities would have found out that the wife wasn't keen and there was an ugly degree of callousness about the whole thing – "I don't want it, do what you like with it", you know? But it does explain why she didn't want to disclose any of this, whatever the risk was. It wouldn't do a lot for "The Brand", as Cassie told me they called it.'

'So her son died and her daughter might have. Always supposing she cared more about them than she did about her first baby, she's gone through quite a bit. Do you think Hammond actually killed Felix?'

Strang shrugged. 'Can't imagine we'd ever prove it. From the sound of it, he'd only have to be offered some of the heavy stuff and the job would be done. But I'm still not sure we've got to the bottom of it even now. Anna's was a carefully calculated statement.'

The road into the town was more or less clear now but there was dirty slush everywhere and the gutters were running with water. The police station car park was crowded; a large contingent had obviously arrived and they had to wait as two badged cars came out and headed in opposite directions along the high street, which left them prey to a jostling pack of media waiting on the pavement, Sascha Silverton among them. Voices rose and there were shouted questions as they got out of the car.

Strang hurried to the side entrance. 'I gave instructions about an incident room and I want to see what they've done,' he said. 'You'd better check in with Wilson since you're officially working here. See me after that.'

Murray followed more slowly. She hadn't expected to find herself in sympathy with Anna Harper at all. She'd never read any of her books and she hadn't even seen the films, but what Marta said, about Anna being important because of her effect on her readers, had made her wonder what it would be like if you knew you had that sort of gift. It wouldn't be the same as being an ordinary person, that was for sure. If Hammond had managed to kill her it would have been an awful waste.

Well, Anna was safe enough now. She'd watched the black-clad guys getting out of the van with their tin hats and masks, and they meant business.

Hammond had seen them too. They always sent them out mob-handed and they were spilling out of the van now; two had split off to go round and cover the front of the house. He was trapped. He had a choice; he could do a Newman/Redford bust out and die in a hail of bullets or he could walk out with his hands over his head and he'd go down for corruption and kidnapping. Cops always got a hard time in jail.

But he'd kill her first. He'd play out the scenario he had crafted so meticulously all these years, then he'd take stock – grab the Burns woman as a hostage, bargain his way out . . . do something. But when he tried to think past Anna's death, there was only a blur, a sort of blankness.

The woman was frightened, constantly casting glances at the larder where he was hiding. If he left her, she had only to open the door and scream. His one advantage was that they were looking for him in the wrong place, outside not inside.

Hammond pushed open the door and beckoned to Kayleigh. She came towards him reluctantly and when she was near enough, he grabbed her, dragging her into the larder with him, and closed the door.

'Sit down,' he said. Trembling, she sank on to the stool as he went on, 'Listen carefully. You stay in here. I will be in the kitchen with my gun pointed at this door. If you make a sound, if you open the door, you're dead. Got it?' Kayleigh gulped and nodded.

Pressed close to the wall where he would not be seen from the outside, he slipped silently out of the room. His hour had come.

'They're out there now,' Marta said. 'There are a lot of them now guarding us. You can relax, *cara*. We're safe enough.'

Anna sat back, rubbing her forehead. 'Oh, I suppose so. But I'll be happier when they find him. How are you feeling?'

Marta gave a little, tight smile. 'Our Cassie is safe, that is the main thing. But not a good morning, really.'

Anna looked at her encouragingly, but she obviously wasn't planning to say anything else. 'There are dozens of emails,' she said, seizing on a change of subject. 'I'd better look through them and see if any really need a reply. I expect there will have been something from James Harrington and it's never wise to ignore communications from your publisher.'

She went across to the desk and logged on. When she heard footsteps coming along the passage she looked up, raising her eyebrows; Kayleigh knew not to disturb her when she was in the study.

Marta got up, tutting in annoyance. 'What now? That girl – she has been all over the place this morning. Come in!'

Hammond opened the door. His dark eyes were too bright, almost feverish, and there was a tight little smile on his face as he advanced on Anna, the pistol in his hand.

'Hello, Mummy,' he said, then, his tone mocking, 'Long time no see, eh?'

CHAPTER TWENTY-ONE

Halliburgh police station was so crowded that DC Murray almost had to shoulder her way through to the CID room. When she got there, DS Wilson was talking to a DI she recognised as one of the Fettes Avenue guys – well, an extra one would come in handy, she reflected wryly, what with their own DI being off running amok with a gun.

DS Wilson didn't seem very interested when she reported in. He was clearly a worried man and she suspected he still hadn't forgiven her for the deception, either. 'They've opened up one of the old offices for an incident room,' he said. 'Your DCI Strang is taking a conference in quarter of an hour, so I expect he'll want you there.'

'Right,' Murray said. That was good – she could look for Kate Graham and bring her up to speed with what was going on. She'd have heard by now that Cassie was all right, but she deserved to know the full story.

After all, if she hadn't told Strang she was worried about Hammond, they wouldn't be hunting him down now.

She was walking along the corridor when Graham hailed her. 'Livvy! There you are. I was hoping I'd see you. What on earth's been happening?'

Murray looked at her watch. 'Conference in fifteen minutes. That's time for a coffee and a bacon roll. I missed breakfast.'

They headed for the canteen together. Graham listened, astonished, as Murray told her the extraordinary story. 'And we don't think we've got to the bottom of it yet. When we told her we knew about her son, they made us leave the room so they could work out what to say. We had to sit there having tea while Kayleigh Burns jittered round us.'

'What was she jittery about?' Graham asked.

'Oh, I suppose just us arriving in her kitchen. I think she'd something else on her mind as well – she barely even reacted when we told her about Cassie being safe—' She stopped. 'Oh no! It couldn't be – please not!'

Murray jumped to her feet and dashed out, leaving a puzzled Graham to look at the abandoned bacon roll. Out in the corridor she asked everyone she passed if they'd seen DCI Strang and tracked him down at last, just as he was taking a phone call.

His face was grim. 'Right, I'll just get across there. Tell someone to announce the conference is postponed,' he said. 'Oh, Livvy, there you are. They've found Hammond's car parked just up the hill from Highfield. You may as well come.'

'I'll tell you something else,' she said, hurrying after him. 'Why was Kayleigh Burns so nervous? She'd no reason to be scared of us, hardly seemed to take in what we said about Cassie—'

Strang stopped in his tracks. 'Dear God – he's inside, isn't he? He was there, somewhere, listening, so he knows what's happened. Get them to warn Armed Response while I get a car.'

Murray ran to reception and gabbled the request, then headed for the door to the car park. Strang was there already, at the badged car with the boot open. He hauled out two sets of body armour and chucked one to her.

'Get that on and get in,' he said.

It was a bit too big for her, but it would do. Better than an imitation suede jacket, when it came to stopping bullets. Murray was feeling very sick indeed as she got into the car and Strang drove off. As they left the enclosure, the reporters surged forward; Sascha Silverton had got herself to the front and had to step back rapidly to avoid being taken out as the car swung left.

Marta Morelli leapt to her feet. Hammond swung the pistol to point at her and snarled, 'Sit down and stay down. This is nothing to do with you – this is between her and me.' He turned back and, holding it with both hands and arms extended, aimed at Anna Harper, still sitting motionless behind her desk.

'I'm aiming for your heart, though that's probably not the best idea, since I doubt if you have one.'

Marta had flushed crimson; she began to say something in Italian, but Anna said, 'Marta, no. Please.' She herself was very pale but her face was calm, expressionless. 'Why don't you talk to us?' she said.

He was still gripping the gun, but he lowered it. 'Oh no! Why don't *you* talk to *me*? Why don't you tell me why you thought I was nothing more than an object to be sold for your own selfish gain? You were my natural protector – my mother, for God's sake! – but you handed me, a helpless baby over to a woman who hated me, who made my life a hell of misery. When I kill you, at least it will be quick. I had to suffer years and years of pain. You did that.'

In his scenario she had started to weep at that point. Then she would beg on her knees for his forgiveness, tell him that she had suffered guilt all her life for what she had done, offer him money, recognition, even love – and maybe, just maybe . . . No, of course not – he would laugh in her face. Instead, Anna just looked at him silently.

He didn't know what to do. He was the man with the gun, the man with power, yet somehow he was helpless. He could shoot her right now, this very minute . . . But why did he feel that it wouldn't solve anything?

Instead, he found himself saying, his voice unsteady, 'But doesn't it mean anything to you – looking at your son, after all these years? Don't you see what you've lost? I was a son worth having. My father knew that, he loved me, even if you don't. You're trash, but at least I am the son of a wonderful man.'

Still Anna didn't speak, but Marta made a little mocking noise. Inflamed, he turned his head and snarled, 'That's it! First her, then you.'

'Why didn't we realise?' Strang said as they drove back to Highfield. 'She was nervous, not acting normally – he must have been hiding right there in the kitchen. He knows we're on to him and he'll have seen the lads outside. He'll move quickly.'

Murray's hands, he noticed, were clasped so tightly that the knuckles were showing white. 'What are we going to do, boss?'

'We are going to arrive at the house, I'm going to assess the situation, then you're going back to wait in the car. I've only brought you in case at some stage the women need support. With fully trained armed officers standing ready you're not going to be involved and I can assure you I'm not planning to do anything heroic either.'

She protested, of course, but he reckoned the protests were token and her hands relaxed. He didn't blame her for being scared; he wasn't crazy about the situation himself. Trying to talk Hammond down would probably be the immediate objective, but from what Cassie had said he doubted that would get them anywhere. This had a very bad feel.

They turned into the Highfield drive and Superintendent Brown hurried over to meet them as they got out of the car.

'We don't know where he is,' Brown said. 'No sign of

him in the kitchen, but I've told them not to go round peering in the windows in case that provokes a reaction.'

'Good,' Strang said. 'We could move into the kitchen and fan out from there.' Then he stopped. 'No, we couldn't. Ms Morelli told me she was resetting the security with a new code. The minute we opened that door, the alarm would go off and we'd be announcing to him that we're coming in. Right. Think again.'

Murray said, 'If he's found the ladies, he's probably in Ms Harper's study. That's where they were when we left them.'

'That's probably right,' Strang said. He looked round; even all these years out of the army it was still instinctive to scope out a sniper's position. 'Up there,' he said, pointing to where, across the drive, a bank rose overlooking the side of the house. He strode across and found that with the elevation, just a little further along, they should be able to look down into at least some part of the room. Of course, anyone there would be able to look up and see them if they thought of it, but it was a risk that had to be taken.

Brown beckoned to one of the officers holding a rifle and he came up to join them. 'Cover the window,' Brown said. 'DCI Strang, stand behind his shoulder.'

Just for a moment Strang felt a real pang at being sidelined, at not being the one taking up his position to get a bead on the target, but he'd no reason to think that the man now bringing the marksman Remington 700 up to his shoulder wasn't just as skilled as he'd once been. He nodded and cautiously they edged forward.

Anna Harper's study window covered only the middle of the room, so that neither the end with her desk, nor the other end was fully visible. He could make out Hammond's figure but he was half turned and Strang couldn't clearly see what he was doing. As he looked, he seemed to be bending down.

It was the perfect shot but there was no legitimate reason for firing it. As the marksman turned his head to look away, Strang remembered the rule; every sniper is well warned about the strange fact that people sense when they are being stared at. He looked away himself.

But the last thing they wanted was to have to shoot. The big question was, if he got the megaphone and tried to talk to Hammond would that simply provoke what he was so desperately hoping to avoid?

Marta Morelli laughed. She actually laughed. Hammond's face turned purple with fury as she addressed him with a volley of Italian. He could shoot her there and then, but he had to know why she was laughing. It made him feel impotent, like the miserable child he once had been.

'You don't know Italian?' the harridan said. 'Well, I'll translate. Your father – he was no "wonderful man". Your father was a liar, a cheat and a murderer – oh, you're his son, all right, looking for revenge. It's bred in the bone, generation after generation of dirty Mafia.'

The words felled him, as if they had been a stun bolt. He dropped the gun, fell forward on to his knees, only managing to grab it back and to point it at Marta as she darted forward. She withdrew again and Hammond turned his head to look at Anna. Still on his knees, begging, he said to her, 'She's lying! Tell me she's lying! I know she is! You are my mother and Oliver was my father – she can't prove you weren't.'

For the first time, he saw Anna's face soften. 'I'm sorry. She doesn't have to. Of course I know you aren't my son. I lost Oliver's baby a month after I went to Italy. I was young, I didn't properly understand what I was doing – a baby to me was just a baby. And Marta was only sixteen; she had been groomed by your father but when she got pregnant, he didn't want to know. So—' she made a helpless gesture with her hands.

He was crying now. He didn't want to cry, but he couldn't help it. It was as if the father he had loved all his life, his one consolation, had just died. But for God's sake, he didn't have time to mourn him now. He had a job to do. He had to be a man. He clenched his teeth, got up again, clutching the pistol.

'Just one thing,' he said, turning back to Marta. 'My *real* father' – he spat out the words – 'where is he now?'

She looked at him with those dark eyes as cold as stone. 'Dead,' she said. 'I killed him.'

All the armed response guys were bunched towards the corner of the house, near the study window where the action was, presumably. DC Murray hadn't actually got back into the car, as instructed, but she didn't feel it would be wise to sneak round there to see what was going on. She was standing looking into the kitchen when she saw something move.

The units in the kitchen were all very sleek, close-fitted, and the door of one of them was opening, just a fraction. With her face now pressed to the window, Murray saw Kayleigh Burns' terrified eyes peering out from what looked like a deep cupboard. Murray dared not raise her voice, but she gestured wildly to the woman to come out.

After a moment's hesitation and an anxious look around her, Kayleigh shot across to the door, fumbled frantically with the bolt and then almost fell out of the house, sobbing with a mixture of fear and relief.

'You're OK, you're OK,' Murray said. 'Do you know where Hammond is?'

She shook her head. 'Ms Harper's usually in the study at this time, if he's looking for her, but he could be hiding anywhere.'

The movement had brought a couple of the officers over. 'Come on, love,' one of them said to Kayleigh taking her arm, 'You're all right now. We'll get you a seat in the van. You're still shaking.'

'What's happening round there?' Murray asked.

'He's in the study with the women,' one of them said. 'They've got him in shot at the moment, but they haven't got much of a view – they're just working out the next step.'

'Right,' Murray said. Then an idea struck her. 'Kayleigh, there's a camera set-up that covers the rooms, isn't there? Where is it?'

She was quick to understand. 'Upstairs. Ms Morelli's room's just at the top, system's next door. Fob for the door by her bed.'

'Right.' Murray turned to the officer, trying to sound authoritative and hoping he wouldn't argue, 'Tell DCI Strang that I'm going to get into the security room and I'll phone him when I've got the study on camera.'

It worked. He nodded and escorted Kayleigh away. Strang would probably be furious but she didn't care. She'd been scared earlier, but she wasn't now, with the adrenaline kicking in. Anyway, as long as Hammond was in the study she was safe enough, provided she didn't make any sort of noise that would attract his attention. She kicked off her boots and on stockinged feet tiptoed across the hall and up the great curving staircase.

She'd been afraid she would have to search for the fob but Marta's room was as spartan as her kitchen, and there it was on the bedside table. A moment later she was in the security control cupboard, looking helplessly at a screen. It was showing the white sitting room at the front of the house in perfect detail, but she had no idea at all how she could make it switch to filming the study, or how she could make it stay there, once it did.

She scanned the desk desperately looking for information – the camera was now panning round the kitchen – and noticed at last a button marked 'pause'. She had to wait to view a rather splendid dining room with a white marble table and cream upholstered chairs before – at last! – the study appeared on the screen.

Then she could see, with shocking clarity, Hammond threatening Anna Harper behind her desk at one end of the room with the Glock, but glaring over his shoulder at Marta Morelli who was standing in front of the fireplace She couldn't hear what was being said, of course, but he looked upset. She pressed pause, and the camera didn't as usual move on after a quick sweep. So she could phone Strang immediately and report, hoping that might at least mitigate her disobedience.

His voice was terse. 'Well?'

Straight to essentials. 'Morelli's at the fireplace, Harper's at her desk. He's between them, pointing the pistol at Harper but he hasn't taken up a shooting stance. He's obviously distressed. He's looking back at Morelli. Now I can see he's in tears. But something else – the door isn't quite closed behind him.'

'Right. I'll take it from there.'

The line went dead. Murray pulled a face, and went on watching.

CHAPTER TWENTY-TWO

Hammond was feeling sick and dizzy now, with his world splintering about him. Those cold eyes fixed on him were dark brown, like his own. The hair was like his, the skin was olive. His mother – not the uniquely brilliant, elegant, sophisticated woman he had always admired even while he hated her to the depth of his soul, but this, this *peasant* who was no more moral than the man she had killed – his father.

What did he have to live for? The little house in Spain, the quiet mind – the sort of fairy story only a child could have believed in. The idea vanished like a puff of smoke drifting away.

And they were waiting for him, outside with their guns. He was too tired, too broken, to think of an escape route now. But these two women, foul with deception – he would get justice for Oliver, who had been their dupe.

'You first,' he said, turning to face Anna. 'You knew Oliver. You knew that he didn't deserve what you did to him, and to me.'

He squared his shoulders, clasped both hands round the Glock. Just at that moment he became aware that the door was moving, very gently, behind him – but he had no time to react before Marta was on him. He didn't even feel the stiletto being driven in; it felt more like a punch in the back, but then the power went from his limbs, his knees collapsed and he was lying on the floor. His finger tightened on the trigger but the shot went harmlessly into a wall and suddenly the room was filled with armed men.

Marta Morelli, unnaturally calm, was led away as DCI Strang bent over his colleague. DC Murray came hurrying into the room and stopped on the threshold.

'Do you – do you want me to call an ambulance?'

He looked up. 'No point. He's gone. She knew what she was doing.' He jerked his head. 'You deal with Ms Harper. Get her out of here.'

Anna Harper had collapsed over her desk, weeping. Murray approached her nervously. She still wasn't clear exactly what had happened, and the situation now was weird. She could never have imagined exchanging small talk with a global literary star, let alone having to comfort her when her son was lying dead at her feet and her best friend, who had obviously killed him to save Anna's own life, was being taken off in handcuffs.

If the person who had told the young Livvy that she would like the police force because you never knew what would happen from one day to the next had been there, she'd have decked him.

Anna was easy to direct, though, moving like a zombie as Murray persuaded her to her feet, drew her through to the kitchen and despised herself that the only thing she could think of to say was, 'Sit down there and I'll make you a nice cup of tea.'

Anna sat obediently, scrubbing at her eyes with a handful of tissues, still shaken by sobs. Murray filled up the state-of-the-art kettle – a more complicated procedure than she would have thought strictly necessary just to boil water – and then she baulked. She hadn't joined the CID force to make cups of tea and she seriously doubted whether Anna wanted one anyway.

She sat down beside Anna at the table. 'I don't know what happened in there,' she said. 'But if you want to talk about it, I'm here to listen.' She wasn't at all sure what would happen next, but Anna gave a ragged sigh and then it all started pouring out, as if she couldn't see how to stop.

'I didn't know until the other day what Marta had done. I knew she hated him, I knew she hadn't wanted his child, but I thought arranging a new life for her would be enough. And yes, I used her: if I'd had to tell Oliver I'd lost the baby he'd have stopped the payment that was letting me write the book I was possessed with, but it solved her problem as well. The bastard who got her pregnant didn't want to know – her family called her a *puttana* and threw her out on the street. And our friendship began there, and—' She broke off, her eyes filling with tears again. 'What will happen to her now? I can't imagine life without Marta.'

Murray made a non-committal noise; struggling to keep up with all this, she couldn't think of anything reassuring she could possibly say.

Anna went on, 'She liked to see herself as my dragon and she could be completely ruthless – whatever I wanted must happen. Sometimes I thought she went too far. That poor, silly young man, Jason – she poisoned any chance his pathetic book might have had because some local critic made a comparison, and he wasn't the only one. I felt guilty about him, but mostly I didn't give it much thought. She cleared the space for me to write and to be supremely selfish with my time and it was all I cared about. Until Felix.

'It was only then I thought of myself as a failure. Oh, my husband had walked out on me, but I didn't blame him and I didn't miss him, and it never occurred to me that it would matter to children who otherwise had everything. They had my love – but it was in theory, I suppose. They didn't have my time or attention. Cassie was strong enough to thrive, but Felix was . . . frail. I don't think she will ever forgive me—' She broke off. 'She is all right, isn't she?'

Murray managed to assure her she was, though her head was reeling.

'Though she probably won't even speak to me now. And the man, Marta's son. I'm to blame for his death, too. He died at her hands because she was protecting me. I stole her love that ought to have been his, I sold him into the life that made him what he was.' She leant forward on the table, burying her face in her hands.

The perfectly cut bob swung forward to cover her face, a huge aquamarine on her right hand glinted. How much, Murray wondered, had this all been about wanting money and fame? You'd never be able to disentangle that one; she doubted if Anna herself knew. She waited, but Anna didn't say anything more and she didn't feel inclined to mutter any of the platitudes that would be an insult to the woman's painful confession.

When DCI Strang appeared at the door with a uniformed policewoman, Murray got up to let her take her place.

'I think she needs a doctor,' she murmured. 'She's in pieces.'

The woman nodded and Murray left with Strang. She wasn't going to enjoy the next bit.

'When I told you to stay in the car, I wasn't making conversation,' Strang said. 'That was an order. Did you fail to understand that?'

'No, sir. I mean, yes, sir,' Murray stammered.

'You put yourself in danger. You'd have been in the direct line of fire if Hammond had erupted out of the study. It is my responsibility to see that you don't take reckless risks with your own safety.'

'Yes, sir.'

She was hanging her head, but he wasn't at all sure that her apparent penitence would make any difference. Acting on her own initiative still seemed to be an irresistible temptation. He couldn't actually claim that what she had done had harmed the operation; he'd no confidence that he'd have had any success in trying to talk Hammond down and Murray's report from the security terminal might have been helpful, even if in the event its effect had been neutral. He was irritated anyway, and they drove back to Halliburgh police station in silence.

As they reached the station, he said, 'I'm not inclined to put you on a charge, because it would only open up another front for the media to rake over and I'll be on the back foot anyway over Hammond's death.'

'But that's outrageous!' Murray protested. She could never stay subdued for long. 'You couldn't have done anything about Marta having a knife.'

'No, nor about some of the other things we'll be accused of failing to prevent. It's pure chance that he didn't get off the shot at Harper before Morelli knifed him, and they'll make a big thing out of that. We might get some credit for finding Cassie, but it'll be forgotten soon enough.'

The media pack was baying louder than ever. There were cameras now, and he got out of the car feeling depressed at what lay ahead of him – the phone call to JB, then the mountain of paperwork, deploying the task force on interviews, the liaising with the fiscal's office about charges, the press statements – days of work lying ahead. This was a story that would run and run.

What was getting him on the raw, of course, was his own failure in observation, the most elementary and arguably the most important policing skill. It was haunting him now, that he'd allowed himself to be so caught up in the bizarre drama that had been unfolding in the study that he hadn't noticed the story that was being told right in front of him in the kitchen by Kayleigh's shaking hands. If he had, Hammond would right now be handcuffed in a police van, not lying on the floor of Anna Harper's study waiting for the attentions of a photographer and a forensic pathologist. Whatever his sins, he didn't deserve that.

Certainly, most of it would be done from Edinburgh. With the task force in place he would be going back to the more standard role of a DCI, reading reports on his computer and having strategic meetings. He could actually arrange to go back to talk to JB tonight and stay in his own home, but after a day like this he wasn't sure he could take the bedtime stories for Betsy and the long explanations for Fin. He hated to think of another night at The Sun, but the chances were that by now the White Hart would have been booked out by journalists.

But whatever happened, he mustn't accept any more hospitality from Kate Graham. He wasn't presumptuous enough to assume that she was interested in him but he couldn't bear to raise further the hopes of her father, a loving and decent man who thought he'd caught a glimpse of liberation from the guilt he felt about his daughter's self-sacrifice.

Propped up on her pillows in a hospital side ward, Cassie Trentham was feeling so tired that she could hardly bring herself to open her eyes and yet she couldn't sleep; when they were shut she had flashbacks and frightening images. They had assured her that her mother was safe, but had been curiously reluctant to say anything else. There was nothing really wrong with her, they said, but they were going to keep her under observation for another night and kept bringing her little snacks of tea and toast and porridge not to overtax her empty stomach, but she struggled to eat even though she felt hungry.

She heard someone coming in. Could she be bothered to make the effort to see who it was? Then she heard Kate Graham's voice whispering, 'Cassie? Are you awake?' and her eyes shot open.

'Oh, I'm so glad you came! I would have phoned you but I haven't got my bag. Please will you tell me what's been happening? No one will say anything, except that Anna's all right. Have they caught Hammond?'

Kate took a seat at the bedside. 'Yes,' she said gravely. 'He's been – stopped. Oh dear, you do look awful – your face is whiter than the pillows. It's a long story – are you sure you're strong enough and that you shouldn't just rest?'

'Too many things whirling round in my head to rest. Tell me, and if I flake out halfway through you can fill it in later.'

As she listened to Kate's gentle voice telling the terrible story of the human cost of *Stolen Fire*, tears slipped down her cheeks. She didn't quite know who she was crying for: for the child who became warped into a monster, for the brother he had killed, for the teenage victim of a cruel society who had finished by killing her own son, for her driven mother who was now paying the price for her obsession.

Kate had several times asked her if she was all right; now she asked anxiously, 'How will you cope with all this? Can you forgive your mother for what she did?'

Cassie didn't speak for a long, long moment. Then she said, 'Hammond talked to me about revenge and I said to him that you had to let things go, and move on. Hatred destroys you as much – perhaps even more than the other person. Anna's going to need me badly. I can't think how she'll manage, without Marta, and she'll be in trouble herself, won't she?'

'It's certainly possible. It'll depend a bit how things play out as the evidence emerges.' Kate got up. 'Now I'm definitely going to leave you to rest. They said you'd be going home tomorrow – I'll pop up to Burnside after my shift.'

'Thanks, Kate. You're a good friend.'

There was so much to think about, but now Cassie knew what had happened she felt more able to rest. As she lay down and shut her eyes, her last waking thought was relief that she did not, after all, share the bond of blood with her captor.

Kate Graham drove back from the hospital looking at her watch. Her shift had finished and she should really go straight home – her father would be looking for his snifter very soon. She wouldn't be needed at the station; with the arrival of the task force the locals were only doing the routine things relating to mopping up after the Beast from the East, like opening up the roads that were still blocked and dealing with a bit of a flooding problem too from the sudden thaw.

She told herself she wanted to check in with Livvy to tell her she'd seen Cassie, but the idea at the back of her mind that she didn't want to admit to was that she might bump into Strang and just casually ask if he'd like supper again. It had been such a good evening last night; her dad had been in great form and Kelso too seemed to be enjoying it. If he was going to be here for a while sorting things out, they might even manage to renew the casual friendship they'd had all these years ago. That was all – just friendship.

When she tracked Murray down sitting in a corner of the CID room, she was looking glum. 'Problems?' Kate asked.

'You could say. I've done it again, and he's mad at me.'

'Kelso is? What did you do?'

'The usual thing – I saw something I could do, and

I did it when I was under orders to stay in the car. It's because I always feel I have something to prove, and even though I know he's more impressed when I'm just working with the team, it's sort of as if I feel that, this time, he's going to see that me taking the initiative was a brilliant thing to do.'

'And was it, this time?'

'Could have been. But as it turned out it was pretty much irrelevant.'

Graham made a sympathetic face. 'Is he going to report you?'

'Don't think so. But he's in a bad mood anyway because he's blaming himself for not realising Hammond had got into the house. My fault too. Oh well, have to wait and see if he's going to forgive me.'

'You really like working with him, don't you?'

'I learn such a lot from him, that's the thing. Maybe if he lets me go on working with him long enough, I'll manage to behave like a proper grown-up detective.'

'And you really like him too, don't you?' Graham said slyly.

Murray tried to sound offhand. 'Of course I do. He's a likeable man. You like him as well, don't you?' she said, turning the tables.

Graham went a faint shade of pink. 'Well yes, he was a good mate. His wife was nice, too. I met her a couple of times.' She took a deep breath. 'I don't think he's got over her, really, do you?'

'Honestly, no,' Murray said. 'He doesn't talk about

her, but I've never heard that he's taken an interest in anyone else.'

'No, that's what I thought. Changing the subject, I saw Cassie. She's looking terribly frail, but they seem to think she'll be fine. She's certainly got a forgiving nature – she was talking about Anna needing her now, with all that's happened. I think she was even sorry for Hammond.'

'Yeah, I suppose you have to be. He hardly got a fair chance in life, poor soul. Cards stacked against him right from the start.'

The door opened behind them and DCI Strang came in. 'I was looking for you, Kate. I haven't thanked you for last night – splendid meal, and good to meet your father. What a great guy!'

'He enjoyed meeting you too,' Graham said. 'You're more than welcome to come tonight as well.'

'Thanks very much, but I'm actually on my way back to Edinburgh. I wanted to see you to say goodbye and thanks. It takes a lot of guts to be a whistle-blower but if it hadn't been for you, we'd never have realised what had been going on. I should warn you that Wilson's being questioned at the moment, but we're presenting it as an incidental finding after the SRCS got involved, so if you keep your head down it should be all right.'

'I'm grateful for that,' Graham said. 'But are you really going back? I thought you'd have a lot to do here.'

'That's the task force's work now. My hands-on stuff is finished and I'll just be stuck behind a desk reviewing what the task force finds. Still, I'm glad to have seen you again, Kate. A reminder of some happy times – and some probably better forgotten!'

'Nice to see you too, Kelso. Maybe see you around if there's another conference.'

'Absolutely. And my best to your dad.' Then he turned to Murray, who was looking as if she didn't want to be noticed. 'Livvy, you exasperate me, you know that? You are such an asset except when you get the bit between your teeth and bolt. The security camera was a good idea; going into a house with an armed man at large was plain crazy.'

'Yes, sir,' Murray muttered without looking at him.

'Consider yourself reprimanded and we'll leave it there. I'll see you at Fettes Avenue sometime later tomorrow, all right?'

After he left, Graham smiled at Murray. 'I guess you're forgiven.'

'Fingers crossed. It's a little on the basis that I don't do it again, though, isn't it? Anyway, could you bear to have me for one last night?'

'Dad would be devastated if I let you go. He's still got some stories you haven't heard – at least he thinks you haven't. And there'll be a bed for you any time you want it.'

Murray was touched. 'You're a good person, Kate. And a good officer too. Right, I'll just get my coat and come back with you now.'

She went out and Kate followed more slowly. It was really nice that Kelso had made a point of coming to see her to say goodbye. Shame that he wasn't going to be around for a bit longer – but when she thought about it, maybe that was all for the best.

DCI Strang's phone call to DCS Borthwick had been mainly about reporting the facts, but tomorrow's conference would be all about damage limitation and presentational issues. She had decided it would be better to have the press statement issued in Edinburgh in the hope of drawing the media presence away from Halliburgh; there wouldn't be much they could write, fortunately, once Marta Morelli was charged. It would all have to come out eventually, of course, but at least they had a breathing space.

JB had been fair-minded as usual but Hammond's death was already overshadowing the success of Cassandra Trentham's release. He'd have some searching questions to answer tomorrow and he wasn't looking forward to it.

After he came back from saying goodbye to Kate, he gathered together his papers. It made sense to get back home tonight, particularly now he'd said to Kate that he was going, but he wasn't looking forward to it. He'd have a lot of preparation to do and after all the publicity there had been there was no chance Fin wouldn't interrogate him when he got back. As long as Betsy was in bed, and her predatory friend wasn't there waiting too, he could manage it.

He'd better phone Fin anyway to tell her he was

coming. He fished out his private mobile, which he hadn't switched on since he arrived in Halliburgh, and saw that there had been several calls from Fin's number. He was gritting his teeth slightly as he dialled.

She greeted him with, 'For heaven's sake, kid, what have you got involved in this time? Are you in one piece? The news has had nothing but stuff about armed response units and a cop running around with a gun.'

'It's been a bit hairy but the worst's over. I'll be getting back tonight.'

'That's good. But we won't be in tonight, actually. Betsy wanted a sleepover with Michelle's Niamh and I'm going to stay too. In fact, I've been trying to get hold of you to tell you – Michelle has an extra bedroom and she's wanting me to flat-share. Would you mind very much if I accepted? I know how fond you are of Betsy and it's been like having a proper family, but there's a lot more space at Michelle's and sometimes I've felt we've crowded you out a bit. You'll see lots of us, anyway – Betsy will make sure of that.'

'I'm sure she will,' he said warmly. 'No one does Daddy Pig like I do, for my sins. That makes a lot of sense, Fin. I'm away a lot and it'll be nice for you to have more adult company. You go right ahead. I'll see you sometime tomorrow, then.'

'But what's been happening—'

'No time just now. Tell you when I see you,' he said.

He sat back in his chair and relief flooded over him. He and Fin had always been such good friends and he had hated that it had become like a bad marriage where every small irritation became amplified. He had little doubt that this went both ways, and sooner or later the relationship would be destroyed.

It was true he would miss Betsy's naughty charm and her extravagant cuddles, but they wouldn't be far away and being the indulgent uncle was a lot more fun than being the enforcer. He was smiling as he went back to his car.

A pale, cold dusk was just creeping in with a hint of mist over the Forth when he got back to the house. There were no lights on, as there had been these past few months, and just for a moment he wondered if he would miss them after all when he always came back to an empty, silent house.

Fin and Betsy had obviously left in a hurry. Betsy's toys were scattered across the floor and there were dishes sitting on the draining board that hadn't been put into the dishwasher. He tidied everything away, poured himself a drink and sat down by the window in his favourite seat to watch the lights come on across in Fife.

He'd have his own space back after they had gone, but it would only be his own space. The last traces of Alexa had vanished; he couldn't feel even the faintest aura of her presence any more.

On an impulse he went to his desk and opened the drawer where a framed photograph lay face down. It had always been his favourite photo of Alexa, one he'd taken himself; he'd called to her and she'd turned her head, looking back over her shoulder at him and laughing. He hadn't been able to look at it since the accident.

Now he set it up on the surface. It looked almost as if she was saying goodbye to him and he found he was able to smile back. Alexa had gone. So be it. He had to let her go.

ACKNOWLEDGEMENTS

My grateful thanks go to my agent Jane Conway-Gordon, my publisher Susie Dunlop and the team at Allison & Busby, especially Kelly Smith and Fliss Bage.

ALINE TEMPLETON grew up in the fishing village of Anstruther, in the East Neuk of Fife. She has worked in education and broadcasting and was a Justice of the Peace for ten years. She has been Chair of the Society of Authors in Scotland and is a director of the Crime Writers' Association. Married, with two children and four grandchildren, she now lives in a house with a view of Edinburgh Castle. When not writing she enjoys cooking, choral singing, and travelling the back roads of France.

alinetempleton.co.uk   *@AlineTempleton*